Praise for H

T0275143

The Magician

"*The Magician's Daughter* is that most rare and precious thing: a brand-new classic, both wholly original and wonderfully nostalgic. It's an absolute treasure."

—Alix E. Harrow, *New York Times* bestselling author
of *The Once and Future Witches*

"Brilliantly imagined. I love the way Parry blends mythic elements with wit and heart. A fast pace, period detail, and an intriguing cast of real, flawed people make *The Magician's Daughter* a book to be absolutely devoured."

—Lucy Holland, author of *Sistersong*

"Innovative fairy tale and deftly researched historical fiction in one, full of captivating magic and richly drawn characters. H. G. Parry crafts an evocative world rife with a struggle for equity, justice, and the occasional miracle that readers won't be able to forget."

—Rowenna Miller, author of *The Fairy
Bargains of Prospect Hill*

"Draws you in and makes you believe that magic does exist. Animal familiars, an island that only appears on certain days, and a young heroine who learns the depths of her strength. I absolutely adored it!"

—Andrea Stewart, author of *The Bone Shard Daughter*

"*The Magician's Daughter* casts a spell with its warm and subtle prose. Parry has created an enchantment of a novel."

—E. J. Beaton, author of *The Councillor*

"A gorgeously atmospheric coming-of-age novel.... *The Magician's Daughter* is a triumph of skill and technique.... [Biddy's] story is a journey of discovery, a coming-of-age into a wider world that leaps off the page in vivid, heart-rending detail."

—*Locus*

"A delightful little fantasy that pulls at all the right heartstrings.... For those who fondly remember the works of Frances Hodgson Burnett or Lewis Carroll, this novel will definitely be your (bread, butter and) jam." —*Wall Street Journal*

"A charming romp of an old-school coming of age fantasy about family and magic that will take your heart for a wild ride."

—*NPR Books*

The Unlikely Escape of Uriah Heep

"If you've ever checked the back of your wardrobe for snow and lamplight—if you've ever longed to visit Pemberley House or 221B Baker Street, to battle the Jabberwock or wander through a fictional London fog—this book belongs to you. It's a star-studded literary tour and a tangled mystery and a reflection on reading itself; it's a pure delight."

—Alix E. Harrow, *New York Times* bestselling author

"Many have tried and some have succeeded in writing mashups with famed literary characters, but Parry knocks it out of the park.... Just plain wonderful." —*Kirkus* (starred review)

"Part mystery, all magical, *The Unlikely Escape of Uriah Heep* is both amusing and perceptive; the novel entertains as it reminds us of the power of words and how fiction can influence real life."

—*Locus*

"H. G. Parry has crafted an imaginative and unique exploration of how words shift our lives in ways big and small. *The Unlikely Escape of Uriah Heep* is a rollicking adventure that thrills like Neil Gaiman's *Neverwhere* mashed up with *Penny Dreadful* in the best postmodern way. Equal parts sibling rivalry, crackling mystery, and Dickensian battle royale, it'll be one of your most fun reads this year."

—Mike Chen, author of *Here and Now and Then*

The Shadow Histories

"A first-rate blend of political drama and magic battle–action.... Absolutely superb."   —*Kirkus* (starred review)

"A witty, riveting historical fantasy.... Parry has a historian's eye for period detail and weaves real figures from history—including Robespierre and Toussaint Louverture—throughout her poetic tale of justice, liberation, and dark magic. This is a knockout."

—*Publishers Weekly* (starred review)

"An absolute delight to read; splendid and fluid, with beautiful and complex use of language."

—Genevieve Cogman, author of *The Invisible Library*

"Magnificent.... [Turns] the part of history class you might have slept through into something new, exciting and deeply magical."

—*BookPage*

By H. G. Parry

The Scholar and the Last Faerie Door

The Magician's Daughter

THE SHADOW HISTORIES

A Declaration of the Rights of Magicians
A Radical Act of Free Magic

The Unlikely Escape of Uriah Heep

THE
SCHOLAR
AND THE
LAST
FAERIE
DOOR

H. G. PARRY

REDHOOK

Copyright © 2024 by H. G. Parry
Excerpt from *The Magician's Daughter* copyright © 2023 by H. G. Parry

Cover design by Lisa Marie Pompilio
Cover images by Shutterstock
Cover copyright © 2024 by Hachette Book Group, Inc.
Author photograph by Fairlie Atkinson

Redhook Books/Orbit
Hachette Book Group
1290 Avenue of the Americas
New York, NY 10104
hachettebookgroup.com

First Edition: October 2024
Simultaneously published in Great Britain by Orbit

Redhook is an imprint of Orbit, a division of Hachette Book Group.
The Redhook name and logo are registered trademarks of Hachette Book Group, Inc.

The Hachette Speakers Bureau provides a wide range of authors for speaking events. To find out more, go to hachettespeakersbureau.com or email HachetteSpeakers@hbgusa.com.

Redhook books may be purchased in bulk for business, educational, or promotional use. For information, please contact your local bookseller or the Hachette Book Group Special Markets Department at special.markets@hbgusa.com.

Library of Congress Cataloging-in-Publication Data
Names: Parry, H. G., author.
Title: The scholar and the last faerie door / H.G. Parry.
Description: First edition. | New York, NY : Redhook, 2024.
Identifiers: LCCN 2024003141 | ISBN 9780316383905 (trade paperback) | ISBN 9780316384025 (ebook)
Subjects: LCGFT: Fantasy fiction. | Novels.
Classification: LCC PR9639.4.P376 S36 2024 | DDC 823/.92—dc23/eng/20240125
LC record available at https://lccn.loc.gov/2024003141

ISBNs: 9780316383905 (trade paperback), 9780316384025 (ebook)

Printed in the United States of America

LSC-C

Printing 2, 2024

To my family, always.

Part One

Camford, 1920

I

In the end, it was four words that changed the course of our lives and the history of the world. Perhaps it wasn't really so surprising. They were, after all, the most important words in any language.

"What are you reading?"

At first I didn't think the words were addressed to me. To begin with, in those days people didn't speak to me without reason. In the week since I had come to Camford, I could count on one hand the number of conversations I'd had with the other students; if I counted only those unprompted by myself, I was down to one finger. That had been on the first day, when somebody had asked who I was. After that, everyone knew, and there had been no more questions. They all pretended not to understand my accent anyway.

For another thing, I was tucked away in a corner of the library where nobody ever came, in the depths of one of the oldest stack rooms, where the shafts of sunlight were clogged with dust and the air had the sweet, stale smell of old paper. The library was the heart of Camford, a great sprawling structure so labyrinthine it was rumoured to be larger inside than out. Some of the students preferred to steer clear of it entirely, not only for the usual reasons students avoided libraries but because they claimed that if the library took a dislike to you it would swallow you up and you would never be seen again. But I never felt the library disliked me—on the contrary, it was the only place among the crooked towers of Camford where I felt instantly embraced. It gave me the books I'd yearned to read since I had first learned of the magical world, and it did so readily, as if they were nothing. It hid me from unfriendly eyes, and admittedly from friendly ones as well. I could hear only the occasional murmur of student voices in the corridors, and I had been confident none would come near.

Most important of all, the voice that had asked the question belonged to Alden Lennox-Fontaine.

Back then, I knew very little of the aristocratic magical Families whose sons inhabited Camford. They blurred into an endless parade of pale faces and well-cut grey suits, smooth accents and smooth haircuts, motorcars and cigarettes and showy spells. I used to tell myself I didn't care about them, when really of course they didn't care about me. Still, I couldn't help knowing, against my will, about Alden. He was the golden child of our year: heir to some vast estate up in Yorkshire, blue-eyed and blond-curled, well-dressed and well-shaped and effortlessly charming. I couldn't even pretend he wasn't clever, because he was. I would hear him behind me before class started, halfway up the stadium seating: laughing with his friends, quick and disarming, the kind of verbal thrust-and-parry the magical Families seemed trained in from infancy. And yet once the lecture began, he would stop laughing and listen; if he spoke at all, it was to ask sensible questions, all trace of irony bled from his voice. A deft, supple intellect, unafraid to want to learn from his teachers yet too full of wit and mischief to be teased by his peers. I had never expected to see him up close, much less to speak to him.

But here he was, so close I could see each strand of artistically tousled golden hair, and he had in fact, despite all logical reasons to the contrary, spoken to me.

He must have thought I hadn't heard him, because he repeated his question again, in exactly the same tone, with exactly the same important words. "What are you reading?"

I found my voice at last. "A book," I said. These were important words too, but in context they were a little lacking in specificity.

Alden laughed his easy laugh. "I didn't think you were reading a map. What book?"

If my cheeks hadn't flushed already, they certainly had now. "Cornelius Agrippa."

"Interesting," he said. "You must have gone quite deep into the library for that."

I couldn't tell if he was teasing, so I chose not to reply. I looked at him and waited for him to move away.

Instead, he looked back readily. I couldn't help noticing, as if it were important, that his eyes had little amber flecks in them.

"I've seen you in here before," he said after a while. I wondered if he was telling the truth: Certainly he had been in the library at the same time as me, but he never had any reason to notice my existence. "What's your name?"

I wished, not for the first time, that I had a name I didn't have to steel myself before declaring. My father had chosen it, liking plant names for girls in general and thinking it would bring me luck. I loved my father, from whom I had inherited my mousy hair and my talent for drawing (my stubbornness came from my mother, according to him). He had died in the Spanish flu outbreak two years ago, and I missed him more than I could say. But honestly.

"Clover," I said. "Clover Hill."

His mouth quirked, as I had feared. "The scholarship witch. I should have guessed."

"What does that mean?" I asked before I could stop myself. "You should have guessed?"

"What do you think it means?"

"It could mean a lot of things." My voice was tight. Tears had pricked my eyes, unexpected and mortifying. I wouldn't normally be so sensitive. The truth was I had been sitting at the desk aching with homesickness. It didn't help that Alden's vast estate was really not so very far from my Lancashire farm. His public school upbringing had smoothed away most traces of an accent, but the vowels held just enough touches of the north to reach my heart. "It could mean that my clothes aren't fashionable enough for me to come from money. It could mean that the work I'm studying is obviously outdated, and that indicates I'm not Family. It could mean that I'm in a library on a Sunday afternoon, and that means I need to study to keep my place here."

"You give far too much credit to my powers of observation," Alden said. "I just meant that you looked clever. I don't even know why I thought that. Probably it was the glasses."

I took them off, and managed to wipe my eyes discreetly in the process.

"As I thought," Alden said with a satisfied nod. "Positively thick-headed now. I'd have taken you for a duchess."

I smiled, shamefaced. God, what was wrong with me? I'd been lonely for days and pretending not to be; I'd been aching for the sound of a friendly voice or a kind word. And the moment someone had stopped to give me one, I'd bitten his head off.

"I'm sorry."

"Not at all. I should apologise. I was being thoughtless." He slid his long limbs into the seat opposite me. I felt his proximity like heat on my skin; suddenly, it became a little harder to breathe. It wasn't purely attraction—though he was undeniably attractive. It was the world he represented. Wealth, breeding, and glamour radiated from him. He was like a burning sun. In my experience, you sneak looks at the sun, careful not to get blinded; you don't expect the sun to look back at you. You certainly don't expect it to pull up a chair, reach across the table, and take up your book with long white fingers. "I *won't* apologise, of course. I was raised badly, and it's far too late to reform now. Still, I'll certainly concede that I should. I'm Alden Lennox-Fontaine."

"I know," I said, and wondered if I should have admitted it. It might have been better to pretend I had no idea who he was. Then again, that might have made me look unsophisticated. The Families tended to know one another.

He smiled, as though he saw full well both halves of my mind. "What do you think of Agrippa?"

It could have been polite conversation. But Alden Lennox-Fontaine had no need to be polite to me. More importantly, I recognised in his face a gleam of real interest, not in me, but in what I was studying. It set me at ease. I couldn't talk about myself; I could certainly talk about Agrippa.

"His theories are terribly old-fashioned," I said. "I know that. They're inaccurate too, which is worse. I think he might be on to something with his binding rituals, though."

"Yes," he said. "Yes, I think exactly the same."

"You've read Agrippa?" I flushed again, realising how that sounded.

He laughed. "We do learn to read at public school, you know. We don't leave all the intellectual activity to those far from the madding crowd."

"I didn't mean that. I just meant—as I said, he's terribly old-fashioned. I know he isn't taught anymore. I only know him because I was taught out of a lot of books that were— well, out-of-date. I grew up in a small village in Lancashire. Even when I found out magic existed, there wasn't a lot of new scholarship."

"He's not on the curriculum," he conceded. "But old houses, like small villages in Lancashire, tend to accumulate old books. I read Agrippa when I was fifteen. Until I met you five minutes ago, I was the only person I knew who had. I came to the same conclusion you just did."

"What conclusion?"

"That he might be on to something with his binding rituals. Now, I've just said that you look very intelligent, and I'm sure you are, but I at fifteen was a relative clod. And yet we both saw that there was something worth pursuing in Agrippa. Why, then, do you think there hasn't been any work on it?"

"Nobody works on faerie magic anymore." My heart was beating fast, and I didn't quite know why. "It's illegal."

"Perhaps. Still, it's interesting, isn't it?" He checked his watch before I could answer and made a face. "I knew it. I have to go to a luncheon. Whenever I start an interesting conversation, I have to go to a luncheon. It's an eternal curse."

I had never been to a luncheon—not a real one, the kind he was talking about. I hadn't thought I wanted to. But I wanted to keep talking to him about Agrippa, so I felt a pang of disappointment.

"Perhaps that curse is Agrippa's influence from beyond the grave." It was my best attempt at Camford student banter. "And that's why nobody's followed his work."

"Hm. But you clearly had no distractions until I came and provided them. The luncheon curse has no power over you. Unless you'd like to join me, of course. Or would that make *me* the curse?"

I blinked. "I'm sorry?"

"You're welcome to join us, if you're not busy." He sounded casual. Surely he could not be. Surely he knew that scholarship students, particularly the only one from an unmagical family, did not attend the same parties as Alden Lennox-Fontaine. "It's just a few of us—a tiresome crowd, for the most part, but one or two good sorts. Hero will be there, if you're worried about being in a room with too many men."

"Hero Hartley?" I asked, trying to match his careless tone. There were few female scholars at Camford, even by the low standards set by Oxford and Cambridge. Of the three hundred undergraduates, only ten were women, and in our entire year there were only two: myself and Hero. I had tried to get up the courage to introduce myself to her more than once that first week, only to lose my nerve and slip away before there was any chance of us being introduced. I had seen her in lectures, always at Alden's side. The two of them were cut of the same cloth: moneyed, powerful, impossibly elegant, with an intellect that cut like a whip.

"Do you know her? I'll introduce you. We grew up together, more or less. Our houses are the only human habitations for miles where we live, so it was the two of us every summer. Oh, and Eddie Gaskell, of course. The Gaskells' land is a few miles north. Eddie might be at the luncheon too, actually, if Hero can persuade him to leave his room." He stood and stretched. "God, I'm still stiff from last night. I wonder what I did. Do say you'll come. I'd much rather keep talking about Agrippa than get drunk on Corbett's mediocre wine at two in the afternoon, although of course we could do both."

"I'd love to come," I said, before either of us could change our minds. I was finding it hard to breathe, as if the air was suddenly thin or I was very high in the sky. "Thank you."

"Don't thank me. You're doing me a favour, and probably Hero and Eddie too."

I didn't, at that point, recognise the gleam in his eye as dangerous. It was the echo of the gleam in my own, and I hadn't yet learned that mine was dangerous too.

That was how it started, the four of us. We never meant any harm.

2

If it hadn't been for the Great War, I would never have gone to Camford University of Magical Scholarship. I would never have known it existed.

I was eleven when my brother went away to war. It was the October of 1914, the autumn after what everyone later called the last golden summer. It was an oversimplification, like most things, but I do remember those months as unusually perfect: the fields of our farm yellowed and dry under an endless blue sky, the ground already warm under my bare feet when I collected the eggs in the morning. Then all too soon the weather was cooling, the call for soldiers was ringing in the streets, and Mum was adamant that Matthew stay exactly where he was.

"Help me talk to her, will you, Clove?" he said, one evening in the barn. We were pitching hay from the loft; he kept his eyes on his work, and I couldn't see his face. "Please. She listens to you."

That was true back then, as much as Mum listened to anyone. Young as I was, I was the eldest daughter, and I was considered the brightest at our small village school. Recently, the schoolmistress had told my father she believed that in a few short years I could train as a teacher at a residential college. To my mother, who could barely read, that gave my opinions a grudging weight they shouldn't have had.

"You don't need her permission." The truth was, I didn't want him to go either. "She can't stop you."

"If she says I'm needed here," he said, "I won't go. You know that. But the war will be over in a few months. The farm will do fine without me until then. It might be the only chance I get to see the world. Besides, I should be out there. Everyone my age is going."

They were, I knew that. Officially, Matthew was still too young, not quite seventeen, but many lads even younger lied about their age and signed up. I also knew the shame that would settle on him if he didn't go with them—not just private shame, although that would poison him more surely, but public ridicule. The country was swept up in a wave of patriotism, and Pendle Hill was being carried away in the flood. I had already seen several young women in town handing out white feathers to any man who looked of combat-ready age, their eyes burning with silent resentment. Last Sunday the vicar had preached the honour of serving one's country, and the usually dozing church had erupted into applause.

I had been caught in the surge of those words too. If I had been a boy and older, I would have gone with Matthew myself, gladly. I longed for new experiences just as he did, and in those days I had read far too many adventure stories to doubt the glory of battle. The trouble was, I *couldn't* go, not even as a nurse. And all I could think of was my brother in some foreign field, alone.

"Do you really want to leave us?" I asked, and hated myself for sounding like a child.

" 'Course not." He stopped and looked at me properly for the first time. "You know I don't. But I can't be here while it's going on. I just can't."

That, in the end, was what got me. Because however much I hated the thought of him going, the thought of what staying here would do to him was worse. I couldn't bear watching him every day of the war, and then beyond it, wishing he was somewhere else, watching regret eat at him until he came to hate himself and us for keeping him here.

I loved all my siblings, but Matthew was mine. It was how the six of us divided up: Matthew and I, the two eldest; Marigold and Holly, the middle girls; Iris and Little John, the babies. The five years between us, the fact that I was closer in age to the middle girls than to him, never seemed to make a difference. Nor did the fact he was confident and fit and eternally optimistic where I was quiet and bookish and sceptical. We shared an older-sibling responsibility for our family, coupled with a burning curiosity about the world away from the farm, and we had muddled through both together since I was old enough to walk. Neither of us said this in as many words—I doubt we could have. It was just there between us, an unbreakable thread woven of work and laughter and childhood adventures and serious late-night conversations in the hayloft. In some strange way, it was really my permission he needed to go, just as I had needed his when I had confided to him, the year before, that I wanted to leave home at sixteen and train to be a teacher.

"All right," I said. "I'll talk to her."

Matthew caught the train to London in October, a month before my twelfth birthday, and we didn't see him for over four years.

Letters came often at first, sometimes spattered with dirt, sometimes scored through with the censor's black lines, always cheerful, filled with allusions to alien places so exciting that I burned with envy and feared for his safety in one confused rush. We would write back telling him all our news, assuring him that we were fine without him, longing for him to come home soon.

Others came home, broken and scarred and hollow-eyed with fatigue, as the war stretched on long past the few months we had been promised, and the stories of horror began to trickle back with them. Matthew never did. Three times he was granted leave, and all three times he was too far away to make it to us.

Twice he was hospitalised, first with pneumonia and then with a minor leg wound, and both times he was patched up and sent back up the line. The gaps between his letters widened, and the letters, when they came, soon said almost nothing at all. That hurt me a little, and frightened me a lot more. Matthew and I had always shared everything.

And then in August 1918, in what was to be the very last push of the war, we received a telegram telling us that he had been seriously wounded in action in Amiens. It was hard to know what to feel: relief, first and foremost, that the telegram had said wounded and not dead; terror that he may yet die; a wrench of the stomach to think of my elder brother, daring and mischievous and invulnerable, lying in pain in a filthy field hospital somewhere I couldn't even picture clearly in my head. France. All I knew about it were the bald facts I had learned in geography, and most of those would have been torn up by war long ago.

The next few months were long, anxious stretches of holding our breaths, punctuated by occasional gasps of air. One breath: a letter from Matthew, three weeks after the telegram, a short scrawled promise that he was alive and doing much better. We knew nothing more—whether he had been sent back to his unit or was coming home or had died the very next day. Another breath, or a sob of relief: The war was finally over, and there was to be no more fighting. There was dancing in the streets, and tears, and celebration mixed with terrible grief. But the soldiers wouldn't be home for weeks, we were told, even months, and however many letters I wrote, we could learn no news of my brother. One day he had been well enough to write, and that was all we had to cling to.

That winter the Spanish flu came in a greater wave than before, and it reached our house. For a time it seemed we might lose my little brother and sister as well. They were spared, in the end. It took my father. He died just before Christmas, never knowing what had become of his eldest son.

It wasn't until January 1919 that we heard a knock at the door. Standing on our doorstep was a small man, fair-haired, with horn-rimmed glasses and a round, anxious face that cleared at the sight of my mother.

"Ah! Mrs. Hill?" His voice was soft, with a Queen's English accent that had formed far from a muddy Lancashire sheep farm. "Please forgive the intrusion. My name is Samson True-love Wells—I served with your son. May I have a word?"

It was there, seated around our heavy kitchen table nursing tea in chipped cups, that we heard for the first time about the magical world that lurked in the corners of our own—the world of mages and scholars, of hedgewitches and spellbooks and old Families. We learned, at the same time, that Matthew hadn't been struck by a bullet or a shell, but by a faerie curse.

"It should never have happened," Mr. Wells said. Beneath his glasses and refined accent, he couldn't have been more than in his early twenties—Matthew's age. But I was sixteen, I hadn't seen Matthew in years, and that seemed old to me. "Magic is a carefully kept secret and always has been. That was made very clear at the start of this war, and for that reason we were all strongly discouraged from signing up. Any mage who wanted to take to the battlefield, on either side, had to swear to never use magic in public, even at the cost of his own life. Nobody, though, was prepared for those battlefields. Most young men don't have it in them to die rather than break a promise to an authority that doesn't care. Things slipped out. And on that day, at Amiens, somebody opened a faerie door. That's difficult magic under the best of circumstances, and it went very wrong. The faerie broke free, and it killed men on both sides. Matthew was one of those hit by its curse. Thank God, I got to him in time."

"Are you his superior officer?" my mother asked cautiously. I think she still hadn't taken in the full measure of what he was saying. She was only wondering why a young man who was so clearly a gentleman cared if her son lived or died.

"Oh no." Mr. Wells understood the question perfectly. "I was a private—I enlisted three years ago. I could have bought a commission, I suppose, but I didn't want to lead. Being what I was, too, I thought it better to keep my head down. Your son and I came through the Somme together. He had been out there longer, even though he was a year younger than I was, and he looked after me, always. And so, when I could, I looked after him. Fortunately, I did an assignment on faerie curses at Camford in my first year, before I signed up. I performed the counter-curse before it reached his heart, inexpertly I'm afraid, but he's safe, and he'll be coming home to you as soon as he's permitted. First, though, I need to warn you—to tell you. To explain to you about our world."

If we'd been in London or even Manchester, among the well-read and well-informed, we might have heard whispers of it before. Magic, it seemed, had been practiced for centuries. It was a closely guarded secret, passed down through families yet forbidden to outsiders. Even so, history was full of moments when things had leaked out, odd miracles and happenstances and glimmers of spellcraft. There had never been more than in the last four years: platoons disappearing into midair, birds summoning help for injured men, nurses who could heal when all hope seemed impossible, deaths that couldn't be explained. The Great War had torn everything apart; it stood to reason it would tear those veils of secrecy too. As Mr. Wells had said, battlefields were no place for half-hearted promises, and trenches left little room to hide. Perhaps, too, this war had been better documented than those before it, with photographs and shaky camera footage bringing unthought-of images home. Nothing damning, but enough to spook the Families. And the incident at Amiens had more than spooked them. It had been an unprecedented disaster, and they were adamant that it should never happen again.

We barely grasped most of this at the time. It was all startling and impossible coming from Mr. Wells's lips—the magical Families, the rules, the secrecy. What I grabbed at and held to, as a drowning person might clutch at a branch, was that Matthew was coming home, and all things considered, he was safe. I had been the eldest child in the house through four years of war and all that had come with it, and I hadn't done that without holding firm to the belief that as long as we were alive there was nothing that couldn't be fixed. Matthew was alive, and that was what mattered. I heard everything Mr. Wells said about the curse, and it didn't faze me. He was going to be all right. I was going to make sure of it.

He wasn't all right. I could see that as soon as he stepped off the train.

It had been six months since he had been hurt, and he had spent them under lock and key in the care of the Families in France, half patient, half prisoner. I don't know if it was that or the years of war that had come before it that had whittled him so thin and pale, that had chiselled new lines at the corners of his eyes and between his brows, that had taken the light from his eyes and from his smile even as both kindled at the sight of us. Either way, it shocked me, and the shock never quite faded. When it was my turn to embrace him, I clung to him, his uniform coarse against my cheek, and felt the weakness in his left arm as he held me. The younger children hung back, shy and a little awed. Even Holly and Mary barely remembered him now, and John and Iris had been babies when he left.

"All right?" he asked as we parted, and his voice at least hadn't changed. "Jesus, Clover, you're nearly as tall as I am. When did that happen?"

"You tell me," I said, and hoped my own voice sounded as steady. "You're the one who shrank."

He laughed, but I wished I hadn't said it.

We saw the damage soon enough that evening. He still needed a hand to shrug off his jacket and shirt in those days, and beneath it we could see the wound the curse had left. I understood then why the Families had been worried—it looked like nothing that could have been inflicted by man or machine. The entire shoulder was withered and cracked and hard like the grey-white bark of a tree. It started just below the collar bone and crept out in dark fingers across his chest and down his arm and up toward his throat. I knew with sickening certainty that it had been reaching, in true fairy-tale fashion, for his heart.

"Does it hurt?" Iris asked, wide-eyed. I didn't have to.

"A bit," he conceded. "It's getting better. It's nothing," he added firmly, seeing Mum's face. "I'm lucky to be alive to feel anything at all."

He meant it, I know. But it was difficult to remember that, as the days turned into months and it never did get better. With our father so recently dead and our mother fully occupied with children and housework, the bulk of the farming fell squarely on him. And the farm was struggling worse than ever in the wake of years of war and sickness. I tried to help all I could, but he made this difficult by insisting that I go back to school. I had quietly not returned after that horrible Christmas, telling myself the farm and my family needed me, trying not to feel as though my future was being ripped away and nobody noticed or cared. Matthew noticed, and he wouldn't have it.

"You're going to go to train as a teacher," he said when I protested. "I didn't fight a bloody war to come home and watch you wither away here."

So I went back to school. I told myself that Matthew wanted it, that I needed to be learning again, that being a teacher would help my family, and all those things were true. It was also true, though, that with my father dead and my brother half a stranger and home so grey and miserable, I longed to leave more than ever. I hated feeling it, I was wretchedly guilty every time I did, and yet I needed there to be more to life than this. There was a shortage of teachers after the war, as there was of so much else, and my chances of being accepted into a training college looked hopeful as long as I worked hard.

I studied every spare second I could. I learned geometry and poetry and the kings and queens of England; after school, for an hour, the schoolmistress gave me extra lessons in Latin and ancient Greek. Then I came home in time to help my mother make supper, and watched my brother grow more frustrated every time he came in. I learned to tell the good days when his shoulder was a dull ache he could ignore, the bad days when every unexpected movement made him wince before he could hide it, the very worst days when he could barely move it at all, and I hated having to learn it more than any lesson school had ever given me. I hated watching pain and worry wear away at him, drip by drip, like water on stone. I hated watching him be brave, knowing he'd already had so much practice at it.

The worst part, though, was the midnights.

The midnights were what Mr. Wells had come to warn us about in person—what we needed to understand and Matthew couldn't explain except as second-hand information. On certain nights of the year, the nights of the old pagan festivals when faerie magic was at its strongest and mages would traditionally work their spells, Matthew would lose his mind.

"In the most literal sense of the word," Mr. Wells explained, his round blue eyes serious behind their spectacles. "He won't be himself anymore. It will last from sundown to sunup, give or take, so you'll need to be ready. During that time, he must be bound—with silver, preferably, though never underestimate a good, sound rope. He'll talk to you, implore you, threaten you, try everything in his power to convince you to release him. You mustn't listen. Keep the door closed, block your ears if you have to. Don't let him go, even for a second. He'll overpower you."

"What will happen if he does?" I asked, my throat dry.

"You'll lose him," Mr. Wells said bluntly. "The fae are always trying to steal human bodies—they can't survive long in the human world without them. That curse will do everything in its power to deliver Matthew to the nearest faerie door. If he made it through, the fae would claim him for their own. The doors are locked now, so that's impossible, but…"

He broke off, looking away for the first time. I had been through a war too. I knew what that meant.

"Your people will kill him, won't they?" I said. "The Families."

My mother stiffened beside me, and Mr. Wells sighed.

"Don't think too badly of them," he said. "They're very scared right now—both of exposure and of faerie magic. If he tried to get to the doors, out of his mind with a faerie curse, they would kill him on sight. You must understand, nonmagical people struck by faerie curses are supposed to die. I'm in a good deal of trouble for saving him in the first place, and a good deal more for using my family's influence to push for him to be returned to you. That's why it's absolutely imperative that he be kept safe on those nights. It will be terrible, I can't deny that. Nevertheless, you must promise me."

He might have been talking to my mother. I was the one who nodded, though, and so his gaze shifted to me.

"I will help if I can," he said. "I promise. Anything I can do, you need only to ask."

But Mr. Wells had left the house before Matthew returned, and he never saw him. We had to struggle with it on our own. And it was every bit as bad as Mr. Wells had said.

It was strange and sickening to tie him up, the first time. It was the night of the spring equinox—Ostara, on the calendar Mr. Wells had given us. We had no silver—the very idea was ridiculous—so we used ropes and chains with heavy padlocks, and shut the doors and windows tight for good measure.

"Go on," Matthew said, when he noticed me hesitating. He sounded calm, but I could read the set of his jaw and the way his eyes never quite met ours. He hated every second of this. "I can't remember what happens on these nights, but I've seen the state of the room the next day. You can't take any chances."

So we tied him to his bed, in the narrow attic room he had to himself, and at his insistence, we stepped out and locked the door behind us. Mum told me to go to bed; I wouldn't. The two of us sat outside on the stairs all night, not speaking, even when Matthew started to call for help.

They were quiet at first, those cries. His voice came, plaintive, asking if we were still there. We didn't answer. Mr. Wells had warned us it was better not to.

"It's all right," my brother's voice said. "I don't think it's happening tonight. You can let me go. Mum? Clover? Is anyone there?"

We still didn't answer. Mr. Wells had warned us of that too.

The calls escalated over the night. The pleading note deepened, then turned to anger. He begged us by name, then he threatened. By midnight the screams had started. Mum gripped my hand in her hard bony fingers, and I gripped back just as tight. The night seemed to last a thousand years.

I only made one mistake. It was almost dawn, the black around us beginning to lighten with the faintest hint of grey. My eyes were gritty, my bones hollow with fatigue. The voice behind the door had been quiet for over an hour. I was half dozing when it came again.

"Clover?" Matthew's voice was soft, almost a whisper. "Are you there?"

I sat up, blinking, rubbing my eyes hurriedly with the heel of my hand. A quick glance beside me revealed that Mum had fallen asleep, leaning against the wall.

"Clover," the whisper came again. "It's all right. It's over now. I'm back. You can come let me out."

It looks so obvious, set down on paper. I knew, really, what was speaking. In that hazy half-asleep hour, though, the world all shadows and uncertainties, I doubted what I knew. It sounded so like Matthew; curses and enchantments were such a new idea to us all. And what if it *was* him? I think, in the end, that was what caused me to get to my feet and creep to the door. What if it really was him—had been him all night, begging us for help, and we had been ignoring him?

"Clover," he said. "Please. Please let me out."

That *please* was the last straw. I pushed the door open.

The predawn haze through the window gave just enough light to see. My brother's body half sat, half lay on his bed, as upright as the ropes and chains would allow. He was not inside it. The familiar lines of his face had sharpened, shifted, contorted; when he smiled, it was a baring of teeth that chilled my stomach. He raised his head, and his eyes glinted.

"It's all right," the thing said with my brother's mouth, while that strange light gleamed in his eyes. "Come here."

I slammed the door shut and slid the bolt home so fast the hem of my dress caught in the gap. The fabric tore as I yanked it in a blind panic, leaving a small scrap of yellow caught against the wood. On the other side of the door, I could hear the faerie-thing chuckling.

I sat there on the stairs, shaking, fighting back tears as Mum dozed beside me. It truly was magic that gripped my brother. I understood it then for the first time, and my world, already in fragments, began to take on a new and terrible shape.

The following night, while my family slept, I carefully crept downstairs to the kitchen. The last embers of the stove were still burning, enough to see to light a candle. I sat at the table and carefully laid out a piece of string with a knot in the middle.

Mr. Wells had shown me the spell right at the end of his visit, almost as an afterthought. I had followed him out to the gleaming motorcar waiting on our driveway, ready to point out the shortcut back to the main road.

"Can anyone do magic?" I asked, right before he got in. "Or only people like you?"

"Anyone, in theory," he said. "Spells are simply a word and a gesture, very precisely performed. It's more difficult for anyone outside the Families, though. Something to do with blood."

"I could learn, though?"

"Slowly, with great effort. You wouldn't be able to do very much." He hesitated, looking at me with mingled guilt and doubt, then dipped into his pocket and pulled out a handkerchief.

"Here." It was the first time I noticed the silver ring on his left hand, though I didn't know then what it was. "Watch closely."

He tied the handkerchief in a loose knot and held it out in the palm of one hand. Then he passed the other hand over it with a twist of his fingers almost too rapid to see, and whispered, *"Behind."*

I felt a shiver in the air, like a breath of wind in the dark—nothing more. Mr. Wells must have seen my sceptical expression, because his mouth twitched as he handed me the handkerchief.

"There," he said. "Try to untie that. You'll find you can't. It's a simple charm, one that renders a knot unbreakable. If you could master it, it might help with the midnights."

I tugged at the knot experimentally, then tried to unpick it with my fingers. He was right. It was stuck as fast as if it had been glued. As magic went, it wasn't spectacular, but it was the first I'd ever seen. My heart quickened.

"Show me how the fingers go again?" I asked.

Now, at the kitchen table late at night, I tried myself. I joined my right index finger and my ring finger together and made the small, tight circle Mr. Wells had shown me; I whispered the Old English word over the knot. It didn't take, of course. I hadn't expected it to. There were a thousand variables—the size of the circle, the pitch of the whisper, the tension in the muscles. The only sure way to learn it was to do it right once, find the feel of it, and keep trying to replicate it until it was perfect.

I tried again. And again. By the end of the first hour my fingers ached and my throat was sore. I kept trying. I wasn't afraid anymore.

It truly was magic that held my brother. As terrifying as it was, that meant one important thing: Magic was real. It was real, and that meant that things *could* be fixed after all. Matthew was cursed—curses, every fairy tale told me, could be broken. I could break it, whatever it cost.

It meant another thing too. It meant that I could learn magic. And that, though I hardly dared to think it, was a doorway to more than just teaching. That opened a whole new world.

By the end of the summer, I was ready.

Anything I can do, you need only to ask. Mr. Wells had said that, and even though he'd never come back, I knew that he had meant it. I found his address in the drawer where Mum kept old correspondence from her relatives. I wrote to him that very night, short and businesslike, assuring him that nothing was wrong but I had a personal favour to ask of him the next time he chose to visit the house. A week or so later a letter came back from him, expressing his regret that he would be unable to visit in the foreseeable future. He would, however, be doing some business nearby in two weeks, if I wouldn't mind travelling to meet him for lunch. Enclosed in the envelope was a round-trip train ticket to Manchester.

Mum wasn't at all sure. I don't know what bothered her

more—the magical world, or the idea of me travelling to the
city by myself to meet a man we barely knew. It was my turn to
appeal to Matthew to convince her, trying to suppress the guilty
memory of where my efforts on his behalf had put him. He
managed it, too, though he came out shaking his head with the
same half-mischievous, half-chagrined air I remembered from
the time I was ten and he had taken me with him into the pub on
Friday night.

"Don't push her too far, all right?" he said. "You have to
remember how this place can be about witchcraft."

Our farm wasn't far from Pendle Hill, where twelve people
were accused of witchcraft during the Lancaster Assizes in 1612.
Superstition clung to the hill like shreds of cobweb—it was the
site of visions and visitations, encounters with fae and with dev-
ils. I knew even then that most of it had little to do with real
magic, only fear. Still, I took Matthew's warning to heart. With
my mother, fear was almost as dangerous as a curse, and just as
inconvenient.

I had been to Manchester only a handful of times in my life,
and never since the war. It startled me: its size, its redbrick solid-
ity, its rattlings and its shouts and its smoke. It seemed in a constant state of construction, exciting and chaotic all at once. The
restaurant to which Mr. Wells escorted me was startling in a
different way. It was sleek and white and modern, its marble-
and-glass interior defying the city outside to smudge it. We sat
on plush chairs at a window overlooking the retail district, and
I knew that whatever would be put in front of me would cost
enough to feed my family for a week.

Mr. Wells looked the same as he had those few months ago—
a little rounder and better rested, perhaps, with his suit sitting
more comfortably on his shoulders. He apologised for making
me come out to the city. It was, he said, difficult for him to get
time away from his work, and I knew at once that he was lying
without knowing why.

I decided to come out with it quickly. "You told me you learned how to counter faerie curses at a university," I said, after the waiter had given us our soups and left. "A magic university."

"Camford," he confirmed. "Or the Cambridge-Oxford University of Magical Scholarship, to give its proper title."

The name bewildered me momentarily. "Is it at Oxford or Cambridge?"

"Neither. Both. Very few people know where Camford itself is situated. Wales, possibly, or Scotland. It's a closely kept secret—most of the magical universities are the same. There are two doors, one at Oxford and one at Cambridge. You pass through one or the other to get there."

I nodded, as if this was the kind of information I received every day. "And it's where people like you go to learn magic?"

"It's where most of the sons of magical Families go when they turn eighteen or so, yes. Most learn very little there, it must be confessed, but it's the custom, and some do stay on to be scholars. I didn't graduate myself. I left after my first year to sign up, and I couldn't face going back. Why?"

"I want to go there," I said. "Camford. I want to learn magic. I want to be a scholar."

"Ah." He had just raised his spoon; he set it down and touched the napkin to his mouth on reflex. "May I ask why?"

"Many reasons." He kept waiting, cautious and courteous. "First and foremost, because Matthew needs help. He can't keep living like this. It isn't fair."

Mr. Wells's face tightened, as at some sudden pain. "Has he said that?"

"No, of course not. I do. I see what he's going through every day. And he isn't the only one, is he? There were others struck by faerie curses in that battle."

"There were," he agreed, still cautious. "Very few are still alive, however, and it won't happen again. The Families across Europe made an accord after the war—no more faerie magic.

The doors between our world and faerie country have been locked for good. Too little, too late, but still..."

"But still," I countered. I hadn't known that, of course, but I was determined not to remind Mr. Wells just how little I knew. I was afraid, in an abstract way, that it would put him off helping me to learn more. "It doesn't help Matthew. And that's what I want to do. If he were injured in the usual fashion, I might train to be a doctor or a chemist. That won't be of any use in this case. He needs magic."

"He does, I agree. But—forgive me, I don't mean any offence. I just want to be clear. I'm not sure he needs magic from *you*. I'm not sure such a thing would even be possible."

It was no less than I had expected, yet it still stung. I drew a deep breath, making sure none of the hurt found its way to my voice. "Mr. Wells—"

"Sam," he interrupted. "Please. I grew used to 'Private Wells' in the army. Mr. Wells sounds peculiar."

"Sam," I amended. "You did tell me, when you first came, that anyone could learn magic. I know people from outside the magical Families would never normally attend Camford—"

"I wouldn't say never," he interrupted, yet again. Normally I would grit my teeth at that; from Sam, though, it didn't feel dismissive. I could see he was ill at ease, and he was one of those people whose tongue runs away with them in such times. "There have been cases of people discovering our secret, just as you have, and attempting the entrance exam. Some have succeeded. Never a woman, though. There are few women scholars at Camford even from the Families. It's a stuffy old place at times, very set in its ways. It's expensive, too, like any prestigious university."

I appreciated the delicacy. He must have known we were poor as church mice. "Don't they have scholarships? Other universities do."

"Well, yes. Most of them are for postgraduate study, though—prizes. The top five graduating students in each year, for instance, receive the Merlin Scholarship, and that pays their way through a doctorate. The only scholarships to enter Camford at first year are hardship benefits, and they're rarely claimed. Most magical Families are wealthy, or at least would rather not attend at all than admit they weren't."

"I'm not wealthy," I said. "And I don't mind admitting it."

That wasn't quite true—I had a healthy degree of pride, as well as trepidation at the thought of how such people might look upon someone like me. I wouldn't let it stop me, though.

"It isn't so simple. They don't give such scholarships out of the goodness of their hearts. It would require you to not only pass the entrance exam but pass among the very top."

"I'd be one of the few who were truly trying, if magical Families are so wealthy."

"They won't need to try to outperform you. You don't understand. Anyone *can* learn magic, Miss Hill, there's no denying that. The truth is, though, those from outside the Families find it very difficult. I don't know why—nobody does—but for some reason, if it isn't in the blood—"

"I learned the spell you showed me." I thought it was only fair I took my turn to interrupt. "The binding spell."

That made him pause, curious, on the edge of sceptical. "Show me?"

I glanced around the restaurant, at the people eating their food and laughing.

"Oh, it's quite safe," Sam assured me, following my gaze. "This is a Family restaurant. You probably didn't notice the spell I performed at the door before we came in? If I hadn't done it, this would have opened to a very old-fashioned shoe store. We can do any magic we like without breaking the code of secrecy."

"Nobody else seems to be."

He laughed pleasantly. "Why would they? I daresay there's some magic being employed in the kitchens. Everyone here is busy eating. Here." He took up the cloth napkin in front of him, tied it in the middle, and slid it across the table to me. "Bind that, if you don't mind. I'd like to see it."

I tried to make it look simple, effortless, as though magic came as naturally to me as breathing and not at all as though I had practiced for hours every night for months until my voice was hoarse and my hands cramped and my head throbbed. I was so nervous that my fingers were stiff and clumsy, and I feared my voice had trembled at the wrong moment. It felt as though my future were hanging on that one incantation, the only one I knew.

Sam picked up the napkin, tugged it experimentally. His eyebrows rose above his spectacles.

"That's very good," he said. "Impeccable. You must understand, though, that the students from Families have been doing magic since they were children."

"I'll keep up, I promise." Hope flared in my chest. He had sounded impressed. "I'll work as hard as I need to."

"I believe you, truly. I'm simply trying to make you understand how hard that will need to be, and that even your hardest might not be enough. Do you really want to go down this path, considering?"

"I want to help my brother," I said.

"I do understand that." I saw that flash of pain across his face again. "But scholars have been working on faerie curses for a long time. Believe me, if anything new is discovered, I'll make it available to you straight away. It's unlikely, though, to come from—"

"Me," I finished, when he looked awkward. "A woman from a nonmagical family. Nobody special."

"Clover, believe me, I have heard all about you from your brother," Sam said. "I know you're special. I know all of you are. Still, the lack of experience and the, well, the *advantage* one gets from magical blood…"

"Perhaps I am unlikely to help Matthew," I said, because I could get nowhere by arguing. "Even so, I want to learn magic."

"Why?" he repeated. "Let's set Matthew aside for a moment. Suppose it transpires that your brother can't be helped, that however hard you study, you will make no material difference to his condition. Would you still want it?"

"Yes." The answer came so swiftly I surprised even myself. "More than anything."

"Because...?"

"Because I've lived my entire life wanting to get away from my home and learn about the world." The words came easily in the end, the ones I had never planned to say. The ones I had been ashamed to admit to, lying in bed late at night in a house filled with dearly loved people who needed me. "I wanted to study to be a teacher because that was the only use I could see for education that didn't feel selfish, that I could use to earn a living and help my family. We could never have afforded to send me to a real university, even if one would take me. But if I can pass the entrance exams to Camford near the top, then everything would be paid for. That's right, isn't it?"

"That's right," Sam said slowly. "If you passed near the top."

"I can. I know I can. If I can learn Latin and Greek and geometry, I can learn magic. I proved that, didn't I? I taught myself that spell on my own. And—"

"And?" Sam prompted gently when I hesitated.

"And I loved it." I hadn't meant to say that either. I wanted to appeal to his reason, to argue my case on its own merits. It just came from me, because it was true. "When it worked—when I did that—I've never felt anything like it before. Like the universe was pure light, and I could run it through my fingers and stir it about like water." That was only a frustrating shadow of what I meant. When I looked at Sam, though, something in his face had shifted. "Do you understand?"

"I do," he said simply. "Any of us would."

I felt the bubble of hope grow stronger. "I know you've already saved Matthew's life. You owe us nothing—"

"I owe your family everything." This interruption I didn't mind at all. "More than you know. Of course I'll help if I can. You never know, after all. With the proper tutelage, you might learn a great deal in the next year or so. And I work for the Board of Magical Regulation now—I'll ask around and see if I can dig up any scholarships that most won't know about. We'll give it our very best shot." He hesitated. "How is your brother?"

"All right," I said. "Tired. The last midnight was hard on him." I wish I could say I didn't know then what I was doing, and on some level I truly didn't, but I wasn't surprised when I saw Sam wince. I was more skilled at manipulation than I admitted, even then.

"I'll help," Sam repeated. "I promise."

We finished our meal in silence broken only by pleasantries, and he walked me back to the train station afterwards. He offered to take me to the Manchester Museum, which I had never seen, but I explained I had to be home to help with the sheep at night.

"Why don't you come and visit us?" I asked him on impulse. He seemed so wistful as the train pulled up, and he had been so kind. "Matthew hasn't seen you since he was hurt."

"Perhaps I will," he said, and I knew that, for whatever reason, he wouldn't. "Either way, you'll certainly hear from me."

Within a week, a letter arrived for me in the post. It gave me the name and address of a house about an hour on horseback from our farm, and told me a witch was expecting me.

She owes my family a debt, he said. *Besides, I believe you've rather intrigued her. Her name is Lady Anjali Winter—her husband was killed in the war. If you go to study with her once a week, she'll give you the benefit of her knowledge. She also has an extensive library, though you may find the books outdated. If by next summer she thinks you ready, you may sit the Camford entrance exam. Do let me know if there's anything more I can do, and give my best regards to your brother.*

I did go to study with Lady Winter. I'll have more to say about her later—at the time, I'm not sure I saw her properly, as scared and in awe and utterly focused on magic as I was. For an hour each week, she taught me basic spellcraft, theory, history, and folklore. In between lessons I practiced harder than I had ever practiced anything before. I immersed myself in books from her library, wrote essay after essay, tried spells over and over until I hit them perfect every time. I kept my eyes on my work, and I never looked up.

In the summer of 1920 I journeyed to Manchester again, this time to meet a red-faced, disgruntled mage and be ushered into a small room. One hour of writing and two of practical tasks later, red-faced myself now and wrung dry with exhaustion, I was informed that I could start at Camford in September, on full scholarship.

3

Camford. I realise I've come this far without describing it, but it's difficult to know how. People say it resembles Oxford or Cambridge, which makes sense, given that centuries ago it was part of them. When Cambridge split from Oxford in the early thirteenth century, the magical department vanished to become its own institute. There was still a Camford staff member at each of those two universities, one to watch over each of the doors that led to Camford itself. The door that led from the Bodleian was still laughingly referred to as "the Oxbridge."

The truth was, the first time I came to Oxford, that sunny afternoon in late September, I disliked it on sight. I had expected to love it—the spires, the cobbled roads, the ancient seats of learning. It represented knowledge to me. I had dreamed of it most of my life, long before I learned there was such a thing as magic or faerie curses. Matthew had found a photograph of it in an old magazine and framed it for my eleventh birthday, the year I had first confided in him I wanted to go to training college, and I had hung it on my wall alongside my print of Tennyson's "Ulysses" and the watercolour of a clover my father had drawn for me when I was born. I had tried to fall asleep looking at those towers, hoping that in my dreams I would soar above them and find my place there as I never would in life.

But the Oxford I saw that first day, as I followed Sam to my new home, was not the one from my dreams. The greyscale of the photograph melted into bright sun, and in the light of it, those famous spires looked mildewed and yellow, in need of a good airing. The architecture, impressive as it was, somehow didn't touch me with anything except rising disappointment. There were too many straight lines and trimmed lawns, too many signs forbidding entry; the buildings had a crumbling, fusty look, as though the place was calcifying. I'd come from slow-moving, rugged hills where little had changed for centuries; in my heart, I'd imagined post-war Oxford as bustling, brimming over with shiny new scholarship, at the brink of a changing world. Yet here I was, and it just looked weary and set in its ways, like an old man falling asleep at a heavy dinner.

"Imposing, isn't it?" Sam asked, perhaps mistaking my silence for awe.

"Oh…yes," I said, truthfully enough. It *was* imposing. It wanted everyone to know it had been important once. "Is—is Camford much like this?"

"Oh no," Sam said vaguely. He was looking about him, my trunk in one hand. I had tried to stop him carrying it for me, until I realised that with a word he had made it feather-light while I would have been dragging a heavy case over cobbles. "Well, the architecture, perhaps. Buildings all look much alike to me. Now, where is that damn library? You'd think in a place where the streets don't move…"

He was right. I knew it immediately the first time I crossed the Oxbridge, and I stepped forward with a rush of wonder and excitement and sheer relief. Camford was not like Oxford at all.

Did you ever see it? I hope you did. I hope you stepped through that peculiar little door in one of the many secret rooms of the Bodleian and felt the temperature drop a few degrees, the wind tease at your hair and clothes and your blood thrill in response, seconds before the sprawling campus filled your eyes. I knew at once that we were somewhere different, somewhere wilder and colder than the mannered countryside we had left, though there was no way of telling where it might be. A high stone wall surrounded it, and beyond those fortifications all that could be seen was mist and haze that persisted even in the brightest sun. The light had a pale, silvery quality, as though filtered through glass, and the breeze brought the smell of rain and stone and autumn leaves. The architecture within it *was* similar to Oxford and Cambridge, in that there were spires and towers and cobbled streets, but it was Oxford through an imperfect mirror. The stone was darker, a silvery grey with odd patches of brick where buildings had been added or repaired. A great domed building rose from the middle—I thought it might be a cathedral and learned later that it was the library. Everything else was crooked, rambling, haphazard. Buildings teetered; paths wound like unspooled thread; a river twisted through the centre, spanned by bridges at random. The doors, for no reason I've ever learned, were all blue.

Strangest of all, it was entirely overgrown with trees. Oak and ash and ivy entwined every inch—holding up the massive walls, peeking through the cobbles, bursting through every courtyard, impossibly green against the stone. If it hadn't been for the students cycling down the pathways, laughing in the courtyards, it might have been a ruin left for a hundred years.

I had come looking for magic and possibility, and here it was. But there was something else here, too, something I had never felt before. History. Tradition. Beauty.

"Oh," I said, completely and wholly inadequately. My heart had risen so far in my throat I thought I might cry.

"It might take you a while to find your way around," Sam warned me, as if from a distance. "The pathways are tricky, especially with all the trees, and some of them move. You'll get there in the end. Everyone does."

I nodded, barely listening. In that moment, I knew I had done the right thing. I hadn't been certain on the train, dressed in my stiff Sunday best, the warmth of my family's embraces still fading from my body, everything familiar disappearing behind me while the world loomed ahead like a shadow. Magic, for God's sake. I was Clover Hill, bright and hardworking and good at drawing but nothing special, and certainly not a witch. Who was I to force my way in here, where nobody wanted me? But looking at Camford opening in front of me like a story waiting to be read, I knew I needed to be here. This place, at least, the war had never touched. It had been battered by so many centuries of magic and scholarship, and it had weathered all those centuries unchanged. From here I could fix everything.

———————⬦———————

Had it not been for that moment, the next week might have broken me.

Camford was a select university, five hundred students and a small staff. Of those staff, ten or so were on the Faculty (it was always capitalised, much like the Board, who governed magic in London, or the Families themselves, and I could hear those capitals whenever it was pronounced). The rest, as far as I could gather, were lecturers, librarians, custodians—it was a long time before I saw anyone who did the cooking and cleaning. For reasons of secrecy, everyone who worked or studied at Camford was housed on the campus; first-year undergraduates, even the few women, lived in a single building at the south corner known as Chancery Hall. All of them, apart from me, were Family.

I had known this before coming, of course. I hadn't understood what it meant. On that first day, as Sam led me down the confusing labyrinth of crooked alleys and winding streets to Chancery, every nook and cranny teemed with young men in the most expensive suits I had ever seen. Sam left me standing in a high-ceilinged entrance hall while he rushed off to ask somebody about my lodgings, and I stood there with the old blue leather trunk Mum had dug out of the attic and watched a group of them by the stairs. My classmates. They had clearly just arrived, too, and yet they just as clearly all knew one another. They called out to each other by name, laughed at old jokes; one moved his fingers too fast to follow and shot a stream of water at another while the others howled with mirth.

I had never been shy at home. Solitary, perhaps—our farm was out in the middle of nowhere, and at school I was always too focused to make real friends, set on learning as much as I could in the short time I had. But I never had trouble speaking up if I had to; I had never worried about what anybody thought of me except the people I loved. It was different here. Whether because I had inherited Mum's mingled wariness and awe of the wealthy or simply because I wanted to belong here as I never had before, the sight of these polished creatures talking and embracing in a sea of dark coats made me want to curl up and hide behind the nearest sofa.

One of them, a cheerful boy with red hair, caught sight of me and grinned. When I returned his smile, weakly, he peeled off from his classmates and came closer. "Hello. I don't think we've been introduced. Justin Abbott. I saw you come with Sam. Are you related to the Truelove or the Wells clans?"

For a fleeting second, I wondered if I could pretend. Sam wouldn't have minded. I could have claimed I was his cousin, from a distant branch in the north. I dismissed the idea almost at once. For one thing, my ring would have given me away. They all had them, like the one I had noticed around Sam's finger the day we had met, and each was emblazoned with a Family crest. I had been given one too—they were enchanted with differing levels of access to Camford, so I would need it to pass through the gates and even my own room—but my crest was blank. I was a nobody, and it wouldn't be long before they saw. Besides, I remembered, uncomfortably late, I wasn't ashamed of my family. I wasn't.

"No." God, why did I sound so young and so provincial? "Sam's a friend of the family. I'm Clover Hill."

His face at once closed off and sharpened with curiosity, a nosy neighbour pulling the window shut yet still peeking around the curtain. "Oh," he said, in a voice that made an effort to be pleasant. Behind him, a couple of his friends turned. "Oh, I see. We heard of you, of course. The scholarship witch."

I didn't know what to say, because I didn't know what to feel. Was *witch* an insult here? It certainly sounded as though *scholarship* was.

Fortunately, Sam bustled back, faintly out of breath. "Your room is this way," he said. "There's a separate wing for female students. Oh, hello, Abbott. Have I interrupted something?"

"No," Abbott said. "Not at all. It's good to see you, Sam. How are things at the Board?"

"Oh, you know," Sam said vaguely. "Boring. Excuse us, please."

He turned to me as soon as we were alone, still moving at a rapid pace down a dark corridor. "He wasn't being unkind, was he? Don't pay attention. The Abbotts are meddling, inconsiderate snobs to a one. I went to Crawley with his brother, I know—"

"Sam!" I forced a smile and shoved him lightly, as though he were one of my own brothers. I hoped he couldn't see my rising nerves. "I can take care of myself."

"I'm sure of it. But—" He stopped, so suddenly I almost collided with him. "If anything goes wrong, or you want to come home, please call me, won't you? I know what this place can be like."

"I will." I meant it. But I was also seventeen, and determined never to need to. "I promise."

My room was on the ground floor, at the far end of the west wing. I'm sure most students would have found it small and uncomfortable. I, however, had always shared a much smaller room with Mary and Holly, the three of us trying to colonise space out of a clutter of old clothes and scuffed Victorian furniture. This bare room, with its blank cream walls and low rafters and window looking out to a paved courtyard, both thrilled and intimidated me. I couldn't imagine ever being able to make a mark on it with the contents of my old trunk. That first night, I lay awake on the creaky mattress as light rain spattered the window and the shouts and laughter of young strangers drifted in, and panic and excitement battled for supremacy in my stomach.

By next morning, panic had won.

Sam had warned me that some of the Camford pathways moved; now, I could also tell you that some walls were false and required a spell to part, some staircases went nowhere, and the outer wall was constantly being made unsafe by the encroaching ivy. On that first day, I couldn't have told you which hazard was which. I spent most of my morning lost, stumbling through mounting terror down streets that made no sense, bursting into lectures conspicuously late, sitting breathlessly in the front row trying to calm down as the lecturers outlined material I couldn't understand and recommended books I hadn't read. In the afternoon, I met my tutor, Everett Dalrymple: a bored, gawky-looking young doctoral candidate, with carefully combed dark hair and a tweed jacket that he probably thought made him look scholarly. I could tell at a glance that I was the last person he wanted to be assigned; later, I learned that I was punishment for some unfortunate remarks about the vice-chancellor, made while drunk at the end-of-year party. He greeted me pleasantly enough, and his cool disinterest warmed marginally when I outlined the authors I had studied. When I mentioned Agrippa and faerie curses, though, he snorted.

"Agrippa," he said flatly. "Well, I don't think you'll find a use for him outside of specialist history courses, and then not until third year. Faerie magic is illegal now in any case. There aren't even any books on it in the library, save in the archives."

My heart sank. "I don't want to *summon* a faerie," I said, as reasonably as I could. "Only study counter-curses."

"Those are off the curriculum too. Anything pertaining to the fae is strictly forbidden since the Accord. It's a pity, I know. A friend of mine had to abandon his thesis because of it. After what happened at Amiens, though, well…"

I bit my tongue before I protested that my brother was at Amiens. It wasn't widely known that a non-mage with a faerie curse was alive in the world, and Sam had warned me to be discreet.

"Leave faerie spells alone, Miss Hill," Dalrymple said, "and Agrippa with it. You'll find a new area of interest. If, of course, you stay past this year."

The underlying threat didn't trouble me. I was used to the idea of having to prove myself, and it didn't occur to me, as it should have, that Dalrymple had the power to fail me whether I proved myself or not. But I was dismayed to find my reading was out-of-date, and the news that Camford wouldn't support my studies into faerie magic crushed me. It seemed that as far as helping Matthew went, I might as well go home. I knew, in the part of my heart I tried to ignore, that I should consider doing exactly that. I could study magic without Camford, or at least I didn't see how anyone could stop me. I could help my family best perhaps with no magic at all. And yet the idea sickened me. I wanted to stay, to learn, to succeed. It wasn't only about magic now. Now I had seen Camford, I wanted nothing more than to belong to it.

It was perfectly obvious to everyone else, though, that I *didn't* belong. Since I had spoken to Justin Abbott, every student in Chancery Hall ignored me. Their eyes slid over me with expressions ranging from kind embarrassment to pity to open contempt, as they might a beggar on the streets. If I asked them a question, they would answer briefly or pretend not to hear. They could have done so much worse, I know, yet part of me would have preferred open cruelty. I could have fought back against bullying. I could have told myself they were jealous or threatened. Instead, my existence was impolite and vaguely repulsive, like a sneeze. After a few hours of it, my skin would prickle and my stomach would tighten, as though I were wearing dirty clothes I couldn't slough off.

By the end of that first week, I was spending every spare moment alone in the library, reading doggedly, trying to cram my head so full of new information there would be no room for doubt or fear or longing for my family. The library, at least, I could always find, standing as it did in the very centre of Camford, and its books welcomed me with open arms. I tried to tell myself I didn't need anyone else.

It was in that state—miserable, homesick, fighting back despair with sheer stubbornness—that Alden found me and asked me what I was reading. Perhaps if I had been less unhappy, I might not have accepted his invitation to Stanford Corbett's luncheon. Perhaps I might have thanked him politely but told him I had more reading to do. I still wonder, in the darkest and most sleepless hours of the night, what would have happened if I had. If it would have been better, after all, though I know it wouldn't really.

It doesn't matter, in the end. I went.

<hr />

When she first learned I would be going to Camford, all my mother had been able to focus on was the notion that I would be dining with wealthy students. The magical world was too far outside her knowledge; she neither understood it nor cared to. Class was real, and so was money, and she was determined I should be defeated by neither. Matthew and I had laughed, watching Mum frantically leaf through a book on the etiquette of cutlery she had borrowed from Miss Darby down at the village.

"Mum, she's not there to mess about with salad forks." Matthew was leaning against the kitchen door, arms folded. I was relieved to see the old playful glint dancing behind his eyes. "She's there to learn magic. She's a student now."

"Students have to eat," Mum said stubbornly. "And if she's eating with the likes of the aristocracy, she needs to do it properly."

I'd learned the salad forks, knowing it was her way of caring for me, fearing she might be right. So far, though I had dined in the student halls most nights, nobody had seemed to care greatly what fork I used or how I ate my soup. That luncheon with Alden was the first time I really, truly, dined with the wealthy students, at their invitation.

Stanford Corbett was a postgraduate with rooms on the second floor of Swan Tower. They were draughty and lavishly decorated and, on that day, already filled with students and scholars. The room brimmed over with them—young, red-faced men who laughed and pushed one another like workers at a tavern; well-dressed men tossing back champagne and snatching up little delicacies from the plates the servants carried; bored men already sitting at the long white table waiting for their food. My own stomach tightened, and I couldn't at that moment imagine swallowing a bite.

"So many people," I heard myself say, and immediately wished the ground to swallow me up. Honestly, I'd just felt that if I didn't say something, anything, Alden would forget I was there at his side and leave me to the wolves.

"Too many," Alden agreed, as if I'd said something astute and not very stupid. His eyes were scanning the crowd. "And too few with anything interesting to say. There's Hero, thank God. Hero!"

At the fireplace, Hero Hartley turned from the small man with whom she had been conversing.

I had seen Hero already. She was difficult to miss. In a room filled with charcoal suits, Hero's dress was white and gold and swept the floor, and there were white feathers in her rippling hair. The new fashion was for hair cut short and framing the face: Mum had cut mine herself before I'd left, using a faded sketch from a fashion magazine as a guide. I had secretly hoped, against all sense, that when it was done I would be transformed, no longer an awkward girl but a sharp, sophisticated young woman who had never brought ailing sheep inside in winter or heaved great bales of hay onto carts in the itchy, sticky heat of summer. It hadn't worked, of course. When Mum had towelled my hair dry roughly and stood back, it had hung limp about my face, which seemed to have grown rounder and pinker as my hair had shrunk. It didn't look like the fashion magazines at all. Hero didn't look like the women in the fashion magazines either. She didn't try to. Nor did she look like the few other women at Camford, who tended to dress soberly and practically, all felt hats and dark dresses. Her hair was long and deep chestnut, swept up in waves at the back of her head. She was tall, at least six feet, and in her heeled boots she rose a head above most of the men in the room. Her face was striking, cool and pale and oval-shaped—detached, I might have said, had it not been for the large dark eyes that glimmered with mischief. There was a sense of fun lurking beneath them that might be equally likely to turn on you or draw you in, and it invited you to try and see what you got.

They warmed as they fell on Alden, even as they brushed against me with curiosity. "Alden," she said pleasantly. "How the devil are you?"

"Rather under the weather, actually," he said.

"I'm not surprised, after last night. How much of it do you remember?"

"You'll have to fill me in." He took a fluted glass from a passing footman and motioned me forward. "Hero, may I present Clover Hill, the scholarship witch. Be gentle with her."

Hero's perfectly sculpted eyebrow shot up, and my stomach

dropped. I had been snubbed too many times since I had come here not to recognise the signs. "What *are* you up to, Alden?"

"I thought you might like to meet one of your fellow female scholars," he said innocently.

"Oh, I would. I'm delighted to meet her. I just can't imagine that would occur to you."

"She's interesting. Not to mention clever."

"I'm sure of that. But what about her is of interest to *you*, Alden Lennox-Fontaine? You have brains enough of your own, after all, and little enough to apply them to. She's very pretty, but not in the way you'd notice."

"I don't have to be at this party, you know," I interrupted. I tilted my chin determinedly, to hide the fact my face was burning. In that moment, I knew I didn't belong here. It wasn't just my family or my sex or my lack of wealth. Nobody wanted me here. I was short, plain, round, bespectacled, and my hair was wrong. Hero's was too, technically, but she looked as though she'd done it on purpose. "Alden invited me. I could go."

Hero turned her gaze on me properly for the first time, genuinely surprised. "Why would you want to do that?"

"You've hurt her feelings," Alden said. He drained the glass and set it on the mantelpiece. "I told you to be gentle."

"I do apologise." Hero's deep, cultured voice did sound sincere. "I'm used to this crowd, who have no feelings at all. I really am delighted to meet you."

"She is," Alden confirmed. "It's me in whom she has no faith. I found her in the library reading Agrippa, Hero, does that satisfy you?"

A look passed between them, so quickly I might even have imagined it: a question and an answer when I couldn't read either. Then it was gone, and Hero was smiling, amused.

"You and Agrippa. That does make things clear. She tolerated your ramblings, and your interest in her is that you believe she finds you interesting. He really isn't, you know, darling."

"I know." I did my best to make my voice as careless as Hero's. "But Agrippa is. He was hanged for black magic four hundred years ago, which is more interesting than anything that's happened to anyone else in this room."

Hero laughed, a generous, unfeminine laugh, not at all the kind Miss Darby in the village had told me was used in polite society. "Well done."

"Don't mind us," Alden interjected. He was grinning too. "Quite apart from the fact it's customary to talk nonsense at these sorts of gatherings, I did warn you that Hero and I were more or less brought up together. Her father and mine were cousins or at school together or saved each other's lives in the Crimean or some combination thereof. She considers it her sworn duty to cut me down to size. You two will like each other, though. I can tell."

"I'm so grateful for your opinion," Hero said. "Please ignore him, Clover, and ignore me around him. Tell me about yourself."

"There's not much to tell," I said awkwardly. "My family have a sheep farm not far from Pendle Hill—"

"Not that sort of thing. I've found that out already, from other people. You're the only student here not Family, which is very clever of you considering you're not supposed to know we exist, but I'm sure everyone involved was punished or pardoned ages ago. What's your specialty?"

"I don't know yet." My heart unfurled just a little. I wasn't quite ready to mention my interest in faerie curses, though. "I tested about the same on all the different branches of magic in the entrance exam."

"Which is very strong, presumably. No wonder they had to let you in."

"What about you?" I meant to ask after Hero's specialty. She misunderstood.

"Oh, there was no way they would ever have been able to keep me out. Even if they hadn't decided to let women matriculate this year, which by the way is about bloody time, they haven't been able to really stop us coming for the last thirty years—not if we have money and brains, and I have both. My father might have stopped me by refusing to pay, admittedly. Fortunately he's an indulgent old thing when the mood takes him."

"And mine doesn't much care if I live or die," Alden added. "You can imagine what we got up to in our youth."

"Our youth?" The eyebrow went up again, but now I could better see the fondness behind it. "What are we in now, our twilight years? We aren't all suffering the effects of the night before, you know."

"I'm glad to hear it." He rubbed his neck and winced. "Well, I hope you bright young things will allow this elderly gentleman to escort you to the table. Corbett will throw a tantrum if we avoid him much longer. After all, he's paying for the food."

It was at that luncheon that I tasted quail's eggs for the first time, and caviar, and wine that was worth hundreds of pounds a bottle. (One bottle, at least. The rest of it, Hero assured me, was decidedly second-rate.) It was there that I received my first polite nods and small talk from upper-class accents, bathed as I was in the glow of Alden's and Hero's approval. It was there where I first saw magic fly freely across a table, in the manner of those who had been brought up with it and had never considered it a privilege. It was there, too, that I met Edmund Gaskell.

I had seen Edmund once or twice, always sitting in the lecture theatre alongside Hero and Alden. He had caught my attention only because he seemed so drab and awkward next to their golden loveliness, rarely talking, his head bent to his papers as though trying to disappear. When I found myself sitting beside him at the table, with Hero on the other side, I was struck mostly by how sorry I felt for him.

"I never know what to do at things like this," he confided to his plate, in little more than a whisper. The Yorkshire burr was even stronger in his voice than it had been in Alden's—not common, like mine, but a little countrified. "Alden and Hero bring me along. I just sort of eat the brussels sprouts and leave as soon as I can."

"Do you like brussels sprouts?" I was grasping desperately for conversation. To my surprise his face lit up. It was a thin, anxious, gentle face: attractive, in its own way, had it been stronger and less sallow against his dark brown hair. The remnants of acne at his jawline didn't help, nor did the fact his eyes never lingered on anything longer than a second.

"I grow brussels sprouts." He almost tumbled over his words in eagerness. "They're a beautiful vegetable. They have all kinds of magical properties, you know, that most people would never expect. Not cooked, of course. Cooked they just taste nice."

"Are you a botanist?" I was genuinely curious now. Spells to do with plants were usually practiced by hedgewitches, not scholars. It was soft magic: its curses imprecise, its healing powers too difficult to distinguish from traditional medicine. There was an optional botany paper, and I was taking it, but even the lecturer had made it very clear that it wasn't something to pursue seriously.

"No—well, yes, I suppose. Not in the usual sense." His eyes met mine for the first time. They were unexpectedly beautiful: the blue grey of a winter sky on the moors. "I believe that plants have a natural connection to magic, you see, Miss Hill, one that we can channel in all sorts of different ways."

His enthusiasm was infectious. "What sort of ways?"

"Well, for starters, you mentioned botanists. Hedgewitches use plants to heal all the time. Their techniques have never been properly studied. It's seen as mundane rather than magical science. But what if, instead of the plants themselves possessing healing properties, some actually draw on magical energy in the same way we do when we cast spells?"

"It would be fascinating," I said, sincerely. "If it were true."

"There's been some work done on it," he said. "I hope to do more myself, one day. Though the Faculty doesn't approve."

It made me think of Alden and his interest in Agrippa, and inadvertently my eyes drifted to where he sat across the table. He was talking to an older student with a ginger moustache, his fingers curled around a glass while his fork lay untouched beside his plate. The glint from the library was in hiding, but I thought I could see it still behind his eyes, and in the corner of his smile.

Edmund mumbled something beside me, and I wrenched my gaze back to him with a pang of guilt. "I'm sorry?"

"I said," he repeated, "I do like your name awfully."

"Did you have a good time?" Alden asked me afterwards. I had lingered by Hero uncertainly, not wanting to leave until I had spoken to him again but not wanting to approach him directly. He might have forgotten all about me. I was far too relieved he hadn't.

"It was interesting," I said honestly. "I'd never had that kind of food before. And Edmund was very nice."

"Oh, you spoke to Eddie? He's mad as a box of chairs, isn't he? Brilliant, though." He checked his watch. "Listen, I have a very tiresome party to go to in a few hours, and before that I desperately need to lie down and sleep away the last of last night, but in between that nap and that party, may I stop by the library and see you for a rational talk about Agrippa? Say seven?"

"I—yes. Yes, that would be fine." I usually had dinner then, but I wouldn't have said that for the world. Besides, I would be full now from the luncheon. "Yes, I'm sure I'll be somewhere around where we met."

He smiled. "Excellent."

"Oh, don't mind me," Hero retorted. "I suppose I'll only get to see you if I come to that tiresome party, where you'll be decidedly irrational and never mention long-dead magicians at all."

"Darling." He kissed her extravagantly. Watching, I couldn't help but blush. "I solemnly promise that if you come to the tire-some party, I will talk to you about any long-dead magicians you wish, as rationally as you could desire."

"With a promise like that, how can I possibly accept?"

"That's what I thought. I'll see you in a few hours and in far better senses, Clover Hill."

"Well, that does it," Hero declared as Alden walked away. "I'm afraid you're stuck with him now. It's a good thing you have me."

"I do?"

"Of course you do, darling. Well, me and Eddie. He doesn't usually speak to new people, you know. I think he's mistaken you for a vegetable. Would you like to come back to my room for a cup of tea?"

Half-formed thoughts and feelings fluttered like butter-flies through my head. This couldn't be happening. People like this were not friendly to people like me. What on earth about Agrippa of all people had drawn Alden to me out of nowhere? It was best not to get involved. Besides, I had left my books in the library, and there was still time to study.

"Thank you," I said faintly. "That would be lovely."

4

It's strange to remember now, but part of me shied away from the idea of having friends. It wasn't that I didn't like Alden, Hero, and Eddie, because I did, very much. They were like nothing and nobody I had ever seen before. But I was at Camford to *work*. I wanted to be a scholar; I wanted to save my brother; the two desires collided and rubbed against each other in my head like a chorus of cicadas. This was my only opportunity, dearly bought. I couldn't justify being away from home if I didn't succeed, and I had enough disadvantages without the distraction of a social life. I needed to immerse myself in lectures, in libraries, in long hours scribbling notes by lamplight with a mug of coffee at my side and the world shrinking to a pen nib on a page. And I did. I really, truly did. It was just that increasingly, day by day, I found that I was not doing it alone.

It started with the lectures.

The Monday after my first luncheon, I came to my morning lecture unsure where to sit. In those days, Camford first-years followed the same core curriculum, with a few optional papers— it wasn't until second year that we were allowed to branch out into specialties. In the first semester we had lectures in Basic Incantations, Linguistics of Spellcraft I (Ancient Tongues), Introduction to Folklore, and History of Modern Magic I (Medieval to Renaissance) several times a week. My usual tactic was to come into the hall as the lecture was starting and sit quickly in the first row. This way I would avoid conversation before the lecture—or, to be more precise, it would be less obvious that nobody was talking to me. Alden and Hero, I knew, sat together halfway up the creaky stadium seating, talking and laughing; possibly Eddie would be alongside them. I wanted to join them. The trouble was, I didn't know if I was welcome. The time I had spent with the three of them the day before seemed part of some enchantment—as though I had briefly stepped into a faerie ring and woken the next morning to find only faded grass. I couldn't help but think they would look at me and not remember who I was.

They didn't, of course. Alden caught sight of me a moment after my eyes fell on him—Alden, I found out later, always felt a glance as though it was a touch. He smiled and said something to Hero; she looked up and waved me over.

"*There* you are," she said as I slid into the seat next to her. It sounded for all the world as though they had been waiting for me, as though my natural place was by their side. "I assumed you'd be here before us, having spent last night somewhat more rationally than we did."

"Speak for yourself," Alden said. "I was disgustingly rational last night. The party was dead before I got there, and for once I went home and let it rest in peace instead of staying on to try to revive it."

"I'd be so much more impressed if you left alone," Hero said dryly. "What was his or her name? I assume you got it?"

"It would have been irrational of me not to."

"Well," I said, before I could stop myself, "impolite, at least."

I was feigning the dry, ironic banter of Camford students, and I knew it. But they didn't, or they pretended not to. Hero laughed her generous cackle, and Alden tore a page from his notebook and threw it at me.

Eddie pushed through the doors last, dishevelled and out of breath. He glanced up, searching for a seat, and his cloudy-sky

THE SCHOLAR AND THE LAST FAERIE DOOR

eyes caught mine like a twig snagging on fabric. The uncertainty in them stabbed my heart, because it was what I tried so hard to keep from my own. I knew at once that he would normally come and join Alden and Hero, but now, seeing me, he wasn't sure if I wanted him there—that he was used to people turning away from him for God knows what stupid reason. I remembered how kind and how interesting he'd been at the luncheon, and how often I'd probably looked away from him toward Alden and Hero. On impulse, with a daring I'd never have mustered for any other Camford student, I smiled and waved him over. His face lit.

"Eddie," Alden greeted him as he slipped into the seat next to me. "How rational was your night last night?"

Eddie blinked. "Well. I watered the plants, wrote a letter home, and went to bed early."

"God. That's not only rational, it's downright healthy."

"Please don't mind him," Hero said tolerantly. "He has a new favourite word."

After that first Monday, I never sat alone at the front of the class again. It felt natural to come in, to seek out the other three, to join them if they were there first or to sit and wait for them if they weren't. We were the ones who were laughing together as the lecturer came in, listening and occasionally questioning when he spoke, disappearing together in a cloud of books and dropped pens after the talk ended. From there, it became natural to stay together afterwards—to walk to the library or to dinner. We started to have places that were ours—our study table on the seventh floor in the astronomy section, our seats in the dining hall beneath the stained-glass window depicting an owl in flight. Our jokes and nonsense, that nobody else would understand.

I still might have been too shy or too proud to let it pass beyond that level of friendly classmates had it not been for Hero. Now

I had come willingly to her attention, she took me up with all the proprietary kindness of an older sister. Rules around male-female segregation were more relaxed at Camford than the outside world—there simply wasn't room for it to be otherwise. Still, male visitors were strictly forbidden in the rooms of female students outside of daylight hours, and even then never unchaperoned. Hero, though, could visit whenever she liked. Within a week of Corbett's luncheon, I was sitting at my desk at midnight gnawing on a pencil and reading the same page over and over when I heard a sharp, unexpected knock at the door.

Truthfully, I almost didn't answer it. My room itself was no different from that of any of the other first-years, and I'd already come to love its old beams and courtyard window. But my belongings were meagre—a red knitted blanket on the bed, my books stacked haphazardly on my desk, my old stuffed bear that my sisters had insisted I take with me. My wall was covered in my own sketches of my family, our farm, Camford. All of these things I feared might draw laughter if word got around.

They would have done, I'm convinced, had others seen them. Perhaps Hero herself might even have laughed, in a different mood, in a different life where our acquaintance began in different circumstances. She could be as thoughtless as any other young girl who'd grown up with everything she asked for. But she had made her mind up about me by then. When I opened the door, her eyes flickered over everything once, taking it in, and all she did was nod approvingly at the blanket.

"I like that shade of scarlet," she said. "Very chic. Clover, darling, do you by any chance have a copy of Richmond's *Rise and Fall of the Augustan Mages*? I need it by Tuesday, and of course so does every other first-year answering Question Three."

Soon, the two of us were in and out of each other's rooms as easily as I would have dropped in on my siblings at home. At first it was for study; then, when there was no study to be done, she dropped by late at night with biscuits and we curled up by the fire drinking tea until we couldn't stay awake any longer. I would have thought, only days before, that I would have nothing to say to Hero Hartley, nor she to me. About some things we didn't: I had never known anything like her wild butterfly adolescence, with its fashions and flings and fast cars, and she had certainly never been to a sheep farm. Her dry sarcasm left me tongue-tied at times; my naive seriousness probably frustrated her. But we had things in common now—not just the big things, like our ambitions and our studies and the fact that we were neither of us meant to be there, but the silly day-to-day ones that were much more important. We would giggle furiously about what on earth was in the pies in the dining hall, which of our lecturers would be the most fun at a party, why that stuffy youth in the front row wouldn't stop asking the same questions over and over again as if he expected different answers. I shared with her a little about my childhood on the farm, then listened with what must have been gratifying wonder as she told me about the summers she and Alden and Eddie spent at Ashfield, the Lennox-Fontaines' estate. It seemed to me a magical place, all old money and stone turrets and wild countryside, the kind of world I had never known and had thought lost forever. And, of course, as I had with Alden the day we had met, we talked about books.

My reading had always been voracious, but books trickled slowly to our small Lancashire village. I had missed the Bloomsbury set's takeover of London, the way words were being stretched out of their meanings to new and wondrous limits. In many ways I was still a Victorian—I had grown up nourished by Jane Austen and Charles Dickens and Elizabeth Gaskell, by Jules Verne and H. G. Wells and the Brontës. Hero led me gently and firmly into the aisles of shiny new volumes. We read T. S. Eliot and Ezra Pound, D. H. Lawrence and Virginia Woolf. She loved HD's *Sea Garden* and Edith Wharton's *The Age of Innocence*; I fell in love with E. M. Forster's *Howards End*. I can't remember which of us discovered Rebecca West—it may have been me for once—but afterwards we soaked up everything she wrote, fascinated not only by her words, sharp and glittering and illusive, but by the possibility of another kind of life. West was an adventurer, a brilliant political journalist and savage critic who had a child with H. G. Wells out of wedlock; her elder sister was a qualified doctor and had been Inspector of Medical Services for the Royal Air Force in the Great War. While my brother had been fighting, she had been a part of the same war, an important person with power to change things. Next time—not that there would be a next time, but if there was—that could be me.

"It will be both of us," Hero said. It was the first time I had told anyone at Camford what had happened to Matthew, stretched out by the fire surrounded by empty teacups and biscuit crumbs and open textbooks. "And we won't be mere medical doctors, the two of us. We're going to be doctors of magic. Witches."

"I need to earn a real scholarship for that," I said, though my chest had swelled. The term *witches* was archaic in the magical world: *mages*, *Family*, or the more modern *practitioners* were the terms currently in vogue. That was the reason people used it to talk about me—not openly cruel, not quite polite either, like most of the snubs at Camford. Yet there was something powerful about hearing it in Hero's voice, something that vibrated deep in the part of my heart that belonged to Pendle Hill. "A Merlin Scholarship, probably. And doesn't your father want you to go home and get married after you have your bachelor's?"

"You'll earn one," she said, as if this was a mere detail. "I've read your essays. And my father is just going to have to learn, that's all. I have no intention of marrying anybody, at least not until I'm good and ready. If he won't pay for it, I'll find another way. Perhaps I'll earn a scholarship too. There are five Merlins, you know."

She sounded so confident, so certain, her chin tilted and the firelight behind her catching her hair as it streamed down her back, that I could see our future unfurling ahead of her. I wasn't so radical as Hero. She was part of the new generation, the modernists and freethinkers who aimed to break the world apart and make it new. She wanted to change things. I wanted only to fix them. If I could be a part of Camford, of magic and scholarship and ideas, it was more than I could imagine. Yet this, perhaps, I could have. It wasn't so impossible, after all. My essays were good—I didn't need magical blood for those. Even practical spells had been coming far easier to me since I had come to Camford. Perhaps, if I worked three, four, ten times as hard as any Family member, I might truly earn that scholarship and be allowed to stay.

"We'll do it," Hero said.

She reached out, and I grabbed her hand and squeezed it very hard.

⬦

By contrast, I can't think of any one thing that drew Eddie and I together. We just seemed to fit, so that as much as I couldn't remember seeing him in lectures earlier, I soon could barely imagine him not being there.

He and I were two of a very small number of students who took the optional Introduction to Botany paper. Frankly, that course seemed designed not to be taken. The lectures were always early in the morning, and the Faculty must have known most students preferred to sleep late rather than listen to an elderly scholar talk about the uses of ragwort. But I wanted to learn all the magic I could, and Eddie would have abandoned every other course on the curriculum before that one. The natural world enthralled him. It wasn't just plants, though that was where his scholarly interests fixated. He could see magic brimming in every leaf and every insect and every change in the weather. Visiting his room was like stepping into something between a greenhouse, a laboratory, and a zoo. Every available space was crammed with potted cuttings from the flowers and trees outside, little brass instruments measuring soil quality and humidity, and in a wire cage, three baby grey-brown mice that he had rescued from the library cat. It reminded me of Matthew, who in every other respect was as unlike Eddie as it was possible to be. He had never been able to turn away a helpless thing in need either.

Eddie and I would sit together in those lectures, at the outdoor amphitheatre in the thin grey mornings, the stone seats cold and the sky often drizzling, and go for a pot of tea together afterwards while we waited for Hero and Alden to wake up. As I'd noticed at the party, he was generally ignored by the other students, sometimes teased and sometimes tolerated. He had, he told me, been at Crawley with most of them for a year. I had to ask him what that meant.

"Crawley's a school," he explained, without a trace of surprise at the question. Eddie was never surprised by what people did or didn't know. "A sort of public school, I suppose. It's not strictly a school of magic, but they teach basic spells there, and most Families send their sons when they turn eleven. More for the prestige than the education, really."

I understood perfectly. "You didn't stay?"

"I hated it," he said—matter-of-factly, but he was looking carefully at his teacup, the Yorkshire burr in his voice stronger than usual. "All those walls, and I never knew what to do or what I was supposed to say or where I was supposed to be. I got sick a lot back then, and I got picked on—just kids, you know. It wasn't as bad as it could have been at first, because Alden made them stop. But one time—you see, I used to grow tomatoes on my windowsill. I had wards on them to make sure nobody could hurt them, and I think that must have been asking for trouble. It's never good, in those kinds of places, to let it show what you care about. One of the other boys found a way to break through them, and he knocked the plants to the ground and trampled them. I lost my temper, there was a fight..." He shrugged. "They sent me home early, and I just never came back the next year. That summer, war broke out, so a lot of boys were kept home."

"That's *awful*." I couldn't imagine gentle Eddie losing his temper. My own rose in response, hot and furious. "Did that boy even get in trouble?"

"Not from the school, no." He grinned, an unexpected flash of mischief. "I bet he was sorry, though. Those wards—I made them myself. Whoever broke them would come out in green spots for a week. I don't think that boy enjoyed the end-of-year dance as much as he'd been hoping."

My laugh caught me off guard, so that I nearly choked on my currant bun. It set Eddie giggling, too, and the fact that heads were turning in our direction made it even funnier.

"Still," I said, recovering a bit of my indignation along with my breath. "They shouldn't have sent you home. That wasn't fair."

"I wanted to go home." He was still smiling, but his eyes were serious. "I loved it at home. Our house is miles from anything, right on the edge of the Yorkshire Dales. There's nothing but moorland wherever you look, just flat countryside teeming with heather and wild things. I'd help out in the gardens and study by myself in the library. I'd still be there now, except my family wanted me to come here. They weren't happy about me leaving Crawley. I'm a disappointment to them."

My indignation deepened a little further, along with my guilt. I'd had my differences with my mother, but they were always rooted in her wanting me to stay home. I couldn't imagine being sent away.

"I'm sorry," I said.

"Oh no," he said, shaking his head. "Don't be. The gardeners at home had run out of things to teach me about plants anyway."

I smiled as if at a joke, but he meant that. I already knew that Hero was irritated sometimes by Eddie's lack of ambition, the way he could so lightly shrug off the very things we had to fight to hold. But I wished I could feel like that: sure of what I wanted to know, uncaring of anything outside it.

━━━━◈━━━━

Alden, it had to be admitted, was the closest to being the kind of distraction I feared. His ridiculous gilded-marble good looks I taught myself to ignore, helped by the fact that Hero regarded them as a source of great humour. ("Alden," she would say dryly, "if you get any more decorative someone will nail you to the gallery wall, and I'll be happy to help them.") And he truly was a brilliant researcher, perhaps the best I've ever worked with. When the mood took him, the two of us would drag out old books in the library and pore over Agrippa and Nostradamus and several of the Renaissance scholars who had fallen out of favour. They were dizzying conversations, unlike any I'd ever had before, ideas and references flying so fast my brain was left fizzing like ginger ale shaken in a bottle. The trouble was, he was also unfocused. One morning, he would be a model scholar, lively and thoughtful, the gleam from our first meeting alight in his eyes. The same evening, he would disappear into a car with a gaggle of older students, get blind drunk, and not be seen until the following week.

This was normal, I reminded myself. People my age did that sort of thing in the modern world. Hero had her fair share of parties and late-night concerts and what seemed to my sheltered eyes to be thrilling excesses as well. Still, in Alden it was different. It was as though he was being chased by a wild black wind, always in motion. He radiated more energy than anyone I'd ever met. Even at his most relaxed it was the languidness of a tiger, all coiled muscle and simmering tension.

Yet it was this, more than anything else, that drew the four of us together into a tight group. When something came into his head, he wouldn't rest until he had pulled us along in its breathless current. I remember one afternoon, about a month into the term, emerging from a lecture debating where to go and get lunch. The dining hall would still be open, but the day was clear and crystalline, and the thought of shutting ourselves in a dark room filled with other people's crumbs and conversations was less than appealing.

"Have any of you been up to the roof of the library?" Alden suggested, out of the blue.

Hero arched a perfect eyebrow. "How and why would we want to be on the roof of the library?"

"Because I know how to get there, and as far as I've been able to find out, nobody else does. Doesn't that sound enticing?"

"Only if it's someplace that's worth getting to."

"Isn't it enough that it's a place we're not supposed to be?"

"That makes it a novelty for *you*, perhaps. You forget, until recently this entire establishment was a place Clover and I weren't meant to be. And there's no food on the roof of the library, as far as I know."

"We can buy it elsewhere and take it with us. I'm sure you've heard of the concept."

"I'd like to go," Eddie said, with what I had learned was his usual knack for cutting through Alden and Hero's banter before it turned into a squabble. "There are strawberries growing in the guttering on the library roofs, or something like them. I'd like a closer look."

"*Thank* you," Alden said, throwing up his hands. "At least someone has a sense of adventure even if it is primarily agricultural."

It took me a moment to realise that they were all looking at me expectantly.

"I'm game," I said as carelessly as I could, as if my heart wasn't pounding. It wasn't as though I had never been out-of-bounds before—Matthew and I had made a game of trespassing on the neighbours' lands when I was little. This trespass could have consequences, though. Camford was looking for any reason to throw me out. It would have been far smarter for me to say no. And yet the thought of being out-of-bounds with these people, as though I had the right to be anywhere they were, was suddenly irresistible. "I'd like to see the view."

"Oh, very well then," Hero said with an amused sigh. "But if I tear my dress clambering up a drainpipe, Lennox-Fontaine, you're buying me another."

There were no drainpipes involved. We bought sticky buns and lemonade from the quadrangle, and then followed Alden up the library stairs to the seventh floor, down a narrow corridor into a tiny back room that even I had never seen before. It was empty but for a stack of dusty wooden chairs and a shelf of yellowing pamphlets; Alden cracked open the filthy window, and sure enough it was easy to step out onto the tiled roof. The incline was gentle enough that I felt no fear of toppling, even when a gust of wind whipped my dress as I climbed out, and we were high enough that I was sure nobody working in the library could look out and spot us. Eddie did stumble once, so that I grabbed his arm on reflex, but that was only because he went forward eagerly to the greenery climbing over the gutters.

"They *are* strawberries!" he declared with satisfaction. "I thought they were. Here, try one."

The strawberries were undersized, at the end of the season, sweet and tangy at once. They would have been nice at the dining table, or on a picnic. Up here, high in the air with the turrets of Camford spread before us, they were a miracle.

"It is nice here," Hero conceded. She balanced as easily as a sea captain on the prow of her ship, boots braced on the tiles, head tilted up to catch the sun. "How on earth did you find it?"

"Thomas told me," Alden said, a remark that meant nothing

to me at the time. He sat down on the edge and cracked open the bottle of lemonade. "Have a seat. You can see all the way to the wall from here."

We sat on the roof, our feet swinging, looking out over Camford.

I hope you saw Camford. I hope you sat up high as we did so often, a strange pale sun at your back. The air was never still, so that the trees rustled and whispered in constant conversation overhead. Sometimes now, when I'm half asleep and I hear the creak of branches outside, my eyes snap open and I'm sure that I'm home.

It wasn't home to me yet, that first time on the roof with Alden and Hero and Eddie. It was still alien and exciting and bewildering, like no place I'd ever been. But I wanted it to be. It hurts me, thinking back to that girl sitting on the roof eating sticky buns with her classmates, and remembering just how badly she wanted what was in front of her.

"What do you think is on the other side of those walls?" I asked. "Sam said Camford was probably in Wales?"

Alden shrugged. "Your guess is as good as mine. Actually, Eddie's is probably the best, because he likely knows where all the plants come from. Do they have strawberries in Wales?"

"They have strawberries everywhere in the British Isles," Eddie said. "Though it's late in the year for them."

I didn't press further. I could see that they genuinely weren't interested in talking about it. To them, the fact that nobody knew Camford's location was so well-established it hardly constituted a mystery. I didn't want to be the outsider asking questions, however much those questions niggled.

I don't remember much of what we did talk about that day. The usual things first-years do when they're getting to know one another, probably. I recall a long, rambling discussion of Shakespeare, of all things, sparked by my explanation of my own name and Hero, in consolation, pointing out that she had been named for the Bard's least interesting female character. ("You're absolutely right," Alden said. "I can't believe they chose Hero when Sycorax was available.") I remember how close Alden and Hero were—the way they picked up each other's sentences, spun them and threw them back to each other, the way each would unconsciously mirror the other's position when one shifted on the roof, the bantering affection that shimmered between them like dust motes in sunlight. I remember Eddie, quiet and almost translucent under his untidy thatch of dark hair, waiting just a little on the outside for his turn in the conversation, casting me the occasional quick, shy smile when he caught my eye. I remember our surprise later at how high the sun had climbed, as though we'd all thought time on the roof would stand still. I remember trembling on the verge of something I had never hoped to find.

❧

Even then, I knew that there were things I wasn't being told. I knew, however much I wanted to believe otherwise, that Alden Lennox-Fontaine did not notice isolated young students and invite them to luncheons—that he was perfectly capable of generosity, even kindness, but Hero had been quite right that something had to catch his eye first. I hadn't missed the look that passed between Hero and him when he had mentioned what I had been reading, however quickly she had covered it. I saw those looks pass between them again, out of the corner of my eye, when I pulled out a book in the library or as we walked down Camford's crooked paths bubbling over with ideas about the lectures we had heard. I even asked Eddie about it once, trusting him not to lie or to mention it to the others.

"Hero and Alden are always up to something they won't tell anyone else about," he said. "Even when we were children at Ashfield. Don't let it worry you."

I tried not to. I loved spending time with them, on any terms—the thought of going back to that first week of miserable isolation made me physically sick. I tried to tell myself that if there was anything underlying our friendship, it would come to the surface eventually, and I could deal with it then.

It did. It just came sooner than I expected.

5

It was perhaps a week or so after that afternoon on the roof when I slipped into a third-year history lecture. The lecture was taught by Dr. James Larkin, a scholar I had never met, and it was titled "Amiens and the Accord: The Last Days of the War."

In the midst of all the essays and group projects and getting to meals on time, I was still trying to the best of my abilities to learn about faerie curses. Everett Dalrymple had been perfectly right about their exclusion from the curriculum and the tight-lipped secrecy surrounding fae magic in general from the lecturers. I was learning, however, that it wasn't quite so simple to make an entire branch of spellcraft disappear. In Folklore, the fae featured heavily in stories and superstitions, and because none of the information was practical, Professor Bolton saw no difficulty with imparting it. Linguistics of Spellcraft was less helpful, though I did at least learn from Professor March's introductory lecture that faerie language was incredibly powerful and no human had yet mastered it. Professor Smallington-Reeve in History of Modern Magic studiously avoided any mention of faerie encounters. It was easy to do—history was vast and nebulous, and this was a first-year survey course that swept past decades in a single hour. A simple thing, to sweep other things out of sight at the same time.

Botany, where I had expected nothing fae-related at all,

actually yielded the most disquieting information, and that was thanks to Eddie. It was a morning of lashing rain after one of the lectures, as we sheltered under the eaves of the library with our hands wrapped around our mugs of tea for warmth. I can't remember what we were discussing, only that it involved the plausibility of using tree bark to heal minor curses.

"The curse that struck my brother looks like the bark of a tree," I said, almost without thinking. They all knew about Matthew now, but I didn't speak of him often.

Eddie only nodded seriously. "What kind of tree?" He must have seen the surprise on my face, because he hastened to explain. "It makes a difference. My grandfather used to study the fae. There are different kinds. The ones you bargain with, those are usually sprites or elves, the mischief-makers. Others, though, are born from trees—dryads, you know. They're the ones whose curses manifest as tree bark. They send out tendrils of their own magic, and the tendrils burrow down until they reach the heart and take root."

My own heart quickened with excitement.

"It's a silvery bark." I racked my memory. I had seen the wound only a few times, when Matthew first came home. Once he no longer needed help, he kept it hidden from us along with everyone else. "A birch, perhaps, or something like it."

Eddie nodded again, as if that made sense. "The theory is that's why survivors of curses like that try to get to faerie country when the veils are thin. The magic inside them is trying to return to its tree. It's a dangerous curse."

"Because it drives them to faerie country, you mean?"

"That too. But I meant because it's alive. It's difficult to heal properly—my grandfather always said the only sure way was to bargain with another faerie, and that's not even possible anymore. And while it lives, it keeps growing. You might find it takes more and more of him as it does."

Unbidden, the image of those green-laced eyes, the smile that turned my brother's face into something else, rose to the surface of my brain.

"Sam never warned us about anything like that," I said, too briskly. I refused to shiver. "He said he'd stopped it."

"He probably did." Eddie had evidently picked up my mood. "Nobody's had much of a chance to study faerie curses over time, and certainly not me."

I found a smile for him. "I'm sorry. I didn't mean to bite your head off. I just hope you're wrong."

It worried me, though. I knew even then that Eddie was rarely wrong about plants.

The truth, and the reason it had been on my mind in the first place, was that Samhain was fast approaching. It was more of a curiosity than a time of serious ritual in the world of modern magic, though there were several loud and competing parties in the week leading up to it and more than one student claiming to have seen a ghost in the clock tower. At home, though, it would be the first midnight since I had left—the first time Mum and the others would be handling things without me. The worry I had managed to quiet my first few weeks at Camford, so sickeningly familiar from Matthew's long years at the front, started to gnaw again.

"Why don't you go back to help?" Hero suggested, when I confessed to her what was bothering me. "You would only need to miss a few days of lectures. You can share my notes—though you'll have to rely on Eddie for Botany. I'm very fond of you, darling, but I don't rise before nine for anybody."

I found a smile. I should go home, I knew. I had promised them I would before I left—had insisted, even when Matthew told me not to be stupid. But I hadn't understood, when I had made those promises. I hadn't counted on how many assignments I would have, how hard I would be working to keep up, how desperately I needed to fight to succeed. Besides, I had thought that by the time I came home, I would have new magic to help. The truth was, I had made almost no progress in breaking the curse. I couldn't go back and tell my family that. They would be so disappointed. They might question whether there was any point in my being at Camford, when there was nowhere in the world I wanted to be more.

So I was more relieved than I wanted to admit when I saw the lecture about Amiens on the third-year timetable—and saw, crucially, that it was slated for the first of November. A lecture about the battle where Matthew had been cursed, the day a faerie had broken free and caused faerie magic to be banned forever. That, of all things, couldn't be missed, and there was no possible way I could be at home for the night of Samhain and make it back to Camford in time. I sent a telegram home at once, informing them that something important had come up and I couldn't be there, telling them (at added expense) how sorry I was and how I hoped everything would be well. I tried not to notice how relieved I was—how my brain shied violently from the thought of one of those long, frightening midnights, and ran toward the safe glow of books and study and magic.

Third-year history papers were usually taught in the Rookery, a large and particularly overgrown stone hall at the south end of the university. It earned its name for its exceptionally high ceilings, in the rafters of which nested a flock of semi-wild ravens. They were a relic of the days when the magical world had used them to send messages—some of the older generation still used them, I had heard, though most now preferred the telephone or the regular post—and nobody had been able to shift them in over a hundred years. Their swooping and rustling high overhead added to the general draughtiness of the building, and that alongside the possibility of an unwelcome surprise splatting onto your papers or head meant that it was usually reserved for less popular theoretical courses. This time, though, the theatre was full as I slipped in, trying not to be seen.

I had been to lectures for which I wasn't registered before, trying to fill in the many gaps in my knowledge, and there was no rule against it. Still, it always felt strange, clandestine, like an act of theft. It didn't help that being one of the few women in the university made it difficult to hide. I snuck into the back row, windblown and surreptitious, and still earned a curious look from a gangly student doing a crossword under the table.

"Amiens wasn't the first breach of the war," the lecturer was saying, down at the front of the room. "There had been many, on both sides."

I had never seen Dr. James Larkin before. He was a sandy-haired, thick-set man, perhaps forty or so, and he held the sides of the lectern in an iron grip that belied his surprisingly light, pleasant voice. I kept my eyes and ears on him as I opened my satchel.

"Scared soldiers throwing fire and ice at their enemies," he said, as though working through a list. "Protective spells thrown in front of bullets at the last moment, water purified and food made good in the rot of the trenches. For the most part they were harmless, difficult to detect or prove afterwards. Sadly, most of them weren't even effective. A bullet is a counter to a good many spells—besides, as I'm sure your practical exams have taught you, magic is easy to fumble under stress. All it takes is a hand too stiff with cold to perform the correct movements, a voice too hoarse with thirst to pitch the words correctly, a mind too blurred by fear to find the right combination, and the most basic cantrip simply won't work. War is not conducive to good spellwork."

He paused, which gave me time to finish rummaging in my satchel and set out my notebook and my pen.

"Faerie magic is different," Larkin said. "When faerie magic fails, it isn't merely ineffective, it's dangerous. And the spell at

Amiens failed spectacularly. Can anyone give me the basic steps of summoning a faerie?"

A whisper of surprise ruffled the room, like a wind across grass. My heart quickened, my fingers tightening so that my pen dug into the paper. This was already far more promising than anything on the first-year courses. I wasn't sure if it was quite legal, and by the sounds of it, neither were my classmates.

He huffed a sigh at our hesitation. "Of course not. The Accord has a good deal to answer for... Yes, Mr. Mortimer?"

A dark-haired young man in the front row lowered his hand carefully. He looked slightly older than the others, from my imperfect view—old enough, probably, to have learned faerie magic before the Accord came into effect. He may have been one of the rare students who had been to war and was only now returning to his studies. "The magic is twofold. You open a door, a door between this world and faerie country. You draw it on a wall, reciting the incantations. The fae are always seeking new ways into our world. One will rush through soon, perhaps at once. Only they don't get very far."

"Why not?"

"Because of the rune circles." He paused, swallowed. "Before you open the door, you'll have made two rune circles on the ground. One is for the caster to stand in. The other is for the faerie. The faerie comes through the door, but the rune circle binds it in place. It can't get free, nor can it go back through the door. A deal is struck in exchange for its safe return home."

"I don't understand," another student called. He was brave— I barely knew this lecturer, and I wouldn't have dared. "Why would the fae let themselves be caught knowing they'll have to make a deal to be let go again?"

"Two very simple reasons, Mr. Adams." Larkin's voice was milder than I would have expected. Perhaps he didn't mind questions—or, perhaps, being a third-year allowed a certain leeway. "The first is that the fae love to deal with humans on any terms. They love the opportunity to twist deals in some way, to make the mischief that they can't on the other side of the veil. A deal is a duel between a mage and a faerie. The mage wants what he wants. The faerie wants the opportunity to give him something else instead. That is the first reason. The second, given what we're discussing, should be self-evident. Mr. Mortimer?"

"The runes," Mortimer said quietly. "It wants to test the runes."

"Exactly. A faerie's greatest hope, when it sees an open door, is that the runes on the other side are incorrect. That it won't be trapped at all. That it will blaze straight through, devour the magician standing there, steal his form, and be loose in the world. And that's exactly what happened on the eighth of August, on the first day of the Battle of Amiens."

There were no questions this time. Amiens was too familiar to everyone here. I remembered reading about it in the newspapers, before the fateful telegram telling us about Matthew had arrived: the start of the Hundred Days Offensive, the turning point for German morale, the beginning of the end of the war. I hadn't known then that the magical world existed, much less that it had just changed forever.

"The spell was cast from within the German trenches," Larkin said, "not that it matters. The soldier was Private Friedrich Koenig. He was twenty-one, from one of Germany's finest magical Families. He had performed faerie summonings three times before, under supervision at the university of magic in Berlin, and done it well. We can only guess at what his intentions were for this one—what magic he would have asked the faerie to perform. It has been suggested that he could see the Allied forces gaining the upper hand, and the attempt was a desperate bid to give his side an advantage. In my opinion, it's more likely he simply wanted to live. As the German trenches were overtaken, he drew up the runes and opened the door. I see no need to elaborate on what followed. The runes failed. The faerie burst through and consumed him in the blink of an eye."

"Why would anyone try to perform complex magic in the middle of a battle?" someone piped up from the second row, with an awkward laugh. "Of course it was going to go wrong."

I was writing notes frantically, my letters hopscotching over the page as I tried to get down doors, runes, binding circles. It took me a moment to notice the silence and look up.

Larkin had grown very still, his gaze fixed down and at nothing in particular. There was an odd quality to the stillness—a tension, an inwardness—that it took me a while to place. I had seen it in my brother at odd moments since he had come back to us, moments when his gaze would shift and for a handful of heartbeats he would no longer be with us, but back somewhere else. It was as stark and recognisable as a scar.

"Most of you in this classroom are too young to have been in the fighting," he said at last. "That was for your fathers, your uncles, your older brothers. Even then, many of our Families thought it was best to keep separate from the entire affair. It was the common people's war, after all, not ours. So I realise it might not be possible for most of you to understand what it was like. But try, please. Try to imagine the relentless barrage of shells and artillery fire and poison gas, the wasteland of mud and tree stumps and barbed wire into which you are expected to run, blindly, until something takes you down. Imagine the person sitting next to you right now falling, their insides shattered, fragments of their bones and flesh spattering your face. Try—and I realise this is a paradox—to imagine the *unimaginableness* of it. There has never been anything like the scale of those battles. There was no way to prepare for them. In their midst, all you can think is that they shouldn't be happening. It feels as though the world has broken, and all reason with it. We don't know, of course, what Private Koenig was thinking in that moment. Perhaps he wasn't thinking at all. Whatever it was, though, I doubt he was concerned with what might go wrong. Everything was wrong."

Matthew had been there, in the midst of that. So had Sam—kind, gentle Sam who had taken me out to lunch and opened the way to Camford. They had been there on a day of mud and blood and barbed wire, one of a very long line of them that they had no way of knowing wouldn't be their last. My throat tightened, and I had to look determinedly up at the high rafters before I trusted my eyes to stay clear. The ravens were silent for once, only a slight rustle of feathers to betray they were even there in the dark.

"In a way, this confusion was what saved us," Larkin said, and the lecture was back on track. But the hall itself had fallen silent now, in a way I hadn't heard before. "The faerie may have had earth-shattering power, but it too found itself in the midst of chaos. It needed to escape if it was to be free in the world. And fortunately, there were a handful of Family on both sides who saw what had happened and moved into the fray. Altogether, in the turmoil of that terrible day, it took twelve mages from different armies to subdue the faerie and send it back to the other world. All but three of them were killed in the process, and of those three, only one was left unscathed. Approximately three hundred common soldiers were struck by fae curses. Again, we were fortunate with the setting. It's barely necessary to come up with an excuse for a few hundred extra dead in a war. Thousands saw the magic, of course, but they didn't know what they were seeing."

Three practitioners left alive. One of those had been Sam Truelove Wells. And three hundred so-called common soldiers dead of faerie curses. Matthew had lived.

"They would have realised soon enough, though," Larkin added. His face was very serious now. "Our world came within a hairsbreadth of being exposed that day. Worse yet, had the faerie truly escaped, there's no knowing what damage would have been done. It's a common misconception that the Accord was drawn up at the close of the war. In fact, it was drawn up within a week of that breach, and as many Family members as possible were pulled out of the conflict. For us, the war was over. Whatever allegiance we had to our countries paled in comparison to our allegiance to our world."

There was more after that: the means by which the borders between worlds had been shut and locked; the way that England, France, and Germany had each performed their own locking spell, so no one country could undo it; the decision to no longer teach faerie magic even as a theoretical exercise. I took notes, but mechanically. For the first time, the enormity of what I was attempting had begun to sink in—and with it, as Sam had tried gently to tell me, just how unlikely I was to succeed. It was one of the many times when learning more only taught me how little I knew.

"Are there questions?" the lecturer asked, minutes before the end of the hour.

Among the third-years taking notes or checking their watches or reading under the table, a familiar hand went up.

Alden. He was in the front row, tucked in the corner by the doors, or I would have seen him earlier. He sat leaning slightly forward, his stance relaxed yet thoughtful, no notebook open in front of him. Beside him, to my further surprise, was Hero. Her clothing was dark and unusually subdued—for the first time since I had known her, she wasn't trying to attract attention.

Larkin nodded at Alden. "Yes?"

"Excuse me," he said, impeccably polite. "I just wanted to know if anyone ever did investigate why the runes failed? Do we know for certain it was a mistake on Private Koenig's part, and if so, what it was?"

"We have no idea," Larkin said, very evenly, "because, as I made clear, there was a battle going on. Any trace of the circle was churned up and trampled over. The general feeling was that whatever mistake was made, the important thing was not to risk it being repeated."

"Of course. Still, wouldn't it be worth exploring what happened? For one thing, why did the faerie in question react so violently to being summoned? Even when the fae have escaped in the past, that number of deaths isn't usual."

Larkin looked at Alden as if for the first time. "It's Lennox-Fontaine, isn't it?" he said. "Yes. I see the resemblance now." When he spoke again, his voice had a curious note to it. "To answer your question: That is a school of thought. There were some who criticised the Accord for suppressing exactly the information that might have enabled us to learn from this disaster. Certainly there are secrets buried in the Camford Library archives as we speak that would help us come to some theories about what went wrong. I suppose it really amounts to what price we are willing to pay for knowledge. Whether a better understanding of a dangerous magic is worth unleashing that danger on the world and exposing us to discovery. Clearly, the reigning magical authorities across Europe felt it was not."

"But if—" Alden broke off, with what would have been for him unusual self-control. I suspected Hero had kicked him under the desk. "I see. Thank you."

Other questions were asked then, half-hearted for the most part and not very interesting. I barely heard the answers. I was watching Hero and Alden. I couldn't help but notice that, though I was staring hard enough to bore a hole in the back of Alden's golden head, he never once turned to look at me.

They were gone as soon as the lecturer concluded his talk, ducking out the door before I had even collected my notebook and stood. I had no chance of catching them and asking them why they were here. But suddenly I wanted to know, very much.

———— ❧ ————

I meant to talk to them at dinner that evening. If we weren't together during the day, which was becoming rare enough, our usual habit was to meet at our table under the stained glass window. When I took my plate to the table, however, only Eddie was there.

"They said they had a party to go to," Eddie said, when I asked after them.

I speared a boiled potato, as casually as possible. "Where?"

"I didn't ask," he said frankly. "I didn't want them to invite me along."

I laughed, because I sympathised. Hero had tried to wheedle me into coming out with her once or twice, and it had taken all my powers of resistance to decline the invitation. I'd said it was because I had work, which was true. I also had absolutely nothing to wear.

I went back to my room after dinner and worked on my Folklore essay late into the night. From my desk, I could always see the light from Alden's window across the quad; I could also hear Hero's footsteps in the corridor and her door open and close when she came home. As the hours wore on, I saw no light; I heard no footsteps. A late party, obviously. Alden often didn't get home until dawn. Still, something about it bothered me, and not just the fact I'd been looking forward to confronting them.

By midnight, my eyes were getting blurry. I'd barely slept the night before, trying not to imagine what was taking place at home, and the print in my book of Greek mythology was small. I took off my glasses, rubbed my eyes, stretched. The problem came to me mid-yawn. Hero and Alden, at the lecture, hadn't been dressed for any party. At some point, they would have gone back to their rooms to change. I should have run into Hero after getting back from the dining hall, if not on my way there. But I hadn't. There had been no sign of them since the lecture.

I sat up, suddenly wide awake.

They had planned to meet Eddie and me for dinner that night. I was sure they had—I had seen Hero that morning, and she had made no mention of any party. That meant that something at the lecture had changed their plans. Something they had seen, or heard.

Or something that had been said to them. All at once, I remembered the look on Dr. Larkin's face—the way his voice had changed at Alden's question.

Certainly there are secrets buried in the Camford Library archives as we speak that would help us come to some theories about what went wrong. I suppose it really amounts to what price we are willing to pay for knowledge.

I knew where they had gone.

6

I knew how to get into Camford Library after hours. The library was open until midnight most nights, and I was frequently there until the last possible moment. Only two weeks ago I had looked up from my paper in a daze to find that the clock was showing half past closing and the building outside the stack room was deserted. I didn't panic—honestly, the thought of being trapped in a library all night gave me a faint thrill, though I did wonder how I would explain it the next day and what I would do for food. I never got to find out, as Hero, Alden, and Eddie came to fetch me ten minutes later.

"I noticed you hadn't got back yet, Eddie remembered where you'd gone, and Alden knew a way in," Hero had explained brightly. "So we formed a rescue party."

The secret, apparently, was a door that opened to the locked gardens outside, which was often left unlatched in the warmer weather, and which could be reached if you were willing to risk life and clothing climbing over the garden wall. That night, when I crossed the quad to the library gardens, I really was just looking for a sign that I was right. If I saw the door unlatched, or even the glimpse of a light inside where it shouldn't be, I would know that Alden and Hero had gone into the library, and my suspicions about what they were doing at the lecture would be permitted to take flight.

I am not the tallest person in the world: I had to jump to peer over the walled garden, and when I did, I couldn't see enough to be satisfied. The door appeared to be closed; that didn't mean it was locked. An idea struck me, belatedly (I wasn't used to thinking in magic in those days). We had learned a spell only days ago in Basic Incantations that revealed echoes and after-images, the imprints that people left on places after they had gone. The imprints lasted only minutes, but the library hadn't been closed for long. Perhaps…

I found a large rock that gave me a better view of the garden and leaned precariously over the wall. My fingers slipped easily into the right positions—steepled together, then parted as I whispered the incantation. The Latin spell, at least, was easy to remember. *"Echo."*

And there they were, hurrying through the darkness, so clear I must have only just missed the real thing. They both wore dark clothing, as they had that afternoon, so that they half disappeared into the shadows of the trees. I saw the phantom door open, and saw them slip inside. The vision ended there—I felt a faint shiver as it departed, like a window opening to a draught.

So. I knew where they had gone, but not why, and not if it had anything to do with me. Perhaps, after all, I was paranoid to think Alden had noticed me for any particular reason, and this was none of my business. Perhaps I should leave well enough alone.

Then, on the lit path leading to the library entrance, a shadow flickered. I turned to look, shrinking instinctively against the wall.

Someone was coming.

I recognised few people at Camford on sight, this early into my time there. I knew this man. He was the sole librarian at Camford, a tall man with a curiously ageless face and wild white hair. The students called him Grimoire and claimed he was ancient as the library itself. I didn't find out for a long time that his real name was Henry Grimsby-Lennox, and he was in his fifties. And yet there was certainly something uncanny about the dry, precise way he could give you the location of any book in the miles of nonsensical shelving, the way he seemed never to eat or drink or go home for the night. I envied it, to be honest. I had never seen him out of the library, and plainly he wasn't staying out for long. Any minute now, he would be inside the front door.

I didn't think—or rather, I had only one thought. I had to warn Hero and Alden. They thought the library was empty; they would probably walk right into him. The fact that I might get caught myself didn't matter, not right now. They had come to get me out of the library, under different circumstances. I couldn't leave them.

The place where we had scrambled over the wall was difficult to climb on my own, in the dark, and I laddered my last good stocking. I didn't care. I landed roughly in the autumn leaves, scrambled to my feet, and rushed as quietly as I could to the door.

Hero and Alden were in the corridor just inside, Hero carrying a flickering candle. They turned, their faces twisting from alarm to astonishment when they saw me.

"Clover!" Hero whispered. "What on earth are you...?"

"Grimoire's coming!" I said, before she could finish. "He's on his way around to the front entrance. He'll see you if you're not careful."

Alden swore quietly. "Then we'd better hurry. This way, come on!"

I ran along with them—I had to, or run back straight into the head librarian myself.

At the heart of Camford Library was an atrium, a high tower

walled by circular shelves and spiralling staircases, all extending
up to a great domed ceiling made of glass. Underneath the dome
was an enormous oak. In a university thick with trees, this one
stopped me still the first time I had seen it: some seventy feet
high, centuries old, its twisted branches reaching to the walls
and in some cases through them. I wasn't surprised to find that
Alden and Hero were leading me to that atrium—uncannily quiet
now, the dark leaves and branches wreathed in moonlight. I was
even less surprised when we ducked into the alcove that held a
heavy wooden door, the door that led belowground. The oak
erupted through the mosaic floor—the tree's roots, far beneath,
were said to begin in the underground labyrinth of the archives
where all the universities' forbidden material was stored. I had
guessed their objective correctly.

We held very still as the circle of the lantern flickered under
the door to the atrium, accompanied by the light tread of footsteps. Then the light faded, and the footsteps with them, going
upstairs.

"It's all right," Hero said, with a quiet sigh of relief. "He must
be going up to his office. Of course he'd pick tonight to leave his
favourite pen there or some such thing…"

"What are you doing?" I hissed as Alden pulled the silver
crest ring off his finger.

"What does it look like we're doing?" Alden asked. "We're
breaking into the archives with a ring I stole from the finger of
the head librarian."

"You didn't steal it *from his finger*," Hero said with a roll of
her eyes. "You requested a book from the Special Collection, he
took off his ring and put on his gloves to handle it, as did you,
and you swapped it out for your own at the end of the hour."

"Grimoire is a Lennox," he explained to me. "Our rings are
similar. Easy mistake to make. I'll come by the library tomorrow very concerned about it. He'll know, of course, but he
won't be able to prove a thing, and anyway I doubt he'll turn in

a distant relative. And by the way, Hero, without me that ring would never have left his finger, so *technically—*"

"Shut up," she said, with a quick look down the corridor. "He'll be back any moment. We need to move."

"Why?" I finally managed to slip a word in edgeways. "What do you want in the archives?"

"This isn't the time or the place," Hero said. "Clover, thank you for the warning, but you might want to make yourself scarce while we both do something idiotic."

"Though you're welcome to join," Alden added. "If you're in an idiotic mood."

Perhaps I was. Seventeen-year-olds often are. I did, at least, consider for a fleeting second what the consequences would be if I were caught. But—they were breaking into the *archives*. I had imagined them many a time, ever since Everett Dalrymple had named them at our first tutorial. Miles and miles of great underground rooms, filled with books that nobody was allowed to touch—books, Dr. Larkin had strongly implied, that held information about the fae, about Matthew's curse, about all the research I longed to do.

And it was Alden and Hero. I don't think I realised then how great a hold the two of them had taken on my imagination. They lived firmly in the modern world, new and exciting and daring in a way that had never reached my rural village, and yet in themselves they were everything I loved about Camford—golden, glowing, elite, steeped in centuries of history and culture. They were what I wanted to be, and they made it look effortless. Perhaps I could have walked away from the archives; I couldn't walk away from them.

"I'll stay with you," I said. "Just…be careful. Hero's right; Grimoire hasn't gone far."

I don't think Alden had for a moment actually expected me to take up his offer. His eyebrows shot up, but he smiled.

"I'll try to be," he said. "This won't take a moment."

He pressed the ring to the lock.

For a moment, I genuinely thought it had worked. The door glowed, a gold burst around the edges, as though a light had passed on the other side of the door. My breath caught; beside me, on reflex, Hero caught my hand. I had just time to imagine those rooms below, the old dusty books surrounded by darkness and the roots of the tree.

Then, the light died, and the door turned black. It was as though the colour had seeped from the wood, darkening it to the ashy grey of a tree blasted in a fire or a badly exposed photograph.

"Oh," Alden said, in a voice that was just a little too calm.

Something struck me hard across the shoulders, knocking me forward; I bit back a curse as I caught myself against the wall. It was on the tip of my tongue to ask what it was, when I glanced up. The answer was obvious.

The books were flying off the shelves. The oak in the midst of that great circular room was thrashing, writhing, as though in a far-off storm; as it moved, the leather-bound volumes that spanned the shelves from floor to ceiling were hurled at us in a great cascade. I flung up my hands on instinct as a heavy volume flew at my face; beside me, I heard Hero cry out as one hit. Absurdly, amidst the panic rising in my throat, I felt a flutter of fear for the books. What if their pages got crumpled, or the spines cracked?

"Back," Hero said. "Quickly. We need to get out of here."

Alden shook his head in disbelief. "That should have worked!" he protested, or complained. "It was the librarian's—ow!"

That one had struck him on the side of his head. He put his hand to it, wincing, and his fingertips came away glistening with blood.

"Come on!" Hero shoved first him, then, more gently, me. "Door!"

We were too late. The shelves continued to pelt us with books as we fought our way across the room, only to find the doors to the atrium had swung closed with a determined clunk. I rattled the handle, desperate, and narrowly missed another impact.

God. We were trapped. We were trapped in the library, and if the books didn't batter us to death by morning, then we would be found, and that was the end of Camford for me. I couldn't believe it had been so quick.

"The roof," Alden said tightly. The blood was coming from a small cut at the corner of one eyebrow—if we *were* found here in the morning, he was going to have a very unglamorous black eye. "Our roof. It's the only way out."

He was right—there was no way to close off the great curved staircases, at least. And there *was* a way to get down from the roof without going back inside, clambering down the trees that grew beside the library. We had done it once, just to see if it could be done. I hated the thought of doing it in the dark, but not as much as getting caught. At least it would get us out of the line of fire from the books.

Hero glanced at me, and I nodded quickly.

"Very well," she said to Alden. "But if this doesn't work, I'll never listen to you again."

"I'm not sure I'll listen to myself," he conceded.

We were at the foot of the stairs when a shiver went through the library. The few remaining books stopped falling, and the giant tree stilled. The stairwell was darkening; in one breath, the candle in Hero's hand snuffed out. Against all common sense, my step faltered. I turned to look.

Far below, a shadowy shape was forming by the old oak. It was huge, the size of a bull; in the darkness all I could see was a confused outline of teeth, horns, long limbs. In the hushed quiet of the library rose a long, threatening growl. Slowly, one by one, the hairs on the back of my neck stood on end. Then I blinked, turned, and ran for my life.

Too fast. My boots were second-hand and the soles overpatched;

one shot out from underneath me on the stone stairs, and I came down hard. My bones jarred sickeningly, and the air was knocked from my lungs. For an agonising second, I couldn't move, couldn't breathe, couldn't *think*, and behind me something terrible was coming. Then a hand grabbed my wrist, strong and sure, and Hero was yanking me to my feet. I stumbled, found my footing.

"All right?" she checked, looking me up and down quickly, and I nodded.

"What is that thing?"

"Grimoire," Hero said. "He's a ward. You didn't know?"

I had learned about human wards only the week before. Certain Family members could be bound to buildings like Family houses or the Camford Library, places rich in magic. Once a mage had been created a ward, the title was theirs for the rest of their lives; a successor could be created only when the old ward was dead and their replacement took their ring. It changed them—gave them new and often unpredictable magic, as long as they were within the walls of the house they had accepted as their own. I had imagined they had new enchantments, stronger spellcraft. I had never imagined anything like that.

We had to get out.

Up the stairs. Down the corridors. The library was all wrong. I knew this section; I could navigate it in the dark, with my eyes closed. Now there were passages that made no sense, stairs where there should be doors, doors that opened out to nowhere at all. I remembered the old claims that the library could swallow those it disliked whole, lost forever among the stacks. Behind us, the darkness pressed, and that terrible low rumbling grew louder.

Please, I thought, to the great expanse of books around us. *Please, I'm sorry. Please let us get away.*

We ran upstairs, through the narrow book-lined corridors, and then, at last, finally, down the familiar path to our study room. I had the sickening thought as Alden tried the window that it would be sealed shut like the door, and we would be found by whatever Grimoire had become and meet our end hovering among the driest tomes in the library. But it was only jammed—a furious push, and the sash window shot up. As I clambered through it onto the pitch-dark slates, I heard a long, echoing howl.

I had never been on our roof at night. It was beautiful—I saw it even as I lowered myself carefully onto the tiles beside the other two, shaking, gasping. The mist on the other side of the great wall glowed faintly silver; by its illumination, the shadows of Camford gleamed like a tapestry of dark blue and grey. Overhead, unfamiliar stars stood out piercingly clear.

We were safe. I couldn't believe it at first. Gradually my heart settled, and my fears with it. We had made it out. Grimoire clearly had no interest in leaving the bounds of his domain. Nobody was following us. But it had been so horribly close.

Hero clearly thought so too.

"We *never* do that again." She sat up, dishevelled, eyes blazing. "I mean it, Alden. I have no idea how you talked me into it this time. It doesn't happen again."

"Well, obviously not." He would have sounded more impressive had he not been struggling to breathe. "It didn't work. That ring can't open the door to the archives. You realise what that means, don't you? The archives are out-of-bounds even to Grimoire. Why? What on earth can be in them that the ward of the library isn't allowed to know?"

"What a shame it's none of our business and we aren't going to find out," Hero said. "No more rule-breaking. We find a different way."

"A way to do what?" I broke in before Alden could reply. I had caught my breath now, and feeling had come back with it.

My shoulder ached where the books had pummelled me; my ankle throbbed and my palms were scraped from the fall up the stairs. I was bewildered and frustrated and angry in equal measures, and Alden's refusal to take things seriously wasn't helping. "What the hell are you two up to? What did you want in the archives?"

"You must have guessed." Alden sat up, wincing. The blood had darkened on the side of his face, and in the moonlight his fair skin was already starting to bruise. "You saw us in the lecture this afternoon, didn't you? I was sure I'd seen you."

"Yes." I wasn't going to betray any surprise. I'd known he couldn't have been as oblivious as all that. "And it's no secret why I was there. I want to find a way to break my brother's curse. I have no idea what you want."

Alden shrugged. "Similar. We want to find a way to safely summon and bind a faerie."

I stared at him. "That's not possible. Ever since—"

"Faerie country was sealed off after the Accord, yes, I know." He actually sounded amused. "We were in the same lecture as you, and certainly lived through the same war. We don't intend to attempt it ourselves, much less tomorrow in the quad. But the reason it's illegal is simply because it's unsafe. They don't know what went wrong at Amiens; they don't want to risk it again. If we could work out what went wrong—if we could come up with an alternative, something that would ensure it never happened again…"

"You don't think they would have found it already?"

"New discoveries in magic are made all the time. The best way is only the best until someone finds something better. And nobody's looking now, are they? The knowledge has been hidden away so well it barely exists. That's why we were trying to break into the archives, of course. It was worth a try, after what Larkin said."

It shouldn't have been a surprise. I had spoken with Alden

about Agrippa—I knew he was interested in faerie magic. But to hear it put so seriously, so simply...It was too much to take in. I looked at Hero. "And you? Do you really want to find a way to summon a faerie?"

"I want to be a scholar," Hero said bluntly. "You were right, you know, about my father. I told you he was an indulgent old thing when the mood takes him, and he is, but he isn't as indulgent as all that. He's willing to pay for a bachelor of magic because university is a wonderful place to meet prospective husbands—assuming I don't marry Alden, which would satisfy him just as well. After that, I'm supposed to grow up and come home. I'm not like you, Clover—my family doesn't believe in earning a living."

Coming off my betrayal already, I felt a flash of irritation. I loved Hero, truly, but she really did seem to think me freer than her, as though having no money was less of a problem than having too much. "My family aren't exactly thrilled about me coming here either, you know! And if they were, it would hardly matter, since they couldn't afford to send me."

Hero shook her head, half-apologetic, half-impatient. "You know I don't mean that. My point is that if I want to stay, I need a Merlin Scholarship every bit as much as you do—you need one because your family can't pay; I need one because mine won't. They won't want to give it to women scholars. Unless we do something they can't ignore. Something brilliant."

"Something like find a safe way to use faerie magic again." My heart was thrumming in my ears like the rattle of an engine. "You think that if you present those findings to the Faculty, they'll have to grant you the scholarship to look into it."

"I don't see that they can help it. Or if Camford are too stuffy, somewhere else will fund the research. Paris, or Rome, or even Berlin. I'd prefer that, in a way. The magical academies in France let women graduate long ago. Either way, I'll have something to trade." I heard the defiance in her voice, careless and brave, and saw at the same time that she was trembling. That was the first time, I think, I realised how much of her courage was sheer bravado, how aware she was that she lived her life in a constant state of trespass. My irritation faded, and something fierce and protective awoke in its place.

I shook my head, trying to clear it, and turned to Alden. "And what about you? You can't tell me you're desperate for a Merlin Scholarship. You're Alden Lennox-Fontaine. If you mentioned you wanted one, they'd probably give it to you for the asking." That sounded bitter, even to me. I didn't care. I couldn't help but suspect that Alden was enjoying this greatly, and of course he was. He had the luxury of not being overly worried about the consequences. "Why are you going to these lengths?"

"Curiosity?" he suggested, unfazed by my anger. "Ambition? Or perhaps I just want to do something brilliant too."

Hero rolled her eyes, her composure back in place. "Alden's always been obsessed with faerie magic," she informed me. "He was the one who roped me into this endeavour last summer, when Father made it clear how much and how little he was willing to allow."

"I don't agree with the Accord," he said, more seriously. "I want to persuade them to lift it, break the seals, and let faerie summonings resume. I think if we can find a safer way to bind the fae, we can make a case for it. Right now, everyone's afraid to so much as look at it."

"*I'm* not afraid to look at it." I tried not to say it accusingly, even though I had realised by now what was bothering me. I had no right to feel hurt. Hero and Alden had known each other their entire lives and me a few scant weeks. Of course they hadn't trusted me yet. But I'd told them about Matthew. I'd thought we were friends.

"We were hoping to tell you, of course, in time." Hero understood at once what I wasn't saying. "We'd almost made up our minds to do it before the Christmas break."

"I *had* made up my mind, personally," Alden said. "I made up my mind the first day we met, do you remember? Hero was kinder than me. She wanted to protect you."

"I know how important Camford is to you," Hero said. "Faerie magic is illegal. We won't be arrested just for trying to study it, of course, but we could very well be expelled if we push too far. At the very least, they would revoke your scholarship, and that would be the same thing as far as you're concerned."

The reminder did stop me in my tracks. Hero was absolutely right. For all the difficulties of being here, I couldn't imagine losing Camford. Camford was my chance to build a new life, a life of magic and scholarship and possibility. My chance to help my family, to fix what the war had torn up.

But they were looking for a way to lift the Accord. The possibility was dizzying. I had been focusing on finding a counter-curse to heal Matthew. If the Accord was no more, I might not need one. I could bargain with the fae for his life, as the old mages had once done. All it would take was research, study, practice, and everything could be put right.

Camford itself was impeding that research. Sam had been right—as much as I loved it (and I truly, truly did), it *was* set in its ways, determined to cling to the mistakes of the past when the world outside was struggling to remake itself. I remembered the books Hero and I had been reading, and their exhortations to set aside the old Victorian values and embrace new ways of thinking and talking and being. Wasn't this what it meant? To not be afraid to smash the world to pieces and make it new?

"I don't care," I said, and almost meant it. "I want to help you, if you'll let me. I know I'm a scholarship girl from a nonmagical family, but I've been looking into this in my own way too. And I'm good at binding spells."

"You don't need to convince us," Alden said dryly. "You out-scored me our last two tests in a row in Basic Incantations. I'd be delighted to have you."

"I am too, of course," Hero said. "But if you want to stop at any time, just say. Don't let this idiot manipulate you."

"Him?" I laughed. "I have the most invested in this out of anyone. You should all be worried about how I might manipulate *you*."

My hurt was receding now, and the gap it left was flooding with unexpected sunlit joy. I had known there was something lurking beneath our friendship, and I had dreaded what it might be. This, though, was everything I wanted myself. Not the sneaking into the archives at night, perhaps—Hero was right, that was too dangerous—but the work, the challenge, the feeling of pushing the bounds of magic in a way that would truly change the world. To do it alongside these people I so liked and admired felt like finding a gift where I'd been looking for a trap.

A thought struck me. "What about Eddie? Have you asked him to help too?"

Alden frowned. "Eddie? I wasn't aware he was interested in faeries."

"He's interested in faerie plants. The curse that struck my brother—according to Eddie, it was from a dryad. We talked about it. He knows a great deal of folklore about using plants to ward off the fae, or to counteract curses. There hasn't been a good deal of literature on them, but they might—"

"They might." Alden sounded interested. "I've brushed against superstitions like that myself. I should have thought of asking Eddie."

I wasn't surprised that he hadn't. Alden, I had already noticed, often overlooked Eddie, despite or perhaps because of their shared childhood. Eddie was too good at making himself invisible to make his presence felt.

"I assumed he wouldn't be interested too," Hero said. "If he is, of course, I'm thrilled to have him. Do you want to ask him tomorrow? You'll see him before us, in Botany."

"Four musketeers," Alden said. "I like it. You see, Hero, I told you we needed Clover's help."

His face had softened, brightened; his eyes twinkled with excitement that bordered on exhilaration. I suspected mine were doing the same. It wasn't that I thought Alden had befriended me just to get my opinion on faerie magic. At my most paranoid I couldn't see Alden cultivating a friendship for weeks on end with a scholarship student he didn't like when he could have just asked. But it made more sense now what had drawn us together. I felt more secure in what bound us, like a harness that had been proven and tested. I was *needed*. We were at last resuming the conversation that had started on the day we met.

"I never doubted it," Hero retorted. "My only worry is that getting it isn't going to be particularly helpful to her. I know how to keep you from getting me into trouble, for the most part. Poor Clover still thinks she likes you."

"And yet you were the one I persuaded to sneak into the archives after dark, and Clover's the one who just strongly implied I was a spoiled idiot who gets everything I ask for." He winked at me. I actually blushed, like my little sister Mary when the boy who delivers the post smiles at her.

"Well, she's right," Hero said briskly. "Unfortunately, she still came in after you."

Eddie was in with surprisingly little hesitation. I cornered him at our Botany lecture, sitting in the drizzle at the front of the amphitheatre. I had brought an umbrella—Eddie never seemed to care about the weather, and in fairness the weather didn't seem to care about him.

"I'd like to help," he said at once, almost before I had finished my account of the night before. "Especially if it might help your brother."

"We might get in trouble if we're caught," I warned him. "Alden promised that we won't break the rules as obviously as last night, but the Faculty won't be happy if they learn what we're doing before we're ready to tell them."

"I don't care what the Faculty thinks," Eddie said, with more bitterness than I'd ever heard from him. He must have caught my surprise, because he gave a small, embarrassed smile. "Sorry. It's just that my tutor keeps turning down anything I give him for my end-of-term project. He says none of them are ambitious enough. What he means is that botany isn't real magic."

I made a face. "What a *skunk*."

Eddie's smile became more real, either at the support or the insult, which was one of Hero's current favourites. My indignation was real, though. I didn't share Eddie's passion for botany— I'd had enough of growing things on the farm—but even I could tell that what Eddie did was real magic, and what's more, it was real science, with a rigour that was often lacking in magical scholarship. The Camford prejudice against the study of plants was ridiculous—the more so given that every inch of the university was entwined with them.

"He's all right," Eddie said, with something more like his usual generosity. "He's only saying what everyone would say."

I gave him a comforting nudge with my shoulder, the way I would one of my siblings. "Well, it's his loss. You can change the Faculty's mind about that at the same time as Hero and I are changing their minds about women in scholarship."

"I don't care what the Faculty thinks," Eddie repeated, with more certainty this time. He turned to me. "So where do we start?"

7

Things changed between the four of us after that. The puzzle pieces that had been hovering cautiously above the board, waiting to see if they fit, snapped into place. We were working together on a project, exactly as Camford scholars should, in defiance of the Faculty, and we were invincible. It was like having the most private of inside jokes, or being in our own secret rebellion. In the dining hall the evening after, the vice-chancellor himself came in to deliver the grave reminder that the archives were strictly out-of-bounds to all undergraduates, and we looked at one another and *glowed*.

Even before coming to Camford, I had been focused on counter-curses. I hadn't thought to research Amiens itself, much less present an argument for lifting the Accord, and I wouldn't have known where to start if I had. But Hero and Alden were directing their attention to what had gone wrong on that day, and Eddie and I quickly fell in line. Hero's passion was spellcraft linguistics, and she spent hours poring over German runespells to see how they might have been affected by the battlefield. Eddie threw himself into superstitions and old wives' tales around dryads. Alden was a wealth of information there as well—his interests ranged widely, but more often than not they settled along the thorny paths of folklore, and he had a seemingly endless supply of fairy tales and old rhymes at his fingertips.

By contrast, I was keenly aware of how little I had to contribute. My background knowledge was sketchy at best, and my unmagical blood was sluggish when it came to the practical spellwork I loved. All I had was determination, the ability to read a very great number of very old books, and a certain skill in plucking out information from multiple pages and drawing them together to make something new. I was good at it, though, and what was more, I loved it. I would spend hours late at night in my room after my own assignments were done, poring over the tiny print in a Middle English spellbook until my eyes grew heavy and I would wake in the thin dawn light with my glasses askew and my face buried in the pages.

"You know, you were right at the lecture," I said to Alden one afternoon in the library. We were in our chosen room on the seventh floor, books scattered between us. He was leaning against the window sill, smoking by the half-open window that led out to the roof. (For Eddie's benefit—Hero smoked like a chimney, and I had learned from my brother after he came home, but the smell of cigarettes gave Eddie a blinding headache.) It was a stormy day outside, and the wind brought the cold smell of rain and pine into the room.

"I often am," Alden agreed modestly. "About what?"

"The real mystery isn't why the spell failed. It's what happened afterwards. I've read through all the documented accounts of the fae breaking through circles that I can find. It happens for many reasons—a lot of different mistakes on the part of the spell-caster. None have ever been so violent. The faeries possess the spell-caster; they don't murder hundreds of people."

"Except in this case they did. I don't suppose your brother could shed any light on it?"

"He won't talk about that day." I tried to say it normally and not as though my insides had twisted into a ball. "Anyway, he isn't a mage. He wouldn't know what he'd seen."

"I see." Alden sounded far from happy about it. There had

been an edge of frustration to him that week, as we moved closer to the term break. "That's fair, of course."

"We know one new thing about Amiens, thanks to Clover's brother and thanks to Eddie," Hero pointed out. I suspected she'd noticed his mood, too, and was trying in her matter-of-fact way to pull him out of it. "We know the kind of fae that was summoned. A dryad."

"A dryad of a silver birch tree," Eddie clarified. "We think." I had gone through Eddie's books and confirmed that the bark matched, although it was still difficult to be sure.

"Exactly. I'd never heard that reported before. And that makes what happened even more unusual. Dryads don't want to come into our world. Their roots are in faerie country. Why would one want to break through enough to kill on such a scale?"

Alden straightened restlessly, stubbing his cigarette out on the window sill. I would have told him off, had the sill not been already well mottled with such marks. "Well, Larkin strongly implied there might be an answer in the archives. The trouble is, Grimoire will be watching us like a hawk from now on. He knows perfectly well that I was the one who tried to break in that night."

I had to admit Grimoire had been keeping a very close watch over us since the break-in. Alden had swapped the ring back the following morning, as he'd promised ("Just as well," Hero had pointed out, "or you'd accidentally become ward of Camford Library if he died"), and as he'd predicted Grimoire had given him a very shrewd look and let it pass. They were distant relations, which meant something to the Families, and as far as Grimoire knew the attempt on the archives had been nothing more than student mischief. Still, he was far from stupid. Any indication that it was anything more serious would come down on us fast and heavy.

"We're not going to give him anything to see," Hero reminded him. "No more archives. You promised."

"Well, we'd better come up with another source of information, then," Alden said tightly. "It's all very well Eddie knowing the botanical classification of the dryad at Amiens, we can address it by its tree if we ever meet it at a party, but that isn't going to help us bind it, is it?"

I felt rather than saw Eddie go quiet beside me, and felt a corresponding flash of irritation. Alden had a tendency to swipe at Eddie sideways when he was frustrated, not wanting a fight with Hero and knowing that Eddie wouldn't fight back. I flicked a glance at Hero; she caught it and answered with an expressive roll of her eyes.

"Alden," she said calmly, "you're being a prat."

"I'm not *being* a prat, I *am* a prat. You're seeing my natural form." The light had come back to his voice, though, and he gave us a rueful smile. "Sorry, Eddie. Don't listen to me. It's the weather or lack of coffee or impending Christmas or something. I just hoped to be further along than this by the end of term."

I couldn't fault him for that. I had hoped the same, with what I couldn't help but think was far more cause.

"You know, there's a possibility we haven't discussed," Hero said. She had put down her book, and the serious note to her voice made me sit up and take notice. Hero was frequently serious, I had learned by now. She rarely let it show unless it was very late at night or very important. "I suspect we've all thought it. And that's the possibility that the Board and the Faculty know exactly why and how that spell failed at Amiens, and that's exactly why we've all been forbidden from looking into it."

"But…" I spoke before I could stop myself. "Why would they hide that?"

The others were kind enough not to laugh. The truth was, I'm ashamed to say, I hadn't thought it at all. I was still so new to the Families. They frustrated me, even angered me, they had imprisoned my brother and scorned me for my upbringing and my blood, but I was also in love with them. They had built

Camford, they had written the books of spellcraft that I pored over every day, they navigated magic with the light, playful ease of a bird through air or a fish through water. I didn't want to believe that anyone could do that and not be trusted.

"Who knows?" Alden said. "Who knows why the Board does half of what it does? Either way, I don't see that we can do anything about it except press on our own. If it takes us there, we'll deal with it then. We're only reading books. What's the worst they can do to us?"

I thought at once of Dr. Larkin. Alden had tried to talk to him, the week after his lecture on Amiens. When he knocked on the door, however, Larkin's office was dark and empty, all his belongings gone. Word got around that he had been suspended from all teaching and placed on research leave effective immediately. It seemed a stretch to imagine it had anything to do with the lecture, much less the break-in to the archives that followed it. Now I wondered if I knew Camford as well as I thought.

Hero was evidently thinking the same thing. "If we start to get anywhere *close* to there, Alden, we're going to back away. Do you understand?"

"Of course," Alden said. "What do you take me for? All I said was that we needed another source of information."

"Such as?" Hero sounded mollified but sceptical.

"I'll think of something," Alden said, and of course we believed him.

The term passed in a dizzying whirl. Soon, the four of us were firmly established around the university as a tight-knit group who did things together, just in time to have little opportunity to do much at all except work. The cold weather set in, and with it the assignments and readings due before the Christmas holidays. Luncheons and parties began to empty of all but the most committed hedonists; even the richest students started to look worn around the edges. They spoke to me a little by then, those rich students. At least, most of them would nod at me if our paths crossed, only slightly less cautiously friendly than if I were Hero or Eddie. They thought we were all strange, of course, even Alden. But it was a glamorous kind of strange now—something other, not something lesser.

I turned eighteen at the end of November, as the term was drawing to an end. I hadn't expected the others to know—I hadn't told them, worried that they'd either feel obligated to do something or that they wouldn't bother, either of which would be embarrassing. I had planned to wake early, to open the presents my family had sent, and sit reading for an hour or so by the fire before going down to breakfast. It was a Saturday, and I wanted to luxuriate in a short time without study. Instead, I was woken by a loud rapping on the door.

Hero stood there, dressed in a spectacular dark green coat with a fur ruff and high boots, every bit as though she were expected.

"Rise and shine, darling," she said. "Happy birthday."

I blinked, dazed, aware for the first time in a while that my dressing gown was threadbare and my hair was in a sleepy fuzz around my head. "What…? How did you know?"

"If you want to conceal your birthday, you really do need to refrain from opening your cards the night before." I had, it was true—the card from my family was perched on the mantel of the fireplace, a drawing from Holly adorning its cover. Hero had been in last night, very briefly, just to borrow a book. I'd had no idea she'd noticed it, much less clearly read it when my back was turned. "And if you *don't* want to conceal your birthday, please do have the courtesy to reveal it a little earlier. A few hours' notice is not a good deal of time to make plans, especially when those plans involve wrangling Alden and Eddie."

"What plans?"

"Get dressed," Hero said, "and you'll find out. Oh, be sure to dress for London."

London. My heart spiked in what was either excitement or fear or both. The four of us had walked into Oxford plenty of times, and I had grown to appreciate its stately beauty and bursts of student mischief. I had never been to London. I had nothing to wear to London, not in the company of someone like Hero. I should say no. I had assignments due—we all did.

"I'll be right there," I said.

The rest of my life, I'll never forget that day. London was grey and dirty, still struggling out of wartime hardship, but I barely saw it. What I saw were the signs of recovery bursting like stars from the grime. I looked in wonder at the playbills, the restaurants, the men and women in their glittering clothes. It was a vision of the modern world and everything it could be. Hero instructed Alden and Eddie to amuse themselves for a few hours and whisked me to a small shop along the dazzling curve of Regent Street, where a brisk, middle-aged woman had me try on outfit after outfit until I couldn't see straight. The one I liked best was soft blue grey, drop-waisted with tiny pearl buttons on the sleeves.

"That's definitely you," Hero agreed. "We'll take it. And the gold one, too, I think—you'll need it for this evening."

"This evening?"

"Well, I should think so. We're going to the Illusion."

My head swam as though at altitude. The Illusion was the most exclusive of the clubs in London for Families, and even I knew that it was very fashionable, very glamourous, and very, very expensive. "We are?"

"We certainly are, darling. We're doing this properly. So you see, you'll need that dress. Consider it my birthday present."

"I couldn't," I protested, even as my hand had clutched the skirt as if someone were about to steal it. I had never much minded about clothes before. This was different. This was as though I was being told I belonged. "It's too much."

"I assure you it isn't," Hero said, and something in her voice told me she understood perfectly. "It's your birthday. Admittedly, I would have found another excuse if it wasn't—I love dressing people up, and we're in a university filled with adolescent boys, for God's sake. But the fact remains that I've bought you these things for your birthday, and you have no say in the matter if you want to be polite."

Hero, I had noticed, was very good at pressuring people to do what they wanted to do anyway. I had no words to resist, so I just nodded tightly and gave her a quick, impulsive hug. It was the first time I had dared to do so, but she only laughed as she returned it.

"After all," she added, with a wicked grin, "we can't have you looking shabby and interesting and showing the rest of us up, can we? Now come on. You'll need new boots to go with those."

By the afternoon, our feet were sore and our arms laden with shopping, so we went to meet Alden and Eddie for lunch and then to the cinema to see *Treasure Island*. It was my first glossy Hollywood epic, and in that new luxurious theatre it was a different kind of magic, the mundane kind that had animated the artillery and tear gas of the Great War, now being used to flicker an imaginary world in front of us.

And then, the Illusion.

I had heard the name swirled around the Camford students' gossip: Like the restaurant in Manchester where Sam Wells had taken me, it was accessible only by magic, a spell performed at a doorway that opened to reveal the top of a long flight of stairs. That, though, was where the similarity between the two places ended. The Illusion was a nightclub, underground and smoky and vibrating with early jazz, and magic was very much on display. The chairs and tables undulated as if on gentle waves; globes of light whirled about the room in time with the music, entwining with the dancers on the floor.

I was thrilled and petrified in equal measures. I had no idea what I was supposed to do or who I was supposed to be. My gold dress and feathered bandeau felt like fancy dress, flimsy and transparent. Fortunately, Alden turned to me before the doubt could grow.

"Care to dance?" he shouted over the blare of the music.

"With you?" I asked stupidly.

"Well, I should hope so," Hero shouted back. "Why else do you think we brought him along?"

He stuck his tongue out at her in a perfunctory fashion, then extended his arm to me.

I had gone to a dance at my school once, to be rotated in a slow circle by one of the village lads; my little sisters, much more fashionable, had shown me the basics of the foxtrot up in our room only months before I came to Camford. I had never truly danced. It didn't matter. Alden could dance well enough for both of us. I needed only to watch him, to move with him and let his hand on my lower back gently move me, and if I put a foot wrong and we tripped and collided, it didn't seem to matter at all. We just laughed, spun, kept going, while the music thrummed in my ears and in my blood and nobody could tell in the smoky darkness that I wasn't meant to be there.

That night seemed to take no time at all and yet to stretch out forever, its own little world. I remember lights flashing; I remember dancing with Eddie, then Hero, then Alden again. I remember collapsing at a table next to Hero and Alden, breathless and exhausted and dizzy, some kind of blue potion in my hand with possibly more alcohol than I had ever held in my life.

"How are you finding your brush with the modern world?" Hero asked me.

I shook my head, not sure how to answer. "I didn't expect it to be so…"

"Modern? Exciting? Loud?"

"Underground."

Hero laughed. "It was a bunker during the war. The Families brought treasures here to keep them from being damaged in air raids—they brought themselves here once or twice too, when things looked risky. Then the war ended, and the Ravenscar brothers bought it and turned it into this. Nice, isn't it?"

I wished, somehow, she hadn't explained. I imagined the ceiling shuddering with the impact of bombs, dust raining down on Families huddled under the tables, and shivered in my new gold dress.

"Clover." Alden raised his voice to get my attention over the music. "This library where you studied Agrippa. Where was it?"

Hero sighed dramatically. "Oh, I'm sorry, were we talking about something other than bloody Agrippa for five minutes?"

"Lady Winter's house," I answered. I didn't mind talking about Agrippa. In the flurry of new sensations, it was something solid to cling to. "She taught me magic. Why?"

"Because most houses threw out their books on faerie magic after the Accord, or pretended to. Ours did. Is it possible she didn't?"

I hesitated, thinking of that assortment of old books that didn't look as though anyone had sorted them for generations. In light of what we had just been discussing, they suddenly seemed more precious and more dangerous. "I wouldn't want to get her into trouble…"

"God no. She has nothing to fear from me. I was just wondering if, when you get home next week, you could look through them."

When I got home. A confusion of feelings swamped me, too fast for me to sift through. I did want to go home. I missed my family, I was wretchedly guilty at being so long away from the farm, and Hero had found a new counter-curse that I was eager to try on Matthew. But I didn't want to leave Camford, and I already couldn't imagine being without the other three. They wouldn't even be with one another for once: Hero's family were spending Christmas in London, and Eddie's family were going to his elder sister's house in Scotland.

"Of course I will. And if I find anything, I'll write to you all."

"You'd better all write to me anyway," Alden warned. "I don't know how I'm going to survive Christmas in that house otherwise."

"God, you're sentimental when you're drunk," Hero said.

"I'm not, actually. I'm sentimental when I'm sober. A few more of these and I won't care if any of you live or die."

"Charming. Speaking of, did you see where Eddie got to?"

"Outside," Alden said, with a nod to the back door. "He never lasts long in places like this. Too many people."

"I'll go find him," I said, pushing my drink aside and getting to my feet. My head was spinning, from the music or the cocktail or the dancing, and since Hero had explained it, the concrete ceiling seemed just a little too low. "I wouldn't mind some fresh air too."

"We'll try not to talk too much about Agrippa without you," Hero promised.

───────◇───────

The back of the club opened to a narrow alley off Fleet Street, littered with old packing crates and broken glass. After the heat of all those dancing bodies, the midnight frost outside was like a splash of ice water to my face. Eddie was sitting on the steps— his shoulders tensed when he heard the door open, then relaxed when he turned and saw it was me.

"Sorry," he said, with his shy, off-centre smile. "I didn't want to leave your birthday. I just couldn't breathe in there."

"No, it's fine." I folded my bare arms against the chill. "I'm not sure I could, after a while. Aren't you cold, though?"

"Freezing," he agreed, without moving. "It might be a white Christmas at home."

I sat down beside him, heedless of the icy step, careful of my dress. The stars were crisp overhead, and I could feel the faint warmth of Eddie's shoulder against mine. I felt guilty, not for the first time, at how I let Eddie fade into the background when the four of us were together. I wondered what on earth was in the blue potion I had drunk, and whether I would feel the cold more when it wore off.

"Here," Eddie said, and I turned to see him digging into his satchel. "I was going to give you this anyway, before I knew it was your birthday. I bought a ribbon for it while you and Hero were shopping, so…" He shrugged as he pulled out a small blue box tied with a white ribbon. "Something to take home with you."

It was a rose, deep scarlet with just a shimmer of purple at the tips. Not a dead rose, of course. It grew in a small pot, surrounded by a wreath of dark green leaves. Something in my heart unfurled at the sight of it.

"It's beautiful. Truly. Thank you."

"I found it growing by the wall at Camford," Eddie said. He drew his long legs to his chest and wrapped his arms around his knees. "Took me a while to get the soil right. The funny thing is, I don't know what kind of rose it is. It's not in any of my books."

I looked at the shimmering tips with even deeper interest. "Do you think it came from over the wall? Does that mean that Camford isn't in Wales after all?"

Eddie gave me a curious look. "You really want to know where Camford is, don't you?"

I was startled that he had noticed, when as far as I could remember I had raised the question only once before, on the rooftop. I shouldn't have been. The mistake people made with Eddie in those days was thinking that his thoughts and feelings were simple. The way he dealt with people always was— at least, it was always kind, and kindness is usually simple enough. Really, Eddie only showed a tiny sliver of what he felt at any moment, and his understanding of the currents of human behaviour ran deep. He was a prey animal, at heart—watchful and wary, curious and shy. Like most prey animals, he wouldn't have survived to adulthood without being very observant.

"Not *really*," I said unconvincingly. "It's just—odd. I've been looking at a lot of old books lately, and there's almost nothing about the formation of the university. I know we split off from Oxford, but where did we go? How were the doors set up, for that matter? When Sam took me through them, I assumed they were common to mages, but there's nothing like them anywhere else, is there?"

"No," Eddie agreed. "That knowledge was lost, they say. The other old universities have them too—I've seen the one in Paris, when we visited my cousins there. Maybe we should rediscover it. We'd be able to study, step through a door, and go home every night."

I laughed, though the possibility was thrilling. Why not, after all? "There are hundreds of students at Camford. That would be a lot of doors. Besides, not all of us want to go home."

I don't know why I said that last part. Probably it was the blue drink.

Eddie only smiled. "Well, I wouldn't try to find Camford based on that rose. Camford has a flora all to itself—the plants are similar to what you'd get here or Wales, but odd colours, and a little more awake. You want to know what I think?"

"What?"

"I think the magic in the air changes them." Enthusiasm warmed his voice. "I've seen that flower respond to magic, you know. Just out of the corner of my eye, when I've been doing homework in my room. It turns toward it the way sunflowers do to sunlight."

I stroked the glittering petals with one fingertip. I was just drunk enough to have the melodramatic thought that I, too, felt myself turning toward magic and Camford and these people like a flower, and not quite drunk enough to voice it out loud. But I decided then and there that I didn't care where Camford was. I looked up at the stars, high above the alley in that smoky London sky, and knew that I, at least, was exactly where I wanted to be.

8

My visit home started when nobody came to meet me at the station.

I had known this might happen, and that it would be nobody's fault if it did. Our farm is a good hour's walk from the nearest train station, or half that on the rattling motorcycle that Matthew bought last year from an army friend who swore it wouldn't break down every five minutes (it broke down every ten). In her last letter, Mum had promised they would try to be there. Sometimes, though, no amount of coaxing or minor spell-craft would get the motorcycle running, sometimes emergencies cropped up on the farm and neither Mum nor Matthew could get away, sometimes the road was blocked by ice or flooding or mud or the old farm horse was needed for work. I'd told her not to worry—if there was nobody at the station, I'd just walk home and it wouldn't matter a bit. I meant it. Still, I couldn't help the eager leap of my heart as the train slowed approaching the plat-form, nor its subsequent plummet back to its proper place when the platform was empty. It wasn't only that I had truly longed to see everyone. It was snowing lightly outside, and the station platform was hard and glittering white.

Well, there was nothing for it. I hauled my book-heavy suit-case off the platform, winced at the wet crunch as it fell, pulled my coat tighter about me with my free hand, and started to walk. At least I'd had the sense to wear my old boots, not the soft grey suede pair Hero had given me for my birthday.

It felt strange to pick my way down the old familiar road, as though I was walking backwards into childhood. It's hard, wild, unforgiving country: On that day, covered as they were in grey wet snow, the roads and stone walls and dark brick houses looked carved by force from the surrounding landscape. In the distance the great flat tabletop of Pendle Hill stood draped in white—the hill where twelve men and women had been accused of witchcraft in the Lancaster Assizes, and which even now felt steeped in a brooding power different to any taught at Camford. I walked through the village, shut up against the winter cold, across the bridge under which the river flowed sluggishly, onto the foot track that followed the great stone wall home. I tried to use a charm to lighten my suitcase, but the hand gestures were precise and my frozen fingers made the result unpredictable—the thing abruptly doubled in weight as I tried to pull it over a stile, and I slipped in an undignified heap on the frozen ground. My newly assured Camford self seemed to shrivel and flake away with every step.

But it was only the walk home, after all. After an hour or so, as the sky was getting dark, I sighted the familiar row of beech trees that stood guard at the edge of our land. Soon, there was our house, small and dark and shivering against the leaden sky. Someone inside had obviously been keeping a watch for me. The door opened before I had a chance to knock, and I was hit by two firm, sturdy little bodies.

"Clover!" Iris flung her arms around me, her hands frozen and her cheeks still pink from the wind. She and Little John behind her would have walked the same road back from school only half an hour before.

"Hello, you two!" I let my trunk fall and dropped to my knees to hug them tightly, and the cold outside melted from my chest. Whatever else I had felt about home, I had missed them so much. "Look at you. You've grown!"

"We were going to come meet you," Mum said, and I looked up to see her tiny figure standing in the hallway in a flour-streaked apron. She didn't smile often these days, but the lines around her eyes softened as I got to my feet. "That useless motorcycle died again this morning, of course, but our Matthew said he'd get it working again or take the horse. Then one of the sheep fell down a gully by the brook. Matthew had to go and get it out—he's been there all afternoon. Marigold and Holly had to get the rest in on their own. And I didn't like to take the horse out in this weather, even if I could have left the little ones."

"You didn't have to come meet me." I returned her brisk hug. I'd forgotten what it was like at home. Everything had to be fine, always, even when it was falling around our ears. "It was a good walk, even with the snow."

"No rain at the moment, that's one good thing," Mum said. If there had been rain, it would have been good fortune there wasn't mist, or sleet, or a tidal wave. "We've made your old bed up for you with Mary and Holly. Go get out of those wet things, and tea should be ready by the time you come down. You're looking pale. Don't they feed you in that place?"

"Not like here," I said, because it was what Mum wanted to hear. In fact, she was the one who looked startlingly gaunt, as though the wind outside had whittled the flesh from her bones.

Iris and Little John were only waiting for Mum to release me. They pounced on me at once and dragged me upstairs, where I barely had time to change before they were showing me three months' accumulated drawings and pressed leaves and stones. Mary and Holly were equally excited once they came in from the shed, though Mary didn't squeal as she would have only last year. I was startled when I looked at her to see not a little girl but a young woman of fifteen, her gold hair pinned up experimentally, her face losing its childish roundness.

"You look so grown-up," I said inadequately.

She looked faintly self-conscious, though pleased. "I'm the

eldest daughter at home now," she said, in a voice that strained too hard for nonchalance. "People look at you different."

"Peter Brooks looks at her different," Holly said slyly, and she and Iris erupted into giggles while John rolled his eyes with the disgust only a seven-year-old could muster.

"No!" I sounded half-delighted, half-horrified, and in truth I didn't know which was closer to what I felt. "Mary, you're not walking out with Peter Brooks?"

"Not *really*," she said, feigning reluctance, drawing the last word out to at least four syllables. "Mum says not until I'm sixteen. He drives me into town sometimes, though, when I go to work at the tea-shop, and sometimes he leaves me flowers when he comes to help with the chores."

I smiled, and wondered at the odd pang I felt at the news. It wasn't that I envied her Peter Brooks—he was a kind lad, a year younger than me, and I had him marked down as the farmer sort with strong hands and not a startling thought in his head. Perhaps it was discomfort to see my sisters settle for life at Pendle Hill, when I felt they could do so much more; perhaps it was guilt that Peter Brooks and my sisters were doing the work for the farm that should have been mine; perhaps, less charitably, there was even an edge of resentment. When I had been their age, the world had been at war. All my spare thoughts and worries had been for the great armies crashing across Europe and our brother and his friends caught in their teeth. I had been clinging to a wreck in a storm, certain any moment that everything would go down forever. I had never had any time or care for the kind of things they were talking about. I could have them now if I wanted them, of course. I wasn't part of Matthew's generation, only a few years ahead, whose youth had been snatched away and would never come back. But still.

"What about you, Clover?" Holly said, with the same sidelong look at Mary. "You're well past sixteen now. Are any of those lords at Camford walking out with you?"

"Or any you want to?" Iris put in.

"Don't be daft," I scoffed. I tried not to think of Alden pulling close to read over my shoulder in the library, Eddie waiting for me in the frost on the night of my birthday, Hero's hand gripping mine and leading me through the glitter of the Illusion. Their friendship was too good to ruin with all that. "I'm far too busy. I'm there to be a scholar, not somebody's wife."

"Can't you be both?" Mary asked, genuinely curious.

I was spared having to answer by Mum's voice calling from the kitchen. "Tea's ready!"

It was toad-in-the-hole with mashed potatoes and peas and gravy, the kind of food that wouldn't have got within a mile of Camford and which unexpectedly brought tears to my eyes. The batter was golden and crisp, the sausages hot and salty, the peas tiny bursts of sweetness alongside the creamy potato. Suddenly I was eight years old again, having my favourite food for my birthday, and the university seemed years in the future and miles from home.

Matthew finally made it back as we were scraping our plates clean and Little John was begging for seconds. I heard the creak of the door and the loud, excited bark of our border collie, then my brother came into the kitchen with Shep at his side, both breathless and triumphant and soaked to the skin.

"The sheep?" Mum asked quickly.

"Safe and well." He took his hat off and ruffled his damp hair. "I put her in the barn to get warm. That's one we're not losing this winter, at least. Speaking of numbers, am I miscounting or do we have an extra here?"

"Our Clover's back!" Iris shouted helpfully, and I jumped up to embrace him. The memory came to me unbidden of his return from the war nearly two years before, when the train had pulled up at the station and we had seen him get off, pale and worn and unfamiliar in his uniform. Perhaps the same memory had come to him, because he tightened his grip on me before he pulled back. He was thinner than I remembered, and there were new lines at the corners of his eyes when he smiled.

"All right?" he asked, and I nodded, pushing my glasses back straight on my nose.

"Better than you," I informed him. Shep was jumping at me, whining excitedly; I ruffled her muddy ears. "You're wet through."

"What, this isn't how they dress for dinner at Camford?"

"Only on Sundays."

"I'd best get dried off, then. Don't go anywhere before I get back, yeah?"

"I've saved your tea in the oven for you," Mum said.

"Good! I'm starving." He looked more than starving, or wet through. He looked tired to his very bones, and once more guilt wrung my insides like a wet dishcloth. I remembered unwillingly what Eddie had said about the curse entwining its way toward his heart.

I could help, I reminded myself firmly. I had the Brackenbury counter-curse to try tonight, and if that failed, I could find others. I hadn't abandoned my family for my own ambitions. It would help them, in the end.

It was difficult to remember that here, though. Camford seemed like something out of a storybook. Part of me was already wondering how I had ever survived there. The other part was already longing to go back.

<hr>

I didn't get a chance to speak to Matthew alone until after dinner. Last thing at night had been my favourite time on the farm, when I was a child before the war. The younger ones would be in bed, the animals would be fed and settled, Dad would be smoking his pipe by the fire, and Mum would be sitting across from him doing a last bit of sewing. Her face would be softer somehow, relaxed from its determined lines. I would make four mugs of tea, set two down on the little table beside Mum, and take the other two out to where Matthew was finishing up at the barn. It would be very quiet as I followed the little track through the field—in summer there would still be glimmers of light on the horizon and the soft rustle of tree leaves and birdsong.

Now, though Mum still sat sewing by the fire, there were only three mugs of tea to make, and her face softened only a little as she nodded her thanks. The fields outside were pitch-black. As I picked my way through, the rain was spitting cold drops from the sky, and the wind snatched at my skirt and whipped my hair about my ears.

But Matthew was still there, forking the hay down from the loft to the sheep penned up below while Shep tried to snatch it playfully out of the air. He looked up at me with a smile as I slammed the door shut behind me, and for a second I had a glimpse of what it might have been like had neither of us ever gone away.

"Those both for me?" he called out.

"No, one's for me and one's for Shep," I returned. "But she doesn't want hers, so you'll have to have it. Here."

I passed the mugs up to him first—we could just manage if he reached down and I stood on tiptoes—then scrambled up the ladder to join him. It was a good thing I had changed into my old woollen skirt before dinner—I don't think I would have made it in my new one, not without snagging the fabric on wood chewed ragged by livestock.

"I put them under my shawl so the rain wouldn't fall in them," I said, taking my mug back.

"Don't you have magic for that now?"

I screwed up my nose at him. "It's too strong for a little thing like that. It would shatter the mugs."

"We can't have that." He sat down beside me with a wince he couldn't quite hide, letting his feet hang out over the barn.

"Magic never seems to get it right, does it? It's either too small or too big."

"Or maybe we're the ones who are too small or too big."

"Maybe we are," he conceded, and though that remark shouldn't have meant very much, I heard something lying beneath it. I saw the light flicker and die in his eyes and his face go quiet. I'd forgotten, or tried to forget, how that had started happening since the war. I hated it. It was like watching him go away again even while I looked at him.

"Matty?" I said, hesitant, and he blinked as if coming out of a dream.

"Mm?"

"Have things been all right here? I mean…did you get through the tupping season? Is there enough feed for the winter?"

Matthew raised his eyebrows, back and teasing again. "Did the farm fall down without you, you mean? We managed fine. And if the lambing goes well, we might be able to hire someone next year." He must have seen something in my face. "What?"

I looked away, flushed. "Nothing."

In truth, seeing my brother for the first time in months, I was shocked by how young he was. He had been an adult to me when we had parted, a returned soldier, experienced and sure. Now he had shifted, the way my vision clarified every morning when I put on my spectacles, and I could see that he was barely twenty-three—younger than Everett Dalrymple, or most of the postgraduates. And yet his face was already so much older. At dinner I had seen the way it stilled into tense, preoccupied lines when he thought nobody was looking, the way the last six years had engrained themselves around his eyes. The old curse marks peeked from his collar, inflamed around the edges by the wind and the cold. Surely they hadn't crept quite so far up his jawline before I had gone away.

"Is it getting stronger?" I asked bluntly. "The curse."

"No. I don't think so." His surprise was just a little too defensive. "Why do you ask?"

I didn't want to tell him what Eddie had said. "You're not fooling me, you know. It's been hurting you all evening."

At least he didn't bother to deny it. "It's been a long day, that's all. And there's another midnight coming soon. It always plays up a bit then." I must have looked sceptical, because he sighed. "Stop worrying! I told you, we've all been managing while you're away."

"Still," I said, "there's something I'd like to try. Do you mind if I...?"

He frowned but obligingly held still as I reached out for the withered mark on his neck. (Birch. I was sure of it now.) I pulled down the collar just enough to find a purchase for my fingers, then I gathered my thoughts, closed my eyes, and whispered the words from Brackenbury. The spell recognised the curse mark at once. An electric shiver rushed to my fingertips; a prickle of cold swept across my skin, like a sudden spring shower.

Beneath my touch, Matthew felt it too. His breath caught with a shiver of his own, then released in a very faint sigh. When I opened my eyes, though, my heart sank.

"It didn't work." I dropped my hand, frustrated, flicking my fingers to shake off the tingling. "That's a different countercurse. Sometimes it's more effective than the one Sam used. I hoped... But I suppose you were struck too long ago now anyway. I'm sorry."

"It's all right." I don't know how disappointed he was. Perhaps he really had managed not to have any hope at all, as he'd claimed. He had always been a natural optimist, though, and I don't see how he could have helped but hope a little. "Thanks for trying."

I brushed this off. It was so far short of what I'd meant that tears pricked my eyes. "Perhaps I shouldn't go back in the new term."

"For God's sake. Where is all this coming from?"

"Well…" I gestured to the dark barn, where the sheep and our old horse munched their hay contentedly beneath the sound of the rain on the roof. "Look at this place. I should be here to help, not running around playing with magic."

He laughed, affectionate, just a little bitter. "Clove, you hate this place. You always have. All you've wanted all your life is to get out."

That stung, whether he meant it to or not. "It isn't *all* I've wanted. I want all of you to be safe and happy, more than anything. Besides, you wanted to get out of this place too."

"Well," he said. "I did, didn't I?"

I didn't know what to say. I never did, on the rare occasions he alluded to the years he had spent away from us. It was one of the many things I hated about the way my brother had come home. I used to know his every mood, as he knew mine. I had known when he needed to be pushed into admitting what was bothering him; he had known when I needed to be teased out of dwelling on what bothered me. I had known what would make him laugh, what would infuriate him, what would fire his eyes with sudden mischief. Now, too often, he became a stranger in front of my eyes. There was a vast chasm between his experiences and mine, and I feared that going away to Camford had widened it still further.

"I just don't want to let you down," I said feebly.

"You're not letting us down, you clod." He looked at me, and his voice softened. "Are you happy at Camford?"

"Yes." I didn't need to think about that, not even for a moment. "It's wonderful."

"Then stay there. I mean that. Don't listen to Mum."

I didn't need to ask what Mum had been saying. "She's right, though. You need my help here."

"You know what helps? Whatever happens, you're happy where you are. I won't have to worry this winter that you're cold or hungry or miserable; I don't have to feel that your future depends on me pulling this stupid farm through the next year or five years or ten years. You took care of that yourself, because you're hardworking and you're clever and you never gave up. So don't ever feel like you're letting us down, all right? We're proud of you."

I'd never heard Matthew say anything like that to me before. We loved each other dearly, that was understood, but our usual means of expressing it was to give each other a shove and call each other idiots. I didn't quite know how to respond to it now. Mixed in with pleasure and embarrassment was a vague foreboding, as though he might be on his deathbed. My eyes burned hot, and all I could do was nod soundlessly and hope my face wasn't doing anything too foolish.

"Besides, you're working twice as hard while you're back to make up for being away," he added, in something more like his usual voice. "Aren't you? Wasn't that the agreement?"

My own voice found its usual tracks as well. "Oh? I don't remember that."

"Well, I'm afraid I do. It's a shame, with all the snow coming this week, but there's nothing for it."

I shoved him and dodged the hay he threw back at me, which gave me a perfect chance to dash my sleeve across my eyes when he wasn't looking. He knew, of course, but at eighteen, I could pretend.

"I wish you could come to Camford too," I said. "Even just for a visit."

"Really?" He gave me a knowing look. "You're telling me you wouldn't be ashamed to be seen with a peasant farmer from the back of beyond, who drops *h*s left, right, and centre and doesn't know how to turn base metal into gold?"

"Don't be daft! Never." Yet some treacherous part of my brain flashed me a picture of Matthew shaking hands with Alden, and the incongruity of it made me want to look away, uncomfortable. It wasn't just that I'd be ashamed of my brother, or for him. In some strange way, I'd be ashamed of Camford too.

He let me off the hook, sort of. "I'm just glad you came home for Christmas. I did wonder, when I got some of your letters."

"Of course I came home," I scoffed.

I didn't tell him, because I couldn't quite bring myself to think it, that I was afraid it could no longer feel like home at all.

⎯⎯⎯⎯⎯⎯❧⎯⎯⎯⎯⎯⎯

That feeling never entirely went away. On the surface, I slipped back easily enough into the old routines, the hurried daylight hours of meal-making and stock-feeding and childcare. My siblings were genuinely happy to have me back, and I was no less happy to see them. But the new distance between us wouldn't close. Everything felt temporary—my suitcase still unpacked, the books from Camford ready and waiting on my desk, my new London clothes folded and ready to be worn back. It was strange: While I'd been at Camford, home had seemed a distant dream. And yet at home, when Camford should have seemed the same distance apart, everything reminded me of it.

Everything reminded me of Alden and Hero and Eddie, everything and anything at all. I missed them desperately—the more so because they were my only line now to the magical world. I wrote to them every few days and haunted the post in the mornings for their reply. Fortunately, they seemed to miss me too. Most days brought at least one letter, sometimes two: Hero's beautiful curling script, stuffed with parties and books and gossip indiscriminately; Eddie's round serious handwriting, the envelopes stuffed more literally with cuttings and pressed flowers from his family's greenhouse; Alden's hasty scrawl, flickering between whimsical nonsense and flashes of serious research. When those letters were before my eyes, the world brightened into candlelit libraries and firelit gatherings, and the pang when

I lowered them to our flat grey farm under snow hurt more every time.

How is your brother? Hero asked as December drew on. *I was thinking of him, with the solstice approaching. I'm still annoyed that the Brackenbury didn't work, but perhaps you'll find it will have made a difference to the midnights. I'll keep looking in the British Museum while I'm here—it will be a merciful distraction from a parade of the dullest young men in creation, all of whom have been visiting the house lately, courtesy of my father. Do let me know how Matthew fares.*

I held off on replying to that letter longer than usual. I had some excuse—the next midnight was only days away, as Hero had said, and it made sense to wait. The truth was, the more time I spent at home, the more painfully clear it was that Eddie's warning had been right. Matthew's curse was growing, and it was taking him.

It wasn't just that the wound in his shoulder was hurting him more every day. He always had an excuse for that—the cold, the damp, the work we'd done earlier that morning. It was the way his smile would fade and he would withdraw into himself when his concentration lapsed, at times too deep for the sound of his own name to recall him. It was the way I would hear him pacing in the attic above my room all night, unable or unwilling to fall asleep; the way he would doze off by the fire in the evenings only to start awake as if at a gunshot. It was the way I would look at him sometimes and see with a chill the green-speckled glint of something else looking back. It terrified me.

It's difficult to heal properly, Eddie had said, those few weeks ago. *My grandfather always said the only sure way was to bargain with another faerie.*

I was beginning to fear he may be right. That if Matthew were ever to be well again, my only chance was for us to persuade the Families to eventually lift the Accord—and even then, it may be too late.

The next midnight was a few days before Christmas, on the winter solstice. The sun was due to set around four that afternoon, but it was only a little after three before Matthew faltered and caught himself against the fence we had been mending.

"I'm all right," he assured me, breathless and distracted. He dashed a gloved hand across his eyes as if clearing them of fog. "I'd best get inside, though. It's starting."

The first midnight I had seen had started after dark. I hadn't noticed the incremental shift earlier every time—or if I had, I had attributed it to the seasons changing. There was no doubt now I was watching for it. The enchantment was swifter, hungrier, more eager. By the time we got to Matthew's room in the attic, it was nearly too late. He collapsed onto the bed, shaking, and Mum tied the knots while I quickly performed the binding spells.

"Thanks," Matthew said, through gritted teeth. He squeezed my hand briefly before I pulled away, and I returned it. "Promise me you won't open the door, all right? I mean it."

I don't know how he had guessed that was exactly what I had been intending to do. I wanted to learn more, to report back to my friends, to see if there was anything that made more sense after our research. But I had forgotten how horrifyingly real this was. The magic at Camford was human magic, carefully regulated, even the pranks and student excesses steeped in tradition. This was wild and uncanny and dark, and it wanted to hurt. I nodded, and he found the faintest twitch of a smile.

"I'm glad you're here," he said quietly, and then his eyes flickered green, he twisted away with a cry, and I flinched back on instinct.

Mum took my hand. "Come on," she said, unusually gentle, and I let myself be pulled away.

The screams started quickly after the door was locked and didn't relent until the morning sun was well over the horizon.

I wrote to Hero that night, telling her in the calmest possible terms that I had seen another midnight and I was seriously concerned. I perhaps wasn't as calm as I imagined.

I am more determined than ever to visit Lady Winter's at the first opportunity, I finished. *Wish me luck, will you?*

Her answer came by telegram the very next day. *Good luck!*

9

Lady Winter had been a figure of awe and terror to me the first time I had knocked on her door. Her house was a few miles away from our farm, and though I knew her by reputation, I had never seen it before. It was a grand redbrick Georgian mansion up a long flat lane, and it had been in the Winter family for centuries. Her husband, William Herbert Winter, had been a pale, clever, delicate man, who other than for his choice of bride had aroused little comment before he had been shot dead at the Somme along with most of his men. Lady Anjali Winter, the daughter of a wealthy Indian merchant from Madras, was another story entirely. The village rumours were that she had come to England to study mathematics at Cambridge, where she had met the young Lord Winter and eventually agreed to marry him. I had never, of course, believed the darker rumours that she was a witch, and so I had been more surprised than I should have been when they turned out to be true. Nobody had dared suspect Lord Winter of being a wizard, even though that was exactly what he had been.

It turned out they had met at Camford, not Cambridge, at the turn of the century; she had been studying advanced arithmancy, not mathematics. That was all she would tell me about herself, the entire year she was teaching me. She never spoke of her husband at all, nor what about him had drawn her from the heat and colour of her home to the damp grey Lancashire countryside. But from the place of honour his portrait kept in the hall, the black dress she wore when the time for mourning was long past, and the tightness that still gripped her face when she was forced to mention his name, I suspected she had loved him very much.

Sam Truelove Wells was a second cousin of her husband's, or something of the sort—the connections between the Families are as tortured and tangled as the roots of an entire forest. It might have been for that reason that she had agreed to tutor me when he asked it of her. I had never been able to work out how deep her interest in me ran. From the start, she was nothing like what I expected. I think I had pictured her tall, ghost-like, mysterious, Lady Dedlock crossed with a princess from the *Arabian Nights* (my reading material truly had been hopelessly old-fashioned). She was even shorter than me, to begin with, and despite her old-fashioned clothes, she had the sturdy, wiry strength of a dancer or a fighter. There was a fierce intelligence in the proud tilt of her head and the glint of her dark eyes; as a tutor, she drilled me relentlessly, her voice with its foreign lilt clipped and precise. And yet nothing she said was ever cutting or cruel, only occasionally impatient. In the right mood, she could talk for hours about the principles of magic, face alight and entire body animated. I grew less afraid of her over the year we had known each other; I never lost my awe.

She was sitting in her study when I was shown in that day, a few days before New Year, reading a book in the green velvet armchair by the fire. I couldn't tell if it was a book of magic or merely the ordinary kind; she looked up from it readily enough, removing her reading glasses to look me over.

"Ah! Clover Hill. I wondered when you'd call on me," she said. "How was your first term?"

"Wonderful," I said, and meant it. The miserable homesickness and exclusion of the first week had dwindled into nothing by now, as a station does when a train pulls away. "I love it."

"I'm glad to hear it. I was concerned you might find it hard going at first. Camford is not always kind to the people it wasn't made to fit."

I started to protest, on reflex, but stopped in time. My memories snagged uncomfortably on the restrictions Hero and I still rubbed against as female students, the way Eddie was lightly pushed aside by students and teachers alike, the sideways looks at my clothes and my hair and my lack of money, the way nobody had spoken to me until Alden had brought me into the fold.

"It isn't," I conceded. "But it's got better, since I made friends. And I'm doing well at the classes, I really am. If I'm good enough, they won't be able to treat me like an outsider forever. Times are changing."

She laughed, not happily. "I hope so. They certainly didn't change fast enough for me."

"Why didn't you stay at Camford after you graduated?" I asked, greatly daring. I was thinking of Hero, and my newfound knowledge that even the wealthy couldn't do everything they wanted. "Was it money?"

"I *didn't* graduate, officially," she reminded me. "It was only this year that Camford acknowledged women who had completed their degrees as graduates. No, in my case, it wasn't money. I was married to Lord Winter by then, and he would have paid for me to study had I asked. Perhaps that was part of it. I had intended to return home with a degree from Camford, whatever my father wanted. Once I knew I wasn't going to put it to that use, it felt unfair to use Lord Winter's money for my own indulgence alone." She paused, considering. "It wasn't truly that, though. Perhaps I simply fell out of love with Camford. That can be the most insidious way to keep someone out of a place: to make it so unpleasant they no longer see the point in fighting to be there."

I should have asked more, I knew even then. But I was eighteen, and Lady Winter was an adult. Eighteen is shy around adults, and yet thinks it can do better than them; it wants to know everything, and thinks it already does. Besides, Lady Winter had been at Camford twenty years ago. That was a lifetime and a world war ago. It had nothing to do with the university I knew.

"I was wondering if I could use your library," I said instead, after an awkward pause. "Just for today. I'd be quiet."

"Of course," she said, her briskness back in place. "I remember the load of assignments they like to give over Christmas break. Take as long as you need."

I didn't quite have that long—it had been difficult enough to get away from the farm for the day, and I'd promised to be back in time to take the little ones to the winter fair in the village that evening. The middle girls were going to a dance, their first night out for months, and Matthew had repairs to make that wouldn't be done in time. Still, that left me hours.

"If you're certain you don't mind…"

"Not at all. It's good for it to be of use again. Is there anything in particular you're looking for?"

I drew a deep breath, hesitated, then plunged ahead. If there was one thing Camford had taught me, I reminded myself, it was that it never hurt to ask.

"I was wondering…Do you have any books on faerie binding runes?"

My offhanded tone hadn't worked. Her eyebrows shot up. "I can't imagine Camford has set you an assignment on faerie magic. Not these days."

"It's…it's for Folklore." I am not a good liar. My entire face forgets basic expressions and flushes pink. "We have an essay on midsummer rites. I wanted to look up the spells. I couldn't find them in the Camford Library."

"I'm sure you couldn't. And I'm sure you know perfectly well why." She studied me carefully, her dark eyes taking in every inch of my face as it probably went from pink to bright red. "You already know I have nothing on faerie curses that might help your brother. You aren't planning to summon a faerie, I trust?"

"No." I was relieved, at last, not to be lying. "Nothing like that, I promise. How could I, with the Accord in effect and faerie country locked off?"

"That's true."

Lady Winter looked at me a moment longer, as if searching for something very particular she would recognise. It was the first time I had ever seen her hesitate. At last, she nodded.

"Very well." She rose to her feet in one sprightly movement. "Come with me."

Lady Winter's library was tiny compared to the Camford Library—only a single room. Yet it was a large room, a narrow gallery spanning the entire length of the house, and it was a beautiful one: lined with oaken shelves, dark green velvet curtains sweeping the floor, leather armchairs by the fireplace, and a matching oak desk in the centre. It had been the first place I had ever seen books of magic, a year ago. Entering it felt like being swept into a familiar embrace.

Lady Winter ignored the shelves from which we had studied for the entrance exams. Instead, she swept over to the wall directly above the flickering fire. I had never even looked at the titles there, thinking the books too old and dusty to be relevant, perhaps even for display only.

"They should be hereabouts. I think I have a copy of Gluckstein here." She studied the spines, frowning. "Most of the Families threw their faerie scholarship out, as I'm sure you know, or at least they pretended to. I didn't. This library was my husband's. It was here long before any Accord, and it will be here long after it."

"You don't agree with the Accord?" It was the first time I had heard anyone of her generation voice any objection. "Most mages do, I thought. I mean—it's meant to prevent accidents like what happened to my brother."

"I'm sorry for what happened to your brother." She meant it, but she'd never met Matthew. Her sympathy was general, not specific. "But practicing magic means understanding that accidents happen when it comes to spells. I studied magic in Bombay before I came to England, you know. There, young mages are taught to respect magic as a force of nature, to be navigated and not tamed. We go into it with our eyes and minds open, the way mariners set sail into the ocean—respectful of its power, knowing that not all will come back. I don't agree with trying to force it to do our bidding and then locking it up when we find we can't."

"So you think we should be allowed to use whatever magic we like?"

"I don't believe *allowed* comes into it. Faerie magic exists, whether the Board like it or not. Sooner or later, if something exists, it will be used. All we can do is try to understand it as well as we can, so we can use it for good." She shrugged very slightly. "Look at Madame Curie in Paris right now. The implications of her work with radioactive isotopes are frightening, terrifying even. That does not stop her, nor should it. Thousands of lives were saved in the war by her X-ray machines."

My heart was beating rapidly. "Does this mean you won't tell anyone if I look at these books?"

"What should I tell anyone? You're doing your Folklore homework, are you not? Ah, there it is." She took a volume off the shelf and held it out. "This is Gluckstein's *Introduction to Binding Rituals*, the one we learned from in our day."

I took it, with more reverence than the tattered textbook probably deserved. "Thank you."

"You're welcome. I'll have the maid bring you some tea down here. Watch you don't let it near the books."

Lady Winter paused just once before she left the room. "I told you that I didn't go on to study further at Camford because it felt dishonest to use my husband's money," she said abruptly.

"Because the university made it difficult and made me unwelcome. I feel differently now. If you want to stay at Camford, then you fight tooth and nail to stay there, by whatever means necessary. If you want to use Camford to help your brother, then you do that too. But be careful. Do you understand?"

I nodded dumbly.

"Good." She nodded at the book in my hand. "The others on that shelf will be along the same lines as that one. I trust you'll put them back when you're done."

God, those books. I still think back to that long afternoon spilling into evening, and the hairs rise on the back of my neck. It was real research, the kind I wasn't supposed to do at Camford until I was a postgraduate, the kind I still try to recapture with every new project. Many of those books hadn't been touched in years—dust rose from the pages when I turned them, and I had to squint at faded writing. My world shrank to a circle of candlelight as the sky darkened outside.

Gluckstein's introductory text was nothing startling, it was true. Most of it I at least half knew already. But I had learned it all sideways, from lectures and textbooks on other magic. Seeing it all laid out clearly and simply in black and white was a revelation, like a light coming on in a half-lit alley. I spent an hour reading the basics from the ground up, feeling my understanding put down real roots and branch out. How to draw a binding ring, and what runes were best for what purpose. How to open a door between the human realm and faerie country. How to lure a faerie out, to trap them, and to bargain a wish for their release. How to bargain safely, first and foremost. Most of the deals that went wrong, Gluckstein cautioned, happened at the bargaining stage. Every word had power, and the fae had centuries to learn the nuances of meaning that could trip a mere mortal.

That hadn't been the problem at Amiens, however. That had been a problem with the binding ring—a rune drawn incorrectly in the heat of battle, most likely, allowing the faerie to burst through its bounds and wreak havoc in the world. Reading this, I could understand why. It was far more precise than we had understood, and every line not quite joined or incorrectly shaped could spell disaster. Alden's theory that we could find something stronger, simpler, impossible to break began to look more unlikely the more I read. There had been so much work done already, and it had all failed spectacularly when the world had gone mad.

The other books were even more interesting. Advanced spell-books, the kind that perhaps we would have studied at third year or postgraduate level. Theories about the nature of the faerie world. Accounts of bargains with the fae, written up as dry and detailed as case studies in a medical journal. Linguistics specialists discussing possible tweaks and refinements to the binding runes (I really needed Hero for the intricacies of that one). A brief reference to an expedition into faerie country in the 1860s, which took my breath away (of course, the explorers never made it back).

And one book—small, shabby, barely holding together—that set my brain on fire.

That's what I really long to recapture, every time I set to work on something new.

That feeling, the one that makes all the hours of frustration worthwhile, of something clicking together. *This is it.*

It was past ten o'clock by the time I returned home, and I was expecting to find everyone in bed. Country hours were very different from Camford hours. I'd been adjusting to the early to bed, early to rise well enough so far. That night I couldn't have been less tired if I had tried. My mind was fizzing with the new ideas I had read, with the notes in my satchel, with, most importantly, the small tattered book that Lady Winter had kindly allowed me to make a doppelganger of by magic. It would last a few weeks, perhaps a month—enough time for me to take it back to Camford and share it with the other three. I wondered if it was worth writing to them tonight. If I could get it to the morning post, then they might have the news by the following day.

You'll never guess what I found, I imagined myself writing, only to mentally discard that page. It sounded too coy, too old-fashioned. *I have something exciting to tell you all*, I tried. No, too much for a mere theory. *Something interesting*, perhaps…

I didn't realise anyone else was in the living room until I had closed the door behind me.

"Back, are you?" My mother's voice came icy from beside the hearth. The fire had burned low, but she was still mending one of the little ones' shirts by the glow of the embers.

I blinked, unsure of her tone. "Yes."

She continued sewing, each jab of her needle like a death-thrust, and I knew I was missing something.

"I'm sorry I wasn't back for tea," I hazarded. I took off my hat and started unwinding my scarf. "I found something unexpected in the library—it might have been important for some research some friends and I are undertaking. I didn't think you'd—"

"We didn't expect you for tea," Mum said. She finally let the sewing drop, and her eyes rose to meet mine with a glare as hot as her voice was cold. "We expected you after, to take the little ones into town for the fair."

Oh. Oh no.

The plummet back to the real world was like stepping through ice.

The fair. The stupid winter fair.

"I'm so sorry." I cast about for the children, seeing only empty chairs. They were in bed by now, of course. I thought of

Iris's and John's worried faces at breakfast that morning when Matthew said he couldn't take them, their immediate confidence when I'd promised to be back in time. They'd believed me. Even Mum had believed me. "I'll do something special with them tomorrow, I promise."

"It's all right." Matthew spoke up from where he was leaning against the doorframe—he must have heard our voices from upstairs and, as always, come down to referee. "I took them. No harm done."

He said it sincerely enough, but there was a certain flatness that might have been disappointment or simple fatigue. Either possibility squeezed my heart in a guilty fist. I'd hoped he'd be better after the midnight had passed; instead, he seemed more exhausted than before.

"There *was* harm done," Mum corrected him. "You didn't have time to take them, that was why Clover was supposed to go. You had a fence to mend before the morning."

Matthew dismissed this. "I'll get up early and do it first thing."

"What do you call getting up early? If you get up much earlier, there's no point in you going to bed at all."

"Well, then I won't go to bed at all! Leave it, Mum."

"I'm sorry," I repeated miserably. "I'll help with the fence tomorrow, Matty, I promise. I just lost track of time. I forgot about the fair."

"You forgot about us." Mum's voice was crisp with anger. "Not for the first time."

Injustice shot through me, momentarily scalding my guilt. "I've never forgotten you!"

"No? You've been gone three months. How often did you write to us?"

"I told you in the letters! I wanted to write more, but it's a school of magic. The post doesn't exactly deliver to our doorstep. I have to get into town—"

"How often did you even think of it?"

"All the time!"

"Rubbish." She got to her feet in a single burst. This was what she had been waiting to say to me since I arrived home, what Matthew's warning glances and my good behaviour and her own forbearance had been holding at bay. "When you did write, we were barely worth a sentence. All your talk was about that place. And now you're back here, it's the same. You think we can't see you looking down on us? Do you think we can't see how much you want to get away?"

"That's not true!"

It wasn't, it really wasn't. I had missed them terribly. I had written when I could, or when I thought I could. I had counted the days before I came home for Christmas. All this was true. I didn't let myself dwell on what might also be true—that my letters had indeed barely asked after the farm, that I had filled them with my own doings out of a selfish and unconsidered thought that what I was doing was new and exciting while this old place was the same as ever, that while I had wanted to come home, I had also seen it as a favour to my family and was already counting down the days before I was to leave again.

"Dad wanted me to go away to study," I said. "He didn't want me to be stuck here forever."

It was a stupid, desperate shot, and it hurt far more than I had wanted. I saw Mum's eyes flash hard as shards of metal.

"Your dad wanted you to study to be a teacher," she said crisply. "Do you really think he would be happy if he knew what you were doing instead? All that schooling, all those books he bought you, and teaching in the village school wasn't good enough. You had to go and be a witch."

"I'm not a witch!" I snapped. "I'm a mage. I'm a *scholar*."

"Try telling that to the neighbours who wonder where you are. Do you think Peter Brooks would ever be allowed to walk out with Mary if they knew her sister was away learning the dark arts?"

I refused to rise to that characterisation, though it stung. "Have you ever thought that Mary might not *mind* that? That perhaps she could do better for herself than marry Peter Brooks to pay your debts?"

"Oh, and you're going to pay our debts for us by magic, are you?"

"I want to! Do you think Camford is just about me? I want to help all of you. I want to be a scholar and earn a living that could help support this farm. I want to have the little ones down to London when they get older so they can find better futures than being farmers and farmers' wives. I want to find new magic to break the curse so Matthew doesn't have to be in pain all the time."

"He wouldn't be in pain if you hadn't encouraged him to go to war."

"Mum, for God's sake!" That was Matthew, sharp with exasperation. I had frozen. I'd known Mum believed that Matthew going away had been my fault. I'd believed it myself. But I'd pretended, for a long time, that I'd been wrong. Now I knew I wasn't.

"Clover had nothing to do with my going away," Matthew was saying. "She might have helped me talk you into it, but I didn't need your permission or hers. I made the choice myself, and I'd make it again. There was a war on."

"Yes," Mum said. "Yes, there was a war on. Now it's over, and the country's in pieces, and the farm's in trouble. And your sister couldn't wait to run away from it all."

"Why shouldn't I run away?" I couldn't stop myself. I didn't even want to. I had just enough self-awareness left to know that I would wish I had stayed silent later, and not enough to care. "Do you think I want to be stuck in this dump? Do you think Matthew would if he had any other choice? Why do you think he went away to war in the first place?"

"Clover, stop it," Matthew said. It was the first time in my life I didn't listen to him.

"He wanted to get away from here so badly he nearly *died* for it! Only he didn't die, Dad did, and now he's stuck here killing himself to try to keep this cursed place alive."

"Oh, and you'd know all about curses, wouldn't you?" Mum retorted.

I started to respond. Matthew got there first. His anger shot out like a whip. "Would the pair of you just *shut up*?"

We stopped, stared, both of us shocked into silence. Mum and I fought often, even if it wasn't usually this vicious. Matthew never lost his temper. He was the peacemaker, the optimist, the one who had taught me that nothing couldn't be fixed. He would stand up for himself and others, but any anger he betrayed was always pointed, deliberate, a weapon ready to return to its place on command. Not this time.

"Rip each other to shreds if you want," he said into the silence. He had pushed himself away from the door, his stance taut and furious, his eyes harder than I'd ever seen them. "But don't you bloody dare pretend it has anything to do with me. Mum, do you think I don't wish every day that things were different? That there had never been a war, that I had never gone, that I had got some ordinary common wound and been sent home in the first few months, that I had never come back, *anything* other than this? Things are the way they are, and there's nothing to be done about it. And, Clover...I'm *happy* for you and your friends and your studies, but you're at Camford for *you*, not for me, all right? I never asked you to fix me. It's my life. And I am so bloody sick of reassuring you both that I'm all right with it all when of course I'm not."

He didn't wait for either of us to respond. He snatched up his jacket from the banister, grabbed his keys from the table, and headed for the door.

Mum found her voice then. "Where are you going?"

He laughed, hard and bitter. "Well, there's no point my going to bed at all these days, didn't you say? I'll be back to mend the fence in the morning."

The door shut behind him with a resounding slam. Moments later, the motorcycle engine coughed, revved, and roared with its usual sputtering hesitation off down the drive.

I didn't dare look at Mum. My insides were a confusion of shame and fury and fear; my eyes were hot with tears, and I knew if I looked in her direction, they would fall.

"I'm going to my room," I said instead, and I walked blindly toward the stairs. I wondered if she would call me back, but she never did.

One good thing about Holly and Mary being in town that night: Our room was empty. I shut the door, not hard enough to wake the little ones in the next room, and threw myself on my bed boots and all. I cried a little then, muffling my face in my pillow, bitterly aware that I was feeling sorry for myself and unable to stop. I had done a stupid, selfish thing, forgetting to come home, and I was furious with myself for it.

But I was furious with Mum too. I had made a mistake, it was true, but she had been waiting for me to make it all holiday, storing up her resentment until it was my fault, and she had loved the chance to release it. She had no right to accuse me of forgetting them when it was for Matthew that I had been researching spells in the first place. She had no right to accuse me of running away when being at home was unbearable.

And I was furious with Matthew, helplessly and unfairly. I understood now how hard he'd been struggling since the end of the war, how much worse everything had been since I had left, how much it had cost him to let me go. But how dare he hide it all from me and then unload it on my shoulders in one terrible crushing landslide? It wasn't fair. He should have told me before I left, and I wouldn't have gone, or he should have never breathed a word of it.

My furious tears must have given way to sleep at some point. All I know is that sometime later I opened my eyes to quiet darkness, and when I tilted the alarm clock by the bed into the moonlight it was sometime after three in the morning. My anger and shame had been extinguished, as was usually the case upon waking after a fight with Mum. Usually the heat of anger was replaced by the soggy ashes of guilt and self-recrimination. This time, though, I felt only cool and calm and hard with purpose.

I couldn't stay there. That didn't feel like a decision so much as fact. I had been fighting the feeling since I had stepped off the train into the snow, and in one blow, my defences had been swept away. I didn't belong. Magic was sparking in my blood now, perhaps not as literally as it would be in the blood of one of the Families, but just as truly, and I couldn't hide it anymore. It was like trying to force myself into ill-fitting clothes, all the while twisting with guilt at not fitting them better. Besides, the thought of facing Mum and Matthew in the morning made me feel sick.

My trunk was easy to pack—most of my things were still inside it. I had only to dump in the last of my clothes and more carefully pack my Christmas presents from my family. The hardest part was wrestling the thing downstairs, thumping it past the bedroom doors and down the creaky steps. It was pitch-black there, and once or twice I nearly fell to my death. But no door opened. The little ones were sleeping, presumably, and if Mum was lying awake, she ignored me.

It was safer to light a candle in the kitchen. I wrote a letter telling my family that I was fine, I was on the early train to Oxford, I was sorry to miss New Year, but I thought it was for the best. I told them I was sorry about the fair, and the argument, and I hoped they would forgive me. I wasn't sorry about Camford, and never would be. It was a child's letter, filled with mixed pride and contrition and sulkiness, and it frustrated me reading it back how contradictory and confused and feeble it sounded when it had felt so clear and reasonable in my head. I had no time to rewrite it. The early train left in two hours, and I needed to be gone by the time the household rose. Matthew still hadn't returned when I closed the door behind me and set off in the dark and the cold.

10

Camford was quiet in the winter break. It was a fair cold day in Oxford, the skies almost the pearl grey of my old sketch, but when I stepped through the door in the Bodleian, I was instantly engulfed in a shimmering mist of rain. It was light enough for the wind to swirl about the courtyard, twisting through the air like a murmuration of starlings. I hurried as quickly as I could through the crooked paths to Chancery Hall, careful not to trip on the roots poking through the cobbles. As far as I could tell, there wasn't a soul in the place.

The lecturers had warned us that the university would be all but abandoned over the winter break. Students were supposed to stay away from Camford during the holidays unless they sought special permission to stay, and that was often denied. I certainly wasn't supposed to return to my rooms without informing anybody. The doors opened readily enough at the touch of my silver ring, but the building was deserted, my room dark and cold.

It didn't trouble me: Camford, overgrown as it was, never wanted for firewood. I went to the wooded copse behind the building, shivering in the icy drizzle, and collected up as many loose branches as I could. I dried them with a charm, imbued them with a spell to help them burn longer, and lit them in my fireplace. It was simple, then, to take off my wet clothes and spread them to dry on the hearth, to wrap myself in the dressing gown I'd left hanging on the door, to unpack my trunk and put my books back on the desk where they belonged. The kettle boiled quickly, and I had a pasty from the Oxford station in my bag. I curled up in front of the fire as the deepening rain spattered the window and, for the first time in weeks, felt absolutely at home.

It didn't last. I spun out the rest of the evening working on my history essay and by nine or so had a passable first draft. Once that was done, the fire was dying even with all the magic I could throw at it, and I decided to go to bed.

It should have been easy to sleep. I'd had a very early start after a disturbed night, and a long, frustrating journey in the cold and wet. The trouble was, I was beginning to realise that my calm, cool state of the night before hadn't been calm or cool at all, but rather a furious sulk. That sulk had carried me all the way across the country; now, job done, it had set me down and forced me to think about what I'd done.

I lay there, insides twisting with guilt, and the darkness helpfully played every scenario of the past day across the low ceiling. I pictured Mum coming downstairs this morning and reading the note, her face like stone; I pictured Holly and Mary coming back from town after breakfast, flushed and alive with last night's dancing, asking where I was; I pictured the little ones confused and upset. Matthew's reaction I couldn't picture at all. I didn't even know if he had made it back safely. He had been so bitterly angry, so unlike himself, that I couldn't help being frightened.

I'd felt like an independent adult extricating herself from an unbearable situation. Now I felt like a child who had run away from home.

I couldn't lie still. I sat up and lit the candle by my bed. I went

to my desk, looking for the train timetable to see how easily, the-
oretically, I could go back to Pendle Hill tomorrow, and found
I'd thrown it in the struggling fire. I got out a sheet of paper to
write a letter home, just to make sure everything was all right.
The trouble was, I'd written my letter already. I could think of
nothing new to say.

I had just climbed under the covers for the second time when
there was a light rap at the window.

At first, I mistook it for the rain and barely glanced up. When
it came again, more insistently, I was startled to see a familiar
face behind the rain-speckled glass.

"Alden!" I struggled out of bed yet again, nearly tripping over
the quilt, and fumbled to unlock the window. He stepped in so
easily he might have done it a hundred times.

"Oh, you *were* in bed," he said, with a glance at the rumpled
sheets. "Drat. I saw your light."

"Only just." I remembered, belatedly, that I was in my pyjamas with my dressing gown out of reach across the room; that
it was after ten o'clock with nobody else around; that as comfortable as I'd become with Alden, we had never been alone
together any place that wasn't a library, and he was emphatically
not allowed in my bedroom after dark or unsupervised. "When
did you get back?"

"I might ask the same of you, and probably will. I came back
three days ago. There's only so much home I can stand. You?"

"Apparently there's only so much home can stand of me."
It came to my lips on reflex, bitter with self-pity, and I regretted it as soon as I saw Alden's eyes narrow. "I didn't mean that.
They're just busy on the farm, and I was in the way, so I came
back this morning. Did you want something?"

I wondered if that sounded suggestive, but Alden didn't seem
to notice. Possibly it was difficult to be suggestive in blue flannel
pyjamas.

"Clover," he said seriously. His curls were dark with rainwater, as were the shoulders of his jacket. "How sleepy are you right now? I mean, are you desperately, irrevocably unable to keep your eyes open, or do you think you could bear to stay up and read a few books with me?"

"Are you asking me to come study with you?"

He winced apologetically. "I can't sleep. The storm's keeping me awake. I'm curled up in my room with a pile of old books and liberal amounts of hot chocolate, working on our project, and frankly I'd love some company."

I wasn't allowed in a man's room after lights-out, of course. If I were found, Alden would be punished in an indulgent sort of manner, and I would be expelled. Suddenly I didn't care. Those rules belonged to an old, safe world—the world that had brought us to war and blown everything to bits. I was so bloody sick of them, and sick, too, of being told what to do.

"I can't sleep either," I said. "I'd love to come study with you. I have something to show you, as a matter of fact." So much for all that agonising about how to write it in a letter. "Though I never took you for a hot chocolate sort."

"There might also be liberal bottles of Madeira in my room. But I feel like hot chocolate. It's a little past ten, it's raining outside, a fire's going, and I'm getting over a cold."

"It probably wasn't a good idea to cross the courtyard in the rain, then, was it?"

"God, you make so much sense." He sneezed. "Excuse me. But I saw your light, so I had to cross if I wanted to add your company to my store of riches, and now I have, and there you go, I've just run rings around your logic. Do you have a coat, or do you want to borrow mine?"

And so, at a little past ten, I found myself sitting cross-legged at the foot of Alden's bed, a mug of hot chocolate balanced precariously on a wobbly stack of books. Alden stretched out reading the book I had brought from Lady Winter's library, his own hot chocolate forgotten as he turned the pages. His room was neater than I had expected, and emptier—aside from the extremely old books that packed every corner, there were few personal possessions at all. It was so much more like being in a library than a bedroom that my thrill of nerves soon settled. Outside, the wind howled around the old stone buildings, and the windows were lashed with rain.

"It's been like this since I got back," Alden said, following my glance outside. "I've scarcely seen a soul about the place—a few teachers, and a postgrad or two in the library. I think this building's deserted. They're not even serving food in the dining hall. I lived on Christmas cake and mince pies in my room for two days before I worked out that we were supposed to go over to Darwin Hall."

"Did you get into trouble about coming back?"

"None at all—so you needn't worry. As long as we don't make any work for the poor staff still working through Christmas, they don't care about a student or two extra. I've just been drifting around the library all day. I found the lost volume of Agrippa this morning, by the way. Apparently someone had it out for their MA. Nothing of interest to us."

"Are you still on Agrippa? He was wrong, you know."

"Wrong," Alden agreed. "By my understanding, his methods would only work in faerie country, which would rather defeat the purpose. But he was looking in the right direction. Why were you looking at him that day we met, if I may ask? If you'd wanted faerie curses, there were more obvious leads even with all the restrictions."

I shrugged. "Honestly, not for any special reason." He raised an eyebrow, and I smiled reluctantly. "If you want to know the truth, I was homesick. I told you, I grew up on Agrippa. When I saw him in the library, he reminded me of home."

"Home," he repeated. "I envy you that."

I tried not to think about the last words that had passed between my mother and me, the finality of that not-quite-slammed door. We had fought often enough, after all. It had never meant anything, not for long.

"You have a home," I said instead. "Ashfield. Hero told me about how you all spent summers there."

"Did she? Well. I do indeed have Ashfield—or will, once my father dies. I assume he hasn't died already. They would have mentioned it, surely, when I was there."

I was used to the kinds of things rich students said by now. "What's it like? Ashfield?"

"Cursed." Apparently I looked sceptical, or just expectant, because he laughed. "Ashfield Manor is a Victorian Gothic property in West Yorkshire," he said, in the dry, overly formal tone of an architect or a real estate agent. "The estate comprises two hundred acres, encompassing a lake and the remains of an historically significant twelfth-century monastery. The land has been in the Lennox family since the seventeenth century. The current house was built on the site of an older Tudor manor that burned down in the late eighteenth century and was reconstructed in 1858 by the grandfather of the present owner; it has upwards of one hundred and fifty rooms and I forget how many windows. Does that satisfy your curiosity?"

I shoved him lightly. What it did, of course, was intimidate. I knew better than to show it. "It must be lovely in winter."

"Let me know, if you're ever there. I try not to be. Certainly I won't be next year while I have a perfectly good room here. I don't know what I was thinking."

Belatedly, I remembered his odd mood in the weeks leading up to the end of term, the prickles and sharp edges Hero had called him on. "You didn't want to go home for Christmas?"

"I told you," he said absently. He was turning the pages more slowly now—I peeked and found he was reaching the part I had underlined. "Ashfield is cursed. Christmas is a dreadful time for ghosts in a cursed house. Never mind, though. I survived, with naught but a lingering bout of insomnia and a mild head cold, and both will melt away with term time like frost on the lawn. Or something. I missed you, Clover Hill."

I felt my cheeks burn, and tried to laugh it away. I never minded when Alden and Hero used my full name, as they often did. I knew they thought it was funny, but I also knew they liked it. "You missed my help with your project."

"I missed that too. The two things are separate, neither mutually exclusive nor dependent upon each other. This book is fascinating."

"Isn't it?" I craned my neck to look over his shoulder, brief self-consciousness forgotten. "Have you got to the part about the faerie doors?"

"I'm just there now. Not a single door at all. Two doors, inner and outer, one in faerie country and one here. When we open a door, we punch two holes in two worlds."

"You know what that could mean for us, don't you?" I rushed on without giving him a chance to answer. "There's a space in between the doors—barely, perhaps a million times smaller than the width of a human hair, but it still exists. If we could trap a faerie *there*, before it reached our world—"

"We could still deal with it," Alden finished, "but it couldn't cross over. It could be exactly what we were looking for. Not a new binding spell—an entirely new approach to faerie binding."

The magnitude of the idea hung between us, luminous and awe-inspiring. In that moment, I forgot my family and Alden's; I forgot who and what we both were. All that existed was magic and possibility.

"It might not be true about the doors," I forced myself to point out. "This is an old book, and the theory wasn't mentioned in any of the later ones. It might have been disproved. We'd never know."

Alden nodded slowly. "Let's test it."

I blinked. "Here? Now?"

"No, of course not. We couldn't do that sort of magic in Camford. We'd be caught at once. We'll have to go out to Oxford—or Cambridge, I suppose, but the Bodleian would be more convenient. Now, though, yes."

"Even out there, we couldn't open a faerie door! The faerie world is sealed, remember?"

"We could open an imp window. Those go to the other world too—the principle should apply. And they're too small to be affected by the seals locking off the faerie world."

An imp window was what had been used to teach students to breach the boundaries between worlds, back when such things were taught. It was a much smaller version of a door, about the size of a saucer; the only thing that could make it through were the tiny imps that ran wild on the borders of faerie country, and they could do no real harm.

"That's still illegal," I said, more doubtfully.

"But not dangerous. We only need to hold the window open long enough to have a good look at it—to test if there really is a gap as the book suggests."

"Hero was very clear that we weren't going to do anything that might risk us being expelled—and definitely not arrested."

He shrugged. "That's her decision, and I respect it. She isn't here. I understand if you don't want to risk it either, of course. But I was going to try it sometime this break anyway. It's difficult to study faerie magic without ever having performed the rituals."

"We study all kinds of spells without performing them, Alden! I've just finished an essay on the death curses of the Civil War, and I've yet to work one of those!" It wasn't the point, and we both knew it. We also knew that if I was resorting to that kind of protest, it was too late. I was already in.

Honestly, I'm not certain I can explain why. Part of it was

the same rush of rebellious contempt for old-world authority that had brought me to Alden's room. Part of it was a desire to prove to my mother and to Matthew that I truly wasn't here for my own advancement, that I was willing to risk losing Camford entirely if need be. Part of it, I'm ashamed to admit, was how much I was enjoying the glow of Alden's company. Truly, though, more than anything, I longed to know if it would work. We had a new idea, glittering and splendid, and everything we needed to test it. The thought of sensibly going back to bed with a few notes to follow up on was unbearable.

"It's raining," I said, very weakly.

Alden got to his feet in a single bounce, sending books tumbling and paper scattering. "We will take," he said, "an umbrella."

It wasn't raining in Oxford, anyway. The long, narrow alley of the Bodleian where the door opened was almost warm after the brisk chill of Camford. It was pure excitement that made me shiver as we closed the door behind us and crept deeper into the library, spellbooks tucked under one arm and my breath misting in front of my face.

I had never spent any time in the Bodleian, only passed through the same corridors to and from the Oxbridge. My impression had always been a dark, formidable space teeming with old books, as straight-lined and secretive as the rest of Oxford. I knew it was really several libraries, and I assumed they were all very different, but I'd been too nervous to explore further. They weren't meant for me. My library was the Camford one: rambling, circular, ever-shifting, with its great oak at the domed centre and its roof to lift us up above the world.

Alden had no such qualms—I doubt he'd ever been told a place wasn't meant for him in his life. He pushed through the long corridor, opened a door, and nodded in satisfaction. "This will do, do you think? Which would you prefer to draw—the window or the circles?"

I had a brief flare of panic—*we'd be caught, this was ridiculous, could we really scribble all over the wall of a library?* I quashed it firmly. For this one night, I was going to break rules. I may as well break good ones. "I'll take the circles."

"Probably for the best," he conceded. "You're the artist. I can barely manage stick figures."

A faerie door needed two chalk circles on the ground before it, connected by a single line. The first was to bind any faerie that stepped through, a complicated ring of spells and runes. The second was far simpler: a plain circle where the summoner stood, which would connect them to the faerie standing in the other circle. It was what enabled the faerie to work its magic on them for the purpose of the deal, when it couldn't touch the rest of the world, but it also made them vulnerable. If the faerie was to slip its bonds, the person standing in the circle would be the first to be taken. That was when, if things went very wrong indeed, the faerie would slip into their body. That was what had happened to Private Koenig at Amiens.

A tiny window like the one Alden was drawing on the wall posed no such threat, but I tried to draw each rune carefully, checking the book frequently. The surroundings were distracting. Apart from the scratch of chalk on wood, the room was utterly still. It seemed to stretch for miles about me, all history and tradition and dust.

"This building's nowhere near as old as Camford, is it?" I asked into the quiet. It was something I had wondered before. "So how can the Oxbridge be here?"

"They've shifted it around over the centuries," Alden explained absently. "For that matter, there was only one door to begin with—this one, at Oxford. The one at Cambridge is a copy. We don't know how to make either now, of course."

"Doesn't that bother you?" Despite my resolution, I couldn't resist asking, just once more. It was that sort of a night. "We step through the Oxbridge all the time, and we don't know how the magic works. We don't even really know where the door opens."

"I'm sure the Faculty and the Board know that, at least. All I need to know is the doors open to Camford." He stepped back from the wall. "And *this* will open to faerie country."

All thoughts of the Oxbridge were pushed to one side. To my unpracticed eye, what he had drawn was perfect. All the runes in place, the circular window right at eye level. It was only a chalk outline yet, but my limbs thrilled.

He was examining the circles I had drawn with the same attention. "Beautiful," he declared. "Shall we try to open it together?"

There was only one answer to that. I nodded.

What does it feel like, the first time you open a window into faerie country? The nearest I can compare it to is like drawing a deep breath and opening your eyes, when your eyes are already open and your lungs are already full. I stood in the circle with Alden, the library silent and cavernous around us, very aware of the heat of him beside me and the quiver of anticipation between us. We spoke the words together, as we had learned during group work in class: The closer you can mirror the tone and stance of a partner, the stronger the magic will be. We had always partnered well together, and we did here. The first few tries yielded nothing, as expected—it always takes at least a couple of attempts to find the feel of a spell. And then, there was a rush of air, rustling the pages of the books of the shelves and stirring my hair; on the wall, the circle glowed with the faint silver of the moon.

There it was. Faerie country. I could see very little of it, just a glaze of light and faint shadows beyond, but I could feel it. Deep in my chest, with an ache like nostalgia or yearning, I knew there was suddenly one less veil between me and the fae.

Alden felt it too—his body tensed beside me, and I heard his sharp intake of breath.

"It works," I said quietly.

He blinked and shook his head, as though awakening from a reverie or a dream. "That's no surprise," he said. "It isn't difficult to open a window or a door to faerie country, after all. We need to see if we can trap a faerie between its layers."

"If there *are* layers," I pointed out, on reflex. Staring at that window, knowing we had punched a tiny hole in the world, I couldn't believe any of our theories might be wrong.

Something flew at the window then, a small winged shape, the size of a bat. We both jumped; Alden snapped the closing spell, and the window vanished as quickly as it arrived. The room already seemed dark without it, even with the glow from our lanterns.

"I think that was an imp," Alden said into the startled silence, and I laughed before I could stop myself.

"It's a shame you closed it so quickly. If it had come through, we could have tested if the binding circle worked."

"Some things I'd rather not test, thank you." He sighed, somewhere between relief and disappointment. "Well. I suppose that's it for tonight. Now that thing's found the window, it'll be waiting to get back through every time we open it again. And... What is it?"

A thought had come to me.

"Did you see?" I asked slowly. "As it approached the door, the window flared a little? The lines began to change from pure silver to a bluish colour."

"Yes," he said. "Now that you mention it, I did. What are you thinking?"

"What if we closed the window as soon as we saw that change?" Excitement and trepidation was creeping into my voice, despite myself. "Just a fraction of a second before it made it through? If there really *is* an inner door and an outer door, that might be the exact moment it's passing through the gap between."

He caught the idea at once. "We'd have to be incredibly precise. There's nothing to measure it by except instinct. But God, if it could work..."

There was no stopping either of us then. I knew I should advocate a retreat for the night—we'd both done a good deal of new magic already, we were getting tired, there was more research to be done. I didn't care. I could do nothing else until I knew if it could work. Neither of us could.

"We can try as often as the imp keeps coming back, after all," Alden pointed out. "If it gets through, it'll only find itself in the binding circle."

Privately, I thought I'd rather not trust my very first set of binding runes, and until a few minutes ago Alden had thought the same, but I agreed that this was nothing to worry about.

We were too quick to close the first time, and again the second. Each time, the imp hurled itself at the window; each time I flinched at the first sign and slammed the window shut as if at the approach of a wasp. By now, we had been opening and closing imp windows for a good half hour. My fingers were sore, my back ached, and my hair was damp with perspiration. Alden looked much the same. He didn't seem to notice.

"I wonder," he said thoughtfully. "Stay in the circle, will you? I want to know if I can feel a difference when I keep my hand on the door. There might be something more tangible than the light."

I frowned. "Is that safe?"

"Is any of this?" he said cheerfully. "Come on. We were close that last time, I know it."

This time, though, when the window opened, the imp was nowhere to be seen. I peered at the window, puzzled, my glasses slightly fogged. I wondered if we'd pushed too far. Perhaps the imp, like my fingers, was starting to get a little bit fed up.

I had underestimated it. Out of nowhere, with the speed of a crow at full flight, the imp barrelled through the window. The door flared; I gave an undignified yelp of surprise; the closing spell burst from my fingertips.

An instant too slow. The imp sprang into the room, a scrabble of limbs and claws, and bounded straight into the binding circle. For the first time, in the mingling glow of the window and our lanterns, I saw it: the size of a large rat, with tiny leathery wings, claws like curved daggers, a jutting overdeveloped jaw, and round yellow eyes. I held my breath, certain that the runes would hold, worried that they wouldn't.

It bounded straight out again. The barest hesitation, and it was through to the library, claws scratching the hardwood floor, teeth chattering angrily. I stared in silent horror. Beside me, Alden swore under his breath.

"No!" Alden stopped me as I started out of the circle. "Stay there, I'll chase it through the window. You be ready to close the window the moment I get it back through."

I nodded, and he circled the imp gingerly, stripping off his jacket to use as one might try to wrangle an angry bird that had flown into a classroom. God, how could this have happened? I had drawn the right runes, I was sure of it. Alden had checked them. Was it the book? Was it too old, out-of-date, had the copying not worked...?

Thank God we had closed the door to the rest of the library, at least. The imp tore about the room, rebounding from walls, floor, ceiling. One minute it was clinging to the beams overhead, the next it had glanced off the bookshelves, its claws sending books flying through the air and landing with a thud that made me wince. I had a horrible image of the librarians coming in the following morning and seeing books scattered on the floor, spines scored by claws, chalk dust smeared on the covers.

Our bodies on the floor with them. I'd always heard imps were harmless, but I had seen those claws. I had seen claws like that before, on a badger defending its home, on a cornered fox breaking into our barn. They were not harmless.

I held my ground. If I stepped out now, there would be nobody to close the window. Just a moment longer.

The imp paused, perched on the back of a chair, sniffing the air with flared nostrils. Alden, hovering with his jacket draped over his hands, seized his chance. He lunged forward. My heart leapt—for an instant, I would have sworn he had it. Then the imp wheeled and launched itself off the chair and into the air toward Alden, with a screeching hiss like an angry cat. Alden took a hasty step backwards, shielding his face with his jacket, and the thing glanced off his hands and knocked him to the ground. Then it turned, ears back, and its yellow eyes lit on me.

It sprang, half flying, half propelled by its long back legs. I held my ground, muscles screaming to run, racking my brains for a spell. There had to be one, surely, to stop it in its tracks. I didn't know it. I had only been studying a few months, my mind was frozen, nothing came to my fingers when I raised them.

I looked about, trying to find some weapon, anything. Then I saw it.

The umbrella. The umbrella we had brought with us across Camford, still slick with rain from the other side of the Oxbridge door, was leaning against the wall, pooling water. I snatched it up, and before I had a chance to think, I swung wildly at the imp.

It dropped to the ground. It was so unexpected it was alarming, like one of those moments when you swipe at a fly and hit it by pure chance. It lay sprawled on the wooden floorboards, limbs splayed, wings crooked. While I was still gaping, Alden swept it up from the ground in his jacket and hurled it back through the window. I had just enough presence of mind to shout the spell, and the window shrank to nothing.

"There," Alden said into the breathless silence that followed. "I *knew* it was a good idea to go out in the rain."

We examined the rune circle carefully, and we couldn't see anything that might have gone wrong. The circle seemed unbroken, the runes correct. At last, Alden stood with a shrug.

"Perhaps it was the grain of the wood, or something too small for our eyes to see. We'll wash it off for now and do better next time."

"I'm so sorry." I ran my eyes over the circle one more time, mortified. "So much for my skill at drawing."

Alden gave me a playful nudge with his foot. "Don't be ridiculous. I'm sure even Agrippa made a mistake the first time. Anyway, there's no harm done." He was still breathless, his shirt torn and his forearm bleeding from a long scratch, but his face was alight. My embarrassment faded. "And I was right. I did feel something. Right as it came through, the lines cooled to the touch, like a shadow passing. That's what we need to wait for. Come on. One more try."

"I thought you wanted to wash the runes away?"

"Yes, and then draw them better next time. Next time being now, I meant. Well?"

"No!" It was a laughing no, though, despite myself. I sounded like a girl at a party who wanted to be persuaded into a kiss. "I think we've done enough, don't you?"

"We were onto something. You felt it too. We were only missing the timing."

"We just unleashed an imp in the Bodleian."

"So we know how *not* to do that the second time." He gave me a winning look, and I rolled my eyes even as I couldn't hold back a grin. "Besides, it was only a small one."

"That's true," I conceded. I stood, brushing the dust from my skirt. "Let's see if we can get a bigger one this time."

This time, it worked.

Alden stood to the side of the window with his fingers pressed to the edge. When his signal came, I knew it was right, because I barely needed it. I could feel when the window was ready, the exact pitch that meant the imp was through one door and not yet the other. It thrummed through me like the chime of a crystal glass flicked with a finger, and I slammed the window shut.

There was a flash of light, and this time the opening in the wall went opaque—as if it truly was a window and the glass was flawed or dusty. On the other side of the sheen, the imp raged. It hurled itself against the window, its shrieks muffled, claws scratching furiously at nothing at all. Alden and I stared at each other, wonder brimming between us.

We had done it. It was shaky and patched together and wouldn't stand a chance against a faerie, but we had the beginnings of a spell that could revolutionise faerie magic. That could make faerie magic safe again. That could fix everything. All it needed was more work, and we had all the energy in the world.

"When we present the paper," I said, "let's not tell the Faculty we did this."

Alden looked at me, then exploded into a fit of helpless laughter. I lasted a few seconds before I joined him.

———— ⋙ ————

It was midnight by the time we slipped back across the Oxbridge, cold and dishevelled, straight into a volley of glittering rain. It drenched us through before I could even think of getting the umbrella up, and in that mad, exhilarated state I didn't want to. I caught my breath at the shock and then laughed aloud, spinning in a dizzy circle as the rain swirled. Alden sneezed violently and laughed too.

"I love Camford," he said. "Always so eager to welcome you back."

"Hero's going to think we're both mad when she hears about this."

"Hero isn't going to hear about this," Alden said, as if it was obvious.

"You don't mean that, do you?" It was difficult to tell with Alden at times. Nonetheless, unease twinged my stomach. "Why wouldn't we tell her?"

"Because you said yourself—she'd think we were mad." He was definitely serious now. "Hero doesn't want to break any rules that would jeopardise her place here—she's said so many times. She wouldn't approve of what we've just done, and she certainly wouldn't want to try again."

"You think we should try this again?"

"Of course. Until we get it perfect. Don't you?"

The prospect was irresistible. We *could* get it perfect, I was certain of it. All we needed was a few more nights over the next term or so, slipping out when nobody was looking and opening up the world. It had *worked*. It could be made to work again, every time.

"Still." I caught myself before my imagination could fly too far. "Even if Hero doesn't want to come with us, that's no reason she shouldn't know. Eddie too."

He smiled briefly. "Believe me, I've known them both my entire life. Hero won't be quiet about something she doesn't agree with, and Eddie won't be able to keep it a secret from Hero if we asked him."

I couldn't imagine keeping a secret from Hero either, nor from Eddie. But it *was* true that Hero wouldn't agree with our rule-breaking on such a scale. Faerie magic was important to her as a way to achieve her dreams and ambitions—she quite rightly wouldn't want those dreams threatened. Eddie, too, was in this only because we had asked him—because he wanted to help us and, if I was honest, to be one of us. The risk wasn't worth it for either of them. It was different for me. I was now all too aware, after my visit home, of how desperately Matthew needed this. The curse was eating him alive. He couldn't withstand it forever. I imagined being able to present this research to Camford, the Accord being lifted. I imagined coming home with a cure blazing in my veins. A furtive, petty thought: Mum wouldn't be able to say I didn't care then.

"Why do *you* want this so much?" I asked Alden, in a flash of suspicion. "You're right—Hero only has her academic future riding on this, not her brother's life. But you have even less, as far as I can tell. Why are you willing to risk being expelled from Camford?"

Alden shrugged, and his eyes glanced off mine. "Perhaps I just don't care about Camford."

I knew there was more to it than that, of course. It was probably true that Alden didn't care about Camford; it didn't explain what he cared about instead. Yet it was all I would get for now. I had to trust his reasons for not telling me, or walk away altogether.

"I'm not saying we don't ever tell them," he said into the silence. "I'm only suggesting we keep it between us until we're a little further along."

In the end, I'm ashamed to say, it was the *between us* that convinced me. I'd felt close to Eddie almost at once; Hero and I had drawn together a long time ago, united by books and struggles and shared laughter. Alden was still on a pedestal, tantalisingly out of reach. Tonight, the distance between us had closed, who we were ceased to matter, and our minds leapt together along new and surprising paths. I wanted it to continue.

After all, Hero and Alden had kept things from me, hadn't they? Even now, there were still things that passed between them over my head, glances that went unspoken. I didn't grudge them it—their friendship had existed long before I was there, and things had grown that I'd had no part of. Surely it wasn't so terrible to keep this one thing from the others, that had its roots in the time *they'd* missed?

"All right," I said, and felt once again the glorious shiver of rebellion. It was like stepping through yet another door, further and deeper, and being hit with the exhilarating sting of rain-specked wind. "Let's keep it to ourselves. For now. But we'll tell them both when we've had a bit more practice?"

"Oh yes." This time I knew he meant it. "We'll tell them then. I promise."

Somewhere in the main quadrangle, the clock chimed. Alden looked at me, his eyes still sparkling with leftover laughter.

"Happy New Year, Clover Hill," he said.

I'd forgotten entirely. The days between Christmas and New Year were always a blur to me, apart from the winter festival, and this year I'd lost track of even that. I'd spent the last day of 1920 travelling across the country—the last hour breaking a hole in the world—and I'd never even known.

"Happy New Year," I said, and saw the new year in a flash, shining and wondrous, glittering with possibilities as the imp window had glittered in the darkness of the Bodleian.

Part Two

Ashfield, 1921

II

We left Oxford early for the drive up to Yorkshire, or at least what Alden and Hero called early. It was almost the same route up through the middle of the country as I had taken when I had gone home for Christmas—once or twice I even saw one of the trains I might have been on pass on the horizon. In every way that mattered, though, the journey couldn't have been more different. Eddie and I sat in the back seat of Hero's motorcar, Hero at the wheel with her long hair caught up under a wide-brimmed hat. I wasn't tied to a train, I wasn't tied to anyone except my friends, and the summer holidays stretched before us like a promise. Summer had always meant long, back-breaking days in the hayfield with sweat sticking dust to my skin; it meant setting the rams amidst the ewes, taking advantage of the good weather to mend the barn roof. I'd never been so free before. The sky seemed much higher overhead than usual, as though someone had thrown the roof off the world and at any moment we all might just spin away.

The others had never worked in the hot June sun, but the last few months of study and exams and last-day essays had been gruelling in their own way, and they had caught the mood of freedom and release too. Our conversation became sillier and sillier as we rattled along the road, until we were breathless with laughter without knowing or caring why. At midday we stopped and ate bread and cheese and cold sausages at a roadside inn, served with lemonade and dark ale, and tried to name the bird-song around us. Unsurprisingly, Eddie was better at it than all of us, even though I had grown up on a farm.

"I spent a lot of time outdoors when I was taken out of school," he explained, as if apologising. "And I had a lot of time to sit and listen. I wasn't working like Clover was."

"You didn't have your nose buried in books like Clover, you mean," Hero said, with a quirk of a smile at me. I wrinkled my nose back, grinning.

"Your family won't mind your not being there for the whole summer?" Eddie asked me, as though he'd only just thought of it.

"No, of course not," I said, as airily as I could. I refused to see Alden and Hero exchange glances. "They'll see me for Christmas."

Eddie nodded and gave me a smile. From what he'd let slip, he hadn't heard much from his own family all year. "Well," he said. "We're lucky to have you."

"For your company," Hero added, "if not for your skill at ornithology."

In truth, I didn't know what my family felt about my absence. I hadn't seen them since that horrible December night, nearly six months ago. I had written to them the day after the imp fiasco, not quite apologising, and Matthew had written back reassuring me that everything was fine. But it was the kind of letter we'd had from him in the war—brief, breezy, uninformative—and I'd heard nothing from Mum at all. When the next term holidays had rolled around, I had written and said that I was staying at Camford with my friends to study, and they had voiced no objection; when I had asked after Matthew in the days following each new midnight, he had told me not to worry and nothing more. We were at a fragile truce. I couldn't break it without returning home, and yet I was afraid that if I did, everything would shatter.

Instead, I'd thrown myself into Camford life, and it was more than happy to swallow me whole. Spring term came fresh and bright, with new papers and new lectures and new magic. The trees turned vibrant green, the undergrowth burst into life so thick that finding a way to class was like fighting through a forest, and the roof of Hew Draper Tower finally crumbled under centuries of determined ivy and needed to be closed for repairs. I had exams to study for at the end of term, I had research to do and assignments to write, I had Hero and Alden and Eddie. And, every now and again, Alden and I had our experiments with the imp windows.

Those night-time expeditions were unpredictable—sometimes we would make plans the day before, in hurried whispers before the others caught us up, sometimes I would simply hear a tap at my window while I sat up late at my desk. My chest would always thrill at that tap, in equal parts excitement and guilt. I knew we shouldn't be sneaking off at night to break the law, certainly not without telling Hero and Eddie, and yet I couldn't wait to find out how much further we could refine our law-breaking this time. Alden was at his very best in those stolen hours: brilliant, perceptive, aglow with energy and purpose that spilled over and mingled with my own so that I lost sight of where my ideas ended and his began. Soon we had the timing of the window perfect. When it was my turn to press my fingers to the edges, I could feel the imp's passing even before I registered the silvery lines cooling and glowing.

Last month we'd hit upon a breakthrough. The imp we'd trapped was alarmingly close to pushing through, the opaque sheen of the window bowing and buckling like a plate of glass about to shatter. In blind panic, I'd cast a locking spell; it had settled over the window like oil on water, and the buckling had calmed instantly. The imp still raged, but the surface of the window was still, quiet, frosted as though by thick ice. We had stared at each other, elated. If he hadn't been standing in a faerie circle and I hadn't been holding a faerie door, I think we would have flung our arms around each other. As it was, our smiles met in perfect harmony.

"Oh," he said quietly. "*Yes.*"

It had been our biggest worry—that only one door might be too fragile, and without the inner faerie door, a trapped faerie could break through. Now we had a solution, and we spent the entire night practicing it until the skies had paled, we were both dizzy and exhausted, and we narrowly missed being caught inside the Bodleian in the morning.

"What are you doing this summer?" Alden had asked that afternoon, out of the blue. We had stepped through the window at the library to sprawl out on the roof, taking advantage of the unusually gentle breeze and the clear, silvery sky. My thoughts, still drowsy from the night before, had wandered from my essay, and I was idly sketching the view of the wall instead.

"Going to visit my family, I suppose." I said it as carelessly as possible, keeping my eyes on the page. "The only summer classes are for third-years and older. Professor Summerdale said I should try to apply next year, though."

"Back to Pendle Hill?" Eddie asked.

I shrugged. "Well, that's where my family are."

They must have noticed I was less than thrilled at the prospect. None of them commented. "Would they object terribly if you came and spent at least part of the summer at my home?" Alden asked.

I was almost as startled as when he'd first proposed opening an imp window in the Bodleian. "At Ashfield?"

"Well, that's where my home is," Alden said, in a credible imitation of my accent. I threw my spare pencil at him, which he ducked easily.

The truth was, Ashfield had become a mythical place to me. I'd heard too many stories of their shared childhoods there, of sealed-off wings and visits to the kitchen and long rambles across the grounds. The thought of seeing it for myself—of being invited to share in it—was both thrilling and unlikely, as though Alden had offered to send me to Neverland.

"Please do come." Hero looked up from her book quickly. "Eddie and I will both be there all summer too. I can't tell you what a relief it would be to have sane company."

"Will your parents mind?" I asked Alden doubtfully.

"Mind? They'd be thrilled. You'd be by far the most civilised guest I've ever brought home. Besides, they'll barely be around. We'll be more or less left to our own devices. Plenty of space for the four of us to try out some of our theories, if we wanted to."

"Is that a euphemism?" Hero asked. "Or did you honestly ask Clover to join us so we could work on our project?"

"Not only for that. I want sane company too." His eyes hadn't left mine, questioning. "Well?"

I understood then what had occasioned the invitation, and with that understanding came a bubbling rush of joy. This was it. Whatever the night-time expeditions had been building toward—and there were times I wasn't certain myself—it was finally going to happen.

"I'd love to," I said, and meant it in every sense.

※

As the sun grew lower in the sky, we turned off the Great North Road and onto smaller unsealed tracks, backways that bumped and wound through hilly country. Eddie, next to me, went steadily paler and quieter as the roads grew rougher, though he staunchly insisted he was fine; up in front, Hero and Alden started to bicker about whose turn it was to drive and why. Everyone began to feel rather grubby and sick of each other. If

I'd taken the train home, I'd have been there by now, I couldn't help thinking. I looked out over the yellow grass and tried not to wonder how the haymaking would get on without me. Matthew had said not to worry. (That was different from saying there was nothing to worry about.)

I almost missed it when the car turned onto a gravel path that I realised belatedly was not another road, but a driveway. I straightened, heart quickening in anticipation, and all thoughts of home fled from my head.

"Is this it?" I asked.

"Just about," Hero said, smothering a yawn. "Thank God. Another few miles and I'd have killed all three of you and then myself."

The car trundled past a building of grey stone, larger than my house ("The stable block," Eddie explained to me quietly) and then came over the crest of the hill. It was early evening, the sunlight beginning to slant and deepen into pale gold, the fields around us gentle green. And then—

The view I glimpse now every time I find myself on a stretch of country road, from the corner of my eye. The great grey stone manor, sprawling and Gothic and ridiculous in the sunlight, the rising turrets against the ocean of yellowing grass, the late-afternoon sky. Ashfield.

"There it is," Alden said carelessly. "It's freezing in the depths of summer, the east wing is falling down, and of course, it's cursed. But it's home."

"It's exactly how I pictured it," I heard myself say, though in fact I had been picturing nothing so clear. I just didn't have the words to explain how familiar it looked when I had never been anywhere like it in my life.

I loved Camford the first time I saw it, but that was a complicated love, its warm glow shot through with ambition and homesickness and determination to belong. It awed and impressed me, and demanded I be worthy of it. My love for Ashfield was unexpected and worn and comfortable from the first, like that for a favourite book. It was, as Alden had once told me, an enormous country estate, with some one hundred and fifty rooms and vast grounds. Yet for all its grandeur, it *liked* me, and it welcomed me exactly as I was hungry to be welcomed. The butler came out to meet us as the car pulled up: a stocky grey-haired man named Morgan, with a stern face and black eyes that twinkled like unexpected stars. Two younger men moved in to take our bags almost before we were out of the car, all brisk efficiency and neat collars. The doors opened of their own accord—a charm, I assumed—and the enormous entrance hall loomed overhead. Everything in it felt like stepping back in time, into some old, safe world I barely remembered.

Alden's parents were away as he had promised, not due to return for another week, and so the house, in all its sprawling glory, was ours alone. The labyrinth of rooms was bewildering, but Alden and Hero and Eddie moved through them so nonchalantly, with such ease, that I was tugged along in their wake. When I think back to that first day at Ashfield, that's what I see. The wide, sweeping staircase, sunlight catching motes of dust that rose at our approach. The long, dark corridors, lined with oil paintings and brass candle-holders. Rooms of dark wood panelling and gilded furniture, porcelain knick-knacks, a grandfather clock, the smell of dust and sandalwood and something sharper I couldn't identify. Alden and Hero's chatter, bright and meaningless as birdsong.

"I told Morgan to put you up here in the Green Room," Alden said to me, pushing open an oaken door that seemed no different from any of the others. "I hope you don't mind that it's a little small. The views make up for it."

It wasn't small, of course. It was a funny-shaped bedroom on a corner, with floor-sweeping white curtains and wallpaper mottled dark green. There was an enormous four-poster in the centre, an armchair by the window, my shabby travelling chest already at the foot of the bed. Pictures lined the walls—landscapes, mostly, and one or two portraits. Outside, the grass stretched forever under a cloudy sky.

"It's wonderful," I said, and meant it. My heart had jumped in my chest as though I'd seen a lover in a crowd.

His mouth quirked at the corner. "I'm glad. Dinner's going to be downstairs in half an hour. Take your time. It's only us tonight."

"I'm not sure where the dining room is," I remembered to say before they left.

"I'm right next to you, in the Red Room," Hero said, turning back. "Come bang on my door when you're ready—I'm sure I'll take longer than you."

In fact, I was still staring at the mirror in a vague panic when Hero came and knocked on my door instead. She took one look at me, standing in my best clothes helplessly brandishing a hairbrush, and laughed.

"What on earth are you doing?"

"I don't know what to wear to dinner," I confessed. I gestured at my dress, which was one of the many Hero had bought me over the last few months, a smoky-grey fabric the colour of mist. "Is this right?"

"Who cares? You heard Alden—it's just us."

"It isn't, though. There's Morgan. There are footmen and things." I didn't know how to explain, and I knew Hero wouldn't understand, that the various men and women who waited the table and cleaned the fireplaces and turned down the beds were far more my class of people than my friends were. I cared far more about their judgement, truly, than I did about that of the pretentious elite at Camford. I didn't want them to look at me and hate me for being at the table and not behind it. "Help."

She sighed, but indulgently. "Your dress is fine, although that colour would do better in the colder months. Face the mirror and I'll do your hair. Where's that bandeau I saw you wearing last week?"

I found it, a slender band with a rose in silver satin, and Hero brushed out my windblown hair with deft fingers and slipped it on at the elusive angle. She, of course, looked perfect—her dress the cool shimmering green of leaves reflected in a lake, her chestnut hair pinned back with a thin gold band. And yet I had come to know her well enough now to recognise when her confidence was innate and when it was battle armour, and I realised quickly that her hands on my shoulders as she adjusted my position were unusually tense. She was a head taller than me, so I could see her face reflected clearly in the mirror, and there was a brittle quality to her eyes that hadn't been there when we said goodbye twenty minutes ago.

"Is something wrong?" I asked.

Hero laughed again, this time a sharp, humourless bark. "Not really." She didn't bother to deny it as she would have eight months ago. "Just a letter from my father. It was waiting in my room just now. He claims he's changed his mind about letting me go back to Camford in the autumn."

"But…he can't," I said foolishly. Hero had hinted this might be a problem once or twice over the last few months; somehow I had never taken it seriously. I couldn't imagine Camford without Hero. "Your marks are wonderful. You're going to come top in linguistics, at least. Why would he…?"

"For that reason, probably, among others. He has no intention of losing me to academia when he wants me married and settled as soon as possible. Which means no degree, and no possibility of further scholarship."

"There must be other funding," I said, as if I didn't have intimate knowledge of every penny available to our year. "Surely you don't have to leave just because of your father."

"Why do you think the only undergraduate scholarships are for those experiencing hardship, Clover? They don't want anyone to be there against the wishes of a wealthy patron."

"Well…What if you and Alden got engaged, or pretended to?" I suggested tentatively. I suspected it was too close to something in one of the novels my sisters enjoyed to really work. Then again, you never could tell with Families. "Then you'd be free to go back to school. You wouldn't have to go through with it."

"It's a lovely idea, darling." She sounded a little tired. "The bare truth is, we're not rich enough for the Lennox-Fontaines anymore. My father's business dealings are failing. That's the real reason I'm not to be sent back to Camford—it's why Thorngate is shut up this summer, by the way, to save money. Camford fees are expensive—providing for an adult daughter is expensive—and the house needs a new roof or floor or some such thing. We're not destitute or anything like that, but I'm supposed to marry to save the estate and let my father restore the family name. Archaic, isn't it?"

I thought of my sister Mary walking out with Peter Brooks, the accusation I had flung at my mother that she was selling her daughter to pay the farm's debts.

"I'm sorry," I said uselessly.

"I'm one-third through my degree already. If he'd only give me another two years, then—" With a shock I saw the hot, angry glint in her eyes as she turned her head aside. I had never seen Hero come close to tears before. In that moment I'd have killed her father myself.

"We'll find a way." It was all I could think to say. "There's always a way."

Hero laughed, I think sincerely, and certainly fondly. "I'd take that as a useless platitude from most people. You actually mean it." By the time she looked back at the mirror, her head was high again. "Never mind. I won't leave, that's all. I doubt he really will make me. And if he does, I'll raise the money some-how. It's just such nonsense to be at war with my own family over something so simple."

"I argued with my family too," I heard myself say. "At Christmas. I've barely heard from them since."

From her complete lack of surprise, they had all guessed as much. She took my hand and squeezed it tightly.

"We're each other's family now," she said. "The four of us. Now, turn around."

I turned, obligingly, and kept my face as still as I could as she tilted my head up to tweak my eye make-up. At last she nodded, satisfied.

"There." She replaced my glasses, careful of my hair. "Look at that. You're wasted on those idiots downstairs. Eddie might notice the flower, I suppose. Come on, now. I'm starving."

I looked back in the mirror, and for a startled second I didn't see me at all. I saw a modern, confident young woman in a loose dress of evening fog, glossy hair tucked back and shaped in a bob. Her eyes were large and starry, her cheeks slightly flushed; a long silver chain glittered at her throat. Apart from the round wire-rimmed glasses perched on her nose, she looked nothing like Clover Hill. She looked like someone who belonged in the overlarge bedroom reflected behind her in the glass, about to go down to dinner with the tall, elegant woman in pale green beside her.

I removed my glasses again slowly, and the world blurred into soft focus.

"I'm ready," I said.

12

That summer at Ashfield was like living in another world. The house seemed to bask forever in the light of the last golden months before the war.

It was the driest summer on record, the heat parching the grass and shimmering the sky. By the end of the first week, the doors and windows of the house were open all day, sheer curtains twisting in the gentle breeze, and we had fallen into routine so simply and sweetly it was difficult to believe we hadn't been here for years. I would wake at nine or so, luxuriously late by my standards, and lean out across the sill to feel the warmth already rising from the roof tiles and blazing across the moorland. Eddie would be already downstairs, and the two of us would walk in the cooler parts of the garden or sit by the fountain drinking iced water and lemon until Hero and Alden finally came to join us. We would breakfast together on tea and bacon and boiled eggs and toast, talking and laughing as the rest of the morning and then the early hours of the afternoon wound away.

Then, right at the hottest, haziest part of the day, when anybody sensible would do as little as possible, we would stir ourselves into action. It was generally action only in the most basic grammatical sense of the word. Sometimes we would go bathing in the nearby creek, its waters brown and glittering in the summer drought, sprawling on the grass to dry ourselves before slipping back in again. Sometimes Hero would drive us into the nearest village for ice creams, and we would wander up and down the cobbled streets looking in tiny shop windows. There was talk once or twice of going for a longer drive to the coast, especially when it was discovered I had never been to the sea, or to York for a weekend, but as each morning dawned scorching and dazzling bright, it seemed too much effort, and there was no real enticement to make it.

Dinner was served at seven, and it was the only time I would ever occasionally glimpse the elusive Lord and Lady Alconleigh, Alden's parents. I never did work out if they were what I expected or not. Lord Alconleigh was a heavy-set man, with a grey face older than its years; Lady Alconleigh was younger, sharper, with Alden's gold hair and the air of careless lassitude he could affect when in large groups. Both were vague and polite to all of us, without much interest. We were Alden's friends come to stay, and it was nice that he had friends to amuse him so they wouldn't have to. It was the way I thought of upper-class families, based on my mother's ideas. Even after a year at Camford, though, I still expected more of Family. As far as I could see, they never even did any magic.

"That's because of the staff," Alden explained with a roll of his eyes. His parents had left the table early, and we were alone in the room as we lingered over dessert. "They don't want them getting ideas."

I didn't understand at first. "But the staff know about magic, don't they?" I felt sure Morgan did—perhaps more than I did myself.

"Of course they do. They've worked for the family for generations. Well, not them, obviously. Their ancestors. Morgan's father was the head groom."

Hero took pity on me. "Houses like Ashfield—Family houses, mage houses—are waited on by common people who have been sworn to secrecy." She speared a bite of her poached pear and waved her fork for emphasis. "Usually their own families have known and worked here for generations, as Alden put it so precisely. The servants have the trust of the Families, and vice versa. But traditionally, the Families have refrained from doing magic around them, lest they work out too much about how it's done."

"Why would that be bad?" I asked, although I was beginning to see all too well. "Why couldn't they learn too?"

"Well, in theory, it wouldn't be possible for them, without Family blood. Though I have to say, I haven't noticed any difference between your abilities and those of anyone from a magical Family lately."

I shrugged, pleased and embarrassed at once. I had felt that myself, and my marks in practical tests had climbed sharply since my first term, but I hadn't dared to hope it was apparent.

"There used to be. When I first started, I could barely fix a knot. It's different since I came to Camford. The magic feels easier."

"It's probably all nonsense," Alden said. "What they say about magic and bloodlines is probably really just the difference between growing up practicing spells and only coming to them as an adult. The way children pick up languages more easily than adults, or riding a bike."

"No, it isn't." I'd felt it, after all, those long months learning under Lady Winter. Probably, though I was so much more skilled now, I still felt it. Camford had unlocked power in me I hadn't known I possessed. When I sat in lectures, I could physically feel my mind opening, expanding, unfurling like a flower whose roots fed on pure knowledge. And yet I was still not Family; probably I would never know what it felt like to pull magic from the ether the way they did, as though it weighed as little as air. "Not entirely."

"It isn't," Eddie agreed. He looked at me apologetically, as though it was me he was contradicting. "I'm sorry, Clover—you're clearly marvellous at all this. But usually it's true. When I was very little, four or five, I was friends with our gardener's son. I could do basic spells then—light globes, flowers growing, that sort of thing. I tried to teach him. It didn't work, not in the slightest. He was very upset with me. I think he believed I was playing a trick."

Hero raised an eyebrow. "Didn't you tell him you'd never told a lie in your life?"

"Well," Eddie pointed out, reasonably, "that's exactly what a liar would say."

I was still thinking about the servants. "Even so, why shouldn't they learn too, the way I did? It might be more difficult, but it isn't impossible. Some of them might even be able to pass the Camford exams. What would be wrong with that?"

"Absolutely nothing in the world," Hero said, "except that would upset the delicate balance of things that people like our parents don't want upset."

"Besides," Alden said very dryly, "if all the servants became mages, where would they get servants from?"

Eddie stayed quiet. I had the impression, without knowing why, that he already felt he'd said too much.

"It's rotten, isn't it?" Alden said, clearly reading my face. "Thank God all that's starting to relax a bit since the war. Shall we go through to the library?"

That put all other thoughts out of my head, because those evenings in the library were the best of all. It was a beautiful library, of course—dark oak shelves extending to a high ceiling, worn reading chairs in dark leather, strange instruments of brass and wood secreted about the place. The far wall was taken up with tall, wide windows that opened out onto a stony courtyard and then to the moors beyond. Its collection of magical theory and folklore was impeccable. There would have been all the time and space in the world to work on our project. Somehow, we never did.

Instead, Hero would put on the gramophone, and scratchy voices and music would spill out into the air; Alden would throw open the windows, and the warm heather-scented wind would rush through. Bottles would be opened, mysterious dust-covered things dug up from the cellar filled with a golden summery wine like none I'd ever tasted. We would talk about the future—the places we would go, the discoveries we would make. Hero was going to travel the world, as soon as she had her Camford degree, and study the spellcraft of different cultures—Africa, China, the Middle East, the Amazon Rainforest. I told them about the Victorian expedition to faerie country I'd found in Lady Winter's library, and we all agreed we would make another someday, the four of us, once the Accord was lifted and the doors between worlds were open again.

By midnight, the room would be thick with spells. We were away from Camford; there were no rules about what spells we could and couldn't perform save those that governed the rest of the magical world; we were young and brimming with magic. We would levitate books and cushions and even each other; lamps would twist and transform into great glowing birds; the ceiling would surge like the ocean and the floors would shimmer like the sky. And I didn't think about the green glint in Matthew's eyes at midnight or the exhausted lines on his face, I didn't think about our farm withering in the record heat while my family battled to save it, I didn't think about the war or the epidemic or everything that had followed afterwards. The four of us were floating through the sky on an island that was only one another, and I let myself pretend it was all there was.

―――――――◇――――――――

But it wasn't all there was. We weren't in another world. Nor, as much as Ashfield itself stubbornly pretended otherwise, were we back in time. As the weeks went by, it became more difficult to ignore it. Midsummer came and went. We built a bonfire and saw in the dawn of the longest day, and that night I couldn't shut out the thought that my family were surviving another midnight. Each morning I checked the post, and this time I had no letter reassuring me that things were fine. I wondered if things truly were fine no longer, if Matthew was simply too busy to write, or if my family had at last given up on me.

Along with the growing dread came the niggling awareness that something was wrong. Alden had hinted very strongly that I was being invited to Ashfield partly to continue our experiments, away from Camford's eyes. And yet we hadn't done so, not once. When I mentioned this, taking advantage of a rare moment alone by the creek with him while the other two went to get drinks, he brushed my questions aside.

"There's time enough for all that. The summer's barely begun."

This didn't sound like the Alden I knew, the one who barely noticed the difference between having an idea and acting on it. I was usually the one urging caution, badly.

"You said we were going to tell the others about the double-door theory when we were further along with it," I reminded him. "I assumed we were going to tell them here."

"Oh, give it a rest, Clover, will you?" he snapped. "If you're really that eager to keep studying, you can always go back to Camford."

It startled me, and later it bothered me. Not because I was particularly hurt—I'd heard far worse growing up in a household with five siblings—but because it wasn't the first time I'd noticed that since coming home Alden hadn't been quite right. Even on our very happiest nights, he was a little *too* wild, *too* energetic, less like he was being swept up in his own feelings and more as though he were trying to outrun them. Occasionally his teasing of Eddie or his quarrels with Hero would take on an uncomfortably sharp edge; he was gentler with me, and

yet I found myself treading carefully around him, to avoid that
edge turning on myself. Just glimpses, like the glint of waves on
the surface of a lake, and then they would smooth over and he
would be himself again. Still, I couldn't shake the thought that
something was lurking in the depths.

As we got ready for dinner together that evening, I asked
Hero tentatively if he was all right. She sighed.

"He gets like this at Ashfield," she said. "It's tiresome, I know.
I'll keep an eye on him. As though I don't have other things to
think about."

I knew now not to take Hero's protestations of heartless-
ness seriously, especially where Alden was concerned, but I also
knew what she was alluding to. Another raven had come from
her father that afternoon. Another thing we weren't thinking
about, just as we never mentioned the complete lack of communication from Eddie's family, and now my own.

We didn't go to the library after dinner that night. We'd made
plans—firm, concrete plans—that we were finally going to the
lake at the edge of the estate for a picnic the next day, and then we
were finally going to go boating. That meant Hero had decided
we were all going to bed at eleven. We had made these concrete
plans at least three times already that summer, and each time we
had slept far too late to make a start. Or Alden had, at least, and
he was the only one of us who knew how to row.

"I don't see why it's my fault," he protested, when Hero
brought it up. "It's not as if rowing is so complicated. We're
practically second-year Camford students, for God's sake."

"Yes, Alden," Hero said patiently. "And believe it or not,
they don't teach *boat-rowing* spells in first-year incantations.
Besides, you were the one who wanted to go. Now you're suggesting we should have left without you?"

"I'm suggesting you *could* have. I would have sulked for a
week, obviously, but you *could* have."

"Well, if we all wake up except you tomorrow, that can be the next plan. I still think we ought to go to bed before three in the morning tonight to make sure it doesn't happen."

I didn't mind. The late half-drunken nights were starting to blur into one another by now. It was a luxury, for a change, to slip into bed in my funny corner room with the early evening darkness cool and inviting outside the window, to wriggle beneath the sheets pleasantly sleepy and yet still awake and sober enough to feel them. It was even a luxury, in a way that surprised me, to have an evening apart from the others. I loved them, and I hadn't for a moment found their company oppressive, but our lives had been very entwined lately. There was no way, for example, we would ever have really left in the morning without Alden.

I was dozing when I heard a noise outside. The creak of a floorboard, the light thud of a footstep; I blinked and saw a glimmer of light slide under the door. My sleepy mind made nothing of it at first. I had grown up in a house crammed with people. I was used to others moving around at night.

I wasn't at home, though. And—I sat up, my head still clearing— none of the others should be passing my door at night. Hero was next door, but there was nothing down my end of the corridor to draw her past. The boys were a floor below, Lord and Lady Alconleigh miles away at the other end of the house, the servants asleep downstairs. On impulse, feeling ridiculous, I slipped out of bed and crept to the door. It was too dark to do any such thing without a lamp: I caught my toe on the rug and nearly fell against an expensive-looking vase. That woke me the rest of the way up. My heart was still racing from that near miss as I opened the door a crack and peered through.

In the darkness, the corridor looked strangely disorienting— too long, too narrow, a twisting tunnel in a rabbit warren. Moonlight poured from a window at the far end, startlingly potent, more liquid than light, although I would have sworn that we had had a full moon only a few days ago and my own room had been dark. And a figure stood there. A man, tall, lean shoulders silhouetted against the window. My heart spiked, a rapid-fire cascade in my chest, before the figure turned his head just enough to catch the light.

Alden. It was only Alden. He wore his old maroon dressing gown, as he often did when he slumped down for breakfast in the morning, and he walked slowly, without his usual lightness. His curls were wild and unbrushed, and his feet were bare.

I must have leaned on the door without meaning to, because the hinges gave a faint, unexpected squeak. I pulled back on reflex; at the same time, Alden turned.

His eyes slid right over me, past the door, searching for someone else entirely. His voice was an uncertain whisper.

"Thomas?"

I didn't know anyone at Camford or Ashfield called Thomas—for one thing, Family names tended to the ornate—but the name in Alden's voice sounded oddly familiar.

There should have been no reason why I didn't just announce myself, go up to him and ask him who Thomas was and what he was doing. It was certainly what I would have done in the daylight. I didn't. There was something uncanny about the scene: the too-strong moonlight, the too-empty corridor, the too-fixed look on Alden's face. I thought, without knowing why, of the night I had opened the door of my brother's room, and seen a faerie smile at me from behind his eyes.

I stayed where I was as Alden turned away, as he walked the length of the corridor, climbed the stairs, and disappeared. Then I drew back from the door and closed it, very carefully, and made my way as quickly and lightly as I could back to bed. The night was still warm, and yet I was ice-cold.

I lay awake for a long time after that. I never heard Alden come back.

13

Had I not seen Alden that night, I probably wouldn't have seen anything out of the ordinary about him the following morning. If he looked paler than he had the day before, if he was quiet at breakfast and came close to biting Hero's head off when she urged us to hurry up, it could easily have been attributed to the fact that Hero's plan had worked and we were all, for once, downstairs and ready to leave the house at a reasonable hour.

But I did see it—and what was more, I understood now what I had been seeing all summer. I was used to watching for signs like it in my brother. I saw how little of the food at the table actually made it to his plate and how hollow his cheeks had become in just over a month. I saw how slow some of his smiles were to come and how brittle they were when they did. I saw that he hadn't slept a wink all night. Little things, things that would soon be worn away by sunlight and conversation, and yet they were there. Something was fraying him at the edges, and he was having to wind himself tighter and tighter to keep from unravelling.

I kept seeing it the rest of that day, which was otherwise perfect. By now we had mastered a spell that would keep a shade cloth rippling above us to protect ourselves from the all-encompassing heat, and we alternated crossing open fields under its cover with casting it off to feel the sun in full force on our faces. We walked a different way across the estate to any we'd covered before, past the old ruins of the twelfth-century monastery that Alden had told me about in his mock real estate mode, and we spent an hour wandering through the skeletal frame, marvelling at the height of it against the blue sky.

"It reminds me of Camford," Eddie said unexpectedly.

"What do you mean?" I asked, startled. "Camford isn't a ruin."

"No, but . . . the way the plants have taken it over." He pointed out the gorse overgrowing the stone walls, the heather strangling the old doorways. I could see what he meant then. It did resemble the way the strange trees and vines and flowers flourished across the university. "I sometimes think Camford is like a ruin that's still alive."

"I know exactly how it feels," Alden said wryly. He was looking rather grey, and I had seen him rub his temples when he thought nobody was looking. I decided then and there, trying to balance on the ruins of a medieval column, that I wasn't going to leave whatever was bothering him to Hero. I was going to talk to him myself.

My chance came sooner than I expected. The lake was over the crest of a hill. We dragged one another up the slope, laughing, taking it in turns to carry the picnic basket as the shade cloth flapped uselessly above our head. The spell was wearing off, and it was becoming wayward. We ended up pulling it down and collapsing onto it, breathless, to use as a picnic blanket.

"Which is just as well," Hero pointed out, unfazed. "We didn't bring a picnic blanket, and this dress is white lace."

The plan was to eat first and then go boating on the water. The boat was there—a rowboat, larger than I had expected and painted a deep green. Before we had finished, though, it was fairly evident that Alden wasn't going to be rowing us anywhere immediately. He stretched out in the shade of the oak that bordered the lake and closed his eyes.

"Alden?" Hero said conversationally.

"Mm?"

"Are you just going to lie there all afternoon?"

He considered. "Mm."

"Well. That was certainly worth dragging ourselves all the way up here for. I could have made other plans, you know. Augustus Carmichael telephoned the other day and offered to take me for a ride in his new car."

"You hate going for rides with men unless they let you drive."

"He would have had no choice."

"You hate Augustus Carmichael."

"True," she conceded. "But he's marginally more interesting awake than you are with your eyes closed. Marginally."

His eyes flickered open, and he sighed. "Give me half an hour. Then I'll row you wherever you like. I had a terrible night last night."

Eddie frowned. "We didn't do anything last night."

"Exactly. It was terrible."

Hero's gaze met mine for just a second, a mute acknowledgement, and then she rolled her eyes extravagantly. "I suppose you'll only drown us all in this state. Though I don't know what you think the rest of us are supposed to do for that half an hour."

"Go for a walk. Pick flowers. Perfect your headstands. Compose a sonata in honour of the ducks. My God, woman, can you really not amuse yourself without me for thirty minutes and counting?"

"May I draw you?" I asked. I kept my voice casual, probably too casual. I had drawn all three of them often enough, especially this summer. There was no reason for anyone, Alden included, to suspect an ulterior motive. "I need a live model, and it's difficult to find someone who'll keep still."

"He'll keep still all right," Hero said. "It just won't be a very riveting picture with his eyes closed."

"It will be mesmerising," Alden said. "How dare you. Everyone knows the eyes are the boring part."

"I like the eyes," Eddie said. "They're my favourite thing about Clover's drawings."

"Strange," Alden said. "I've never seen a drawing of broccoli with eyes."

Hero swatted him with a napkin.

The eyes were my favourite too—when I drew my brothers and sisters, they were what I always did first. But there was something about Alden's face when his were closed that was indeed mesmerising. The lines of it softened, smoothed, as though a guard was being lowered. Most people's eyes gave away more than they concealed; Alden's never did, even at his most relaxed. It was only when he wasn't looking at anything at all that it was possible to get a glimpse of what he might be like when he wasn't being looked at.

"It's fine by me," Alden added, and it took me a moment to realise he was answering my question. "I'll try to keep still. Feel free to kick me if I start to snore."

"I suppose I'll go and look for fungus down by the lake, then," Eddie said. He said it without a hint of recrimination, or even disappointment, and yet guilt twinged my stomach. I had promised to go with him to sketch the specimens he found. I'd done so last week by the river, and I'd unexpectedly had a wonderful time. It was cool and pleasant down by the water, and the delicate, soft-coloured folds of mushrooms were beautiful against the bark. I'd sketched them quickly, while Eddie measured them and took samples and lit up with enthusiasm at my every question, and made notes on the pinks and yellows and reds to fill in with watercolours later. The mushrooms would still be there another day, though. I would make it up to him.

"I'll come along for a walk," Hero said. She stood, picked up her hat, and dusted off her long white skirt. I wondered if she minded my staying—she'd known Alden her whole life, after all, and she'd as good as said his problems were hers to deal with. The grateful wink she gave me set my mind at rest. "Enjoy your nap, Fontaine, and try not to outshine the *Mona Lisa*. Clover, don't feel you have to flatter him too much. We both know his ears are too small."

"That's slander," Alden said with a yawn. "My ears are exactly right. The rest of my head is too big."

In fact, I discovered as I started to sketch, his proportions were unfortunately and inevitably perfect. I hadn't often drawn Alden except in brief snatches—partly because he was rarely still; partly, though I hated to admit it, because I still tended to blush if I looked at him for too long. But he truly must have been tired, because his face relaxed into sleep as soon as the others had left, and much as I wanted to talk to him, I couldn't exactly kick him awake to do it. So I shaded in his high cheekbones, his sharp chin, the quirk of his eyebrows. The hollows under his eyes, too deep and dark lately; the fine eyelashes against the curve of his cheek; the gentle tumble of his curls, darker at the roots, lightening to fine gold. It's an oddly hypnotic experience, to sink so deeply into the details of someone else's face. The world slowed down around me as I drew, and my breathing slowed to match his. I tried to tell myself this was no different to drawing anybody else, and almost succeeded.

After a while he twitched, then his eyes blinked open. "Sorry," he said drowsily. "There's a tree root digging in my back." He wriggled against the bank and scratched the back of his neck before settling back down. "That's better. Is this still all right?"

The shadows had shifted on his face. I looked at the paper, then at him. "Tilt your head down a little? And to the left?"

It wasn't perfect, but it was close enough that I nodded. "Thanks. You can get up and stretch first if you need a break."

"I'm comfortable." His eyes had closed again. "How long was I asleep?"

I had to check my watch myself. The time had unspooled slowly and gently as a skein of thread. "About twenty minutes."

His eyebrow quirked. "That long? You're a restful person to be around, Clover Hill."

"You mean dull," I said dryly.

"Not in the least. Dull people make me fidgety. You're restful."

"You're exhausted," I countered. I shook off my reluctance to speak further. I was a scholar, after all, and so was Alden. We believed in answers. "I saw you in the corridor outside my room last night."

He grimaced. "Did you? I didn't see you. I wasn't sleepwalking, was I?"

"You might have been." The thought, foolishly, hadn't occurred to me. "I stayed out of sight."

"You should have come and said hello. I'd have appreciated the company."

"I didn't like to. You seemed—"

"Yes." He sighed, and his eyes opened to meet mine. "I can imagine. I'm sorry if I worried you. I don't sleep very well at home."

"This is why you left at Christmas, isn't it?" I had been wondering that ever since, on and off. It had never seemed right to ask. "Why? What bothers you about this house?"

"Oh, old memories. Old curses. You don't feel them?"

"I love Ashfield." The breeze stirred my hair gently, as if in response. "It might be haunted, but it isn't cursed."

"Well." His voice was getting drowsy again. If I wasn't quick, I was going to either lose him or have to actually kick him after all. "Perhaps the memories and curses are all mine."

"Who was Thomas?" The words came from my mouth before I could bite them back.

Alden didn't so much as blink, and yet something in him woke all the way up. "Are you asking if Thomas was cursed?"

"No." I looked down at my paper, flustered, which wasn't very helpful since Alden was there as well. "No, I just—I heard his name somewhere, I was just wondering—"

"It's all right," he interrupted with a smile. I couldn't tell how forced it was. "It's not a secret. Thomas was my older brother. He disappeared at the end of August 1914—almost a month after the war broke out. He was eighteen."

Of course. The first time on the library roof: Hero had asked how Alden had known about it, and he said that Thomas had told him. No doubt it was Thomas who had taught him to get into the library after hours too; probably the name had passed between them a few other times without my noticing it.

I was such an idiot. Of course Alden didn't like being at Ashfield, for the simplest and most commonplace of reasons, the same reason I hated being on the farm and seeing my father's empty chair. So many of us these days had missing elder brothers or cousins or fathers whose absence haunted our homes. I should have guessed.

"I'm sorry," I said.

"No, why should you be? *I'm* sorry. I forgot you didn't know."

Alden was clearly waiting for the next question, the obvious question, so I asked it as tactfully as I could. "I— Did he go to fight?"

"I still think he must have done. Nobody really knows for certain." He propped himself up on his elbows with a faint sigh, as though resigning himself to a story he'd prefer not to tell. "He intended to enlist with a few of his friends from Camford. My parents didn't want him to—they thought the war was none of our business and the Families should stay out, from what I could gather. I was twelve years old and hopelessly self-centred, so it all went over my head. But Thomas wanted to go. He and my parents argued; he insisted on his right to fight for what he believed in, and he was determined to enlist. Then, the night before he was due to go, he disappeared. Nobody ever saw him again."

"Could he not have run away to enlist, as he'd said he would?"

"That's what I believe. I think he left after we had all gone to bed, so that our parents couldn't stop him. But he never reached his friends. Perhaps something happened to him on the way. Perhaps he signed up without them and was killed thousands of miles away under a different name. Some of the more malicious Families, especially the ones who had lost sons in the war, started a rumour that he had simply run away. It nearly broke my mother's heart, hearing him branded a coward. Strange, isn't it? When she didn't want him to go in the first place." He fell silent. "Anyway. His friends swore they left without him. One of them died in the trenches, one lost a leg. One came back whole. I suppose we'll never know what happened to Thomas."

"I'm so sorry." I fumbled for something to say. "If he *was* afraid—if he *did* run away—then it wouldn't be shameful. Those trenches were terrible."

"I suppose your brother told you about them?"

I shook my head. "Not really. He won't talk about the war. But he lets things slip sometimes, and the rest I can guess. He came back different, and only some of it was the faerie curse." I was saying more than I'd meant to now, and yet Alden didn't seem to mind. He was still listening. "I hate it. I hate watching him try to pretend everything's fine. I hate hearing how he did his duty and we should all be proud of him. I hate remembering that I argued with our parents that he should be allowed to go, and that he thanked me for it. I hate that it's my fault."

"Clover, my love, it was a war." The endearment was meant lightly, but there was real softness in his voice. "It wasn't your fault. You couldn't have stopped him."

"I could have tried. He trusted my judgement. He might have listened to me if I'd really insisted we needed him at home."

"You'd have felt guilty about that too, believe me."

I'd always thought so. Lately, I wasn't so sure. "Would your parents have felt guilty? If they'd made Thomas stay?"

"You know, when it came to it, I don't believe they really

would have stopped him. Oh, they argued with him about going, they said all the right things and might have even believed them, but they would have given in. My parents believe in duty, country, glory, and all that."

"And you don't?"

He laughed a little. "I'm a disappointment in that regard. That's considered quite normal for a younger son at this time of his life, though, so they aren't worried. I don't get anything like the rubbish that Eddie gets from his family. There's still hope for me, so long as I do my time at Camford, graduate well but not too well, possibly go into politics. Marry a nice girl."

"Not Hero anymore, though."

I wondered belatedly if I had betrayed a confidence, but Alden only rolled his eyes. "Oh, she told you about that nonsense? Mother's never trusted Hero—she's thrilled that she has a reason to argue for a better match. The irony of course is that Hero never intends to get married, so they have nothing to hope for or to worry about on that score. What about you?"

"Do I intend to marry, do you mean?"

"Well, I could be asking if you'd marry *me*, but I'm not that brave."

"It's a no on both counts, I'm afraid," I said, as lightly as I could. I refused to question how much I meant it. "I want to be a scholar. That's difficult enough for a single woman. Marriage would rob me of my time and independence."

"Hero would agree with you. The difference is, and forgive me for being blunt, she's at least only trying to break into one world, not two."

I didn't mind the bluntness at all. It was refreshing, after all the sideways snubs of the Families. "I'm already in your world," I reminded him. "Whatever my background, I've made it. All I need to do now is be so good they can't make me leave."

"I have no doubt you'll be that good, but you know things like that are rarely dependent on merit alone in this world."

I shrugged. "I can't do very much about the world. If Camford won't keep me, I'll study independently. They can't stop me."

"No." His lips curved into something that wasn't quite a smile. "No, I don't imagine they could."

Hero's voice came up the slope. "Have you *really* not moved since we left? God, you're going to grow into the tree at this rate."

"I *have* moved, I'll have you know," Alden replied, raising his voice to match. He sat up as Hero and Eddie came back, looking far more like his usual self. "Ask Clover. I ruined her picture, didn't I, Clover?"

"It takes more than that to ruin one of my pictures," I informed him haughtily. "It's come out very well."

In fact, when I drew back to look at the picture critically, the results were frustrating. The features were all recognisably there under my pencil. There was something missing nonetheless, some elusive secret that I couldn't put on the page.

"Let's see?" Hero bent to look at the drawing over my shoulder. "Excellent, given the limitations of your subject matter. Fortunately, Eddie found some toadstools for you to draw next. I suppose we can go rowing now?"

"I could have a go, if you don't want to," Eddie suggested. He sounded serious. It was difficult to tell with Eddie. "I've seen it done. Once or twice."

"Don't you dare." Alden got to his feet with alacrity. "You'll see some pond weed or something and send the boat to the bottom for a closer look."

Hero's hand tightened on my shoulder as she straightened, a mute thank-you. I had no doubt she knew far more of what the two of us had been talking about than she had let on, and that she had taken Eddie away especially to let our conversation happen. The trouble was, she vastly overestimated how much good I could do.

What Alden had told me made perfect sense. It explained his

distraction, his night-time wanderings, his reluctance to come home to Ashfield, and even his parents' distance when he did.

It didn't explain the moonlight.

⸎

That night, I couldn't sleep. We had gone to bed before midnight again this time, worn out after the golden afternoon on the river and the velvet walk home in the evening. I told myself that was why I was lying awake: I wasn't used to two relatively early nights in a row. I twisted to my left side as the sheets warmed beneath me, then my right; I lay back and tried to think of nothing at all.

Then, in the early hours of the morning, a faint glow played across the ceiling, a sliver of silver, moonlight where there was no moon. I heard the light tread of footsteps outside my door, the creak of a loose floorboard. I knew this was what I had been waiting for all along.

Alden was outside the door when I opened it, the features I had drawn that afternoon once again cast into relief by that peculiar shaft of light. This time, he gave no sign of hearing me, even though I made no effort to conceal my presence and the door squeaked again. He was moving in the same direction as before, quicker this time, his footsteps unusually heavy and rapid.

This time, I didn't go back to bed. I followed him.

We walked a long way, farther than I was expecting. Down the corridor, up a short staircase, then a sharp right, headed slowly but certainly toward the east wing. We hadn't been to that part of the house that summer. The rooms were smaller there, less fashionable, the wallpaper showing signs of age. Alden gave no sign of knowing I was there—that, and the occasional uncharacteristic stumble, made me increasingly sure that he wasn't really awake. He'd warned me I might see him sleepwalking; he hadn't told me what to do in the event it happened. I knew common wisdom was not to wake someone in his state, yet surely it wasn't safe for him to walk around the house all night? Hero would probably know. If I went for her, though, I would lose him. It wasn't only that I was afraid of where he might go on his own. I wanted to know where he was going.

When he did stop, I nearly missed it. The door was no different to any of the others we passed; abruptly, out of nowhere, he simply turned the doorknob and went in. I stopped, startled, as it closed in my face.

I hesitated only a moment before opening it again.

I had assumed, without quite realising it, that the room Alden was visiting was Thomas's. Perhaps it had been once, but there was no sign now it had ever been a bedroom. It was a sitting room of some kind: a long low couch in faded green, two armchairs in front of an unlit fireplace, a shelf filled with odd books. An ordinary room by Ashfield standards, somewhat shabby. The only strange thing about it was the glow of moonlight that filled it, and that Alden stood in the centre.

There was no doubt now that he was still asleep. His eyes were open, but they weren't seeing me. They were wide, their blue almost translucent, and they were filled with fear. His body was taut, his chest rising and falling at double speed. Whatever landscape was playing in his head, it was filled with terror.

"Alden." I said his name as calmly as I could.

He didn't hear me. But, as in the corridor the night before, he heard *something*. His head twisted sharply in the direction of my voice, eyes flickering over me without seeing. His brow furrowed.

"Thomas?" he said.

"No." I swallowed. "No, it's me. Do you know where you are?"

He didn't answer. He was breathing even faster now, his face glistening with perspiration.

I reached out, tentative. "Alden—"

He wrenched away abruptly, shoving me backwards. *"Get away from me!"*

The cry was startlingly loud in the silence of the house, loud enough that I thought for certain someone would hear and come. At home, when the younger children woke screaming in their various infancies, the whole house had always woken with them. In the early days after the war, when my brother had woken from nightmares crying out for people who were dead, the sound had travelled from the attic and brought us to him. This was Ashfield. We were several floors above the staff, several locked rooms away from Lord and Lady Alconleigh or Hero or Eddie. We might as well have been in another house entirely. For the first time I was aware of the loneliness of this vast estate, suspended alone with nothing but the moors and the sky for miles in either direction.

I don't know whether I was afraid of Alden or for him— perhaps both. Either way, I took a slow step back. My heart thrummed in my ears, a frantic beat of warning.

"Stay there," I said to him, uselessly. He didn't move. "I'll be right back."

I waited until I was safely in the corridor before I started to run.

<hr>

Fortunately, Hero didn't sleep with her door locked, and she didn't sleep heavily. I needed only to shake her shoulder lightly before she stirred and twisted around.

"Clover," she said hazily. She sat up, frowning, and brushed her hair back from her eyes. "What's wrong?"

"Alden," I said. "He's in the east wing—sleepwalking, I think. I tried to wake him, but—"

Hero swore quietly under her breath and threw back the covers. "Not again. Where did you say he was?"

14

Alden hadn't moved from the room when we got there. He stood more or less where I had left him, his eyes open and glassy, his breath coming hard and fast and wild. Once again, I found myself pulling back, afraid of something I couldn't quite name. I remembered, anew, that he had said Ashfield was cursed.

Hero didn't flinch. She stepped forward as though going to greet a friend for dinner, took Alden's hands in hers, and looked him in the eye.

"Alden," she said, gently yet firmly. "Alden, it's all right. Wake up. It's all right. Alden, look at me."

She said it a few more times; he tried to pull away, and she only held on more tightly. Slowly, his breathing calmed, and the terror on his face softened. He blinked rapidly a few times, and when he opened his eyes, they were his own again: bewildered, exhausted, no longer behind a glaze of fear.

"What...?" It came out husky; he cleared his throat and tried again. "Was I asleep?"

"You were." She released him. "You were sleepwalking again."

"Oh, bloody hell." His hands were shaking as he rubbed his eyes, but his voice was returning to normal. "Sorry. I didn't mean to wake everyone."

"You didn't. You woke Clover, who woke me. She's the one who deserves your apology. You frightened her to death."

"I'm sure I did. I'm sorry, Clover." He drew a deep, shuddering breath, like a child coming down from tears, and shook his head. "I think I need to sit down. I don't suppose there's a glass of something around?"

"Just this once, I'll fetch one. Don't think I'm making a habit of this." She glanced at me. "Will you wait with him? Make sure he doesn't fall asleep again before I get back."

"Of course." I was embarrassed now to have panicked so completely. I knew what night terrors were. Iris had been prone to them when she was three or four, and I had often been the one to calm her down. I had sat awake with Matthew in the kitchen for many long nights after his homecoming until he was ready to go back to sleep. But I'd never seen anything like Alden's nightmares. They looked a lot less like nightmares and a lot more like a curse.

Alden looked around when Hero left, and some of the bewilderment came back to his face. "Where—?"

"You're in one of the rooms in the east wing," I said quickly. I hoped he wouldn't ask how I had been able to hear him all the way from my room, and fortunately he seemed far too dazed to think of it. "Come and sit down."

I took him gently by the arm, and he let himself be led to the sofa. The floorboards underfoot creaked as he sank onto it.

"There's really no need to be frightened," he said, with a quick smile, as if remembering me or himself again. "I'm all right, I promise. Just a bit confused."

"You shouted at me. You told me to get away."

"I'm sure I did." His eyelids were starting to droop. "Sorry. I'm saying that to you a lot today, aren't I?"

I sat down next to him, carefully, and lowered my voice. "What were you doing here?"

"I don't know," he said vaguely. He forced his eyes open with effort. "I walk all sorts of places in my sleep."

Hero returned with a bottle and two glasses. "Here," she said.

"You're in luck—your father's drinks cabinet was unlocked. This one's water, this one's a shot of whiskey. Take both and get back to bed, Fontaine."

"You're an angel." He swallowed both with such speed that I had no time to see which was which, and suspected neither did he. "I'll try to get some real sleep. Thank you, both of you."

I breathed a deep sigh after he left, without knowing why. The room without him in it seemed suddenly harmless—a bookshelf, a sofa, little else. Even the moonlight had dimmed. I felt, irrationally, as though a crisis had been averted.

"Here." Hero refilled one of the glasses, somewhat more generously than she had for Alden, and held it out to me. "We need it more than he does. He'll barely remember this in the morning."

I doubted that somehow, but I took the glass and swallowed without question. It was stronger and harsher than the wine we usually drank, and it burned going down. I coughed, and drank again.

Hero poured the other for herself and knocked it back with far more practice. "Well," she said dryly. "That put paid to an excellent dream I was almost having."

"I'm sorry I woke you," I said. "He warned me he sleepwalked. I should have tried what you did first."

"No, you did the right thing. He's more used to my voice in that state." She stretched, yawned, and leaned back against the wall by the fireplace. "He used to do that all the time when he was younger. When he was fourteen, he wandered out into the fields in the middle of a storm. God knows how the rain and the cold didn't wake him. It was one reason they used to have me over to stay such a lot. I was supposed to keep an eye on him."

I stared. "He seemed fine at Camford."

"Oh, he is fine at Camford. He was fine at Crawley, as far as I know. This place is bad for him. I have no idea why he wanted to spend the summer here."

"Why does he hate Ashfield so much?" I thought I'd understood, this afternoon. But his brother's loss didn't account for this level of fear. I found it hard to be on our farm these days; I didn't spend every minute there hanging on to sanity by my fingertips.

"He loves Ashfield—or he used to. That's the problem. He thinks Ashfield doesn't love him back. His brother was meant to inherit it, you see."

"Thomas?"

"Mm. Alden loved him too, but he was also jealous of him. Thomas was always his parents' favourite, and he resented it; he resented, as well, that Thomas would have Ashfield one day when he didn't really care for the house at all. The three of us made it our playground, Alden and Eddie and I, and Thomas was always off with friends in London. When Thomas disappeared and the inheritance passed to Alden after all, he felt that it was somehow his fault, and that the house knew it and blamed him. I know this because we got blind drunk together after his brother's funeral, and he told me—we haven't spoken of it since. Completely barmy, of course. Houses can't blame."

I tried to take this in. "Is he all right now?"

Hero snorted. "God no. He's a mess, but aren't we all? Well, possibly not you." She paused as if struck by a thought, then looked at me more seriously.

"Listen, darling," she said. "I know the temptation with Alden is to swoop in and try to save him from himself. Don't swoop too close. If he looks like he's drowning, throw him a rope, by all means, then step back and let him pull himself the rest of the way. He can, you know. He doesn't need you to jump in after him, and you're more likely to drown trying than he is. Did that metaphor hold? It's very late at night."

"Yes." I didn't know what else to say. "It holds."

"Good." She finished her glass, then set it down on the mantelpiece. "Well, I suppose I'd better be off to bed myself. Good-night."

"Hero?" The sound of my own voice surprised me. It was

that time of night, when things were spoken aloud of their own accord. "Are you in love with Alden?"

"I think everyone's a little in love with Alden, if he wants them to be," Hero said, without batting an eye. "Not beyond reason. If you're asking if I would mind you sleeping with him— no. Not for my own sake. For one thing, I already slept with Alden, when we were sixteen. It was nice enough; I don't think it meant very much to either of us. Sex doesn't ever mean very much to Alden, as far as I can tell. He enjoys it, and he's good at it, but there's something not quite there."

I wished I didn't blush so easily. "No, I meant—"

"For your sake, though, I'd wish you better than Alden." She sounded serious now—or perhaps it would be closer to say she sounded thoughtful. "I love him dearly, even if I'm not *in* love with him, but he's a careless driver. People around him tend to get bowled over unless they stand very firm. Oh look, another metaphor. Eddie's devoted to you, you know."

"I know. I love him too."

"But you're not interested in him that way. It happens like that sometimes, doesn't it? Never mind."

I didn't know how to say that I wasn't sure Eddie was interested in me in that way either—I had suspicions about Eddie, but they were nobody's business, not even mine. Besides, I wasn't sure if I was interested in Alden in that way, not really. I loved all three of them, and I couldn't untangle in my head where that love started and ended. I loved *working* with Alden more than anything. I loved the way his mind worked: lithe and supple, all flash and daring, snatching up and playing with ideas that I was inclined to stand back from and dissect. Beyond that, I only knew that I cared for him; more than that, I was pulled to him, the way I might be pulled toward a forbidden book, with mixed fascination and wariness and wonder.

Well, that wasn't quite true. I have never to this day seen a book with Alden's cheekbones.

"I'll just warn you of this," Hero said into the silence. "You're very clever, as I'm sure you've noticed. It doesn't surprise me at all that Alden values your collaboration so much. But I'm sure you won't mind me saying that I am very clever too—at least as clever as Alden. So whatever you and he are doing together that you haven't told me about—and please don't think I haven't noticed—you might want to think about why he doesn't want me to know."

The nights in the Bodleian. The imp windows after dark. My insides squirmed guiltily.

"Do you mean that he's using me?" I tried to keep the hurt from my voice.

"No, not at all. Not in the way you mean. I think, though, there's something in all this nonsense about Agrippa and faerie doors that he doesn't want me to see—and I would see it. I've known him all my life. You don't know him so well, and he's aware of that. Try to watch out for it, if you can."

I went back to bed, through the corridors that had become shadowy and strange into the funny-shaped room that had become as familiar as a favourite jumper. I kicked off my slippers, lay down on top of the rumpled blankets, tried to close my eyes. This time, they wouldn't stay closed.

There's something in all this nonsense about faerie doors... Try to watch out for it, if you can. Now Hero had said it, I could no longer pretend not to see it. I had known the first day we had met that Family heirs like Alden Lennox-Fontaine didn't notice people like me without reason. That reason had been Agrippa, and faerie doors, and because that had suited me perfectly I had asked no further questions. But Family heirs also didn't obsess over faerie doors for no reason.

There had been something in that room with us both. I didn't let myself think beyond that, not then, lying awake in the dark. I knew, though, that I had seen that silver light before. It glimmered in the lines of every imp window Alden and I had ever opened. Every window he asked me to keep secret, even from our friends.

The night was waning when I accepted that I wasn't going to sleep. I sat up for the second time that night and, with a sigh, got to my feet.

There was no mistaking the silver glow now. It hung in the air as I mounted the stairs into the east wing, so thick I could almost taste its bitter cool on my tongue. When I came back to the room where I had found Alden, it blazed through the gap beneath the door. And yet when I pushed the door open, it was gone in a single fleeting glimmer, like a rush of mice dashing for cover when you open a pantry.

In its absence, the room looked just as it had a few hours ago. A cluster of furniture and oddments, ill-matched, like a life-size dollhouse waiting to be played with. I loved Ashfield dearly, loved how its size made it a self-contained world, but I did have to concede that it had far more rooms than it had a use for. The glasses Hero and I had used still sat on the mantelpiece, the only sign that anyone had been there for years.

I drew a deep breath, trying to calm my heart, and looked around. It was only a room, I told myself. A room like so many others. All I had to do was look and put my own fears to rest. In a few short hours, the sun would be up, and I would feel ridiculous to think I had done this. There was nothing to see.

There wasn't, at first. I was almost ready to leave when my eyes caught on the far wall. The grey predawn light from the window opposite was just beginning to illuminate the dark green wallpaper. Amidst the floral patterns, a few faint marks were visible. Chalk.

Nothing incriminating, not yet. The traces were too faint to make anything out. They could be marks for hanging pictures or God knows what else. Still.

I knew a few different spells to unmask something concealed. Their effectiveness, of course, depended on whether they were more or less powerful than the concealing spell. The one I felt surest of was the one we had learned in Basic Incantations, and I decided that, performed well, it had a greater chance than a more complicated one I would doubtless get wrong. I crossed my arms over my chest, fists closed, then slowly parted them. *Manifesto.*

Power coursed through my veins, so strongly that I wondered if something outside of me was trying to help it along. What was hidden wanted to be seen, and had a will of its own. It was the only explanation I could imagine for the light, and the only one I've ever been able to find for why in the very next breath the far wall blossomed into lines of silver. They spidered across the green wallpaper, ornate swirls like those in fancy garden gates. Last of all, they twisted into a doorknob, and stopped.

My heart stopped with it.

A door. It was a faerie door.

15

I had never seen one before—there had never been any left to see—and it should have been impossible for there to be one now. Yet there was no doubt. The silver designs were exactly as I had seen them in Gluckstein's *Introduction*, only they weren't true silver at all. They gleamed starlight and mist, the light from another world.

It looked closed to my eyes. Surely it had to be—it was impossible for this door to be here at all, much less open. And yet a faint breeze teased my hair and nightdress, bringing with it the smell of salt and pine and rain. I took a step closer, against my better judgement, almost against my will.

Who are you?

The voice rustled through my head like the wind in the trees. I stiffened at once.

The door might not be open, but it wasn't wholly closed. There was something on the other side.

The voice came again. *Who are you?*

I knew better than to give my name. Still, it rose to the tip of my tongue. I had to bite down on it and swallow.

Another susurration, another breath of air. *Come closer.*

My feet took one step forward, then another, and this time there was no doubt they were doing so without any guidance from me. Something was reaching out, stirring the tangle of my nerves and bones, drawing them closer. I should have been frightened, should have been fighting, but the silver drowned out any feeling except wonder and a vague melancholic awe. It was impossible, and so beautiful.

The door was close enough to touch, close enough to see the faint lines of chalk beneath the silver, to make out the grain of the paper beneath even that. I wondered if I would die when I reached it. I wondered what that burning light would feel like beneath my fingers, and what lay beyond.

The crash of a door behind me. A voice, breathless and familiar. *"Occultare."*

There was no sound, no spark of light. The lines of the door simply retreated into the wall, spidering back into the corners as though they had never existed. The sudden dark hit me like a physical blow, and feeling rushed back with it. I fell back, gasping, shaking, my mind reeling from what I had seen, what I had nearly done.

Hands caught my shoulders deftly, comfortingly. "It's all right," the voice was saying. "It's safe now. You're safe."

I turned and saw with no surprise at all that I was looking at Alden Lennox-Fontaine.

"You know, all you had to do was ask," Alden said, after the silence had stretched out to the thinness of a scream. "I would have told you."

Even then, I knew that he believed it, and also that it wasn't true.

"It's a door." Saying it out loud made it even more impossible. And yet I had known what I would find, hadn't I? I must have. I wasn't a fool. "A faerie door."

"I've warded it." He let go of my shoulders, gently, and I pulled away. "As long as it's hidden, nobody knows it's here; even when it's revealed, as you just found, I don't think anything beyond it can do very much. It's safe."

"It's a faerie door, Alden! It isn't safe." I had felt that grip on my mind, that silver light flooding my body and drowning my will. I shook my head, trying to settle my thoughts. "How can it be here? The Board closed them all. They locked the faerie world away."

"They did. But you see, this door was still open when the Accord came into effect. It had been open for a long time by then—four years."

"Opened by whom?"

"Me," Alden said, as I'd known he would. "I opened it. I was twelve years old. Clover, can we please sit down and talk this over?"

"Why can't we talk this over standing?"

"Well, we could, but these are new slippers, so it would be less than comfortable for me."

I couldn't help it—I laughed. It was a burst of nerves, nothing more, and I regretted it when I saw a touch of relief in his eyes. It was only then that I realised how frightened he had been to find me there—how his breathing was still slowing, and his hands curled up into fists to keep them from trembling.

"I didn't mean for this to happen," he added. "Please believe me. I didn't mean any of this."

He sat down on the couch, raising his eyebrows in mute inquiry; after a moment, I sat beside him. I was still trembling myself, after all.

"I want an explanation," I said.

"And I want to give you one. I always intended to give you one. Not this soon, though, and definitely not at four in the morning after a very strange night, so please give me a second to get this right, will you?"

I waited, watching as he gathered his thoughts and organised them behind his eyes. I was close enough to see every inch of him, in aching detail. I tried to reassemble those features, the ones I could have drawn blind, into someone unfamiliar. I couldn't. I had always known there was a secret behind that face, one I couldn't reach. Knowing the shape of it at last should have altered him in my eyes, but it was too late. I knew him too well, and not well enough.

"I told you about my brother, Thomas, didn't I?" he said at last. "I told you that he meant to go to war, that my parents argued, that he said it was no use, he was leaving in the morning."

"Yes. And in the morning he was gone."

He didn't respond to that. "That was the longest night of my life. I lay in bed, as wide awake as I've ever been, and all I could see was Thomas getting on a train and vanishing from our lives. I don't know how it was, but I never had illusions about war. I never believed in glory. I knew it was violent, and filthy, and that Thomas would come back broken or not at all." He caught himself. "Well. I don't have to tell you."

I thought of the night before Matthew left, the way every rustle of the leaves outside had seemed the wail of a banshee heralding his death, the way I lay awake and listened because my dreams would be worse. I think we all did, even Matthew.

"It came to me, at three in the morning, as all the very worst ideas do. I didn't have the power to keep Thomas from war. But something did. All I needed was a book, and the magic to punch a hole in the world."

"A faerie door." I shook my head again, this time in disbelief. "It was idiotic."

"I was an idiot," he said bluntly. "I think I barely understood that faerie deals were dangerous, and I wouldn't have cared if I had. Crawley teaches all sorts of bad behaviour, but the worst thing it teaches is that we're exceptional, not bound by the rules that govern ordinary people. Either way, it was almost dawn when I crept up to this room—it was our playroom, back in the day, although you wouldn't know it now—and drew the chalk lines of that door." He looked at the wall, where the lines had recently glowed in silver. "I'm still not sure how I did it. You know my abilities as well as anyone alive by now—I'm talented,

not exceptional. The only explanation I can find is that something else was pushing from the other side."

I felt sick.

"It didn't go wrong," he said, reading my face. "Not the way
you think. The runes worked. The faerie came through and
was trapped, exactly as it was supposed to be. It was perfectly
polite—amused, I think, to be summoned by someone so young.
I made my bargain for its freedom, and it accepted that bargain.
I thought I'd done so well. It hadn't escaped, after all."

"They don't only want to escape, Alden. The fae make deals
in the hope of causing mischief and pain. You must have known
that."

"I thought I was being clever. I thought I was outwitting it."
He laughed a little, that bitter self-deprecating laugh I was beginning to understand now. "All those stories of plucky young boys
tricking the fae. Not that I blame the stories. It's right to tell
children that monsters can be defeated. I was just far too slow
to grow up and realise that most of the time they aren't. And so
I pulled open a door to faerie country and wished for whoever
was on the other side to keep my brother from the war."

"And it stole him away." It seemed obvious now. I should have
seen it before. I might have, had the light of Alden's friendship
not been so blinding. But I had believed him that afternoon when
he had told me he didn't know what had happened to his brother;
I had believed, too, that there were no faerie doors left in the
world. Now I knew that neither of these things was true, the last
ten months were beginning to make a new and terrible sense.

I tried to collect myself, to speak as normally as I could. "I'm
sorry about your brother, truly. I just don't understand what
you've been trying to achieve with our research. Even if we
could safely deal with the faerie behind that door, your brother
is lost. The fae never give back the people they take."

"Thomas isn't lost," Alden corrected me. "He's a hostage. Or
perhaps it would be more accurate to say a reward."

"A reward for what?"

"For doing what it tells me." He paused, and again I saw that familiar sifting and organising, that decision of what to tell and how. "That's the one thing that went wrong with the spell, on a technical level. I couldn't close the door again. Not all the way. Somehow, the faerie managed to keep a crack open. It can't come out, don't worry, but it can whisper through it, as I'm sure you heard. Every night I'm here at Ashfield, it speaks to me—sometimes in my brother's voice, sometimes in its own. It tells me that Thomas is suffering, lost in faerie country, growing no older and forgetting who he is, and if I don't help him, he will stay there forever. But I can free him. All I have to do is open the door and let the faerie in."

My throat was dry. "Let it into what? The world?"

"Into me. It wants me. It's hungry for a physical form."

"And you've been trying to close the door all the way." I put all the warning I could into my eyes—as though, at this late stage, I could shame him into sense. "Of course you have. You wouldn't be so monumentally *stupid* as to think you could do anything else."

"If I close it, Thomas really will be trapped forever. The door will be subject to the Accord—it will never be opened again. I need to get him out. The trouble is, I also needed to make sure it would work this time, especially after what went wrong at Amiens. I need it to be safe when—"

"When you let the faerie behind that door out," I finished flatly. "When you make a bargain with it."

"It was what you wanted too, wasn't it? To make a bargain that would save your brother?"

"Not like this! I was going to write a proposal and present it to the Faculty for further study! We all were."

"And how seriously do you think the Faculty will take it? A proposal presented by four undergraduates, two of them female, one of them not even Family? Oh, they might look closely enough to see that the spellcraft is sound, they might put it in

the library, they might award someone a *grant* to *look into it*."
The bitterness in his voice startled me. It was my own, reflected
back—only in my case it had grown from years of being looked
down on for my gender, my upbringing, my family; from seeing
my brother used as a weapon in someone else's war and thrown
aside broken when he was done; from a thousand dismissive
glances and sniffs and shoulders turned aside. Alden had never
had any of that. He was the golden child of our year. I couldn't
work out on what soil his resentment could possibly have taken
root. "Nothing will be done for years, if it's done at all. Even if
they agree to lift the Accord, what would be left of your brother
by then? What would be left of mine?"

That stopped me short. I remembered against my will the last
midnight I had seen, the tendrils of bark devouring muscles and
bone and skin, the green glint in Matthew's eyes.

"We can do it now," Alden said. "We know how to trap a
faerie safely between worlds and force it to do our bidding. Next
week is Lughnasa. That's a powerful date—the magic will be
stronger then."

"The faerie is stronger than the imps. I doubt the two of us
could trap it."

"Not the two of us, no. But there are four of us. Two to open
and close the door and make the bargain, two to signal the right
moment and to hold the gate closed."

"Is that why you asked us here?" Strangely, this of all things
felt like a betrayal. Our friendship, this summer, the four of us at
Ashfield...Those were sacred things. The thought that they had
an ulterior motive was sickening, like a church being used for
money laundering. "Asking Hero to help research faerie doors,
then me, then Eddie...Have you been planning this all along?"

It must have sounded terrible to him too, because he winced.
"Not like that. I mean—yes. I have. I've been planning it since
I was twelve. I asked for Hero's help, because I needed it and I
thought it could help her too, and I did the same thing to you

and Eddie. I didn't mean to drag you all into it as far as I have. If the spell could be performed by a single mage, I would have taken our research and done it alone."

"You could have told us earlier."

"I meant to talk to you all about it as soon as we came up here. I just kept putting it off. I knew what you would say. And…at Camford, it doesn't talk to me. The faerie. I forget what it's like. The thought of actually opening that door at last, well…" He caught himself with a shrug, a little embarrassed, and I knew he thought I wouldn't understand. In fact I did, all too well. I remembered how my plan to stay in the room with Matthew over Christmas had broken down at that first glint of faerie light. "Never mind. I've always been a coward about things that matter. But I really do think we can do it."

"We can't." It sounded weak to my ears, and probably to Alden's as well. He had seven years of obsession behind him. I was pushing back with the reflexive thoughts of a few minutes. I drew a deep breath, trying for firmness once more. "I understand why you opened that gate, Alden. Truly. I would have done the same thing to save my brother."

"You wouldn't have. You let your brother go, as you should have, because he asked you to."

"But I didn't *want* to!" It came in a burst of frustration and guilt, like water pushing through a broken dam. "I don't even know if I should have—whether I did the brave thing and respected his wishes, or the cowardly thing because I was more afraid of losing his approval than I was of losing him. If I had known about magic back then—if I could have just made a wish, and he could have stayed safe…" I bit back the words pushing at my throat, knowing that they would bring tears with them. "You see, I do understand. I understand why you need to save him now. But—"

"No, you don't understand." Alden was quiet for a moment, lost in thought or memory. "We communicated well," he said at last. "The faerie and I. Too well. I was twelve, and my soul was open for inspection. It saw not just what I wanted to tell it, but what I wasn't saying. I told it I wanted Thomas to be kept from the war. It saw that I was jealous of him—for being older and better than me, for my parents' favour, and above all for Ashfield. In those days I loved this house with every piece of my heart, and perhaps some of those pieces didn't love my brother, or at least didn't think it was fair that he should have what he never seemed to want. And so when the magic kept Thomas out of the war, it listened to all of my heart. It took him away. That's what it taunts me with every night I'm here. That's why I have to put it right."

I didn't believe it. Still, I remembered what Hero had told me about Alden and Thomas, only hours ago.

"You didn't want your brother taken away," I said, and willed myself to be convinced. "Of course you didn't. You would have let him go to war if you did. You were trying to keep him safe."

"Was I? Or did part of me just hate the attention he was getting and want him to have to stay here if I did? I'm not a good person, Clover. You believe I am because I'm clever and charming, but neither of those things are virtues."

It couldn't be true. It couldn't. "You've always been kind to me," I said, with effort.

"That isn't a virtue either. I've never had cause or desire to be otherwise. I like you very much, and always have. And you've never tried to cross me in anything I want to do. On the contrary, you've helped me every step of the way." My face must have shown something, because his softened. At once, he looked more like the Alden I had known for almost a year, and not the cold, strange young man who was talking about wishing his own brother dead. "Please don't look at me like that. Believe me, it would be so easy for me to say you're absolutely right, the faerie tricked me, I wasn't specific enough in my wishes and it deliberately twisted them to what I didn't want. I'm trying to be honest with you. But I'm not a monster. I want to undo the mistake my worst impulses may have caused."

"You can't," I said bluntly. "Whatever you did, whatever reason you had for doing it, it's done now. The best thing we can do is to close that door. Once it closes properly, you're right, it should fall under the umbrella of the Accord and lock for good. No more harm will come of it. We could do it ourselves, if you don't want to report it. We know how now."

"We know how to do more than that, Clover. We know how to safely bind a faerie and force them to obey us. Hero and Eddie will help if you agree, I know they will."

My voice was coming out strangled, as though there was a hand to my throat. "Why would I agree?"

"Because you can bargain with it to release your brother from his curse. That's what you want, isn't it? We can save both your brother and mine."

"There are safer ways to help Matthew. There have to be."

"Perhaps. But we haven't found them, and he can't wait forever. Besides, you want to do it this way. I know you do."

"Really?" I found a laugh that sounded more like someone being murdered in a West End play. "Because I'm insane?"

"No. Because you're clever and you're ambitious, and you love this." His answer came promptly. He really had been thinking about this a long time. He had been thinking about *me* for a long time, perhaps more deeply than anyone had before. "You haven't been helping me all these months because you like me, or because I tricked you. You haven't even been doing it for your brother, not entirely. It's your research too. I've seen you working on it, and every time we discover something new, your mind and heart and soul catch fire. You're a scholar to the core. Imagine what it would mean for magical scholarship if we succeed in this. Imagine what it would mean for you."

It would be revolutionary. The kind of magic that could change the world. The kind that would give Matthew his life back. The kind that would let me stay at Camford for the rest of my life. At that moment, I couldn't tell which of those things weighed more.

"I can't force you to help," Alden said into the silence. "I can't even persuade you—I know you too well for that. But you want to open that door too. If we closed it without trying, you'd never forgive yourself."

"Perhaps I'll never forgive myself for opening it."

I realised, as I said it, that it was an admission. Not *I would never*, but *I'll never*. I was already speaking as though opening that door was inevitable, as though I had made exactly the decision I was pretending I would never make.

If Alden noticed, he didn't show it. There was no flash of triumph behind his eyes. His face was soft, serious, imploring.

"Not as much as you'd regret never opening it at all," he said.

It was what I had told myself when Matthew had asked me to help him go to war, and I had imagined him staying behind, eaten up with bitterness. If we didn't do it, the rest of our lives would be haunted by what could have been.

I understand now, as I didn't then, what Alden meant when he said how easy it would be to pretend. Because writing this, it would be so easy for me to do the same. I could tell you that it was all Alden's fault—that I was nothing but foolish, that he persuaded me, tricked me, manipulated me. I could even say, as he could have done, that I only wanted to help my brother. It wouldn't be true. I knew what I was doing. I knew what we saw to gain, and I knew what could be at stake if we lost. I was eighteen years old, a scholar of magic, and I was as clear-headed in that moment as I have ever been before or since. I chose, and I have to live with that for the rest of my life.

"All right," I said. "We'll do it."

I think even Alden was surprised. "You're certain?"

"No. No, not at all." Excitement was bubbling in my chest where disbelief had been only minutes before, and it was impossible to stop a faint smile creeping to my face. Alden obviously saw it—his own lips curved in response. "We need to take every precaution. Even if we plan to trap it between worlds, we still

need the binding circle just in case. And we'll need Hero and
Eddie to help. It's too much for just the two of us. If they don't
agree…"

"Yes, yes, of course." He wasn't really listening to me, or to
himself. "We can do it, Clover."

"I hope we can." In that moment, though, I believed we
could. I saw Alden's brother returned, Matthew restored, faerie
magic revolutionised, our work revered. I saw myself a Camford
scholar, now and forever, part of the world I loved. I was still
being cautious, or I thought I was. But the dream of success had
slipped under my caution like a blade under armour and stabbed
me in the heart. The magic was sound, after all. I knew somebody could do it—I was willing to publish to that effect. Why
not us?

"We can," Alden said. His eyes were alight now, and in their
light I could see everything in him that I hadn't been able to
draw. He was incandescent.

I didn't think. I kissed him.

Another lie it would have been easy to tell: that he seduced
me, that it was part of a plan, that it was why I agreed to what I
did. I know some said it later. It wasn't like that. I had already
agreed, and so had he; our plans were made, they were glittering
like stardust in the gap between us, and I reached out and closed
the gap. He hadn't been planning that kiss, or even expecting
it—I felt his breath of surprise, a pause that might have even been
hesitation. Then he fell into it, willing and urgent and tender,
meeting me exactly as I wanted to be met, giving me back what
I gave. His hand went to my waist as it had at the Illusion, firm
and gentle; mine went to the back of his neck, fingers burying in
his hair, and then there was no gap between us at all.

We made so many mistakes that summer, the four of us, and
so many more after. So many dangerous choices, because we
were young and clever and invincible, and I regret almost every
one. But not that one. Never that.

16

"You must be insane," Hero said bluntly.

The four of us were sitting under the oak tree by the stables, shaded from the scorching midday sun. A barely touched spread of cold bacon-and-egg sandwiches and fruit sat in front of us. Inside the stone building, I could hear the faint *thwap* of a horse's mane being shaken and the low comforting crunch of hay being devoured. Otherwise, the open land was eerily quiet. Alden had cast a ring of silence to keep us from being overheard, but it was scarcely necessary. There was nobody here except us.

I had come downstairs very late that morning, still muddle-headed from the long, strange night. The other three had already been awake, packing breakfast into a picnic basket in a triumph of determination over skill. We were going out, Hero had explained to me, to get out of the servants' way and find cooler air. I had known, even before Alden caught my eye meaningfully, why we were really leaving the house, and what was about to be proposed once we were far from curious ears. Yet it had still been a shock to hear what we had discussed last night spoken aloud, dragged into the light of day. I had been expecting Alden to tell the other two about the imp windows for weeks; I hadn't realised, until I saw the surprise on their faces, just how dangerous our experiments had been, and how much we had been keeping from them. And that was without taking into account the truly disturbing news: the existence of the faerie door itself. Not only was I now doubtful that the other two would agree to our proposal to open it, I was becoming uncomfortably aware that in their position, I would never agree myself.

"That's what you said when I said I was going to wear a gold waistcoat with a green suit to the Christmas party," Alden answered Hero blithely. "And it was brilliant."

"That's a matter of opinion. This isn't. And don't you bloody dare act like this is nothing, Alden. Do you think I can't see now what you've been doing?"

"What have I been doing?"

"You manipulated me. You persuaded me to help you investigate the fae, right here, last summer, because you told me that making a breakthrough like that would be to my advantage. You swore to me that it was a purely theoretical exercise."

"You didn't really believe me," Alden said. "You know me better than that."

"I thought I did," she agreed. "I thought you would try to do something stupid sooner or later. I had no idea you *already* had a faerie door open down the corridor off your bedroom, and had done since you were twelve. That seems like something you might have mentioned to me years ago."

"I would have liked to have known too," Eddie remarked, with just a trace of irony. He was sitting cross-legged, quiet, twisting a blade of long grass in his fingers. He didn't look at any of us. "You know, at some point."

I thought it was time to step in. "We can do this." Hero turned to face me, and I immediately wished I'd stayed quiet. I'd seen Hero's disapproval in action before, often employed on my own behalf. Having it directed my way was withering. I couldn't help but feel she could see exactly what had happened between Alden and me the night before, and the thought made me blush to my soul. Nonetheless, I pressed on. "I know we can. The four of us have been working on faerie magic for months now."

"I know exactly how long we've been working on it, Clover Hill." The use of my full name, strangely, stung. I could tell it wasn't affectionate this time. "I've been working on it longer than you have. But I thought we were working on it with the intention to present a paper to the Faculty. That's quite a different prospect to opening a door and trapping a faerie for your own ends. I don't appreciate being lied to."

"I thought that was the intention too! Believe me, I thought this was as insane as you did last night. I was as surprised as you are now when I found the door."

"You might not have known about the door. You might have told me you've been opening imp windows all over Oxford."

That stopped me short. I realised far too late that Hero wasn't simply shocked or disgusted or even angry. She was hurt. I remembered the sting of seeing the two of them in the archives all those months ago, of learning the secrets that had been kept from me when I'd thought we were starting to be friends. This was a much deeper betrayal. We were more than friends now—we were family. I *had* lied to her. And the worst thing was, a part of me had been enjoying it. I had felt as though I were circling the outside of the group in that first term, and this had brought me inside.

Was that why I had invited Eddie into the project too, all those months ago? So that someone would always be just a little further out than me?

"I'm sorry," I said weakly. I turned to Eddie, trying to include him in the apology. He wouldn't look up. "I promised Alden I wouldn't. And until last night I didn't realise it meant anything."

"It isn't Clover's fault," Alden said firmly. Any lightness had fallen from his voice now. "I made her keep the imp windows a secret, and I never said a word to her about the Ashfield door. Perhaps I should have told you all earlier, I know, but it truly was for your own protection. You two, especially—if you'd known the door was here when the three of us were growing up in this house, you would have drawn the faerie's attention the way I did, and believe me, you wouldn't have wanted that. It's a nasty piece of work. It nearly had Clover last night, before I got there."

Hero raised an eyebrow. "And…you want to bargain with it?"

"Yes!" He ran a hand through his hair, frustrated. "I do. I want to force it to put things right. I want it to give me Thomas back. Is that so difficult to understand?"

"The desire? No, not at all. It's the part where you genuinely believe you can succeed where so many before you have failed that baffles me. The Accord exists because the fae aren't safe, Alden. Not only the circles—the fae themselves. Changing the method of dealing with them only changes that so much."

She wasn't going to agree. I could see it in her face, in the straight-backed stance and the glint in her eyes. Despair settled on me like a blanket.

"Please," I heard myself say. "It's my brother too. I have to help him. We fought, the last time I went home. About Camford, and the war, and everything. I just…" I wasn't making sense, and I knew it. I couldn't put into words how it all tied together—my guilt over Matthew going to war, my shame over leaving them for Camford, the need to prove that I had been right. The urgent feeling that the world had broken, and we had to fix it now or it would just continue to crack further along the same lines. But Hero was looking at me again, her face softened, and I blinked away tears.

"Please," I repeated.

Hero sighed. "It isn't that I don't want to help your brother," she said, in a gentler tone. "You know I do. I want to help Thomas, for that matter—I loved him too. But what you're proposing—"

"What *are* you both proposing?" Eddie interrupted, looking up for the first time. His jaw was set; his eyes met mine directly, without flinching. "Exactly. What do you need the four of us to do?"

I looked at Alden, my heart unclenching just a little. Perhaps it wasn't hopeless after all.

He returned my look, and I saw his own relief flicker before he turned back to Eddie.

"The trick," he said, "is to close the door at the precise moment the imp—or, in this case, the faerie—has passed through one door but not the other. The only way to find that moment is to have someone stand with their hand to the edge of the door, and signal as they feel it start to cool. In practice, one of us has stood in the circle while the other stands by the door. This time, though, Clover and I will both need to be in the circle to make the deal, and to ensure the spell is strong enough. We need one of you—preferably two, one on each side—to stand by the door and give us a signal. And once we have it trapped, we need you both to hold the door with a locking spell. That, I imagine, will definitely take two of you. It took one of us to hold the imp window."

"Why does it need to be held? The fae can't usually break through a closed door."

"They can't break through a door closed on *both* sides. This will only be at half strength. And judging by the imps, they can summon a good deal of will when they're truly trapped."

I remembered how the door had shuddered and blazed under my fingers, the first time I had been the one to hold it. I said nothing.

"That's all you need to do," Alden added. "You won't be in the circle—it can't take you. You're just telling us to slam a door shut, and holding it shut once we've done it. It sounds simple enough, doesn't it?"

"I think it sounds dangerous," Eddie said frankly. "A second too late, and the faerie would be through."

"It wouldn't get far," I said. "The usual circles would be there, if the worst happened. There's no reason to assume that what happened at Amiens would happen again. This isn't a battlefield."

"No, just four people who have never summoned the higher fae before, making God knows what kind of mistakes. I want to help Thomas and Matthew, I do. I just don't think this is the way. Hero—"

He turned, looking for support, but Hero's lips were pursed thoughtfully.

"If this does work," she said slowly, "then it really would be momentous. Forget the kind of research the Faculty couldn't ignore—we could take this straight to the Board, to the papers, to anyone who would listen. We needn't tell them we'd done it, of course, not yet. But we'd know for sure it would work."

"Exactly," Alden said. "It wouldn't matter what happened at Amiens anymore. We'd have the ways and means to safely deal with the fae. The Accord could be lifted, because of us."

Hero nodded, and her face hardened. "I'd like to see my father take me out of Camford then."

"Except," Eddie reminded her, "it *isn't* safe. If the faerie does come through—"

"It won't," Alden said. "Clover and I have practiced this for months. We can practice again now, all four of us. The two-door method will work."

"Will it really?" Hero asked suddenly. "No, Alden, you shut up, I'm asking Clover. You'll just tell me what you want to believe. Clover, is the scholarship sound? Is there any reason for it not to work?"

Here is where I have to make another confession: I knew what I should have answered. If Alden had told Hero what he wanted to believe, as she quite rightly predicted he would, it would have been because he had truly made himself believe it. That was how Alden's brain worked, what made him so convincing and so difficult to resist. He was absolutely capable of persuading himself. I wasn't. The scholarship *was* sound, as far as it went. But the scholarship was far from perfect, especially when we were learning out of scraps from old books and illegal experiments. I remembered the moment when the imp had broken through, all claws and snarls and flashes in the dark; how helplessly we had laughed afterwards, when it was one umbrella-strike away from being not funny at all. That *could* happen again, of course it could. Our timing was still an instinct, not a science. I remembered the jolt of fear when it had leapt from the circle as though the chalk lines on the floor held no power at all—and we never had determined for certain why that had happened. All of this rushed to my mind in a surge like a landslide, and I pushed it away with the same force.

"If we do everything the way we've planned," I said evenly, meeting her gaze, "then there's no reason in the world it won't work. The scholarship all checks out, Hero. I promise."

She sighed. "I'll have to see the notes for myself," she warned. "But if I agree, then very well. I'm with you."

Relief swept over me in a wave. I nodded tightly, eyes suddenly hot. "Thank you. And I really am sorry—"

"Don't thank me," she interrupted, but her voice was more resigned now than angry. "This is my best chance of staying at Camford, as you well know. As far as you two go, I haven't forgiven you quite yet for keeping things from me. I probably will, though. Give me until this evening. And for God's sake, don't let there be any more secrets."

"Believe me," Alden said with a wry smile, "opening a faerie door and accidentally wishing my brother through it is as far as I go. I'm not *that* interesting. Thank you."

She allowed him a faint twitch of a smile in return.

"Eddie?" Alden prodded, not unkindly. "Are you with us? It would be a lot more likely to succeed with your help."

"I know." Eddie's voice was unexpectedly bitter. "That's what's unfair. Do you think I don't know what will happen if I say no, and you don't attempt this? Thomas will stay trapped, Matthew will stay cursed, Hero won't be at Camford next year, and you'll all blame me. How could you not? It would be my fault."

Even Alden looked taken aback. "Well," he said, after a pause. "Possibly. Although by that logic, you refusing could be saving our lives."

"We'd never know for certain, though, would we? All we'd know for certain would be that I'd stopped you. *If* I stopped you. If I actually thought I could, then I might do it, and let you hate me—I've survived worse. But I wouldn't, would I? You'd go ahead without me."

He was looking at Alden, and Alden answered. "If it was up to me," he said, "then yes. I can't do this on my own—the trap won't work. Even two would be difficult. But if Hero agrees, and I have Clover on the inner circle...I would try it without you."

"And then," he said, "whatever happened would be my fault too."

I forced my throat to work, my tongue to move. "It wouldn't be your fault," I said. "And nobody's forcing you to do anything. If you don't want to help, then..."

My voice dried up. Because that had already come out wrong, hadn't it? Of course he didn't have to join us in breaking the most important law of magic—of course no one had any right to force him. It wasn't a question of *not wanting to help*. I simply couldn't quite bring myself to tell him not to do it. I wanted it too badly, and I feared that he was exactly right—without him, it either wouldn't happen or it wouldn't work.

Eddie looked at me for a long time. His face was still, and it was impossible for me to see what thoughts were turning behind his cloudy-sky eyes. "No, I'll do it," he said at last, abruptly. "If there's a chance, then...I do want to help. Of course I do."

I reached out and squeezed his hand on impulse, and he smiled faintly as he squeezed it back.

"Thank you," I said. "Only if you're sure. I mean that."

I didn't, really, and he must have known it. The most I can say for myself is that I tried.

"It's only a faerie, after all," he said, with his best attempt at bravado. "My grandfather always said there was no real harm in the fae. You just have to be firm with them."

"Well, then," Alden said, and if he sounded calm, I could see the excitement brimming behind his eyes and fizzing under his skin. "It looks as though we're summoning a faerie."

We did it at midnight.

It was the most powerful hour, according to the textbooks, the space between one day and the next. For the same reason, we also decided to do it on the first night of August, Lughnasa. It was one of the nights my brother's curse was strongest, when the veils between worlds were thinner, when deals between mortals and the fae had traditionally been brokered. If we were successful, I told myself when my nerves wound so tight they threatened to break, it would be the last night it would ever have any hold over him again.

I had worried our friendship would be poisoned after that morning by the stables. The first day or two, it was—there was a faint unease, a lingering distrust, an occasional hesitation before one of us would speak that hadn't been there before. But, like a fever rising to combat a toxin, once we started to prepare for Lughnasa, the wild secret rush of it submerged everything, and we fell back into the old patterns of research and brainstorming and practice as though nothing had ever happened. In some ways, we were closer those few days than we had ever been. Hero visibly cast off the weight of her father's plans, now we had a plan of our own to thwart them. Eddie said nothing further about his doubts and threw himself into the research as though determined to look neither back nor to the side. Alden was lighter, happier, freed from years of secrecy; I, in turn, was freed from the guilty secret of our nights in the Bodleian. I hadn't noticed the subtle tension those silences had created between us until it dissolved like a sigh of relief.

Neither Alden nor I spoke of what had happened between us the night I had found the faerie door. That seems odd to me now;

at eighteen I was glad of it. I wasn't sure what it had meant to me, what I wanted to come of it, whether I was more afraid of Alden wanting more from me or wanting nothing at all. Yet the energy between us had changed, blazing and tangible like the silver light that had flooded the room. I would be aware of his movements a heartbeat before he made them; I suspected, by the way he would pass me my glasses before I reached for them or shift to make room for me before I sat down, that the feeling was mutual. We barely touched, but every glance we shared was a shiver on my skin.

Midnight at Lughnasa arrived hot and dry and airless, the kind of night that feels breathless with anticipation. All four of us had been the same all evening, so high-strung and over-excited that I'm sure every member of staff knew something was happening. Fortunately, Alden's parents were away again, and Morgan was too well-trained to give us more than a very shrewd look as he served us our supper and we burst into giggles for no reason.

Any laughter had died by the time we stepped into the room with the faerie door. It was dark, without that eerie silver sheen, and when we lit the oil lamps, the shadows were ghost-like and trembling. I wished, not for the first time, that we were doing this in one of the rooms at Ashfield that had electricity.

"I never did like this room," Hero said with distaste.

"That's utter rubbish," Alden said absently. "You never gave this room a second thought in your entire life."

"If I don't like something, darling," Hero said, at her most Hero, "then that's exactly how I treat it."

Their bickering would have been comforting, had it not been just a little too fast and too glib. I could hear the nerves beneath it.

We set to work like clockwork, books sprawled on the floor for reference. Two circles. The simple ring for us to stand in, the ring that would allow us to receive and channel faerie magic.

The second ring, the binding ring. The ring that had broken at Amiens and caused so much trouble. It shouldn't be needed, of course. We drew it anyway, just in case.

The faerie door we didn't need to draw. It had been there, waiting, for years.

"Hero, Eddie, can you two stand on either side of the door?" Alden stood from where he had been putting the finishing touches on the runes, brushing chalk dust from his hand.

I checked the runes yet again, just to reassure myself. To my unpractised eye, they were perfect. Even if a faerie made it through, it would get no further than most. Faerie bargains used to be made all the time. It had rarely been dangerous before Amiens. It would be even less dangerous now. Surely. Surely.

"Is everybody ready?" Alden asked briskly. He was addressing all three of us, but his eyes were asking me.

It wasn't too late to stop all this. And yet the thought was unbearable. It was like being poised on a rope, waiting to swing out into the river. The anticlimax of stepping down, of missing that thrill of weightlessness, was so much worse than the niggling worry that the water was dirty and I just might drown.

I stepped into the circle beside Alden. His hand slipped over mine, held it, and I felt a quiver of electricity before he squeezed it and let it fall.

"Thank you," he said quietly, then looked over at Hero and Eddie. "All of you."

"Well, go on," Hero said, but softly. "We haven't got all night."

Together, as we had the very first time we opened the imp window, Alden and I spoke the words of the spell.

We had pitched well together before. This time, after months of practice, we were perfect. Our voices blended, strengthened each other, and a surge of power spilled through me and out into the world.

The lines of the faerie door glowed bright silver, and the

air was suffused with light. Its cool metallic scent coated my tongue—and something sharper this time, a tang like salt air or petrichor. Faerie country.

The faerie was waiting. The door was barely open when the silver glow turned its cooler blue. Eddie caught his breath; Hero snapped, "Now!"

We didn't need the signal after all. We could see it: a shadow against the door, tall and slender, human but for the head that tapered into fragile antlers.

Alden and I spoke as one. The door slammed shut.

"Hold it!" Alden ordered, and Eddie and Hero flung their spells against the door.

Not a moment too soon. There was a shriek like the wind on the moors, a flash like lightning; the lines buckled, swayed, shuddered. Then the faerie door was translucent as a pane of frosted glass, and there was a faerie standing behind it.

I had seen illustrations of the fae in Lady Winter's books. I had seen pencil sketches and engravings, watercolours and oils, even one blurry photograph. I had known what to expect. And because of that, all I could think was it looked utterly unreal. The long, thin limbs, almost insectoid, glowing a soft silver white; the gossamer-thin wings; the wild white hair and green eyes enormous in the pointed face. It was like the first time I had seen the Houses of Parliament in London, that perfect postcard image, and couldn't shake the familiar thought that I'd like to see the real thing someday even as I stood before it. I thought of the Cottingley faerie pictures that had taken the country by storm the year before, the eerie superimposed, paper-thin quality of the tiny figures. This faerie had exactly the same painted look—only it was transparent, at least six feet high, and unquestionably alive.

There was only one unexpected thing. The fragile antlers I had seen weren't antlers at all. They started at the shoulders, entwined around the forehead, spiked above it in a silver-brown crown delicate as spun sugar. Branches.

"It's a dryad," Eddie said, very quietly. "A silver birch."

"You can't get through," Alden said, in what seemed to me in that moment more wish than fact. "You're trapped in the space between doors. We want to negotiate."

It spoke. I had always imagined the fae to have upper-class voices, soft and precise. I don't know why. Perhaps Camford had tricked me into thinking magic the sole province of the aristocracy. This faerie had a voice like the rustle of leaves, or the trickling of water, and I know, I know what a fanciful simile that sounds, but if you ever meet it, you'll understand exactly what I mean.

"At last. It's been a long time since any doors between our worlds opened. I was starting to think you didn't need us anymore."

"It's been illegal since Amiens," I heard myself say foolishly. "All the doors were locked."

My voice caught the faerie's attention for the first time. Its head tilted to regard me. "I know you, don't I?" it said. "I'm sure I do. Have we met before?"

"I found this door, earlier," I said. "You spoke to me."

"I remember. It isn't that I mean, though. You weren't there when I last came through, were you? At the battle?"

Amiens. My breath caught in a rush.

"You were the faerie who broke through at the front," Hero said. Of all of us, her voice sounded the most sure, which I knew meant she was at her most scared. She was the same at university events and college dinners, when the older men would sneer at her and me as though we didn't belong, and she would raise her head a little higher and plant her feet a little firmer. "The one who killed all those people."

It wasn't just a dryad. It was the same dryad.

"They didn't all die," it said. "There are three still on this earth. I can feel them. Oh!" Its eyes went back to me. "One of them was yours, weren't they? You're too young to have a son there. A father?"

I had to swallow before I could speak. "A brother."

"That's what it is. I've tasted your blood. My curse is running through his veins. Is he why you're here?"

I glanced at Alden, whom we had agreed should make the first deal; he nodded at me, encouraging.

"Yes," I said.

There was no time for second thoughts now. This was it, the moment of the bargain, at least on my part. Yet I had never been expecting to make a deal with the same faerie that had cursed Matthew and killed so many others besides. I had thought for days about how to phrase the deal, and as I spoke the words they still sounded like the beginning of a folk story of how yet another stupid farmer's daughter was tricked by the fae. I could practically hear children groaning as their mother read it to them around the fire.

"I want you to tell me how to break the faerie curse that binds my brother Matthew Hill." That wasn't enough, of course. "I want you to let me use that knowledge to break it. And I want him to survive the breaking with his mind and body and soul intact."

It considered, head tilted to one side like a praying mantis. "And this is why you summoned and bound me? This is your condition for my release?"

No going back now. "It is. On my part. Alden will make his own terms."

"I can give you the spell you ask for. Be warned, though, from a human it can only be so powerful. If the curse is too close to his heart, there will be nothing you can do." It paused. "Of course, if you were to let me inhabit your form, I could perform it. It would work then, even were he moments from death."

I shook my head firmly. That mistake, at least, I wasn't going to make. "No. I'll perform the spell. That, and the guarantee he'll survive it sound in body and mind, will be enough."

Matthew's curse had been far from his heart the last time I

had seen it—surely it couldn't have progressed so far in the last few months. Either way, it was the best chance he had.

"Very well." The faerie seemed to expect my answer. "Then I make that deal. Do you know how to make it binding, human girl?"

"Don't do it," Eddie said abruptly. It was the first time he had spoken since the dryad had appeared. "I know we agreed, but that was before we saw it—before we knew who it was. I understand the reason for the Accord now. It wants something."

"It's too late now," Alden said, without looking in Eddie's direction. "We've trapped it. We can't hold it forever, and we can't release it without at least ensuring its promise to depart. We have to make a deal."

"Both of you don't. And not so dangerously. You could just make a deal to let it go."

Alden laughed, a short bark without humour. "Let it go? Do you have any idea how long it took me to trap it?"

"Do you have any idea how long it took the oak tree at our house to grow?" Eddie returned. "Two hundred years, give or take. But when it was old and dangerous and liable to fall on the roof, my father had it cut down. It doesn't matter how long something's taken to grow when it's rotten at the core."

The faerie ignored this exchange. It was looking at me, its green eyes fixed and unwavering. I have never been looked at like that before or since. It made the rest of the world recede into white noise.

"Do you know?" it repeated.

"Yes," I said. "I have to give you permission. I give it."

I felt nothing. The faintest contact across my forehead, more like the brush of a leaf than a human finger. But with a shiver like an epiphany, I *knew*. I knew the words to release a human from a faerie curse, and the steps that went with it. I knew how to free my brother. It felt less like being told than remembering. I fell back, breath catching.

"That's it?" Alden asked. "You have the spell?"

I found a nod. "I have it."

I had done it. I had bargained with a faerie for my brother's life, and I knew how to save him.

The faerie turned its head slowly, deliberately toward Alden. "And you? I know what you want, don't I?"

"I want Thomas back," Alden said. "Alive, unaltered, and unharmed. You stole him from me."

"You asked for him gone."

"I asked for him to be safe from the war."

"And he was."

"The war's over now," Alden said. "We're in a new world. I want him in it too."

"And you know what I want from you in return." Its voice was flat, even by fae standards. "I've told you many times. Your body in exchange for your brother's safe return."

He shook his head. "I'm only offering your release, as Clover did. Make the deal, or be trapped here forever. Those are the terms."

"I might be prepared to agree to them," the faerie said. "Under certain conditions."

Alden opened his mouth to ask the obvious question. He never had the chance. Hero's voice broke in sharply, "Look out!"

For a second, I couldn't see what she meant. Then I saw, and my heart stopped in my chest.

The door was opening. The great silver lines were wavering, parting; the light from beyond was spilling out. All our careful spells were pinging away like buttons from a coat.

That was why it had been talking to us—why my deal had come so easily. All the while our attention was focused, it had been eating away at the clever new magic we had devised to trap it.

"Hold it!" Alden snapped—at Hero or Eddie or both, I didn't know.

"It's no good!" Eddie shouted. His face was pale and slick with perspiration. "The spell isn't strong enough. Not for this."

Another crack, and the door split farther. Beyond it, against silver that scalded my eyes, I caught a glimpse of a vast landscape. It was windswept and overgrown, all vines and thorns and wasteland for miles and miles. Wind ripped through the room, an endless scream of cold and rain and the heady scent of pine; my hair was torn loose and my skirt billowed about my legs. I couldn't breathe.

Alden's face was absolutely white. He was saying something, something about the circles. I could barely hear him over the noise. I could barely hear myself when I shouted back.

"The circle." I raised my voice even further, past breaking point. "It'll hold, won't it? We're still safe."

I heard him this time.

"The circles don't work!" It was what I had suspected, for a long time. But Alden wasn't voicing a suspicion. Somehow, he knew. "They haven't worked since before Amiens. I should have told you, I know, I'm sorry. They're useless."

This was what had happened at Amiens. It came to me with a flare of pure terror, the worst spark of understanding I had ever felt. Private Koenig had made no mistakes. The fae had found a way to break through the binding spells. Had we not left one door closed, this one would have torn through at once. Now we had only moments until the door cracked all the way and the faerie stepped through, in and then out of the useless circle, to the world beyond. And Alden had known it all along.

Had Camford known all along too? Was this why the Accord had truly been brought in?

No time to worry about that—or rather the time had passed. We had one hope, and only one. I raised my fingers, braced against the wind.

"*Beclysan*," I said, and twisted them into a fist.

I had performed the spell a hundred times—on imp windows, to shut my door behind me at Camford, to lazily close a book sitting on my desk. It should have worked. This time, though,

I felt the wind fighting against it, the spell reverberating back at me. I gritted my teeth, and tried again.

Alden saw at once what I was doing. He fell into line, mirroring my stance, pitching his voice exactly to mine. Our spells blended and entwined, strengthening like a twofold cord. Again, and our voices wound tighter, so that I could feel the edges of Alden's mind pushing against mine. It was the closest I had ever synched with another mage, and in the midst of terror it was intoxicating.

It was working. The door was closing. Little by little, inch by inch, the silver was rebinding, knotting back together. My muscles throbbed, my dress was soaked with perspiration, and I gritted my teeth and performed the spell again.

Beclysan. Beclysan. Beclysan.

Then, mid-spell, Alden stopped. His magic pulling away from mine was a physical blow; I stumbled and had to grab at his arm to stay in the circle. He was burning fever-hot through his shirt, and I could feel him trembling, a thin current under the buffeting of the storm.

"Thomas," he said, soft with wonder.

I looked up, squinting through the wind and the flare of silver, tears from both fogging my glasses.

"There's nobody there, Alden! It's a trick. Keep going."

"He's there. I can see him."

"There's nobody there!"

Except—was there? Behind the terrible winged shape of the faerie was a faint shadow—a trick of the light, of magic, of the faerie itself, I couldn't tell. It came closer. Still closer.

We had paused too long. The door was opening again. The light behind it was blazing, brightening, burning.

"Alden!" I grabbed his arm tighter, willing him back, and he shrugged me off with a force that nearly had me out of the circle again. The roughness I had seen as he sleepwalked was back, the glazed look that had been pure terror and now was a horrible sheen of hope.

He wasn't going to help. As long as there was a chance his brother was coming through the door, there was no way he would close it. He would let the door open, or even open it himself, and the faerie would rush into our circle. It would slip into one of our bodies—Alden's, probably, he was the one it had been waiting for all these years—and then it would be able to walk through the world unhindered.

I didn't think. I shoved him as hard as I could, out of the circle, where he could neither do any harm nor come to any. His attention was all on the shadow beyond the door; he stumbled and fell to the ground with a cry of shock. I didn't stop to watch him fight to his feet, against the roaring wind. I turned to face the oncoming faerie, moved my hands once again to position.

My voice was something between a scream and a sob. *"Beclysan!"*

The room was filled with silver now. It glowed so brightly I couldn't see, so thick it was almost liquid; the buffeting of the wind and rain was a living, bruising force. Black things shot across the air around me, and I couldn't tell if they were leaves or branches or books or bits of the house falling down. I could no longer feel my feet on the floor. I could no longer feel my fingers to work the spell.

The spell wasn't going to be strong enough with me working it alone. It couldn't be.

"Beclysan!" I cried, one last time.

I can't describe what happened then. I have only fragments, all flashes and gaps, like a film montage or a letter scored through with a censor's black pen.

The wind tearing at my clothes, endless and hungry. Light like the stars had split apart. A sharp cry and a crack like the fall of a great tree.

I felt an impact on my shoulder, a single hard blow, the floor rushing up to meet me.

I felt the world billow and snap like a sail in the wind.

And then I felt nothing at all.

17

Clover.

The voice came from a long way away—so far, in fact, that I wondered if it weren't from my own head. I couldn't place it. I couldn't place myself. The world beyond my closed eyes was slippery, amorphous. I had a vague sense of being home, in my childhood bed and my childhood body, in those safe days before the war, but when I reached out to draw it closer, it slipped through my fingers.

"Clover!"

My name again, more insistent. Not from inside my head. Outside it. My head itself was pounding in sick glass-splintered waves; I forced open my eyes and saw only a vague blur. I rolled over with difficulty, wincing, stifling a moan, and the blur resolved into something not entirely unlike Alden Lennox-Fontaine.

"That's it." His voice was a sigh of relief. "You're fine."

I wasn't sure if it was a question or a command. I nodded, putting a hand to my throbbing forehead as I did so. "Ow… Yes. Yes, I'm all right."

My glasses were on the floor beside me. I fumbled for them, put them on. My surroundings came back into focus, painfully sharp—not my old bedroom at all, but the east wing at Ashfield. The sun was peeking over the horizon, and its grey light illuminated the battered state of the room. It looked as though a storm had ripped through, thrown everything in the air, and set it down again crooked. The floor where I lay was littered with dead leaves.

I sat up, and saw Eddie doing the same by the wall, white and clammy and dazed. Hero was sitting on the couch, her head in her hands, looking very much as though she were fighting not to be sick. The edges of the world felt wrong, off-kilter, and my entire body throbbed. My mind fumbled for what we had been doing.

"The door." The touch of the memory was like a shock of electricity. I straightened at once, ignoring the stab behind my eyes. "Is it—?"

"It's closed. For good, this time."

I let my eyes shut, partly in relief, partly against the spinning of the room. God, what we had nearly done... I thought of that vast, teeming mirror-kingdom seething behind the wall, the burning force of will pushing through, the shimmer of magic in the air, and my stomach churned. How had we been so stupid? We'd had no idea. We could have split open the world.

Alden was saying something I couldn't hear, or at least understand. I had to ask him to repeat it.

"I said, why did you do that?" The relief that I was alive had faded from his voice. It was hardening, solidifying, settling somewhere between accusing and hurt. "Thomas was right there! We were so close."

I blinked, too surprised for the moment to feel anything except dull confusion. "We were *close* to that thing getting out! It was going to take your body, or perhaps mine. It wasn't going to give you Thomas back."

"He was there. I could see him."

"There was nobody there, Alden!" My confusion was beginning to sharpen into anger as the memory of those last few minutes bled through. "I'm sorry about Thomas, truly, but we hadn't made a deal. What do you think? The faerie was just going to let him walk out on his own?"

"Well, we'll never know, will we? You closed the door. It's subject to the Accord now. It won't open again."

"Please," I said, far too calm, "tell me you didn't already try."

"If it's closed, then so much the better," Hero said, looking up for the first time. "It should have been closed years ago—we should have closed it this summer. I can't believe you were so unutterably *stupid*—"

"And you tried to stop us from opening it, I suppose!" Alden snapped.

"I never said I was any better!" Her voice had been shaky; now it was stronger, surer. "I'm the stupidest of the lot, if it comes to it. You trusted your own ego, as always. I trusted you, and I knew better than that. You knew the circles no longer worked, didn't you?"

He sighed, and just a little of the fight ebbed from him. "I suspected. I should have told you, I know. I didn't think it would matter."

"You more than suspected," I corrected him. He had as good as admitted it, in the frenzy of those moments when the door was opening. "That's why you were so focused on finding a safe way to summon the fae, weren't you? How long had you known? Before the imp window?" A terrible thought struck me, like a blast of cold. "Alden. You opened this door at the start of the war. You said the circles hadn't worked since before Amiens. Did you know before Amiens?"

There was a just a fraction of a pause. It would have been unremarkable in anyone else. But I had never once heard Alden lost for words.

"It warned me," he conceded. "That last summer of the war. It was always trying to get me to open the door when I was home from Crawley, to bargain again. I wouldn't. I wasn't worried about the circles then—I was only trying to perfect the deal, to make sure I could save Thomas without letting it free. That summer, its tactics changed. It told me that it had learned how to escape the circles on its own—that the next time someone opened a door, it would be free. It told me that if that happened, and I hadn't dealt with it by then, I would never see Thomas again. Last chance. Amiens was a week later."

"And you never said a word to anyone."

"I never thought it was telling the truth! It said all sorts of things—it always has. Even after Amiens, I hoped it was just… I don't know, a different faerie, a mistake, a coincidence, somehow. It wasn't until that imp broke through that I knew it wasn't. I couldn't have prevented Amiens."

I tried to accept this. I almost could. There was enough to blame Alden for without adding Matthew to the list. Still, I couldn't help but understand the real, unspoken reason why he had told nobody: He couldn't have done so without admitting he had opened that door in the first place. He had kept quiet to save himself, as much as anything else. If he had only told somebody what he had done, what the faerie had threatened… If the possibility could have been investigated, if there had been advance warning…

"You knew," Hero repeated. "And you let us open those doors."

"You knew too," he returned. "At least, you guessed. Clover certainly did. Eddie told us it was dangerous."

"That's right," Eddie said. He had pulled himself into a sitting position in the corner, quiet and watchful, his grey eyes impossible to read. "I did. And none of you listened."

"For God's sake." Alden had recovered some of his equilibrium. "Nothing bad happened to any of you! Clover made her deal. She can save her brother now, just as she always wanted. I'm the one who's lost mine. Seven years of waiting and planning and that thing trying to drive me mad, and it's over."

"It was already over, Alden!" I retorted. "I had to close it."

"And if it had been your brother on the other side of that door," he said, "would you still have had to?"

I never had the chance to reply. There was a knock at the door.

It was almost comical—the way the four of us froze, silent and rigid, as though we'd been caught stealing from the local shop or in a compromising position behind the library shelves. My eyes swept the room, looking for anything that might betray what we'd been doing. The room was in a mess, but that could be for any reason. The leaves, similar, in a house full of magic.

The circles on the floor. The evidence that someone had been performing a faerie spell.

Alden had the same thought. "*Mundo*," he whispered, and with a sweep of his hand the chalk lines shook themselves and disappeared.

It was Morgan, the butler, at the door.

"Forgive me," Morgan said. If he noticed we were all in our clothes from the night before and the room behind us was in chaos, he was far too well-trained to show it. "There's a telephone call downstairs for Miss Hill."

I'd never had such a thing in my life. It took a moment for the words to even make sense. "But…I don't know anyone who owns a telephone. Present company excepted."

"Well, perhaps somebody bought one," Alden said. He was very good—it sounded light, inconsequential, the barest hint of an edge. Nobody would have guessed they had interrupted a furious row. "Why don't you go find out?"

I hesitated, torn, unwilling to leave. But if there really was a call, it had to be from home. Nobody else knew or cared where I had gone for the summer. If home were calling me, they had gone to trouble to do so—the nearest telephone was at the post office in town. It would have to be an emergency.

"I'll be back soon," I said, to Alden or Hero or Eddie or all of them. I couldn't work out why that sounded almost a threat, and then I realised. I was worried about what Alden might do left in the room with the closed door.

The phone was in the downstairs hallway, an incongruous object of brass and wood amidst the oil paintings and old furniture, the wide round circles of the bells and receiver giving it a look of perpetual surprise. I raised the receiver to my ear uncertainly. This, of all things, felt like magic.

"Hello?"

"Clover?" It took me a moment to identify the voice—one of the middle girls, but they sounded similar enough in person, much less funnelled through acres of wire. Then I heard the tiny stammer and knew with a tightening of my chest that it was Holly. "Is that you?"

"Yes. Yes, it's me. Are you all right? What's happened?"

There was a rush of static as Holly sighed. "Oh, thank God. Clover, how far away are you? You need to come home right now."

<hr />

I could hear Alden and Hero arguing all the way up the stairs. It should have been a familiar sound, but there was an edge to it this time, a sharpness that pushed beyond exasperation. I didn't care anymore. My heart was pounding; everything else was numb. Last night already seemed a terrible dream.

Nobody noticed me as I opened the door. I had to clear my throat before I could speak.

"It's Matthew," I heard myself say. My voice sounded very small and far away to my own ears; everything else seemed to be receding down a long, dark corridor. Far away at the other end, the others quieted and turned to me. "That was Holly—she drove into town to use the telephone. Something went wrong with the curse last night. They couldn't wake Matthew this morning. They think it's taking him."

"My God," Alden said softly. His anger at me drained away at once. "I'm sorry."

I couldn't stop to acknowledge the sympathy. I was walking a tightrope—if I didn't keep my eyes fixed ahead, I'd fall and break.

"I have to go home," I said. "At once. I hate to leave you after all this, but—"

"I'll come with you," Eddie said. He was already standing, pale yet composed.

"You don't have to—"

"I want to." I couldn't remember the last time he had ever interrupted me. "Please. It's your brother. Two Camford scholars there are bound to be better than one."

I couldn't answer, just nodded quickly around the lump in my throat.

Hero got to her feet, gingerly. "I'll drive you to the station."

"Thank you," I managed.

Alden was looking at the wall where the door had been with great attention. As the three of us started to leave, he seemed to suddenly remember our existence. His head snapped around.

"Wait!" He sounded brisk now, almost businesslike, and that was far more disconcerting than his earlier grief and fury. "Before you go, we need to agree on one thing. We all need to promise never to mention what we've done tonight to anyone. If anyone asks, we went to bed early last night, around ten, and nothing happened. All right?"

"Obviously," I said, as dryly as possible.

"I mean it, Clover. I need you to promise."

"I said yes!" The numbness from the telephone call was starting to wear off. "What do you want, a binding curse?"

"It might be an idea." He must have seen the disbelief on my face. "Of course that won't be necessary. I trust all three of you with my life. We just need to be sure, that's all."

"Alden, my brother might be dying!"

"Mine might be dead!" His anger flashed unexpectedly to meet mine, like a blade. "Yours you at least made a deal to save.

There's still a chance it might work. We closed the door before we could do as much for Thomas."

"It doesn't look like the deal's worked out so well for Matthew, does it?"

He didn't answer that. "I'm just trying to keep this from causing any further damage. It's for your sake as much as mine. We could be arrested if this gets out. At the very least, we'd be expelled from Camford."

"I don't bloody care about Camford right now!"

"And that's why I need you to promise," he said. "You will, sooner or later. I need to protect all of us."

"You need to protect yourself, you mean." I was truly angry now. It might have been at least partially self-defence—anger was a far easier emotion than fear or shame or the horrible dread curdling my stomach—but not entirely. "Would you really care if I told, as long as I kept you out of it? I don't have time for this…"

Alden's fingers were around my wrist before I could turn. I pulled back, furious and indignant, and they held fast.

"It's better for everyone if there's nothing to be kept out *of*," he said. "Please, Clover. It may be that nothing comes of this. If it does, though, then we need our stories straight."

"Get off me," I said coldly. He didn't move.

A frightening doubt surfaced. Alden had been standing right in the centre of the ring beside me, after all, and the faerie had come very near to breaking through. I had pushed him from the ring; he would have just had time to get back in. Perhaps it had been too near. Perhaps…

But it was Alden. I was looking him dead in the eye. This wasn't the faerie in his body. He hadn't been possessed. I had seen Matthew in the grip of enchantment; I knew what it looked like. I knew my friend; I recognised him now. And I wished with all my heart that I didn't.

"I promise," Eddie said into the silence. It might have been his usual talent for keeping the peace coming to the fore, but there was something in his look—a darkness, a flash of warning—that I hadn't glimpsed before. I remembered, out of nowhere, that he had been expelled from school for fighting. "Let her go, all right? I promise."

"So do I, of course," Hero said. If my voice had been cold, hers was ice. "I have no burning desire to incriminate myself, especially when we're more likely to be arrested than expelled. I suppose I may leave in my own car now?"

Something wild and trapped flickered in Alden's eyes. Then he heaved a sigh, frustrated, and it was gone. He dropped my wrist and stepped back, raising his hands in surrender. "Of course. I wasn't going to *kidnap* you, for Christ's sake. I was only saying—"

"I know exactly what you were saying. Come on, you two, before I change my mind and walk out on all of you."

"We went to bed around ten," Alden repeated. "That's the story if we're asked. Do you all have that? Eddie?"

"I'm not stupid." Eddie turned unexpectedly. His fists were clenched. "You never quite believed that, did you, even back in school? I'm really not. I was the one, if you remember, who told you not to do this."

"I know you did. But—"

"And I'll tell you something else, now we've seen it. That was the same dryad that was at Amiens. I couldn't have guessed that—neither could Hero or Clover. But you could. You'd seen it before. Dryads almost never come through the doors. The moment we worked out that it was a dryad at Amiens, you had no more excuses not to know that it was the same one. And you never said a word. Why not?"

Again, that uncharacteristic hesitation. "I didn't know. I never saw it properly when I was twelve—I never realised what it was."

"Right." Eddie snorted. "Now I know you think I'm stupid."

"I don't think you're stupid." He had gathered himself again quickly, but not quickly enough. The cracks had shown, and something had peeked through. "I think you've never told a lie in your life."

"Well, I'm about to start, aren't I? We went to bed at ten o'clock and we didn't nearly let a powerful faerie into Ashfield. Will that do?"

"Yes," Alden said quietly. "That will do. Clover—"

I couldn't give him my word. I was too furious, too hurt, too sick with worry and magic and the blood-metal taste of betrayal. Instead, I gave him a short, sharp nod. Then I turned on my heels, and I left.

It was a silent drive to the train station. God knows none of us felt like talking. My head was pounding and my stomach was acid—I had to close my eyes once or twice when the car took a tight bend or bumped over a pothole. Hero's face was pale and set, fixed on the road ahead; I couldn't see Eddie in the back seat, but I was willing to bet he didn't look good. It was more than that, though. The air shimmered with resentment and guilt, like a heat haze. Talking about it would only solidify it further, and yet I couldn't imagine talking about anything else.

"Do tell us how he is, won't you?" was all Hero said as I clambered out of the car. Her voice was strange—coolly formal, when Hero's anger always blazed hot—but I took comfort at least that she had spoken.

I nodded, miserable. "Thank you. And—I'm sorry."

I didn't know what I was sorry for—for convincing them of this nightmare, for being convinced myself, for knowing the risks and lying about them, for running out on them now, for some vague unspecified harm I didn't want to think of—only that I was. I was so, so sorry.

The train was half-empty—we found a carriage easily, and as soon as we did Eddie curled up against the window, buried his face in the crook of his arm, and closed his eyes. I sat opposite him, back to the engine, and rested my head against the glass as the track receded and the wheels picked up speed. I was going home, I reminded myself. I had the faerie's spell—that at least I had gained from last night's adventure. Perhaps I could save him.

Please. Please, let me save him.

"Your plants," I said to Eddie, at least three miles too late. We had each grabbed a very small bag from our rooms. Everything else was still back at Ashfield. "The ones you brought with you. Are they—?"

It took him a moment to stir. "They'll be all right. The gardeners at Ashfield will take care of them for a day or two. When I get a chance, I'll send word home and one of our gardeners will go and pick them up."

Eddie always seemed so beyond class and money and Family. I forgot, sometimes, that he was as wealthy as Alden and Hero, that his home was a great house like Ashfield and had gardeners too. I had a flash of him, younger than Little John, crouching by their sides as they trimmed hedges and planted herbs.

"Are you angry with me?" I tried to say it as reasonably as I could. "I just want to know—I understand if you are. I know you didn't want to go ahead with the door, and you agreed because of us. Because of me. And I misled you. I told you it would be safe."

"I'm not angry at you." I think he meant it. It was difficult to tell with his face hidden in his sleeve and his eyes closed. "You didn't mislead me. You misled Hero, maybe. I didn't believe you."

I wasn't sure if that made it any better. "What about Alden? Do you really think he knew who that faerie was all along?"

"I don't know. He said he didn't. Please, I really don't feel well. I just want to sleep."

I left him alone. I still felt sick myself, but there was no way I could rest.

⎯⎯⎯⎯◇⎯⎯⎯⎯

There was nobody to meet us at the station again, of course. They didn't know when I would be here, and none of them would leave Matthew's side to wait. It occurred to me, in a brief flicker, that this was the first time any of my friends were seeing my home, that I should probably worry about what Eddie would think of the bare platform and the dirt road leading to town. But I didn't care, and anyway, Eddie showed no sign of thinking anything in particular. He had recovered himself by the time the train stopped; as it pulled away, he took my hand comfortingly. His face was back to normal—only a little pale and quiet, as if privately resigned to something he was going to put out of his mind for now.

"It'll be all right, Clover," he said. "I'm certain it will."

I found a weak smile. "Come on. It's this way."

The walk was long and hot, the grass dry in the summer sun. Fortunately Eddie was used to walking for hours in the country. He kept up easily, even when my house at last came into view and I broke into a run.

Someone was obviously watching for me. The door burst open before I could reach it, and Iris and Little John were there. It was like my last homecoming, only so very different. Their faces were tear-streaked and frightened, and they clung to me as if to a life buoy at sea. I dropped my bag and wrapped my arms around them, my heart thrashing like a caged bird in my chest.

"It's all right," I said, trying to be calm, torn between wanting to comfort them and longing to know what was happening. "I'm here. Where's Mum?"

And there she was, standing in the doorway, her face tight and worn, her hair falling from its pins. Her sleeves were rolled up—they always were when things were serious, as though she could pull us through with hard work alone.

We had spent months not speaking; I had spent those months reliving our last fight whenever I had thought of her, alternately furious and guilt-ridden and self-pitying. It didn't matter. I knew that as soon as our eyes met, and in the midst of everything I could have sobbed with relief.

"You came," she said.

"Of course I did! This is Edmund Gaskell," I added, though I wasn't sure if Mum had even seen he was there. "He's a friend of mine from school. He wanted to help."

"Hello, Mrs. Hill," Eddie said. "Don't mind me, really, I don't mean to be any trouble."

"We're glad to have you," Mum said, but absently, the way she might offer a cup of tea. Her mouth found the right pleasantries; her mind was up with Matthew, and her eyes were fixed on me. All her worries about the posh students at Camford, and when it came to it she didn't even care that one was standing right in front of her.

I took a deep breath. "I'm sorry for what I said—"

Mum was already shaking her head, grabbing my hands in hers. "Never you mind that. Water under the bridge. I'm sorry too, for what that's worth. Our Matty will be so glad you're here."

I knew things were bad if she was calling him Matty. "How is he?"

Mum's hands tightened around mine, the only sign of any strong feeling. "Poorly," she said. "Very poorly. He's been unwell all year—spring was very hard on him, and the midnight at midsummer lasted nearly two days. I almost wrote to you afterwards, even though he wouldn't have it. This was different, though. I did what we always did: I tied him up, I waited outside the door. It was a lovely night, soft and golden, nothing sinister at all. Not until twelve, when the winds picked up. Strange winds, they were, and when I looked out the window, the fields were covered in silver. Shep was barking, and the sheep were screaming. Matthew never made a sound. Maybe that's how I should have known. Maybe I should have opened the door and checked on him. But we never open the door."

I didn't have the words to ask.

"When I went in to let him out at dawn, I couldn't wake him up," she said. "And the...the mark's spreading. The curse mark, the part of him that's turning to wood." I couldn't remember her ever saying that aloud before. It was too strange, too surreal. She preferred to think of it as a war wound and nothing more. "It's been creeping up his neck and across his chest all day. It hasn't got far to go before it touches his heart. He'll die then, won't he?"

"I don't know," I said faintly, then shook myself. "Yes, he will. Is he awake?"

"Not since I found him. He called out a few times in his sleep at first. He's gone quiet altogether now." She hesitated. "Can you do something?"

We had done something, the four of us. We had opened a door. And straight away, the message had come from home that Matthew was dying.

"I'll try everything I know." I returned the squeeze of Mum's hands and found a smile. "Let's go see him."

18

He wasn't going to be glad I was here. That was the first thought to cross my mind, brief and nonsensical, as I opened the familiar door and saw him. He wasn't going to know I was here, or that anyone else was. He had already gone somewhere else.

Mary and Holly glanced up from his bedside at my approach, their eyes anxious and hopeful at once. My brother lay there, the bindings that had held him all night untied beside him. As a scholar, I probably would have advised keeping them on, but I could see why my family hadn't. His eyes were closed, his chest barely rising and falling, his face ashen. Despite all I had been imagining, my stomach still clenched in shock at how gaunt and frail he had become since I had seen him at Christmas. His shirt was unbuttoned to mid-chest, and for the first time since he had come home after the war, I could see the extent of the curse that was turning his flesh to wood. This time, there was no doubt that it was growing. It was happening before our eyes. Inch by inch, long fingers of bark crept out from his shoulder, up his neck, over the curve of his jaw. And, slowly but surely, to his heart.

If the curse is too close to his heart, there will be nothing you can do. The faerie had warned me of this. I should have realised the warning was a threat.

This was my fault. I had let the faerie into the world, despite all my efforts to the contrary. The door had opened—only a crack, but enough. Enough for the faerie to complete the curse that had been halted so long ago on the battlefield at Amiens. Enough to make sure that the counter-curse I had bargained for would come too late to save him.

"Clover…"

I shook myself at Holly's voice, so small and so helpless, and found a smile. "It's all right," I said. "I know what to do now."

I did. I had ripped open the world for exactly this. Perhaps, after all, I had reached him in time. But all I could think, over and over again, was that I was in a story in which the foolish farmer's daughter makes a bargain with a faerie that ends in her losing everything she loves.

I sat on the bed and placed my hand over Matthew's chest. I had to find his heart precisely, I knew that without knowing why. It wasn't difficult. It was struggling frantically against my palm, racing for its life while its owner lay far too still.

The words the faerie had given me knew the feel of a human heartbeat. They pushed at my throat like a scream. I closed my eyes, opened my mouth, and let them out.

Most of the magic we use is rooted in Latin, Old English, medieval French and German. Other cultures have their own magic, rooted in ancient versions of their own tongues—we had covered some of these in the second semester, and Hero in particular had always revelled in their differences. Yet even these feel shared in some way, shaped by human minds and driven by human needs. This was different. It was magic in the fae language, entirely alien and strange. My mouth spoke it without a trace of understanding, the words themselves shaping my tongue and teeth and breath. It was thrilling and frightening, like being possessed by something I had invited in. I knew in that moment just how arrogant Alden and I had been. No amount of study would ever have got me here had we not opened that faerie door.

The power of that spell was like nothing I'd ever felt. It rushed from me in a great wave, flexing my back and shoulders, throwing my head back, leaving me breathless. It hit my brother with the same force. His body twisted on the thin mattress; a sharp cry was wrenched from somewhere deep. His eyes flew open, and they gleamed bright green. They looked at me, a short, sharp contact that froze my insides, and then he fell back, shuddering, fighting for breath.

I watched, waiting, holding a breath of my own. The horrible grey fingers of bark faltered, stilled. Then, like a creature shaking off an imagined threat, they kept going. They moved forward one inch, then two.

"It didn't work," Mum said, too calm, too gentle. She was crouched beside him now, her hand smoothing his hair from his forehead as she did Little John's when he was sick. As she had my father's, right at the end. "He's going."

"No," I said numbly. "No, that's not possible."

It was. Of course it was. His heart beneath my hand was growing weaker, struggling for each beat; each breath was coming with more and more effort, with longer pauses in between. And the look in those green eyes—it had held nothing but triumph.

If I hadn't made the deal, the curse would have taken months or years to devour him. Now it was swallowing him whole, and it was all my fault.

"I'm sorry," I heard myself say. "I'm so sorry…"

"Clover." Eddie's voice, trembling right on the brink between calm and panic. "Here, take this, here…"

My free hand reached out for what he was offering and clasped it blindly. A flower. A rose, scarlet and full-bloomed, with a long stem. It was from the plant I had brought home from Camford and left behind in my room, my birthday present from Eddie. I could see it now over by the window, much larger and repotted into an old bucket with a broken handle. I should have known.

My sisters were hopeless with houseplants, but Matthew never could resist rescuing a living thing.

"Try again," Eddie said. "Just try."

I should have asked why, or at least wondered. I didn't. It was a plant, and Eddie, who was so uncertain of everything else but knew everything about plants, was handing it to me. I gripped the stem as tight as I could, heedless of the thorns biting my palm, while my other hand pressed tighter against Matthew's heart.

"Please," I said aloud, as though it was a spell in itself. "Please."

Then I drew a deep breath and spoke the spell again.

The force of it tore through me, less violent this time, just as powerful. Matthew's back arched; he drew a sudden sharp breath, as though at the thrust of a knife. His body creaked and groaned like a tree in high wind. I nearly snatched my hand back on reflex. Then I looked again and held tight.

Because the tendrils reaching for his heart were truly receding now. Little by little, like poison drawn from a wound, the long fingers of bark crept away from my hand, back toward the wound in his shoulder, leaving bare flesh in their wake.

It's working. I held the thought at arm's length, not daring to hope. But it was. It was working.

Farther back, farther—now the silver bark that covered his shoulder was shrinking too, like watching a patch of damp spread in reverse. The patch was little more than the size of a fifty-pence piece when his body shuddered just once more, and then was still.

My mother's voice broke the silence, unusually quiet. "Is that it? Is the curse broken?"

I looked at Matthew, still half convinced we had killed him. Yet he didn't look dead. His face had a flush of colour now; his breathing was gradually becoming more regular. Mary and Holly were staring at Eddie and me in awe, as though until that moment they hadn't believed either of us could do magic.

"I think it is," I said. "I don't understand how, but…"

"You're bleeding." Eddie's hand was on mine, very carefully removing the flower from my hand. I uncurled my fingers at his touch, reflexively; they were sticky with blood, and yet I felt no pain. My mind was dazed, past relief, past astonishment, well past noticing a few scratches from a few thorns.

There was no time to ask Eddie what had happened. Matthew was stirring awake. His eyebrows quirked, his brow furrowed; his eyes blinked once, twice, then stayed open. The sight of them, fogged and exhausted but unstreaked with green, was the most welcome thing I had ever seen.

"What—?" he asked huskily. He started to push himself up on one elbow, then fell back with a wince. "Is everyone all right?"

"Why wouldn't we be?" Mum demanded, in the over-accusatory tone she takes when she's very happy indeed. "You were the one we all thought was going to die."

"Why?" His eyes fell on me, and he blinked again, this time in surprise. "What are you doing here?"

"Hello to you too," I said, as airily as I could through a throat thick with unshed tears. "Aren't you pleased to see me?"

"I'm pleased to see anything, to be honest." His voice was clearing, becoming his own again. "It's been a very weird night. Is anyone going to tell me what happened?"

What *had* happened? I didn't know how to answer. It was too big, too confusing, there were far too many questions and all of them entangled with guilt and worry and doubt. I looked at Eddie and saw it all mirrored in his eyes as he looked back at me.

"What happened," Mum said firmly and unexpectedly, "is that your sister saved your life. You did, Clover," she added, as though I'd opened my mouth to protest. Perhaps I had. "You said you were going to, the last time you were home, and I said things back that weren't fair. I'm sorry for it."

I had waited a long time to hear those words, and now I didn't deserve them. "I said things too—"

She shook her head before I could go on. "That's as may be. But you saved your brother, just as you said you were going to. I'm proud of you. Your dad would be too."

There was no question then of what I was going to say. All at once, the worry and tension and miseries of the last seven years broke the dam I had built for them. I burst into tears. I cried helplessly, as I hadn't since my father died and perhaps not even then. Mum didn't know half of why I was crying—I didn't myself. Nonetheless, I felt her arms around me, and with them the touch of the old, safe world before the war had come and shattered us apart.

―――――――――――――⟨⟩―――――――――――――

We didn't stay like that for long. We weren't a demonstrative family, and besides, there were chores to be done. Mum went to get everyone a bite to eat and prepare somewhere for Eddie to sleep; Mary went to give the stock their supplementary feed, it being the parched summer months of drought; Holly went into town on the motorcycle to pick up supplies, and Eddie went with her to use the only telephone for miles. I took Iris and Little John in hand: They were worn out after the long day of panic and confusion, and they hadn't eaten since breakfast.

Matthew had fallen asleep almost before we had left his room—real sleep this time, deeper and more peaceful than I'd seen since he had come home. It wasn't until everyone else had gone to bed that I had the chance to talk to him alone. I hesitated on the ladder leading up to the attic, unsure of my reception. We still hadn't spoken since that terrible Christmas.

"It's all right," Matthew's voice came, soft and drowsy. "I'm awake."

"I know." I could tell the difference—I had a lot of experience sharing rooms with my siblings. "I just wasn't sure if I was welcome."

"Of course you are, idiot." I heard the creak of the bed as he sat up, then the lamp beside the bed flared. "Come here. I never really had a chance to thank you for saving my life, did I?"

"Don't," I said, before I could stop myself. "Please."

"Why?" He frowned, his eyes still adjusting to the light. "What's the matter?"

"Nothing, I hope." I clambered through the trapdoor and sat on the bed beside him; he shifted to make room. "How are you feeling?"

"Good," he said, and the wonder in his voice told me that this time, for perhaps the first time in years, it was true. "I mean, sort of like I've had the flu and then been turned inside out, but...it doesn't hurt."

"Can I see?"

Matthew pulled down his shirt collar willingly, which more than anything told me he truly wasn't worried. His exposed shoulder was flesh again, slightly pink and tender. Only where the curse had struck was a small knot of silver-grey wood.

"It's not all the way gone," I said, and couldn't dismiss a twinge of unease.

He shrugged his collar back into place. "I'll take it. Like I said, it feels fine." He hesitated. "I used to hear it whispering all the time, in the dark. There's nothing now."

A shiver went through me from head to toe. "What did it say?"

Matthew looked away, uncomfortable. "Nothing, really. Just rustlings. Like a forest when the wind shakes it."

"You never told me that."

"Why would I? You couldn't have done anything."

"I did, didn't I?"

"You did." A smile tweaked his mouth. "Thank you."

He didn't know what he was thanking me for. But just then, in that moment, I didn't care. I let myself hope that it was worth it—the long hours of study, the terrors of the long, dark night, my still-throbbing head, and the fears of what worse might have happened. I had done what I had said I had gone to Camford to do.

"Why did you take off that night last Christmas?" Matthew broke the silence. "I know I bit your head off. I'm sorry. I'm doing that to everyone lately, and I never used to. It didn't upset you that much, though, did it?"

"It wasn't just you," I said. "Mum was furious at me."

"What else is new? She'd have got over it by morning."

"But she was *right*." The words came out painfully. "You both were. About Camford, and about me looking down at you all, and about me pretending I was there for some noble reason when really I just wanted to do magic and build a life for myself. And I was so ashamed."

"You're eighteen. You're allowed to want your own life. You're allowed to want to do magic. Who wouldn't?"

"You said—"

"I know. That wasn't about you, all right? That was…" He paused, frustrated. "I don't know what it was about. Just that sometimes I'm sick of pretending everything's fine."

That struck me with the physical force of an epiphany, like learning the term for a concept in magical studies that had been vague and nebulous and now suddenly made sense. Because we were all pretending, weren't we? It felt like since the war and the epidemic that followed it the world had been irreparably broken, and we were all trampling barefoot through the shattered fragments as though nothing had happened—as though we weren't all broken too.

Last night we had come so close to breaking the world again. Somehow, despite everything that told me otherwise, I couldn't quite be sure we hadn't.

"What happened to you when the curse took hold last night?" I asked. "Can you remember?"

Matthew started to shrug the question off, but something

in my face must have told him I had a reason for asking. "Not really." He shifted uneasily, and the bedpost creaked. "I remember my legs binding together and digging down into soil; I remember branches and vines creeping around me until my bones cracked; I remember a voice screaming in a language I couldn't understand. It was cold—proper cold, the kind that stops your heart—and I couldn't breathe. Things like that. The usual. Why?"

It was my turn to shrug. Unlike Matthew, I took it. "I just wondered."

He gave me a long, hard look.

"I'm getting married," he said, out of nowhere. "Next spring, probably."

"What?" I glanced at him sharply, and whatever my face showed, it made him smile. "How? Why? To whom?"

He snorted. "Well, there's an insight into your priorities. In the usual way. For the usual reasons. To Jemima Piper, in the village. We got engaged before I went away. You really didn't guess?"

I shook my head dumbly. Jemima. I knew her, of course, but only vaguely—she had been four or five years ahead of me at school, and had left to work for the post office when the older girls were still a bewildering blur of half adults to me. Fair-haired, short, kind, smart, and efficient at her job, she had given sweets to the little ones when I brought them in on errands... I had never given her more thought than that. I was starting to realise how self-centred I had been the last few years, and how little I knew anybody who had been around me at the time.

"Does she know about...?"

"The curse? Yeah, she does. It's a little difficult to hide, when you're turning into a tree and lose your mind at set dates. She grew up on Pendle Hill, you know. Witchcraft runs in her family. She says she doesn't mind if it's now in me as well, but I do. I've been pushing the engagement off again and again, because

I wanted better for her and our family. So please, Clover, if you know something—if something worse is coming—tell me."

"Nothing else is coming," I said, and willed it to be true with all my heart. "It's over. I promise."

He didn't believe me—I could see that. But he must have decided that I did at least think I was telling the truth, or at least that he was too tired to argue about it. His eyes were already growing heavy once more.

"Well," he said. "That's something, I suppose."

<hr />

The kitchen was quiet when I came down. A single candle was burning at the table; Eddie sat perched on a chair in its light, his fingers curled around a mug and a plate of biscuits in front of him.

"I said I'd sleep here on the sofa," he said softly, so as not to disturb anyone upstairs. "Your mother left me all these biscuits. Do you want one?"

I shook my head and sank down on the chair opposite. I was bone-achingly tired, and my stomach was still queasy. "No, thank you. They're meant for you, to make up for all the other hospitality she can't offer you. She'll be mortified that a young gentleman is in her house and consigned to the sofa."

"She did offer to swap me her bed," he admitted. "Quite a few times. But I like the sofa. I like your house awfully, you know—and your family. Is Matthew well?"

"He's fine. Better than I've seen him in years."

"Good," he said. "I'm glad."

"What happened?" The question burst from me. "The flower. What did it do?"

"I don't know." Eddie shook his head, tired and bewildered. "Not really. The plant was there on the bedside table. I just looked over at it, and it was straining toward your incantation like mad, as though it wanted to be near it. I remembered that when hedgewitches treat curses, they use roses, and I just thought what if...?"

Only Eddie, in the midst of a life-or-death act of magic, would look toward a plant on the bedside table. I didn't know whether to laugh, cry, or hug him very tight.

"Thank you," I said quietly.

The corner of his mouth twitched in the faintest possible smile. "I'm glad it worked," he repeated.

There was something he wasn't saying. I could see it in his hesitancy, the long gaps between sentences as if each time steeling himself to say something different.

"What is it?" I asked. "What's wrong?"

Eddie sighed gustily. "I telephoned Ashfield, as I said I would," he said. "Hero had already left. I told Alden that Matthew was safe."

"Was he pleased to hear it?" That came out more sarcastic than I meant. Actually, I was worried.

Eddie understood. "He was. He's upset with you about Thomas being locked on the other side of the door. He didn't want Matthew to die."

"No, of course not." I rubbed my aching temples, annoyed at myself for being so melodramatic. "I'm sorry. So what's the problem?"

"Well. It turns out it wasn't just Matthew."

I froze. My stomach, already sick, went cold. "What wasn't?"

"The curse reawakening. It was all of them. The other soldiers from Amiens, the ones who were struck with the curse and lived. Three men altogether, like the faerie said. Your brother, Charles Perowne, and Gerald Drake. The other two died this morning. The curse took them."

I hadn't even known the names of the other surviving soldiers from Amiens until then. We had a Drake in our year—Harold Drake. Gerald must have been an older brother of his, or a cousin. And one of our lecturers was a Perowne—John Perowne, in History of Modern Magic, an older man in tweed, perhaps Charles's father or uncle. All these thoughts raced through my head, confused and disjointed, and overlaying them all was the image of the tendrils of bark creeping toward my brother's heart.

We had killed them. We had let that door open too far and let the faerie who had cursed them snake strands of magic into the world, and they were dead.

My God, Alden had said. *I'm so sorry.*

"Alden said to remind you not to say a word," Eddie added. "Especially now."

"I'm sure he did," I said, with a welcome shot of irritation. "It was what he did, wasn't it? He never told anyone that he had opened a door, that his brother was stolen, that the fae could break through the circles. Then one broke out and murdered its way through a battlefield."

The same faerie. Eddie had been right—it wanted something. Presumably it still did. I just couldn't see what it was—what any faerie could want badly enough to kill on such a scale.

"Do you really blame Alden for that?" Eddie asked. "For Matthew?"

I sighed. "Not really," I said, and tried to mean it. "He was twelve. He didn't know."

"There's nothing to stop us from telling someone, you know. The Faculty or the Board. We promised, that's all. Promises can be broken."

"Do you think we should break this one?"

He thought about it for a long time. I couldn't read what those thoughts might be, or where they would take him.

"If it was just me, I might," he said at last. "But it isn't just me. It's you, and Hero, and Alden. I don't want to betray you all."

"I feel the same." I also, though I didn't say it, felt a rush of relief. I knew then that I was as bad as Alden. I didn't want to lose

Camford because of what had happened at Ashfield. "Not when I can't think what good it would do. The door's closed now—the danger's come and gone, and it can't come back. And...and then there's Matthew. I don't know what the Families would do to him if they knew I'd saved him. Nothing bad, perhaps..."

"Oh, nothing good," Eddie said, and his voice was surprisingly grim. "I forget sometimes. You don't know them like I do. It might be different if you could tell them how it was done— you can't, can you?"

I shook my head. It was gone. The spell that had made so much sense only hours ago had unravelled in my head like a ball of wool. The deal had been one use only.

"No." That, above all, seemed to make up Eddie's mind. "No, I think Alden was right after all. We'd best put it behind us."

"For now, at least." It was a weak compromise. As though I truly thought we might change our minds. "We can talk about it again later. Back at Camford, if we don't go back to Ashfield. The four of us."

"Yes," Eddie agreed. He looked very, very tired. "You're right. Whenever we're next all together."

〜

But we never were all together after that. I think, even then, we knew that we would never be together in this world again.

Part Three

The Magical World, 1929

19

I was giving a lecture in Advanced Summoning Spells when the news came.

I had started lecturing only that year, the last year of my PhD. It was always a struggle—there were very few women on the teaching staff, and though I had considerably tamed my Lancashire accent in recent years, I still had students complaining that I could be neither heard nor understood. They were snobs, like most of the Families, yet I couldn't help fearing they had a point. Teaching didn't come naturally to me. I had gone through school addicted to learning, through Camford entranced by magic—I didn't know how to make my subject sound interesting to bored young people who didn't want to hear about it. This, combined with the fact that it was a bright spring morning and I was outlining a particularly fiddly and complicated piece of magical theory, meant I was sensitive to the restlessness of the class and more than a little worried I was going to lose them. So when I felt a ripple of interest coming from the back of the hall, a whisper spreading like wind through grass, I knew it didn't have anything to do with me.

I didn't see any point in ignoring the disturbance; if I did, it would only get worse. I put down my papers, looked at them over the rim of my glasses, and let my voice tighten with disapproval. It was a trick I'd learned from Lady Winter, a long time ago. "I'm sorry, is there something you'd like to share with the class?"

As it happened, this wasn't very effective, as there was exactly that.

"It's the German lock," a boy at the back spoke up. He had come in late, a copy of the *Practitioner* in his hand, and his face was flushed with excitement. "The one that seals off the borders to faerie country. It's been broken."

My heart skipped as the murmur across the classroom escalated to a roar. I didn't know why I felt suddenly sick—except that it was worrying news, of course, and anything to do with faeries was an unearthing of everything I had spent almost eight years trying to bury. The locks. They were all that stood between our world and faerie country, all that held the world to the Accord. One broken was not a disaster in itself—the entire point of the Accord was that all three would need to be smashed for the doors to be able to open again. And yet…

"Does this mean another war?" someone asked in the front row, and I snapped back to myself.

"No, of course not. The war wasn't Family business—it was between the governments of the world." Just over a decade since the war had ended, and already these students could barely remember it. I felt impossibly old, a relic of a lost generation. "I'm sure the Board won't be happy that the Germans broke their lock, but that's why there are three to start with. Even if they wanted to, they hardly have the power to declare war on Germany."

"It wasn't the Germans who broke it, though." Someone at the back was still reading. "It was an Englishwoman. Lord Beresford's wife, it says. He had access to the lock, as a cultural attaché. She murdered him, and she broke the lock. Now nobody can find her."

It was at that point that I knew exactly what I had been fearing, without letting myself think it. My head spun; I had to grip the sides of the lectern for support.

Lord Beresford's wife. Lady Beresford. I still had trouble keeping the Families straight in my head, but that one I would never forget.

Lady Beresford was Hero.

I hadn't even heard about Hero's marriage from Hero herself. After Eddie and I left her at the railway station, I never heard a word from her all the rest of that shattered summer. I heard nothing from Alden either, and I told myself that suited me fine, since I had no desire to write to him. Hero, though, I wrote to several times—and received no reply. I asked her if she was safe, then I begged her to forgive me. I understood her anger. She had warned me that there were to be no more secrets. I may not have known that circles wouldn't work so certainly as Alden had, but I had suspected. She had agreed to the experiment only because I said it would be safe, and I had lied. Now our project had come to an end—there would be no proposal to the Faculty, no way to stop her father from pulling her from Camford. I had betrayed her trust, and I knew it. Clearly, she knew it too. I returned to Camford that September not knowing if I would find her there.

When I knocked on her door, it was answered by another young woman: Gretchen Ingalls-Fletcher, a dark-haired scholar in the final year of her degree. I knew her to say hello to, and she had been friendly enough in return, but she wasn't in our classes, and Hero had always been vaguely scathing of both her commitment to her studies (limited) and her choice in footwear (ostentatious). Her face, which had been puzzled and suspicious, relaxed when I asked after my friend.

"Oh, you don't know," she said. "Hero isn't coming back to school. She's getting married next month."

"What?" Whatever my face had shown when Matthew had

told me about his engagement, it was now showing it twice as hard. "She wouldn't! To whom?"

"Um... I can't remember his name. Someone in the government, quite rich, a lot older than her." An understandable trace of satisfaction crept into her voice. Gretchen hadn't liked Hero, possibly because Hero kept looking at her shoes. "Her father's pleased, from what I hear. They announced it in the paper this week. I suppose you don't get the *Practitioner* where you live..."

We didn't, of course. But I got it at Camford, and I saw, two months later, the photo in the society pages of Hero's marriage to Lord Beresford. She looked radiant, naturally—a tall, veiled figure draped in gauze, arm in arm with a short, middle-aged man with a walrus moustache. Lord Beresford was, according to the *Practitioner*, a widower and a foreign diplomat in Europe with a tidy property in Bournemouth and an upcoming post in Berlin; Hero was only described as the daughter of the honourable Mr. Horatio Hartley. I wrote to her once more, this time congratulating her on her marriage, and finally received a letter in return. It was gracious, formal, and utterly impersonal. Only the postscript had any trace of our old warmth.

Don't blame yourself for what happened, she said. *It wasn't your fault, and in the end it worked out well. I don't suppose we'll see each other again. Good luck with your studies, darling, and I really do wish you all the best.*

I knew she had to speak in veiled terms, in case the letter was read. But the drawing of a clear line—*we do not speak of this again*—broke my heart more soundly and surely than it had ever been broken before or since. That line cut off our entire friendship and left it floundering and dying on the other side. By the time I received it, Eddie had left Camford and gone home, never to return. Alden and I hadn't spoken since Ashfield. Now I had lost Hero, and it was all my fault.

The wedding had been the toast of the season, or perhaps the scandal. Rumours had flown as to why a beautiful, intelligent, headstrong young woman had given up the university she had fought to attend in order to marry an uninteresting middle-aged Board member when there were far richer suitors available. Then the months passed, no mysteriously premature baby had arrived, no blackmail plot emerged, and everyone lost interest. There was an underlying feeling that Hero and the Hartleys had somehow got what they deserved, though it was unclear what crime they had committed and why Lord Beresford was a fitting sentence.

I tried not to think about Hero—or, by then, Eddie or Alden. I wanted Ashfield firmly behind me, with all its loveliness and heartbreak and terrible, crushing guilt. Certainly I had more than enough to occupy my thoughts. My results in my first year had been good, but the time spent on friendship and faerie doors had taken a subtle toll on the final exams. The following year, I was ill a good deal and had to come back in the summer term to make up for lost papers. I didn't mind—the extra work gave me something to do and a place to be at a time when I would otherwise have sunk down into memories of the golden summer the year before. By third year, my scholarship was in jeopardy, and I needed every minute of every day to save it.

I spent all my free hours in the Camford Library once more—not our room this time, and certainly not on the roof. I found my own corner, an alcove overlooking the atrium, where I could see the students come and go and nobody ever looked up to see me. The only person who knew I was there was Grimoire, and he would move past me with barely a nod, pausing only to quietly deposit a book on my table that I hadn't known I needed. There were no more friendships, no spiralling late-night conversations, definitely no excursions across the Oxbridge to chase imps in the night. Every fibre of thought was spun into essays and practical tests and independent research, and if those studies were a little dull now that my sole focus was trying to give

Camford what it wanted, at least nobody was going to get hurt this time. I had broken enough rules, pushed the bounds of magic far enough. Two men were dead.

I earned my Merlin Scholarship, against all odds. I earned my master's in the magical arts. I started a PhD, focusing on summoning spells of the late eighteenth century. Theoretical magic, a fresh take in a well-explored field. I was now shrewd enough to know that Camford would not grant a scholarship to a scholar who wasn't Family to study practical spellcraft, however high her marks had become, and certainly not to attempt anything revolutionary. There was no way my blood could be strong enough—and if it was, they wouldn't trust it. My success was measured by how well I could assimilate myself into Camford despite my shortcomings. I couldn't afford to challenge it, and after Ashfield I didn't want to. I wanted to belong to this old world of dusty tomes and ancient stone. I especially wanted nothing more to do with faeries.

I started to believe that the summer at Ashfield and everything that had come before it had been a dream. It had been such a different time, when the long dark nightmare of the Great War was still a fresh scar on our minds. It had been a new, bright world, a world that had been smashed apart and that so many were determined to put back in a different shape. Now the pieces had fallen to earth, and already many had settled into old familiar grooves. Camford had done exactly what it had hoped to do and survived the social upheaval intact. My students today barely remembered what the generation before them was trying to forget. It was easy to consign that summer and even my friends to the same forgetfulness.

But now one of the three locks had been broken, and it had been Hero who had broken it. I couldn't ignore, anymore, what that meant. It meant that the voice I had been trying to silence for eight years had been right, and we were all in terrible trouble.

Camford, unsurprisingly, was not on the telephone. The nature of the door meant it didn't receive letters or telegrams either; even to send a raven meant smuggling the poor bird into Oxford under your coat. The lack of communication was irritating, but it was surprising how infrequently it mattered. Camford really was its own little world. Sometimes I went weeks without leaving its grounds and never even noticed.

Today, though, Camford was very much interested in the outside world, and I was at a disadvantage, having had a lecture to finish before I could get free. By the time I stepped through the door, both the Oxford and Cambridge phones were being used by students and staff talking in low, serious voices. I had to go out into the streets and find a public telephone box in Cambridge to make my call to the Boardroom.

"May I speak to the minister for magical enforcement, please?" I said, when I finally got a voice at the end of the crackling line.

The woman sounded flustered, and I could only imagine the chaos pressing in at her back. This was probably the worst day they'd had since the war ended. "He's very busy, I'm afraid. I can check with him. Who should I say is calling?"

"Tell him it's Clover Hill." I paused, hesitating. "Tell him I can call on him in person if it's easier."

Telephones, after all, were hardly amenable to private conversation. Half the Board would be listening in impatiently on this line right now.

"I doubt it will be." I couldn't tell if that was meant to be helpful or condescending, and it didn't matter. I'd learned long ago that I wasn't going to get far in the magical world if I stumbled over every perceived slight. "Hold, please."

I held.

When she came back, the woman's voice was faintly surprised. "He says he'd be happy to meet you this evening, if you'd like to call at his apartment around six o'clock. Would that be convenient?"

It would be a long drive from Oxford, where my car was parked, and it would mean missing an afternoon tutorial. I didn't hesitate. I doubted my students would be very interested in discussing magical history today anyway.

"Tell Mr. Lennox-Fontaine I'll be there," I said.

———※———

I hadn't seen Alden in six years. It had been at graduation, a drizzly grey afternoon lining up in the Great Hall to have our bachelors of magic conferred. We still hadn't really spoken since Ashfield, but what had begun as mutual burning resentment had mellowed into cool civility. He had kept things from us; while I hadn't quite forgiven him for that, neither could I wholly blame him when I had willingly taken the risk and Matthew's curse had been broken as a result. On his part, I knew he hadn't forgiven me for closing the gate and leaving Thomas on the other side. I don't think he ever quite believed I would have done the same had Matthew been at stake. And yet he had never turned the school against me, as he could have done, and he treated me with courtesy when we met in public. I hoped he had come to understand that I had done what I had to do.

I watched him walk across the stage that day, golden and glowing; he would have watched me too, neat and serious in my green dress and hired robes. (I had learned to dress myself by then, but I will never have Hero's style.) We exchanged brief congratulations at the reception afterwards, tentative, as though we barely knew each other. I had been surprised to hear he wasn't coming back for postgraduate study, and even more so to hear that his father had a job lined up for him on the Board of Magical Regulation.

"And…you want to work there?" I asked.

He shrugged. "There's nothing else I'd rather do. I might as well make my father happy for a change."

I understood the veiled reprimand. Alden had never cared about research for the sake of it. His only ambition had been to save Thomas, and I had thwarted it.

"It's interesting, isn't it?" he said, and he genuinely did sound interested, rather than bitter. "Of all of us, you're the one who got everything you wanted in the end. You didn't even have to give up Camford."

My hands curled into fists of my own accord; I forced myself to draw a breath and release it. He had no idea what I had given up, and I couldn't expect him to, since I had never told him.

Alden had done well in government, to nobody's surprise. He was clever and charming, as he had warned me once, and that, along with his wealth and his Family name, had taken him where he needed to go. In the last Board shuffle he had come out as minister for magical enforcement, a position only a few tantalising steps below the first minister. There were rumours that he would be taking those few steps very soon. I wasn't interested in politics—especially magical politics, which as far as I could see meant nothing at all outside the Families—and I saw it all as a tremendous waste of potential. Research was where he had flourished, and he could have done great things rather than legislated them. There was no doubt he was an important person, though, as such things were reckoned, and a successful one. Exactly the sort of person to one day inherit Ashfield—although, from what I heard, he was scarcely ever there now.

The penthouse flat in Mayfair that I came to that evening was about as different from Ashfield as it was possible to be while still boasting the same wealth and status. It was the flip side of the gold coin: sparse and stainless and shining, where Ashfield was steeped in tradition, all polished metal and white marble and glass. It certainly wasn't as welcoming. I rode the gleaming elevator to the top with folded arms, afraid that everything I looked at would spontaneously smudge.

To my surprise, Alden answered the door himself.

"Clover." Even guarded as it was, his voice—warm, light, a verbal patch of sunlight—was just how I remembered it. I hadn't known what kind of welcome to expect, and this was better than I had anticipated. "Come in. How are you?"

He had aged well but visibly—more visibly than I had imagined. His marble face had sharpened and thinned, an impression aided by the crisp cut of his suit and the more severe slicked-down part of his curls. Their gold was threaded through with the occasional streak of premature silver now, and there were fine lines at the corners of his mouth and eyes like flaws in porcelain. He could have passed for a good deal older than the twenty-seven I knew he was. He was still, regrettably, achingly beautiful. I was no longer an eighteen-year-old girl awed by glamour and class, but I had to take a moment to remind myself of this for the first time in a while.

"I'm well, thank you," I answered him automatically, as if talking to some friendly stranger—or, perhaps, to the minister for magical enforcement. "How are you?"

"Oh, fine." His mouth twisted in the familiar self-deprecating smile, and my heart gave a treacherous little jump to attention. "Busy. It's the election next month, you know. And of course there's this business with Hero, which I assume is the reason you've come to see me."

I smiled back ruefully, against my will. "It is."

"You'd better come inside."

The sitting room looked larger than the entire flat had any right to be—a wide expanse of white and gold, with a circular staircase curving up to a second floor. Alden gestured for me to sit on a long green velvet couch and sat down himself in the armchair opposite. The lightness left his manner as he did so. I saw the extra years settle on him, or perhaps it was the extra responsibility. Perhaps it was just the first chance he'd had to sit down all day.

"I can't tell you much more than the papers reported, I'm

afraid," he said, without further preamble. "You'll have heard about Lord Beresford."

I didn't mince words either. "They're saying Hero murdered him and broke the Berlin lock. How? What happened?"

"They found his body in his study, at their apartment in Berlin. We don't know how she did it, not yet. A curse of some kind."

"It can't be true. Hero wouldn't murder anyone. Self-defence, possibly…"

I could see that—Hero straight-backed and cool, pointing a pistol at a highwayman on the road at night. Or defence of some-one else, that too made sense. Hero would tear the sky down for the few people she truly loved. She wasn't a murderer.

"Perhaps it *was* self-defence," Alden reminded me. "Perhaps her husband caught her in his study, and she had no choice. Or perhaps the murder was committed by someone else entirely—an accomplice, or somebody threatening her. We won't know until we find her. Whatever else may be in doubt, she *did* break the German lock afterwards. Her husband's ring opened the door, and she was seen leaving the building. Nobody's seen her since. The assumption is that she's headed to Paris, then London."

"To break the other two locks."

"She won't get that far. Every mage in Europe is after her now. There are armies waiting at both sites."

"What are the orders? To kill her?"

"If we have to." He pinched the bridge of his nose. "I don't want it to happen either, Clover. You know that, don't you?"

"Of course I do! That's why—" I hesitated. "Can I speak freely?"

"Why do you think I haven't offered you tea? I gave all the servants the evening off when I knew you were coming. Hold on, though." He muttered something under his breath, and his right ring finger and left little finger joined together. A very neat silencing charm; I noted the faint echo as the air around us closed. I thought of the one he had cast around us that morning under the tree by the stables, all those years ago. "There. Just in case anyone's listening at keyholes, literally or metaphorically. Go on. I suspect I know what you're about to say."

"This is our project at Ashfield again," I said. "Isn't it? Hero is breaking the seals because she wants to open a faerie door."

"I don't know. Truly."

"If you had to guess."

"I would guess the same as you do," he conceded. "If Hero has refined the double-door method, then she can bargain for anything she wants, as long as she can open a door. The trouble is, faerie country truly is sealed, since you closed the Ashfield door. If she wanted to deal, she would first have to break those seals open."

There was just a hint of recrimination in his voice, the first since I had come in. I ignored it. "But why? Hero was never interested in faerie magic, in a practical sense. She thought it was too dangerous, and what happened at Ashfield proved her right. What would possess her to take a risk like that again?"

"I don't know," he repeated. "I could suggest a few things, but I'd be speculating. Hero made it very clear that she held me responsible for that night at Ashfield and wanted nothing more to do with me. I haven't spoken to her since before she was married."

Married to Lord Beresford. One of the very few men in England who had access to the Berlin lock. Had she been planning this, even then? Or had she pieced it together later, as the opportunities arose? Was this a plan years in the making, or a desperate flight?

I couldn't even speculate. I knew nothing about what Hero's life had become in the years since we were undergraduates and the world, broken as it was, was all before us to make new.

"We need to tell them," I said into the silence that followed. "I don't mean we need to make it public—as few as possible is fine.

But the Board, the first minister, the Faculty, anyone who needs to know. We need to tell them what we did at Ashfield."

He didn't pretend to be surprised. He must have known when I had called what I had come to say. "Would it really help? Whatever Hero is trying to do, it's unlikely she'll succeed in breaking all three locks. Not with the forces of the magical world against her."

"She obviously thinks she can. And what if she does manage it? What if the double door fails and that dryad comes through again? Hero won't be able to hold it back, especially not on her own. She'll be killed, or enchanted, and then it will be loose in the world. We can't take that risk."

"Everyone knows about Amiens already. Everyone knows the dangers of a faerie incursion. If the dryad breaks through, knowing that we nearly let it through once before will scarcely help."

"We're scholars, Alden. It's not our job to keep back information that might be important."

"You may be a scholar," he said dryly. "I'm a politician. We keep back information all the time."

I refused to smile. "I can tell the Faculty, if you like, and they'll pass the information on to the Board. But I think it would be quicker and simpler if it came from you, the minister for magical enforcement. Soon to be more, I'm told, after the election."

"It's too soon to say," he said absently, on reflex. "The votes will be very close. Certainly not if I tell them I opened a faerie door when I was eighteen and two Family members died as a result."

"Is that really what matters to you?"

"No." He looked at me properly, perhaps for the first time since I arrived. "Of course not. You know me better than that."

I did. Alden had never cared about position in Camford; I couldn't imagine he cared about it now. The trouble was, I no longer knew what he cared about instead.

"You can blame me, if you'd rather." The thought of my academic career, my little rooms in Chancery Hall, my family, all crossed my mind in a painful wash like acid. I blinked them away. I had been thinking of those the entire road down. This was more important. "Tell them I did it."

"You would really let them think that?" It was difficult to read his face. "You know they'd come down harder on you than on me—though God knows they'd be hard enough on us both if this went to the courts. And there may be consequences for your brother."

"I'll deal with those, if they happen." Sam Wells was still working for the Board, albeit in a capacity that was little more than a clerk. He would do everything he could to protect Matthew, I felt sure. They still hadn't spoken since the war, but Sam asked after him all the time.

Alden appeared to come to a decision. "Very well. We'll tell them."

I blinked. Somehow, I realised, I had never expected him to agree.

"Really?"

"Really. Don't tell anyone yourself, not yet. I'll speak to the first minister in confidence tonight. For what it's worth, I think he'll keep both our names out of it. Nobody wants a scandal this close to elections, and all that rubbish."

I didn't like the political gloss that cast on matters, but I had to admit to a flicker of relief. I had spent years getting to where I was and carving out a life for myself there. I was willing to throw it away, truly; that didn't mean I was eager.

"Thank you. It's the right thing to do, Alden." I felt compelled to keep convincing him, even though he had made up his mind. "It isn't just the danger to the world, you know. We need to stop her before she gets into serious trouble. This is Hero, for God's sake."

Something shifted in my mind all at once. I'd been focused,

since I'd heard the news, on the problem at hand, the dangers and the hard, necessary steps we needed to take to make sure what we had done all those years ago would cause no further harm. Now the thought of Hero Hartley broke through, the Hero I had known and loved all those years ago. Hero at Corbett's luncheon the first time we had met, white and gold in a sea of grey. On the library roof, braced like an explorer against the sky, her long hair spilling down her back. Curled up on the rug by my bed, reading Rebecca West by lamplight and laughing her generous laugh at what had happened in class that morning. At Ashfield, stretched out on the grass on those impossibly hot afternoons as the sky went on forever. My heart ached as though it were trying to snap in two.

"I wish she'd told me what she was planning," I said, without knowing I was going to. "I wish she'd told me anything, ever."

"So do I." Alden's voice was softer than it had been. "But it isn't your fault."

"Isn't it?" I'd had a long drive to think about that too. "We just left each other alone after that night. I know we were all angry and bitter, but we were friends. We should have tried to make amends. Instead we all went our separate ways, we barely looked at one another after we came back to Camford, like first-years after a regrettable one-night stand, and I can't help but wonder if we—well, if I at least knew something like this would happen and was trying not to see."

"You would never do that," Alden said firmly. "You always looked at things directly. It was one of the things I admired about you. If anyone's to blame, it's me. I've known Hero my entire life. I was the one who should have seen if there was something awry. But as you said: We all went our separate ways afterwards. I haven't seen Hero for years—nor Eddie, for that matter."

"No. I heard he was living up in Scotland, a few years back…"

"He still is." Alden sat back. "In a cottage his family own. I called on him once, after graduation. He's happy enough. Eddie never really did like the world—or Camford. You're not planning to make him a part of this, are you?"

I shook my head. "No. It wouldn't be fair. He didn't do anything except try to help us—help *me*, if that's the way you want to play it."

"Even if I did, they'd never believe it," he said, with a ghost of his old smile. "The door is at Ashfield. It may be closed for good now, but there's enough of it left to read. If anyone goes near it, they'll see it was opened long before you even knew magic existed. We're in this together, Clover Hill."

The teasing familiarity of my full name steadied something unexpectedly. Everything felt real, for the first time since the news about Hero had broken, perhaps for the first time since Ashfield, and it was world-ending and disastrous but reassuring too. We had been pretending for years that none of it mattered. Now we knew it did.

The sky was darkening by the time I left. Alden offered to walk me down to my car, which was parked outside on the road. He offered to take me somewhere for dinner too, but I told him I had to drive back to Oxford. As surreal as it seemed, I was giving a lecture the next morning, and I still had notes to go over if I wasn't going to be arrested.

"I read your paper last month on summoning charms," he said. "It was excellent, as always. You're no longer working on faerie curses?"

"It didn't seem the path to a great career, when nobody would publish it," I said dryly. I was taken aback that he had known about it, much less read it. "Besides, I started to research those to help Matthew. He's been doing very well lately."

"I'm glad to hear it. He married, didn't he?"

"Yes. He and Jemima. They have a little girl now—Rose. Holly and Mary are both married now too. Iris is at university in Manchester, training to be a doctor, and Little John's working on the farm."

"Good." He said it absently. He never met my family, after all. "That summer was the best time of my life," Alden said, out of nowhere.

I found a laugh, though my throat had tightened. "You were sleepwalking most nights. We all thought you were losing your mind."

"Oh, I was. But I was used to those nights at Ashfield. I didn't mind them that year, because for the first time it seemed it might be over soon. And when the nights faded and the sun came up, there were the three of you. You know, after my brother, you three are the only people I've ever loved."

"Yes." I could have said more. I didn't have to. He understood.

"Telephone me from Oxford tomorrow morning," he said, before I got in my car. "I'll have news for you. I'll handle this, I promise."

It was the last time I believed him about anything.

20

I always liked the drive from London to Oxford. My dreams of paying for my family through my glittering career as a scholar had been laughable—I was paid a pittance for the teaching I did and usually told to be grateful for free room and board. But when I had won my Merlin Scholarship, I had given every scrap of the money I had saved for tuition fees in case of failure to my family. They, in turn, had given it back to me with interest in the form of a battered yet beautifully functional two-seater motorcar. I had protested roundly, even as I had stroked the smooth green bonnet.

"I meant for you to put that into the farm or Rose's schooling!"

"Rose is fine," Matthew had said. "So's the farm, at the moment. Tell you what, if that ever changes, I'll steal the car back; would that make you feel better?"

So I had taken it, and the freedom it gave me as I rattled along the highways was a continual delight. I loved being able to drive to Pendle Hill for Christmas or a week in the summer holidays, or up to Manchester to visit Iris, or down to London with some of the other Camford postgraduates to see a play and have dinner. On a summery evening like this, with the wind tugging at my hair through the open window and the narrow roads through the Chiltern Hills curving ahead of me, it seemed impossible to hold on to the panic that had followed me down. Alden had eased that, anyway. He was telling the first minister that very evening—by now, he may have told him already. Hero would be safe. Nothing bad would happen. Surely what we had done as thoughtless eighteen-year-olds couldn't be so hard to undo.

I knew better than that, really. Two men had already died—three, including Lord Beresford. Thomas had been stolen away and locked out of this world. It was already too late to undo anything. And yet I was still startled, as I turned down a country lane framed by hedges and overhanging trees, to see that lane start to slowly spin in the distance.

My mind recognised it at once for what it was: an illusion. I knew exactly how to construct it myself. My eyes didn't believe me, and my hands swerved the car on reflex before I mastered them and put us firmly back on the road. It was supposed to disorient me, to force me to stop the car, that was all. I had to pass through it and out the other side. It couldn't hurt me. The real danger was whoever had cast the spell.

The spell was a strong one. The road ahead twisted in a circle, the enclosing trees spiralling into a long green tunnel. It resisted any attempt at a counter-spell, and when I drove toward it, the car too began to swivel and rotate as though the laws of physics had turned to nonsense. I closed my eyes and floored the accelerator. Dizziness swept over me in a single nauseating wave, and then it lifted, and my eyes opened to a mercifully clear stretch of road.

The sky, though, was no longer clear. Above the rattle of my own car I heard a reverberating thrum, like a swarm of bees overhead. I craned my neck to look up through the trees, expecting to see the shadowy form of another illusion. Instead, I saw something far worse.

I had never been very interested in the various aircraft that had fought in the war—Matthew and all the other village lads were infantry. But my sister Holly had always had a weakness for machinery, and she had taught me enough to recognise the various types by their markings and silhouettes. Bearing down on me from overhead was a Bristol Fighter.

I knew then, with a certainty like death, that this was very serious. An illusion could have been a robbery attempt—they were not unprecedented among mages. Highway robbers, though, did not fly in old wartime aircraft. I could see two men in the pilots' seats, and they were no criminals. They had the matching headgear and grim, focused concentration of professionals.

They were directly overhead, too late to try to evade them. I braced myself for gunfire and bullets. None came. Instead, the second pilot leaned out the side of the plane, raised his hands, and began to throw spells.

I could hear some of them over the roar of his engine and my own—binding spells, freezing spells, spells designed to incapacitate. All of them required far more precision than was possible from a plane aiming at a moving target, but all it would take was a lucky shot.

I tried to swerve the car back and forth, as much as was possible in the tight lane enclosed by trees and stone walls on either side. They had chosen the location of their ambush well. Spells hit to my left and right like falling stars, and there was very little I could do to avoid them. Even so, I thought they had missed me entirely, when a sharp, deep sting jabbed my right bicep.

I cried out and swatted it on reflex. My hand brushed metal; I glanced down, just in time to see a gleaming brass pellet burrow into my upper arm. It was the size of the nib of a pen, shaped like a tiny insect—I felt the wriggle of tiny legs and the buzz of filmy wings under my skin before it stilled.

My heart plummeted. I had read about these in a journal only last term—a new way to deliver spells, one that required far less precision on the part of the caster. So far, it had been used exclusively for tracking spells. From now on, whenever I did magic, the caster would know exactly where I was. No sense in worrying about that now, of course. The mages overhead knew exactly where I was already, and if I wasn't careful, I wouldn't be going anywhere for them to track ever again. What bothered me more was that only one group of people were authorised to use that spell. These were Guards, the small branch of police that investigated crimes for the Board of Magical Regulation. And there was only one reason why they would come for me.

The plane was turning, coming in for another barrage.

Before I stopped to think, my fingers twisted and I spoke the words for flame. Every culture has a version of that particular spell—I tended to use the one in Latin—and it throws just enough fire to ignite a bundle of wood or coal. This one ascended in a sharp curve into the air; the plane swerved, just in time to miss the flames scraping the tail. I gripped the wheel, trembling. God, what was I doing? If that had struck, it would have gone up in a fireball—I had seen enough footage of planes crashing on the news reels at the cinema. I would have had two murders on my hands, and no way to proclaim my innocence. I couldn't strike back. I had to get away.

Another cascade of spells dropped my way, great invisible comets that shimmered the air. I veered the car sharply to the right, scraping the thick trees that lined the path. The misfired enchantments fell, close enough to heat my face, one glancing off the bonnet with a chime like cymbals clashing. Some small part of me found it interesting—I had seen powerful spells displace the air before, I had read the theories on the phenomenon, but I had never been in a position to observe it so clearly. The rest of me was more concerned with the fact that I had to get off the road. As long as I was stuck in this narrow lane, I wouldn't last.

Only one thing for it. I opened the door on the driver's side in preparation, then with a deep breath, I wrenched the wheel to the side.

At this point, the road was lined with thick hedges, not stone walls. Even so, the impact was bone-jarring. My head crashed forward to the steering wheel; my mouth filled with blood as my teeth split my lip. I had barely the presence of mind to slip out the door and crawl through the gap in the hedge my car had opened, fighting my way through the thick gorse as best I could, keeping low to the ground. With luck the trees overhead would hide me from sight.

It wasn't enough, though. The plane was turning about, coming in for another attempt. If I got to my feet and ran, they would see me; if I stayed where I was, I would be hit by another, far more incapacitating spell, or the plane would land and the Guards would dig me out of the hedges like a particularly stubborn weed. I had only one idea, and it was a desperate one. It just had to work.

The rattle of the plane's engine was louder now, its shadow falling across the road. I was ready this time. Pressed to the earth, heart pounding, barely feeling the prickles and twigs biting my skin, I stretched my hand out and waited. I couldn't see the spells themselves, but I heard the high scream as some of them fell, and saw the sparks hit the ground as they failed, one by one. I waited as they came nearer, nearer still, and then I whispered the words and twisted my fingers, and my car was suddenly a ball of flame.

Even I was startled at how swift and dramatic it was. It was noiseless, no warning, just heat and fire and smoke. I choked as the acrid smell reached me, and deep beneath the adrenaline my heart cried out. I had loved that motorcar.

I held very still, and waited. With any luck, the Guards in the air above would believe that their magic really had accidentally struck the car and set it alight—and me with it. The way spells reacted with machinery was still unpredictable and unexplored. Even if they didn't, though, they would have no choice but to abandon the chase for now. Soon there would be cries from the surrounding farms and people coming; already the haze was enough to make the ground difficult to see from above, and by the time they landed, the fire would make it impossible to get close. Besides, they had me marked now. The next time I used magic, they would find me.

The fire was spreading, hot fingers stretching out to the trees and creeping across the grass. I stayed pressed to the ground, mouth buried in my sleeve to stifle coughs, flames inching toward me. The thrum of the aircraft roared overhead, closer, closer—then, at last, it spiralled away. When I dared to raise my head, the plane was a faint dot on the horizon, headed back to London.

I should have felt relief, tempered by far greater fear. I was safe for now. I was, suddenly and unexpectedly, not safe for much longer. The life I had built for myself was over, and something new and desperate had begun. But just then, my chest was burning with such fury there was no space for anything else.

Only one person on the Board could have sent that plane. Only one person had known where I was going to be.

"You bastard, Alden," I said out loud. "You bloody coward."

———— ◇ ————

I couldn't go back to Camford. They would be waiting for me there; I'd be arrested as soon as I went near the Oxbridge. And soon that would be true of anywhere I went. Those same newspapers that had told my students about Hero would tell them about me by morning. My face would be splashed over the covers, the pages filled with stories about whatever terrible thing I had done. It wouldn't be the Ashfield door—Alden was right that there was no way he could pass that off as my work alone. Perhaps the story would be that I was helping Hero, or that I knew where she was. There was only one place I could think to go.

I had one advantage over the Families. They had grown up in a magical world. By adulthood, they used spells constantly, thoughtlessly, like drawing breath. The tracking spell they had managed to cast on me relied on the assumption that I would be unable to refrain from using magic too. The difference was, I had lived the first two-thirds of my life without magic. I knew how to get by without it, if that was what I had to do.

I spent the rest of the night walking, following the road as best I could, ducking down into the hedgerows at any flare of head-lights or unexpected snap of a twig. I was some twenty-five miles out from Oxford—a long walk, it was true, but my family would have laughed at me for thinking it a hard one. Matthew would have covered that in a day during the war, in far worse conditions.

It *was* hard, though, despite what I told myself. The roads were rough and overgrown, and my stupidly nice going-to-London shoes were scuffed and blistering within an hour. Hunger set in, then thirst, and both were tormenting. As the night crawled on, it was all I could do to keep one foot in front of the other and my legs pushing grimly forward. I had always heard that a tracking spell was painless; this one kept up a niggling, burrowing itch that deepened to a throb after the first few miles. Worst of all was the fear. It was a constant shadow companion, freezing me when a light from a car appeared on the horizon, nipping at my heels with sharp teeth when the roads were dark and silent, until I thought I would go mad. In many ways, those long, lonely hours were the worst of my entire life.

I don't wish to dwell on them. Suffice it to say, by the time I made it to Oxford station, the sun already hot and high in the sky, I was grubby and footsore enough to draw surprised glances from the crowd, and I had to swallow several times before I found the words for the ticket officer. "A one-way ticket to Manchester, please."

I'd have to change trains there or find some other form of transport, but I didn't want to declare up front where I was going. Too dangerous. It was all dangerous now.

Thankfully, the train was almost ready to leave. I bought some wilted sandwiches and tea from the station, bolted them too fast on board, and then settled back as the train drew away from the platform. I dozed with my head against the window of the carriage, body exhausted and mind reeling, watching a blur of grey skies through half-closed lashes.

I should have known. The words went over and over in my head with every turn of the wheels until the train took on its own voice. *I should have known. I should have known.*

I had known Alden hadn't wanted the Ashfield gate exposed. He had made that very clear on that terrible morning, and nothing that had happened since had ever changed his mind. I knew he was capable of lying, of keeping secrets, of persuading others to keep them too. The only thing I didn't know was to what lengths he would go if someone went against him.

He'd warned me, all those years ago, when his words were still able to be taken for adolescent exaggeration. *I'm not a good person, Clover. You believe I am because I'm clever and charming, but neither of those things are virtues. And you've never tried to cross me in anything I want to do.*

I was crossing him now. But I was exhausted and angry and scared, and I couldn't help grieving bitterly not just for Hero and the collapse of my entire life, but for what Alden had once been to me and what he had become.

⬥

It was after dark again by the time I reached Lady Winter's square redbrick house. The windows were dark too, its inhabitants long since asleep. And yet I felt the tickle of security charms against my skin as I climbed, stumbling, over the fence that bordered the property, and wasn't surprised at all to see the door open and a flicker of candlelight appear at the top of the stairs.

"Please," I said, before Lady Winter could say anything. "I know this is an imposition. But I haven't anywhere else to go."

She must have hesitated. The entire country was looking for me. This wasn't refusing to get rid of some old books on faerie lore. Hiding me was more than an imposition, it was a terrible risk. It never showed on her face.

"Well," she said calmly. "You'd better come inside."

21

Lady Winter dealt with my arrival out of the darkness as briskly as if she'd helped half a dozen fugitives. I told her everything in full, seated on her sofa by the fire with a glass of water cupped in my hands, and she listened gravely and without giving anything away.

"I'm sure you know now how foolish you were" was all she said. "And fortunately I'm neither your mother nor your teacher that I need to lecture you about it. Young mages always do try to summon faeries, and it often does go wrong, so that part is nothing new. Your worst mistake was trusting a Lennox-Fontaine to act in anyone's interest other than his own."

"I never thought he would go so far," I said, and knew I only sounded naive. I pressed the cool glass to the bridge of my nose, willing my thoughts together. "My family. Are they safe? Do they know the Guards are looking for me?"

"They know." There was an odd note to her voice, one that I was too hazy to place. "The Guards came to your house last night—or rather, in the early hours of the morning."

I sat bolt upright, pain and weariness momentarily forgotten. "Are they all right? What happened?"

"They're safe. Don't concern yourself. Sam Truelove Wells managed to warn them, less than an hour before they arrived. Your brother had already taken little Rose and left."

"*Sam* warned them? But...why did Matthew leave? And Rose? If they were looking for me—"

"They weren't looking for you," Lady Winter explained patiently. "They had come to take your brother."

No. Alden wouldn't. Even if the worst was true, and he wanted me out of the way, surely he would never be monstrous enough to hurt my family. Even if I had, in his eyes, lost him his own brother. Even then.

"I doubt Lennox-Fontaine was to blame for that," Lady Winter added, as though I had spoken aloud. Perhaps I had. "The Board never were happy with letting your brother go free after the war. The locks being under threat would be enough excuse to move on him. And of course with Rose sharing that same blood, your family feared the Guards would take her too—especially if they found how much magic she knows."

My heart was racing—the echo of it throbbed in my head and my arm. "Are you sure they're safe? Where are they?"

"They're close by. The Guards didn't stay at your house long. Your mother told them that Mr. Hill and Rose were in Manchester, and they had no idea where you were. When they didn't find anything, they left. I think your mother rather frightened them."

I didn't smile at that, as I usually would. Images flashed before my eyes as though on a cinema screen: summoning spells ripping through my family home, my mother's stiff-necked fury, fingers pawing through my family's lives. Rose, torn from sleep, wide-eyed and fearful in the dark, told to run.

"I'll fix this," I said uselessly. "I promise I will, somehow."

As long as we were still on this earth there was nothing that couldn't be fixed. I had said that so many times growing up, to my younger siblings, and later in the dark to myself. I had believed it; I still did. I just couldn't see a way to fix this. For the first time since Ashfield, magic felt impossible, wild as the sea and infinitely more dangerous.

"We'll discuss all that tomorrow," Lady Winter said firmly.

"I told you, they're safe now. First things first. Let's get that spell out of your arm."

I was too far beyond exhaustion for real surprise. I only blinked. "Can you do that? I was always taught a tracking spell could only be removed by the caster."

"In the old days, that was true. If I'm not mistaken, though, that spell wasn't cast on you directly. That would have been difficult magic, far too precise to be flung from an aircraft."

"No." I caught on, thankfully, to the familiar intricacies of practical magic. They, at least, made sense. "It was cast on a metal casing, which embedded itself in my arm. You could draw it out with a summoning spell?"

"Like a bullet being pulled from a wound—or so I assume. It will hurt, though. Stay very still."

It did hurt. The pellet proved stubborn, and every fraction of an inch it gave was like having red-hot wire drawn through my flesh. I sat rigidly still, gritting my teeth, willing myself not to cry or flinch as Lady Winter pressed her fingers to the sting and repeated the spell once, twice, three times. When at last she pulled her hand away, the world spun into a red blur. Lady Winter caught me before I hit the floor.

"There." Her arms tightened on my shoulders, firm and reassuring. "All over." She held out her hand, and I caught the glint of metal and blood between her fingers. It looked like a small bullet, at first; as it woke to the air, its wings unfurled once more, and its tiny legs scrabbled furiously for purchase. "Nasty little thing. And lazy spellcraft, I might add. I appreciate the blending of magic and science, but the Board are getting slapdash with it. Like those airplanes they've been using instead of broomsticks since the war. All noise and flash, no precision."

I had thoughts on this issue myself; I had attended a lecture on it only last month. I kept my mouth shut. Not only could I not remember any of them, I was fairly certain I was a wrong breath away from being sick.

The rest of the evening was a dizzy haze. There was a waiting bath of hot, fragrant water and then a clean nightgown and a bandage for the still-bleeding wound in my arm. A bowl of hot porridge sprinkled with sugar and a cup of tea. A door, old and worn, that turned out to lead to a cellar. It was charmed, Lady Winter explained, to open only to those with the counter-spell, like the Illusion with less glamour. It was a relic of the very earliest foundations of the house, constructed during the English Civil War, when not all the Families were on the same side and there was frequently need to hide some mages from others. If I stayed down there, only those who already knew the room was there would ever find it— which did not include anyone presently on the Board. The Winters were a small family and had always kept to themselves.

"I'll tell your family where you are," Lady Winter promised, before she closed the door. "They'll be very glad to hear you're safe."

I nodded faintly. The world was swimming in and out of focus, and I was shivering even after the bath and warm clothes. "Thank you," I managed. "I'm so sorry to put you at risk like this. If the Board found me here—"

She laughed bitterly. "The Board have been getting away with far too much for far too long, Clover. If I can help them not get away with this, believe me, the risk is welcome. Now lie down."

I barely heard her. There was a small camp bed made up down there, sagging precariously under the weight of thick quilts and pillows. I curled up under them, burrowing into their warmth, and fell as immediately and deeply asleep as though I'd been hit with a brick. My last, vague thought was that I didn't care if the Families found me now. I had done my best.

⸺⊰⊱⸺

The rap of knuckles on the door must have woken me, although I was barely aware of it. My dreams had been of faerie doors and rattling engines and spells flying overhead. I came out of them bolt upright on the bed, heart hammering, hand poised and a spell on the tip of my tongue. I had never been in a fight, but I had a degree in magic. I knew how to throw fire, I knew how to freeze water, I knew how to send pain shooting through nerves. If they wanted to take me, I wouldn't make it easy.

"Clove?" The voice was so familiar that my body relaxed before my mind caught up. "It's Matthew. Let me in."

I'll tell your family where you are. I cursed as the memory of where I was settled around me, and Lady Winter's words came back with it. I should have told her not to let them come to me, whatever it took. My resignation of the night before had melted away with the morning, and all my fears had come crashing back in its place. All the Families in England if not beyond were looking for me, and now apparently for Matthew too. He couldn't be here.

The knock came again. I disentangled myself from the quilt, wincing, every ache and throb of the last day and night blossoming painfully along my legs and back. My feet were swollen and blistered; I gave up any hope of hobbling up the stairs and opened the cellar door with a twist of my fingers.

My brother came down quickly, two stairs at a time, his brow creased with concern. He stopped when he saw me and looked me up and down.

"Well," he said conversationally, "you look like death warmed over."

"Oh, thanks very much," I retorted. It was the best I could do, under the circumstances, with the familiar sight of him bringing a lump to my throat. Even now, part of me still believed he could protect me, and in that moment I ached to be protected. I folded my arms tightly against it and forced steel into my voice. "What do you think you're doing here, Matty? It's not safe."

His eyebrows raised. "Thank you very much yourself. Remind me again, of the two of us, which one spent their youth at the front and which one spent it at a magic school for young toffs?"

"That's exactly why I'm the one—"

"Aunt Clover?" a small voice from the top of the stairs cut me off. A small head peeked around the door—a fair head, with the Hill family eyebrows above wide blue eyes.

"Come on down, Rosie," Matthew called. "It's safe."

I shot Matthew a look, part fury and part bewilderment, which he returned with the wide-eyed innocence he knew always got up my nose. Regrettably, I couldn't kill him in front of a child. Instead, I bent down and held out my arms to the little girl in the gingham dress, pulling on my old role as the interesting aunt who definitely did not have the forces of the magical world trying to kill her.

"Hello, Rose!" Her little body was warm in my arms; I breathed in the scent of her fine hair, soap and smoke and the fresh air from outside, and the terrible pressure in my chest eased. "Gosh, you've got so big!"

"I was seven in April," she informed me, as though I could forget—as though, in fact, I hadn't sent her a book of fairy tales, an oversized box of chocolates, and a pen enchanted to write in whatever coloured ink she was imagining. I had meant to visit, but the day had coincided with a three-week research trip I was taking to Rome, so I'd promised to see her again in the summer.

I was meant to present that research at a seminar this weekend. The thought cudgelled me out of nowhere. My paper was sitting on my desk, fully written. The Guards probably had it now, along with everything else in my small, neat office and my crooked little bedroom overlooking the quadrangle. I had missed my lecture yesterday, the one I had been driving home to prepare for, and I might never give another one at Camford again.

"Well, that explains it." I don't *think* my voice wobbled. "Seven's a big age."

"Rose, love, how about you go look for a new book in Lady Winter's library?" Matthew suggested, as Rose opened her mouth to reply. "Your aunt and I need to talk for a bit."

"I'll see you soon," I promised her, and she nodded, disappointed. I waited until she reached the top of the stairs (she stopped and blew me a kiss, which I caught and returned), then turned back to Matthew.

I meant to go on scolding him for coming, for bringing her, for anything. I meant to push him as far from me as I could, back out to the edges of safety. But fear and grief and the clasp of Rose's tiny hands around my neck had dissolved any steel I'd managed to summon. I caught Matthew's eye, and in one stroke I forgot that I was a grown woman and a mage who could handle things herself, I forgot that this was all my fault and I had already put him in far too much danger. All I could think was how glad I was to see him.

He must have seen it, because he softened too. "Come here," he said gently, and I clung to him as I had the day he came home from war. His arms were stronger and surer now, and his coat carried with it the comforting home smell of hay and dirt and spring rain.

"All right?" he asked, as we pulled apart.

I found a deep, steadying breath and nodded. "I'm fine, honestly. What about you? Where are you hiding?"

"Not far away. We got into the woods for the night—remember that old hut we found when we were little? Rose was a bit bewildered, but she did well. In the morning I came to Lady Winter to find out if you were safe. We're in an old labourer's cottage out on the edge of the estate for now—it's been empty since Lord Winter died. Nobody's come looking again—at the moment they're more worried about you and Hero. Clover, what the hell were you thinking all those years ago?" Now that he knew I was safe, his voice was growing serious. "Surely you knew better than to go messing with the fae?"

"I know." I sat back down on the bed, cold once more. He was right. We had all known better. "I'm sorry."

"I *knew* something was wrong back then. I just didn't want to ask. Just what did that spell cost? Nobody got hurt, did they?"

Gerald Drake. Charles Perowne. I hadn't thought of those names in years—I couldn't. I couldn't name them now. I didn't need to—Matthew read my face and swore quietly.

"Great. And it's my fault."

"No!" I was startled into speech. "I opened the door, not you."

"You did it for me. That makes it my fault."

"Oh, shut up." I admired my brother's willingness to take burdens on himself, truly, but sometimes it got on my nerves. "I wasn't a child, Matty. I was old enough to make my own choices. Besides…it wasn't all for you, not really. That was just what I told myself, to give myself the excuse. I wanted to see for myself if it worked. I wanted to be the one who made it work." I fumbled for words in the dark, and found only his own. "I was sick of pretending everything was fine since the war too. I didn't just want to fix you. I wanted to fix everything."

He made a noise that might have been a sigh or a laugh. "Well, you didn't do a great job, I have to say."

I didn't have a chance to reply. A soft knock, and Lady Winter was coming down the stairs.

"No trace of any Guards this morning," she said to me without preamble. Her dress and hair were unchanged from the night before, both slightly rumpled, and I knew she had been watching all night. Yet she didn't look tired. She had the firm, brisk energy of a commander on a battlefield. "The morning papers arrived, though."

They landed beside me on the bed with a slap, face-up. A grainy photograph taken at a conference last May, my face very round and the glint on my glasses obscuring my eyes. *Scholarship Witch Still Evades Capture.* I tried to open my mouth, to make some light remark about how the journalism in the *Practitioner* got more sensationalist every day. I couldn't. I felt sick. I hadn't been called a scholarship witch in a long time.

"Those bastards," Matthew said softly. "I'm sorry, Clover."

"You'll be safe enough here for now." If Lady Winter objected to Matthew's language, she made no sign. "They'll hesitate to intrude here, on a Family house, without cause. I'm Family by marriage only in their eyes, though, and foreign to boot. They'll find cause soon enough, and the spells around this cellar won't hold against everything."

"I just can't make sense of any of it." I took off my glasses to rub my eyes, hoping it looked like weariness and not the dashing away of tears it was. "Hero *did* know better than to mess with the fae. She only did it years ago because the door was right there, and Alden and I persuaded her it was safe. I can't think what would possess her to do it now, when it means tearing down the veil between worlds. What deal could be that important? Matthew, did Sam give you any hints when he spoke to you?"

"Not about Hero. And he didn't speak to me, exactly." He caught my questioning look and sighed. "The evening before last, about when we were heading to bed, there was a rapping sound at the window. Outside there was a large black bird—a raven. There was a note wrapped to its leg. I thought it might be from you."

I had sent a raven to Rose once or twice, just because I thought it would be more fun for her than a telegram. She loved birds. But that evening I had been running—or at least walking—for my life. "It was from Sam?"

"First time I've heard from him in ten years. It said something about a German ambassador being killed by a faerie curse, and that the Families wanted me back in their custody. It said to take Rose, just in case, and be gone by the time they arrived. That was it."

It took me longer than it should to work out what my attention had snagged on. When I did, everything stopped.

"Wait—the German ambassador was killed by a faerie curse?" Beside me, I heard Lady Winter's breath catch. "Are you sure?"

He raised his eyebrows. "It's the sort of thing I'd remember, isn't it? Considering?"

"Do you have the note with you?"

"I remember what it said. Lord Beresford was killed by a faerie curse. The same one that…" He shifted, uncomfortable, and his eyes flickered away. "Well. You know."

There was only one that Matthew wouldn't want to talk about. "The same one you survived. The curse from Amiens."

"Yeah," he said quietly. "That one. Is it important?"

It was more than important. It changed everything.

Human mages, however talented, couldn't perform faerie curses.

"It isn't her," I said. Hearing my own words didn't seem real. It was as though the bottom had fallen off the world, and everything was drifting. "Hero. It's the faerie. The one who tried to break through at Ashfield."

Lady Winter nodded very slowly. "The faerie from Amiens. It's here."

I felt rather than saw Matthew tense, freeze, the terrible involuntary stillness of a rabbit when a hawk screams down from the sky.

"I closed the door." My own voice seemed to be coming from very far away. "That night at Ashfield—I *know* I closed the door."

"It's been many years since then," Lady Winter reminded me. "There may have been other open doors, like the one at Ashfield. There are any number of ways it could have broken through."

It was true, I realised as my panic ebbed enough to think. After all, I had been the one standing in that circle at Ashfield—if it had broken through then, it would have taken me, not Hero. Besides, it had been eight years since then. Faeries stole bodies, and sometimes even pretended to be those people, for short bursts of time, not for eight years. It must have come through another door, perhaps only the same night that Lord Beresford had been murdered.

But if there *was* another open door, then why was the dryad going to such lengths to break the locks that separated our world from faerie country? Why, for that matter, had it spent so many years trying to come through at all, when it clearly had none of the usual faerie interest in experiencing the human form? We never had found out what its plans were, only that it would step over any number of broken bodies to fulfill them.

Now it had taken Hero. I thought of that terrible winged shape, silver birch twisting into a crown on top of its head, and my insides turned to water. Whatever had happened, it was the fault of that night somehow. Ashfield had loomed in my memory too long for me to shake the conviction that everything came back to it.

Another thought came to me, almost as unwelcome. "Alden said the Board didn't know how Lord Beresford died," I said slowly. "Matthew, what time did the raven come from Sam?"

Belatedly, I looked across at Matthew. He hadn't moved; I'm not sure he had released the breath he had drawn at the mention of Amiens. His face had the frightening remoteness I had once thought was part of the curse and now knew was just how men of his age looked sometimes when a nightmare came on them without warning in broad daylight. I hadn't seen it in a long time.

"Matty?"

He blinked; I saw him drag himself back with the convulsive shiver of someone coming up from deep water. "I'm here. I'm listening. I just…" He drew a breath, released it. "The raven… It would have been half past eight, maybe, no later. The sun was still setting. Why?"

It would take a raven a few hours to get to Pendle Hill. I had been sitting in front of Alden at seven o'clock that evening.

"Alden knew." I heard myself sounding far, far too calm. "He must have. He's minister for magical enforcement. If Sam knew in time to send that raven, then Alden knew by the time I came to him. He sat there, he talked to me about Hero and why she might have committed murder, and he never told me it wasn't her at all. He lied to me."

"He's lied to everyone," Lady Winter said. "Or at least the Board has. There's nothing in the paper about a faerie curse. The story is that Lady Beresford is acting upon her own free will. I don't like that. They should have no reason to hide that information."

"Perhaps they don't want to panic the Families?"

"Perhaps." She sounded doubtful. "Even if that's the only reason, it makes things very dangerous for you. If the Board truly are trying to keep a faerie incursion secret, this is a good deal bigger than Lennox-Fontaine trying to protect his career, and they'll look that much harder. I doubt you'll be safe here another night. You need to leave."

"Where? Where is she supposed to go—my lady?" Matthew added belatedly. "They're wizards. They'll find her."

"Your sister is a witch," Lady Winter reminded him. "They won't have an easy job of it. As for where she's supposed to go—Clover? I assume you have a plan?"

Until then I would have said it was less a plan than a growing conviction about what I had to do and a doubt whether I could do it. Lady Winter's calm assumption of my competence steadied me, as perhaps she intended. I forced myself to concentrate, to think about this academically, the way I'd test a new hypothesis. Whatever had happened to Hero—whenever and however it had happened—I couldn't help her if I didn't keep my head.

"I do." The headlines in the paper were still glaring up from the bed. I turned them over without looking at them. No distractions. "I need to find Eddie."

I had told Lady Winter of Eddie's involvement; it couldn't have been a surprise to her. Still, she looked troubled. "Nobody's seen Edmund Gaskell for years. Do you know where he is?"

"The last I heard, he was staying in one of his family's cottages somewhere in Scotland." That had been from Alden, but I doubted it was a lie. There would have been little point, and being caught out would have only made me suspicious of what else he was lying about. "He knows more about dryads than anyone I know. Perhaps he can work out what this one might want, and how it might be bargained with. At the very least, I have to warn him that he might be in danger. I have to tell him about Alden, and about Hero."

"And then what?"

"Then I need to find Hero." It came as simply and naturally as anything I'd ever said. "I need to stop her before she—before the faerie inside her—achieves whatever it's set out to do."

"It sounds like Alden and the Families have every intention of doing that themselves," Matthew said. His arms were folded, as they often were when he was thinking harder about something than he was pretending. In this case, I think he was also keeping himself together. "Why do you need to volunteer?"

"Because they'll kill her," I said bluntly. "She's in terrible trouble, and it's my fault. However that thing got inside her, at the very least she never would have met it if not for me. She trusted my judgement, and I let her down. I need to save her."

"Clove…" His own voice had the same calm I forced into mine only moments ago, and I suspected it came at even greater cost. "Listen to me. You don't understand what these people can be like. I learned when I first met them what they'll do to keep their secrets. You've been living with them for years, but you've never stood against them."

"Well, then I have the advantage." I heard Hero's ringing bravado in my own voice. "They don't know what to expect."

Normally that would have made him at least smile. This time, he only shook his head, frustrated.

"It isn't only the Families. I—" I watched him pause, gather himself, forge ahead. "I've seen that thing face-to-face, you know.

I saw it murder an entire battalion. I watched those men go down beside me, screaming, their flesh turning to wood, until their hearts stopped and they died in no-man's-land. I heard it whisper to me every night for years, and when the curse had me, I knew what it was saying. Whatever this faerie wants, it's not like the ones you tell Rose stories about, the meddlers and mischief-makers, the ones who think bargaining with humans is a game. It hates us. If it sees you, it will kill you without a thought."

In all the years since he'd been home, Matthew had never once told me anything like that. I had seen the way his mind swerved from those years, like a car on an icy road. It was true what I had told Alden: Matthew was doing well, more than well. The splinter left in his shoulder that still troubled me didn't seem to bother him, the midnight enchantments had stopped, his body had gained weight and muscle and his face had lost its constant tension. The farm was surviving, the family were thriving. I had broken the curse. But I hadn't *fixed* him, as he'd accused me of trying to do. Like so many of his generation, he had seen and done too many things, things that ran deeper than curses, things that had broken his world and put it back together a different shape, and the only way he lived with them was by keeping them in the dark and refusing to look. If he was dragging them out now, for my sake, then I had better listen.

"I know," I said, when I could trust my voice. "Or at least, I can't know, but—I believe you. But, Matty, can't you see that all that is exactly why I need to fight back? You saw how dangerous that faerie was on the battlefield, how much it wants us all dead. Hero has it in her *head*. It's trapped her in her own body. You of all people must be able to imagine what that's like."

He started to speak, then stopped. I saw his eyes flicker, toward me then away, as he turned my words over in his mind.

"Edmund Gaskell, at least, I can help you with, if what you've been told is true," Lady Winter said into the silence. "I know where that cottage in Scotland is. It came from my husband's family—it went to the Gaskells when his great-aunt Camilla married in. It's in the Highlands—I can find you the exact address."

Relief washed over me. At least Lady Winter thought I was doing the right thing. "Thank you."

"Don't thank me—thank the way Families interbreed. You can thank me for this next part, though. Tell me, have you ever flown a broomstick?"

I shook my head, taken aback.

Her lips twitched. "Well. I have some clothes for you to change into. When you're ready, meet me in the orchard. Mr. Hill, you might want to bring Rose. She'll want to see this."

I had seen broomsticks before. They had been in fashion last century, and some of the older lecturers at Camford still favoured them. We would see them propped up outside lecture theatres occasionally; at Ashfield, one unusually showery day spent exploring the attic, the four of us had found an old broom belonging to Alden's great-grandfather, although we couldn't get the flight spell to work. Eddie had had one as a child, at his own house. Hero used to laugh about them affectionately, the way I might at our old fat Shetland or the plough my father had used before we'd bought the tractor.

The broomstick Lady Winter gave me felt no different than the one I had used often at home to sweep the floor: the handle thin and cracked, the brush a thick bundle of fibres clogged with dust. And yet with a word and gesture, it came alive in my hand. The broom was suddenly lighter, supporting itself rather than supported by me, and it hummed with repressed energy: the difference between touching a twig on the ground and a living branch. My blood quickened in response. Just for a moment, the grip of dread clutching my stomach loosened.

"Try it," Lady Winter said. "It should respond to the slightest pressure of your hands, as a horse might."

The farm horse had never listened to a word I said, but I didn't say so. This, in the midst of all the confusion and guilt and fear, was something I could learn. It was *magic*. My brain snatched at it, and my hands grabbed the handle. I straddled the broomstick and kicked off.

I understood now why Lady Winter had told us to meet her outside in the orchard. The broom rose gently into the air, and I rose with it, not perched on it precariously as I'd feared but part of it. It was exhilarating. The trees above screened us from any prying eyes, even had there been anyone to pry. The broom and I made three great wobbly circles of the garden, at first with my toes skimming the top of the grass and then increasingly higher as my confidence grew. I wove through the trees, narrowly missing a branch, and thrilled at the cool breeze on my face and the sunlight overhead. I'd thought my car was freeing. This was the same freedom, the same impossible speeds, but with the encasement of metal fallen away, just the broom beneath me and the magic in my blood. I couldn't imagine why it had fallen out of favour with the modern world.

Down below, Rose and Matthew watched, Matthew sceptical and little Rose's face alight with wonder.

"Can I try next?" she begged, as I landed with a slight bump and stumble on the ground. "Please?"

"When you're older," Matthew said, on reflex. He was still unhappy, I could tell, but he was pulling together a good impression of himself for Rose's sake. Lady Winter had been wise to suggest he fetch her. "Are you sure about this, Clove? You can always borrow the motorcycle."

"Does it work now?" I asked, still breathless from the ride. Despite everything, I had to fight the wild desire to laugh.

" 'Course it does! Well, usually. With a good kick or two."

I made a face at him. "I'll take this, thank you. We know they found me on the road last time, anyway. This way I can stick to the trees and hedges and stay out of sight. Are you sure I can borrow it, Lady Winter?"

"I'm not likely to use it again." Lady Winter hefted the broomstick in one hand and gave it an affectionate spin. "Everyone rode these when I was at Camford—though already a good bicycle was faster and more comfortable, especially when you applied a few judicious spells to make the wheels spin without the aid of your legs. Then motorcars began to creep in shortly before the war, and they were all the rage. The convenience and the comfort—and groups could travel together. Brooms are thoroughly out of fashion these days."

"I'm not surprised," Matthew said. "I don't mean any offence, but I wouldn't like to perch on that. I'm surprised those Family gentlemen ever produced any heirs at all."

I definitely snorted that time.

"Ignore your brother," Lady Winter said sternly. "The broom will take care of you. It won't be able to take you to France, unfortunately—the flight spell can't cross large bodies of water—but it will get you to Scotland."

Scotland. France. London. I'd been so focused on Hero, on the dangers and the stakes, that I'd forgotten the sheer enormity of the distances involved. My exhilaration faded. "I don't even know where the lock in Paris is."

"Ah. Eddie Gaskell might be able to help with that, in fact. The Gaskells have relatives on the Conseil—the French Board. Tell him to call in a favour with a second cousin or something."

I nodded.

"In the meantime," Lady Winter added, "I'll see if I can reach Sam Wells. Clearly, he knows more about what's going on than most. He wouldn't take my call this morning, but let's see how long that lasts. He owes me a favour, after he called me up out of the blue all those years ago and asked me to educate you."

I hugged her, on impulse, the way I had never dared before.

"Thank you," I said. "Not just for the broom. I know the risk you're taking, and I don't know how I can—"

"I'm not only helping you," Lady Winter interrupted. For the first time that morning, her brisk cool melted, enough to glimpse something dark and furious lurking beneath the surface. "I *am* fond of you, Clover, and of course I want you to be safe. But this is more important than your safety alone. Do you know why I attended Camford? Because the British Raj is rife with the younger sons of English Families, and my father saw the best way forward was for us to ingratiate ourselves with them. I was bright and reasonably attractive and of good blood, as these things are judged by the Families, so my father pulled strings for me to go to England and study at Camford in the hope that I could meet and marry an English lord. It was not my reason for going. I wanted to gain an education in magic that I could bring home and use to help my own country, and a British one would carry more weight over there than one from an Indian university. I was there for three years. I studied hard, I did well, I endured all the sneers that came my way, and because I had powerful patrons, no real harm came to me. But it wore me down, in the end. I met William, soon to be Lord Winter, and let myself do what my father wanted and marry him. I don't regret that. We were happy together, truly, until he died in the mud in the Somme, and he made certain I had money and independence after his death. I do regret that I didn't stay at Camford longer, and that I didn't go home as I intended. I regret most of all that all the time I've been here, the British held my people in a tight and bloody grip, and every time they've tried to wriggle free, that grip has squeezed even tighter and thousands have died while I've done nothing."

I must have looked about to speak, though I'm not sure what I would have said, because she raised a hand.

"I don't mean to give you a lecture. Suffice it to say, the English Families and those on the Board of Magical Regulation in particular are steeped in lies, and I would prefer they not get away with this one. Particularly as it seems likely to result in a faerie breaking down the barriers between worlds."

Lady Winter had tried to warn me, obliquely, about her time at Camford. As a girl I hadn't listened, focused on my own studies and experiences. I remembered now the faint tension in her eyes as she'd wished me well there, the mingled relief and disappointment as she'd looked me up and down when I'd returned and observed that it seemed to suit me. I remembered the bitterness that had always been in Matthew's voice when he'd spoken of the Families, who had kept him for several long months as they argued whether he should live or die or be locked up forever to keep their secret safe. I remembered that Sam's worry when he asked after Matthew was based on very real dangers, and the fae had always been the least of it. I was beginning to feel as though I'd walked through Camford blinkered, and the worst part was that those blinkers had been worn willingly. I thought I'd been accepted there as long as I didn't look at it too hard. And yet when it came to it, a single word from Alden and it had all fallen away.

Matthew nodded slowly, as though accepting an answer to a question he hadn't asked. "Leave Sam to me," he said abruptly. "I'll talk to him. He's in London, isn't he?"

"You can't go to London!" I protested, alarmed. "The Board are looking for you!"

"Well, they won't be looking for me in London. Rose, you don't mind staying with Lady Winter for a few days, do you?"

I shook my head at the same time as Rose. "If Hero breaks the lock in Paris, she's coming to London next. You'll be face-to-face with that thing."

"As far as I know, I'm still the only one in this room to have faced this thing in battle."

"You were struck by a fatal curse."

"But I didn't die," he countered.

I growled, frustrated, and the first smile I'd seen since the mention of Amiens twitched his mouth.

"Let me help," he added, more seriously. "I can't promise Sam will talk to me either. Until that raven, I hadn't heard from him in years. But if he broke the rules for me that time, he might do it again. I'll do my best. You were right, you know." He looked at Lady Winter. "You both are. I *can* imagine what having that thing in your head must be like—I've had it there myself. And the Families shouldn't be allowed to get away with it. Not this time."

"All right." I had to swallow very hard. "Thank you."

———————⟨≫⟩———————

I left Pendle Hill behind within the hour, broomstick laden with saddlebags of food and warm clothing, goodbyes from Lady Winter and Matthew and Rose echoing in my ears. I tried not to wonder if I would ever see it again.

———————⟨≫⟩———————

The Gaskells' Scottish cottage was some three hundred and fifty miles north, and though a broom felt very fast skimming the air with the wind in my face, it would still take an inexperienced rider like me the better part of a day to get there. Over the hours, the joy of soaring above the great curves and contours of the Lancashire countryside was eroded by monotony and discomfort. My muscles, still sore from the day before, began to cramp painfully with the effort of holding the same position, and the wound in my arm throbbed under its dressing. Worst of all, the broom required concentration. Every time my attention began to drift, I would take a quick nosedive into the grass, and come up cursing and brushing uselessly at grass stains on Lady Winter's dress.

My attention drifted often, unsurprisingly. I was far better off than I had been the night I escaped London—then, I had simply been fleeing, frightened and confused, trudging in the dark with no plan and no clear path forward. Now I was at least headed toward something. I could tell myself that Hero needed my help; I could steel myself with the reminder that all this was my fault and I had to set it right. Yet the enormity of it kept intruding, and with it sickening flashes of what Hero was living through every minute while the Board tried to kill her. It hadn't truly sunk in yet—I wouldn't let it—but it pressed its barbs to my mind and stabbed.

As the skies deepened to late afternoon, I landed close to a small village. It was the closest hub of civilisation to the Gaskell cottage, some ten miles away, and I wanted to find an evening paper—it would be an ordinary paper, not the *Practitioner*, but I wanted to see if I could glean anything about Hero's activities nonetheless. I also, I had to admit, longed to step into a shop and get something hot to eat and drink. I couldn't guarantee that Eddie's place would be safe, and I was almost too stiff and cold to walk. I tried a simple cantrip to shrink my broom to conceal-able size, and to my relief it folded to the length of my forearm—small enough to fit into my satchel.

I never got to eat. I found a small newsagent, where I paid for a newspaper and leafed through it quickly. The photograph on the second page was so familiar it took a moment for it to settle into my brain. When it did, my heart chilled.

It was me. Me, except according to this paper I was a dan-gerous poisoner who had killed two men and was wanted by the police. Except that the picture, which was from a confer-ence, was now claimed to be at the village school where I taught. Except that the number the public were supposed to contact would doubtless take them straight to the Board of Magical Regulation.

It was no longer the magical world that was looking for me. It was everyone. My name glaring up from that perfectly mundane newspaper gave everything a horrible new layer of reality. Even now, somebody could look idly up from reading the evening news, see me, and freeze.

It was at that moment that I saw the car outside. A large, dark green monster, parked by the side of the road. The driver stood beside it, a red-haired man my own age, smoking a pipe. It could have been anybody, just passing through on business. Except that I knew him. It was Justin Abbott, from my undergraduate class. The last I heard, he had gone into the Guards.

I left quietly, straight-backed, not too quickly, my legs trembling now not from weariness but from fighting the urge to run. My hands shook as I mounted my broom once more and kicked off into the darkening skies.

<hr />

There were no cars around the Gaskell cottage for miles, at least. There was only one road through the hills, and that was narrow and winding, built for horses rather than motorcars. The cottage itself was smaller than I had expected, a grey stone house like my family's, perched at the top of a steep hill overlooking a deep blue loch. It was so enclosed by trees that I almost flew past it, though to be fair that was partly my own fault. It was late evening by then, and with the long journey and the prolonged mental strain of keeping the broom in the air, I was desperately tired. I understood now why motorcars and motorcycles and even bicycles had taken over bloody broomsticks. I never wanted to see one again as long as I lived.

I landed the broom amidst the thick woodland, just out of sight of the house. It was cold now, with an evening bite in the air, and my legs and arms had locked painfully around the broom; when I straightened, it was with an involuntary groan as my back spasmed. I stretched my shoulders and tried very

hard not to think of my armchair by the fire at Camford, the
dinner being served in the dining hall this very minute. I needed
to focus.

The difficult thing was finding a way to talk to Eddie without
attracting anyone's attention. The Guards were bound to have
called on him. The fact they were in the village so near was not
a good sign. There would probably be others in the cottage—if
not Family, then certainly a gardener and a servant or two. I
wondered, vaguely, about working out what room was his, waiting until he'd gone to bed, and flicking a pebble at his window.
At least he went to bed early—or had when I had known him.

That, of course, was if Eddie even wanted to see me. We had
parted on strange terms, a long time ago. And I had dragged him
into enough trouble already.

God, what was I *doing* here? How on earth did I think I could
find Hero and chase the faerie from her body when I couldn't
even find a way to knock on a door?

I was still standing there, fighting the urge to burst into tears
like a three-year-old, when a small dog came barrelling out of
the undergrowth.

If I wasn't a former farm girl and well past being scared of
anything short of another biplane right now, I would probably
have panicked. It was a scrappy little fox terrier, barking at the
top of its lungs—not only could it draw attention to me, but
from the flash of its teeth, it was more than inclined to bite. As it
was, I stood still and folded my arms, firm, not aggressive, as if it
were a neighbour's working dog.

"Down!" I ordered.

"Scruff!" I heard the call, the whistle, and then a man strode
into the clearing.

I think we were both just as surprised to see each other. Certainly we both started, stopped, stared. I must have looked
a sight: a bespectacled woman, bedraggled hair and an old-
fashioned white dress stained with grass, holding what was

undeniably a broomstick. He looked, quite frankly, as though he'd strolled forth from a John Constable painting. A strong-figured man about my age, dressed in work clothes and a broad-brimmed hat that half hid dark curls. Just a groundsman or a gardener of some kind, really, no different to some of the lads I'd grown up with at home. At Pendle Hill I would have passed him working in the fields with barely a glance, and he would have done the same to me. In the clearing, in the fading light, I think we both believed the other a figure from a dream.

The man recovered first. "Excuse me," he said, and I heard the Yorkshire lilt to his voice. The dog ran back to his heels, tail wagging, and he crouched down to ruffle its ears absently. "You wouldn't happen to be Dr. Hill, would you?"

I hesitated, but took a chance. It was unlikely that a Guard, whose members were selected from the best Families, would have such a regional dialect. And I knew only one Yorkshire-man in this part of the world. "I am. Well, Miss Hill, technically. Clover. I'm not submitting until October."

The man's face relaxed into a surprisingly boyish smile. "Ah! I thought so. I'm Richard Sutcliffe. Would you be looking for Eddie? He thought you might drop by, though he was expecting you to come by road. I can show you in, if you'd like. You look like you could use a cup of tea."

I knew now he was a real person. But in that moment, he was more dreamlike than ever.

"Please," I said faintly.

22

The last time I had seen Eddie had been through a crack in the door at Chancery Hall, a few months after we had opened the Ashfield door. It was the same day I saw the news of Hero's wedding in the paper—a grey, miserable day, the overgrown trees and stone of Camford damp and dripping. I hadn't seen Eddie in lectures for weeks, not even in Botany. I'd heard that he was ill, and the few times I had knocked on his door before, he hadn't answered; I was ill and exhausted myself most of that autumn, and I reasoned that if he didn't want to see me, nothing would come of making him. But on that day I missed all three of them more than reason, and Eddie was the one whose loss I least understood. I knocked, and I kept knocking, ignoring the wear on my knuckles and the dirty looks I was getting from people passing.

"Eddie?" I called. "Please. I just want a word."

The door, at last, had creaked open. The gloom behind it startled me. I had never, in all the time I had known him, seen the curtains closed in Eddie's room. There were too many plants in there that needed the light.

"What is it?" Eddie's voice had come, husky and wary. He did sound ill, which I supposed was unsurprising. Eddie could weather a blizzard unscathed, but what we'd been through had been a storm of a different kind.

"It's me." Suddenly, after all that knocking, I hadn't known what to say. "Did you see about Hero in the papers?"

He sighed. "I really don't want to talk, Clover. Please."

There wasn't a lot I could say to that. "I just wanted to see that you were all right," I said weakly.

"I'm fine. Well, no, I'm not. I'm probably going home next week. Thank you for asking, though."

The door had closed, and next week Eddie had gone. It was one of many things that year that shouldn't have happened. I had known Alden was still angry at me for closing the door on his brother; I knew, or thought I did, that Hero blamed both of us for what had gone wrong. Eddie had forgiven me. I never expected to lose him too. But there had been nothing to be done.

Now, when the back door to the cottage opened, I was struck by the double blow of the similarities and differences. The door opened wider this time, enough that I could see the person behind it, and a flickering firelight glowed from within. Eddie was dressed roughly, old work trousers and a dark brown jumper with a hole starting in one sleeve. His dark hair and beard had grown out unfashionably; his face beneath it had rounded and softened. It would have suited him tremendously, had his expression not been tight with worry.

"Clover." The greeting wasn't unfriendly, but his grey-blue eyes darted to my face and glanced off without meeting my eyes, as they had the first time we had met. They did that to people he didn't know well, I had learned long ago. The first time his gaze had settled on me had felt significant, as though he were giving me his trust to hold. Plainly, I had dropped it.

"Hello, Eddie," I said, too bright and chipper. "It's been a while."

It's been a while. For God's sake.

"Come in, quick." He shepherded me in, gently, and I felt absurdly relieved at the touch of his hand on my arm. At least I wasn't entirely a stranger. "Are you all right? I saw the papers..."

"I'm fine, really. Just tired." It was an understatement. My arm throbbed, every muscle ached, and I had to swallow a yawn as I shrugged off my wet coat. "I'm sorry to bring trouble to your door."

"No, no," he said, but distractedly. He and Richard exchanged a look I couldn't read. "Go through, get warm by the fire. Can I get you anything? I'll check the kitchen."

"I'll keep an eye on the road," Richard said to Eddie quietly, then nodded to me. He, at least, gave me a smile that was real. "Lovely to finally meet you, Dr. Hill."

I didn't correct my title this time. "And you," I said, with a smile of my own.

***

My idea of decorating is to rearrange all the books on my shelves and nod in satisfaction, often, but even I could see that the sitting room into which Eddie led me was exactly right. It was a country sort of room, wallpapered in Victorian pale floral print, with low dark beams and heavy dark wood furniture and yellowing books stacked haphazardly on shelves. The pictures on the walls were eclectic, a mixture of botanical sketches and landscapes and scientific drawings of birds. And, of course, it teemed with plants in every convenient nook and crevice—ferns, ivy, rose trees, aspidistra, philodendrons, basil, all in earthenware pots. I sat down on an armchair between the fire and an overenthusiastic maidenhair fern, grateful beyond measure for the softness against my aching back, and fought the urge to close my eyes. I was a scholar now—this was more physical activity than I'd had in an entire year. I was starting to worry I would drift off before I had the chance to talk. Scruff trotted to the rug by the fire and settled there with a sigh that belonged to a much larger dog.

When Eddie came back from the kitchen, he brought with him half a seed cake on a plate in one hand and a pot of tea in the other. He poured and passed me a cup himself, sloshing a bit into the saucer. His hand was shaking.

"Sorry." He sat in the chair opposite, carefully. "There's no housekeeper here, I make do on my own. Well, not quite on my own, you saw..."

"Richard," I finished, and knew I was right when Eddie flushed pink.

"Yes." Some of the old warmth crept back into his voice. "You don't... You aren't annoyed I didn't tell you about him, back at Camford? There really wasn't anything between him and me, during those years, but I still felt odd never mentioning him. I know most people thought I fancied you..."

"I knew you didn't," I assured him. "I sort of thought there was someone else, too. I just couldn't guess why you wouldn't tell us. I understand now, especially if he wasn't Family. He isn't, is he?"

Eddie shook his head. "He was the gardener's son at my family's house. The one I tried to teach magic when we were both young, do you remember?"

"The one who thought you were playing a trick on him?"

"He didn't think that for long." His eyes lightened, not a smile but the memory of a smile. "We practised magic together a fair bit, in those days. I meant what I said, he couldn't get a hold of spellcraft the way you have, but he got quite good at it after a while. My family would have thrown him out if they'd suspected any of it—the fact I was teaching him magic, the fact we were friends, the fact we might be something more. And as I said, there wasn't anything to suspect, for a time. We fell out just before I went away to Camford—my fault. I pushed him away to protect him, when he didn't ask for my protection. We didn't really speak again until—well, until after I dropped out. He was one of the groundsmen by then."

"The groundsman." I couldn't hold back a grin. "That's very Lady Chatterley of you."

Eddie's mouth quirked in response for the first time. "I thought that book was banned."

"Not in Paris. There's a copy being passed around Camford. I read it last month. I don't like forbidden knowledge."

"How was it?"

"A bit metaphysical for me. Hero would have loved it." The mention of Hero faded the smile from my face. I set my teacup down carefully, though it was barely touched. "You know why I'm here, don't you? You saw it in the papers?"

"I did." He sat forward, serious. At least he was looking at me now, although he wouldn't quite let our eyes meet. "About Hero first. I nearly contacted you then, but it's difficult to get a private message into Camford, and it had been so long since we'd spoken…Then the next day I saw the news about you."

"It wasn't Hero, Eddie." I decided to come out with it as quickly and bluntly as I could. "Sam Wells told Matthew that Lord Beresford was killed by a faerie curse. The same one that struck Matthew. The faerie from Ashfield."

I waited for disbelief, or at least for surprise. What I saw was the faintest possible hesitation, like a flinch. "Oh," he said.

I should have known. Eddie always did see things nobody else did. "You knew."

"Not about the curse, no. I definitely would have been in touch if I'd heard that. But I knew about Hero—at least, I suspected. You see, I saw it."

"Saw it? Saw what?"

"That night at Ashfield." I saw him draw breath, release it, the way my brother did when steeling himself to speak about Amiens. "You were standing in the circle alone, and the door was opening. I tried to reach you—the wind from faerie country was too strong. Hero was closer. She pushed you out of the circle, right as the door shut."

I had suspected it, really. I had wondered for years what that faint memory meant—the hands on my shoulder, the fall from the circle, the cry. Perhaps I had always known, as I had said to Alden, and hadn't wanted to know. Yet hearing it spoken aloud as a certainty, no room for comfortable doubt, was an agony like tearing back a curtain and being scorched by the light.

"Eight years ago." The words tasted like ash. "Eddie...You're saying that she's been under faerie control for eight *years?*"

"Yes." Now, of all times, he sounded surprised. "When did you think it had happened?"

"That can't be. The fae don't keep up pretenses that long. Someone would have noticed Hero wasn't herself."

But this was no ordinary faerie. Nothing it did was ordinary faerie behaviour. It had plans. If those plans entailed breaking all three locks, it would have needed to find them all before it acted. That could well have taken eight years, even with a husband in Berlin.

Hero had been coming to Ashfield her entire life. All the years the door had been here, the faerie had been able to watch her—more than enough time for it to learn to impersonate her, at least for long enough to get her away from everyone who knew her well. Camford, of course, would have seen the enchantment on her and kept her from its gates, which is why it had known better than to let her go back to school. It had accepted a marriage proposal, moved her far away from her family; it had cut ties with us, the people who knew her best. And we had let it happen. We had left her, when she was trapped in her own head begging us to come back.

I had known Hero. I knew that beneath her cynical airs and toughness, she would have walked through fire or into any faerie ring for the people she loved, and she loved the three of us. I had punched a hole to another world to save my brother; I had no doubt that Hero, seeing us in danger and with no time for thought, would run into a faerie circle for us. For *me*. I had been the one still in the faerie circle. She had done it for me.

Eight years.

"If you saw this," I made myself say to Eddie, "then why didn't you say anything?"

"I didn't think anything of it at first. The door seemed to have closed, with the faerie on the other side. It wasn't until Hero didn't come back to school and her engagement was announced that I wondered. I worried it wasn't like her—and I suppose, then, I worried that it really wasn't her at all. I wondered if we really had closed the door fast enough."

"You never said anything to me."

"No." His hesitation was palpable this time. He shifted uncomfortably in his seat, as though fighting the urge to stand. "I went to Alden. I told him I was concerned, and we should tell someone what we'd done. He—well. Let's just say he wasn't very happy with that idea."

I swallowed. "Did he threaten you?"

"No," he said, but unconvincingly, with too many syllables. "Not in so many words. He said I was wrong, and telling anyone now would ruin everything. He said the evidence of the door was gone now, and if I tried to tell anyone, they'd find no trace and he'd deny it ever happened. He said they'd believe him over me, which they would, of course. I was expelled from Crawley for violence and instability; Alden was the golden boy of our year. And…he knew about Richard, or suspected. They'd met a few times, when we were all children. I don't think Alden would have said anything, he's not like that, but…"

"God." I shouldn't feel sick, I reminded myself. I knew what Alden had just done to me when I had threatened to tell the Board about Ashfield. I knew he had convinced me to keep the imp windows from Hero and Eddie long ago, and because I had agreed I had never found out what he might have done had I not. "But I would have backed your story. You must have told him that."

"Oh yes." Even Eddie couldn't hide a touch of irony there. "He said I should be very careful about that. Your position at

Camford was precarious enough—did I really want to drag you into scandal? They'd believe you even less than me."

Now I really did feel sick. "Is that why you dropped out of Camford?"

He shrugged. "It just started to get too difficult, the way it did at Crawley, only without the fighting or the tomato plants this time. I didn't know how to talk to you without talking about Hero, so I stopped talking to you, and so I never really talked to anyone. And I couldn't even look at Alden, after that. I would sit in lectures with my chest going tight and my head spinning too much to see my notes, and soon our classes stopped making sense. I stopped going to lectures, even the ones Alden wasn't in, and then it became easier not to leave my room. That was when they sent me home on medical grounds. My parents were furious, but I didn't care. I didn't care much about anything for a long time."

I should have seen it. I knew Eddie as well as I knew my own siblings. I had watched him change, and been bewildered and hurt by the changes, and yet somehow I never asked. It had made depressing sense at the time: My friendship with Hero and Alden had dissolved after Ashfield, so of course Eddie would go the same way. Besides, I had problems of my own. When he had gone home unwell, I had been relieved—because he was getting cared for, of course, but could I swear there hadn't been an element of selfishness to it as well? Had any part of me just found it too difficult to have him around?

"To be fair to Alden," he added, as an afterthought, "I think he truly didn't believe Hero was under an enchantment back then. Or he didn't want to, which is always the same thing with him."

"I'm sorry," I said weakly. "I didn't know."

He shrugged again. His gaze was firmly on the floor. "It wasn't your fault. Just one of those things."

I wasn't happy with that, but I didn't have time to probe further. I couldn't even think of any of this mess too carefully, or I would fall apart and take everything with it.

"Well, I know now," I said instead. "About Hero, and about you. And I need to put it right. I say *I*; I really mean *we*. I'm asking for your help. We need to find her."

His face stilled, as it always had when presented with a new plan. I'd forgotten that: the way part of him retired to turn a proposal over while the rest of him gathered more information. Unexpectedly, my heart ached. "Do you know where she'll be?"

"If the Board are right, then she'll be headed for the Paris lock. Lady Winter seemed to think you might have relatives in France who can tell us where that is."

He neither confirmed nor denied it. "And then? There's no way to cast out a faerie once it's taken possession of a body."

I'd had a long broom ride to think about this. "But the faerie can choose to leave. There's clearly *something* it wants, something it's been planning for a very long time. Perhaps it might be willing to accept a deal: our help for Hero's freedom."

"We don't even know what it wants, much less what helping it would mean. There are a lot of things that could go wrong."

"I'll work out how to deal with each of them on the way. I understand if you can't come with me—I'd never ask you to. If you could just contact your cousin, tell me anything you can about the dryad...Please. I need your help."

He muttered something, too quiet to hear.

"I'm sorry?"

Eddie looked up at me then, and anger flashed across his face. I had seen that flash only once before, that terrible morning after the door had opened. "That's what you said to me at Ashfield." The words tumbled out and over one another, fast and unstoppable, like opening a door to a flooded room and being swamped by icy water. Or, perhaps, a door to another world. "It's what you always did to me, the three of you. You know, don't you? You all asked me to help you find a safe way to summon a faerie, and I agreed. You asked me to open a faerie door with you, and I agreed. I knew it was wrong, and I did it anyway, because your friendship and Alden's and Hero's was the most important thing I had and I didn't want to lose it. I'm not blaming you," he added, as I opened my mouth to—what? Protest? Explain? "It was my choice. I wanted to help. But that night broke me apart. When I got home from Camford, I didn't leave my room for three years. I was in pieces. It's only been this last year or so, coming out here with Richard, that I've started to feel some of those pieces come back to me. And the only time I've heard from you, in all those years, is you showing up out of the blue and asking for my help again. It isn't fair."

I sat there in silence, bitter guilt flooding my chest. He was right. I had always known that Alden tended to use Eddie to vent his frustrations, because Eddie would take it and never hit back. I had never realised, or at least never admitted to myself, that I had used him too, in far worse ways. I had used his intelligence, his loyalty, his desire to help. I had told myself I was bringing him into our project, when I should have been protecting him from it. I had even, in some dark unacknowledged corner of my brain, used the fact that he was there because I had asked him to be and not because Alden and Hero had. The four musketeers, Alden had called us once, but that meant someone had to be D'Artagnan, the outsider, and as long as Eddie was around, I no longer felt that was me.

"I'm sorry." The words fell flat—thrown into the air like a failed spell, drifting uselessly to the ground. "You're right. I was selfish and stupid, and I should never have got you involved in this. But we're all involved now, Eddie. We need to put it right."

"I know." He sat back with a long, shuddering sigh. The anger had faded now. He looked a lot more like himself than he had since I had come to the house—only very scared, and very, very tired. "And I do want to help. I really do. Or at least... I *want* to want to. I just don't think I can, not anymore. I've been out of the world for a long time now."

"You can. You've always been the strongest of all four of us, when it's come to it." I meant it. At the same time, though, I was worried. The Eddie I'd known had always been gentle, vulnerable, but with a core of steel. That core seemed bent now, fragile, as though it had really been made of some far softer metal. Gold, perhaps—the best substance for a heart, according to tradition, but perhaps the most malleable as well.

"I'm not," Eddie said, and now it was his turn to sound guilty. "Clover, there's something I have to—"

He never got any further. A quick knock at the door, and Richard stuck his head in.

"Sorry to interrupt," he said. "There are five cars coming up the road."

———————◈———————

They were some distance away yet, I saw when we went to join Richard. He had been at the upstairs window, in a little alcove that overlooked the hills. In the distance, a few miles below, I saw the edge of the loch, with the main road following its edge before climbing toward the house. The cars rumbled along that road, going slow on the uneven ground but certainly heading our way. Their lights glittered yellow on the darkening waters.

"I don't understand," I said. "How did they know I was here?"

Richard started to answer. Eddie got there first. "It was me."

I turned to look at him, shocked. He stood in the doorway; he seemed to have shrunk, so that his jumper was too large for his frame, his eyes too large and dark for his face.

"I'm sorry, Clover," he said. "That's what I was about to tell you. Alden arrived up here yesterday morning. I think he'd been driving all night—he looked shattered. He told me that if the Guards didn't catch you, then you would likely show up here. He gave me a coin, a doublet charm, and told me to make it burn hot if you arrived."

We'd used doublet charms often, in the old days. It needed two similar artifacts—coins worked well—that could be linked by a spell. From then on, if one grew hot or cold, the other would change temperature to match. It was an easy signal. It would have taken a second in the kitchen for Eddie to perform.

"He said he wanted to talk to you in private, without the Guards involved," Eddie added, when I didn't speak. "He said he wanted to help you."

I found my voice. "Did you really believe him?"

With anyone else, I would have assumed so, and I would have understood. Alden was very plausible when he wanted to be. I had believed him myself, far more often than I should; he knew how to give people what they wanted to believe and help them fool themselves. But Alden had shown Eddie who he really was a long time ago. I doubted he had been fooled now.

"*I* didn't," Richard broke in. He was staring at Eddie too, somewhere between disbelieving and exasperated and concerned. "Bloody hell, Eddie."

"I understand," I said, as calmly as I could. "You were angry with me. You had every right to be. You didn't owe me anything."

"You *don't* understand." Eddie's head snapped up, frustrated. "Neither of you do. Of course it wasn't because I was angry with you—do you really think I'd betray you because of a stupid thing like that? I didn't believe him either, not exactly. It's just…I've always done what Alden says. Right from when we were at school together—before. At first it was because I loved him and wanted his friendship, then it was because I was afraid of him and scared not to have it, and now I don't know where those two things start and end. But I swear, Clover, he told me that he only wanted to talk to you without the Guards about. I hoped he meant it. I tried to tell myself he did."

I understood exactly what Eddie meant. Right until that point, I too had held a faint hope I might have been wrong, that Alden had told the minister exactly what he'd promised and everything afterwards had been out of his control. I hadn't even realised it, until it flickered and died in my chest, and the world got a little more grey.

"How long until they get here?" I asked.

I was asking Eddie, but Richard answered. "About five minutes. We'll lose sight of them around the hills for a bit, then we'll see them on the driveway."

Thank God for the highland geography. "Then we need to get moving. I'm sorry, Eddie, but we both need to get out of here now. The broomstick can take the two of us—in five minutes we can be long gone."

I said it firmly, though every nerve in my body quailed at the thought of getting back on the broom and taking off into the night. So much for falling asleep in the chair where I sat. I wasn't even sure if my legs could bend again so soon.

"I can't." Eddie shook his head, as if I'd argued otherwise. "I mean it, Clover. I said downstairs I didn't think I could, and now, like this…"

Richard spoke before I could. "Eddie," he said. "For God's sake, get out of here. I could understand being afraid of the fae, but you're not. You're not even afraid of the world, whatever you say. You were exactly right: You're afraid of Alden Lennox-Fontaine. You always have been, even when you were friends, and you need to stop it. He can't do anything to you worse than he makes you do to yourself. If you won't listen to me, will you please listen to Clover and go do what you've known you have to do for the last eight years?"

I don't know what convinced him, in the end. I knew so little of their long, secret history together. But I saw the moment it worked. Something flickered behind Eddie's eyes, and then caught. He nodded, without a word, and I breathed again.

"Thank you," I said, to both of them. I pushed my glasses up my nose, trying to think. "Richard. Um…"

He made it easy for me. "What do you need from me? I could buy you time, if you like. I'm the groundskeeper, they won't question my being here alone. I'll say Eddie's gone back to his family, or on holiday, or anything you want them to hear."

"No," Eddie said, before I could. "If Alden sent those Guards, there's every chance he told them to bring you in as well. You need to run. Get across country—you'll be safer under trees. Don't stop, and don't come back." He paused, struck by a thought. "Take Scruff, and the hedgehog, it's still not well. The cats can look after themselves for a while, and anyway they're out prowling at this time of night. You'd never find them."

He nodded seriously. "Where shall I meet you, when it's all over?"

Eddie looked at me, questioning.

I thought it was unlikely we'd be meeting anywhere, ever again. I didn't say it. "Do you know Lady Winter's house at Pendle Hill?"

"No, but I reckon I can find it," Richard said. "I've got family not far from there."

"She'll hide you, I'm sure of it. And you can tell her I made it here safely, and we're off to France."

"Stick to the woods yourself," Richard advised. "It'll give you the best cover, all the way down to the coast."

I nodded, ignoring the screams of my lower back. "I'll go get the broom," I said to Eddie, before he could change his mind. "I'll be waiting out back. Bring something warm, and food if you can."

<hr/>

We barely made it.

I was waiting outside when I saw the first glow of car headlights cast the house into shadow. Eddie came out a second later, his worn old clothes covered by a much smarter grey coat, a leather bag over his shoulder, harried and frightened and determined in one glance.

"They're at the bottom of the driveway," he said, as he swung himself up on the broomstick behind me. "Go, go."

I kicked off at once. The broom wobbled precariously; Eddie grabbed my waist but made no protest. And then we were up, in the midst of the trees, skimming their topmost branches. Behind us, gravel crunched under tyres, and the woods flickered with the light from twin headlamps.

The trees had barely enclosed us when a shriek split the sky: the high, whistling scream of a defensive spell. I had heard it only days ago, propelled toward my car; I ducked on instinct now, and the broom hit the undergrowth. We both hit the ground, spluttering at the taste of dirt and leaves. I started to rise, half-ready to apologise. Eddie caught my wrist.

He didn't say a word. He didn't have to. The heat had reached us now, and the fiery light danced through the woods. Eddie's cottage was on fire. Hungry tongues of flame, red and yellow tinged with green, had already licked their way halfway up the blackened building; as we watched, wide-eyed, a hunk of the roof fell to the earth and smashed.

They had thought we were inside it, or at least they hadn't known we weren't. There had been no time to search the house. They had wanted us dead.

That sitting room, alive with books and greenery, all crisping and dying. The wallpaper curling and the curtains turned to sheets of flame. The alcove where we had crouched to watch the cars invading, fallen to the ground.

"It's all right," Eddie said in a low voice, before I could say anything. I suspected he had cut me off deliberately; I could feel him shaking and knew a stupid or sympathetic exclamation from me would push him over the edge. "It's all right, Richard got out, everything living got out, except the plants, and they can be grown again. The house doesn't matter. Just go, quick."

I didn't say anything. There was nothing I could say that wouldn't cut through his own attempts to hold himself together. I fumbled for the broom in the dark, found it, mounted it. Eddie got up behind me, and we turned the broom away from the glow and the heat, and into the night.

23

We flew on the broomstick through the night, most of it in silence, taking it in turns to steer. Eddie was far better than me, having grown up flying his parents' old brooms, as opposed to having just learned that morning. We made much better time under his guidance, and it was a relief for me not to have to concentrate furiously every mile. But my limbs were still locked stiff, and I could relax very little without tumbling off the broomstick. It rained in earnest around midnight, and by the morning I was chilled and exhausted and my entire body was in agony. I was secretly glad we couldn't travel that way across the Channel. I'd be seriously afraid I would arrive in Paris unable to move.

Instead we caught the ferry, like every other ordinary citizen, and I paced the rain-speckled deck as we skimmed the water. Hero would reach Paris first, having started from Berlin days ago, and she presumably had the advantage of knowing where the lock was kept. We knew only that it was somewhere in the city, probably deep in the vaults of wherever the French equivalent to the Board, the Conseil, was located. There was a very good chance she would be crossing the Channel in the opposite direction already.

"Perhaps we should have gone straight to London," I said aloud. "We might have had a better chance of intercepting her before she breaks the lock then."

Eddie shook his head. "We can't just sit in London waiting for her to attack the Paris lock and come to us. The French Guards could kill her. She will certainly kill many of them. That's not the sort of thing you just…let happen, as a strategy."

"I suppose not."

I looked at him, pale and distracted, gripping the railing of the ship just a little too tightly. Despite his best efforts and the near-empty deck, the outside world was overwhelming him. It was what I was used to seeing at a nightclub or a crowded party, right when his tolerance for noise and conversation and the proximity of other bodies was pushing against his threshold and he would have to step outside. I remembered his warning that he had barely been among people since he had left Camford, and guilt squeezed my heart anew. I would have had the right thing to say to him once. Now there was too much that was uncertain and awkward hanging between us. It was strange that I only realised just how much I missed him when he was standing right next to me.

I tried to find an encouraging smile, which probably looked daft. "I'm sure Richard's safe."

Eddie managed a smile back. He never was good at pretending. "I'm sure he is too. The Guards won't have any reason to be hunting him."

The Guards wouldn't, it was true. We both knew that Alden would, if he wanted to get to Eddie. My own family were in danger for the same reason.

If Alden touched any of them, I swore I would kill him.

"We'll get there in time," Eddie added. "You'll see. Hero won't attack in Paris as soon as she arrives. The dryad's waited eight years—it will take the time to plan, now the Board know it's coming. Trees are patient."

It wasn't convincing, but the effort at least was comforting. We were both doing our best to mend what had broken between us.

"Yes," I agreed. "We'll get there first."

⎯⎯⎯⎯✎⎯⎯⎯⎯

And in fact, we did. We had been in Paris nearly a full day before an explosion rocked the city.

⎯⎯⎯⎯✎⎯⎯⎯⎯

We were a few miles away, at a café near the Tuileries. Lady Winter's old broomstick had taken us from Calais to Paris; we had checked into a motel that was only marginally less grubby and tired than we were, and Eddie had telephoned his cousin at the French Board to arrange a meeting. Understandably, his cousin was less than impressed at being phoned by a distant relation she barely knew, especially one the English Board was trying to find; she also, more worryingly, had the same rush and panic in her voice that had been in that of the telephone operator at the Boardroom the day word of the Berlin attack had reached Camford. But she had agreed to meet us for lunch in an hour on the Right Bank, and we had made ourselves as presentable as possible to join her.

"How well do you know Paris?" I asked Eddie, and he laughed.

"Me? I don't like cities, remember. My parents took us to the South of France when I was seven—we stopped here for a day. What about you?"

"I came here for a conference," I said. "Last summer."

It had felt important, that week-long conference. The streets were sunlit and crooked and charming; the Seine sparkled green brown, and the pale buildings with their twisted iron balustrades looked like illustrations from a picture book. The French university of magic was through a portal door off the Sorbonne, its white stone and ordered streets the polar opposite of Camford, and the Faculty there had welcomed us with open arms. With only a few exceptions, I was spoken to as though I was a scholar and not a scholarship witch; several fellow scholars came up after my paper to congratulate me and ask questions, and the conversation had flowed over into dinner and then into the night. I had dared to hope that I truly had made it.

"Well," Eddie said, before I could spiral any further. "I'll follow you, then."

He might have been oblivious to what was going on in my head, but from the quick smile he gave me, I doubted it.

There was an unsettled, restless air to Paris as we found the café, asked for a table in our hesitant French, and were seated with the waiter promising, in English, to be back soon. The sky was grey, yet the pavement exuded stormy heat. We sat without talking, keeping an eye on the street for Eddie's cousin, although he had only the vaguest idea what she looked like and I had none at all. And I kept an eye out, too, for anyone else that might be looking for us. The broomstick was inside my satchel once more—in desperate need, it could be used. Spells that might help us raced around my head, reflexive, ready to burst from my fingertips at the slightest twitch. It didn't feel enough.

"Do you think the Conseil is near here?" I asked once, just for something to say.

Eddie shrugged. The tight, anxious look had crept back into his face, and his feet were twitching uneasily under the table.

"Perhaps," he said. "Not too close, though. She won't want to be seen with us."

If I replied, I don't remember.

It was then that all of Paris shook.

The impact rattled the plates and glasses, sent the chairs skittering on the cobbles and customers leaping up with startled cries. Eddie and I looked at each other, eyes wide.

"She's here," I said.

Smoke and dust were rising in the distance, across the Seine, behind Notre Dame. By the time we had pushed back our chairs and stood, the screams had started.

The smoke was coming from across the city. The broom was too conspicuous, though I pulled it from my satchel and held it at the ready just in case. Instead, we flagged down a passing cab, argued furiously in a mixture of French and English to take us toward the commotion rather than away from it, and threw far too much of Eddie's money at the driver before he would carry us across the bridge. In the end it bought us only a little time. As we drove into the Latin Quarter, the traffic and the crowds coming the other way were so thick that they spilled across the road, and we were forced to get out and push through them as best we could. I heard words in lilting French, high with panic: explosion, bombing, war. Cracks like gunshots or fireworks split the air, and each time I flinched.

By then, it was obvious we were going to be too late. It was also obvious exactly where the lock had been.

I had visited the Panthéon during the conference last year. Matty had been to Paris on leave at the start of the war, and while he claimed he had mostly learned where best to get drunk, he had at least told me how spectacular that monument was. And it truly was. The ornate classical front loomed impossibly large, the Grecian columns as thick and tall as ancient trees; inside, the high ceilings, the blank-faced sculptures, the great swinging pendulum that had been marking time since the middle of last century, all pressed down on me with a hushed awe that felt indistinguishable from magic. Now the enormous domed roof had split apart as though cleaved by a giant axe, and the remains were a blazing wreck. Ash drifted slowly from the sky; smoke filled my lungs, harsh and acrid, and I coughed painfully.

I had read the reports of the bombing raids on London and Norfolk and the Midlands by German zeppelins in the war, seen the photographs and the public service posters, and in my visits to London I had witnessed the buildings still being repaired. The dust and the wreckage and the noise looked exactly as though a bomb had struck. There was just one difference. The site was covered with trees. A forest of silver birch rose up from the ground, cracking the cobbles apart. Ivy and bracken draped the rubble, as though it had lain as a ruin for centuries. It looked like Camford, I recognised, and once I had thought it, I couldn't shake it. The ground before us was littered with dead leaves.

It was littered with something else too, something more terrible. There was a dark shape draped over the wreckage, a coat or a bundle of old cloth; when I looked closer, rubbing the soot from my glasses, I saw with a chill that it had a face. A body. A human body. There was another lying discarded on the footpath beside the gardens; another being dragged out to join it. I had to stifle another cough, this time because my stomach curdled and bile rose in my throat.

At least I knew for certain now. Hero couldn't, and would never, do this. This was something else, something that had reached through and taken her. We had opened a door in the world, and this was what had spilled out. I thought I had realised it, but it hit me now like a stab to the heart. I couldn't breathe.

"Josephine," Eddie said quietly, and it took my dazed brain a moment to remember that this was the name of his cousin. "Do you think she was here?"

"No." I said it without thinking, grabbing for reasons to fit the answer, exactly as a scholar shouldn't. "No, she couldn't have been. She was coming to meet us. She wouldn't have been here."

He said nothing. I'm sure he knew that the answer I'd given him wasn't honest.

We were too late. The battle was over—the second lock was

broken. The faerie had been right here, only moments before, and it had killed everyone and left before we had arrived. Such a narrow margin, and we had missed it.

And then I saw it. A figure, walking tall and straight-backed from the rubble, head held high and step brisk. I had last seen that figure eight years ago, watching from her car as we left to catch our train. I would have known it anywhere in the world.

"Hero!" I cried, as loudly as I could. "Hero, stop!"

Slowly, as if against her will, the figure faltered, turned. Through the crowds, she saw me.

The Hero in my memories had always been an adult, poised and sophisticated. In reality, though, she had been nineteen, little more than a girl, really, only months older than me. This Hero was grown. She was dressed in an elegant black suit, streaked with dust; her hair, fashionably short and crimped, framed a face that was still young and yet had hardened into something cooler and more austere. A faerie, I reminded myself, but it wasn't, or not entirely. There's a good deal of debate on where a host ends and a faerie begins in philosophy of magic, and I'd never quite seen the point. I did now. A faerie has no human body—the one it had now, by definition, was still Hero. In taking her form, it had in some very real way become her.

I had that one glimpse to take her in, as I assume she did me. Then she spoke. I recognised the high, wild lilt of the faerie tongue, and the ground beneath me erupted into twisting vines.

The suddenness and the scale of it was shocking; more to the point, it was *wrong*. Magic was secret. It always was, always had been, no matter who had needed to die to keep it that way. Now it was loose, tearing up the cobbles of the Latin Quarter, sending the crowds screaming and scattering as it streaked toward us like the flash of a snake. It stopped me still in my tracks, staring in horror, for just a moment too long. I raised my hands to strike back—with fire, with ice, with anything—and then the great tendrils were upon me.

They wrapped around my legs and then my body, pinning my arms to my side, and then they kept growing. My feet left the ground—I was being lifted in the air, suspended above the streets, almost to the roof of the ruined Panthéon. Beside me, I saw Eddie in the same position, struggling to no avail. The vines were the thickness of cord, and they blossomed with scarlet flowers. Their grip, though, was like the bite of iron.

I couldn't cast a spell. It wasn't just that my hands were bound, that my voice was constricted by the vines at my throat. Magic drained from me at the touch of the plant. It was like losing my hearing or my vision; I hadn't realised until that moment how accustomed I had become to *something* coursing through my veins and sparking in my fingertips, something that hadn't been there before Camford and now was in every beat of my heart. I panicked, gagging, thrashing wildly even as their hold clenched tighter and tighter. My glasses fogged; I couldn't draw breath; dark specks danced across a world grown pale and transparent.

"Don't fight!" Eddie's voice came to my right, muffled around the edges. "It'll relax if you do. Let it hold you."

It went against every instinct I had, but I had seen cats hunting mice often enough to grasp the sense in it. I stopped fighting the vines and started fighting myself. I closed my eyes, forced my limbs to stop thrashing, and tried to breathe evenly and slowly even as it felt my ribs would crack. In my head, as I often did when struggling to fall asleep at night, I went to the library roof at Camford. The four of us stretched out on sunbaked tiles, the crooked paths and buildings and canals far below, the university walls encircling us and shielding us from the mist beyond. *Breathe. Just breathe.*

Slowly, inch by inch, the vines relaxed their grip. I was still held, suspended high above the cobbles, but the hold was no longer painful. My breath came at last in ragged gasps, and for a moment the sweet rush of air filling my lungs blotted out everything else.

"What do you want, Clover Hill?" It was Hero's deep, beautiful voice, from Hero's body, but it wasn't Hero speaking. I could see it now, as she walked toward me glowing with faerie magic. "I fulfilled my bargain with you. You have your brother alive and well."

I could have pointed out that the faerie had had no intention of Matthew being alive or well. I didn't. It wasn't just that the accusation would be stupid. I didn't want the faerie thinking about Matthew.

"I want Hero," I said instead. I tried to sound firm when I was still struggling for breath. "We've come for our friend."

Her head tilted to one side. It wasn't Hero's gesture at all. I recognised with a chill the insectoid twist from the faerie we had held in the door.

"A little late now, isn't it? You left her to me for eight long years."

"We didn't *leave* her." It was ridiculous to be so defensive, I knew that even as I spoke. It was a faerie, it was being cruel on purpose, it didn't care—but the feelings of my eighteen-year-old self came back in a rush. "You took her."

"And you never even noticed."

"How could I? She drove us to the station and dropped us there, and then I never saw her again."

It hit me with a rush then, everything I had been trying not to picture. Hero pushing me to safety as the world buckled around us; her cry as the fae had sunk its talons into her flesh and burrowed into her mind. Hero trapped in her own body, screaming at us to see her as the train pulled away. Year after year, moment after moment, watching while her body was used by something alien, realising that we were never going to come.

Had I really not suspected, even for a moment? Eddie had guessed, after all. Alden had convinced himself that nothing was wrong. Had I done the same, without even having the honesty to lie to myself about it?

"You kept her away," I said. "You let me believe she blamed me, so I wouldn't see what had really happened to her."

"It wasn't for that reason," the faerie in Hero's body said. The words felt involuntary somehow.

"Why, then?"

There was a hesitation, the tiniest breath before she spoke that felt human and not fae. "She bargained."

"Who did?" It came to me a beat too late, in a painful rush. "Hero. Hero bargained. She made you leave us alone."

"If I'd been worried you would see the truth, I would have killed you all. I might have done it anyway, just to be safe. But she fought me, every breath. It would have meant nothing in the end, but her will was strong. Fighting back takes time, and as long as I was in her body, hurting her meant hurting myself. If I left you three alone, she agreed to stay quiet. She's been quiet for years now. I'm not sure how much of her is left. And it didn't matter, did it? None of you noticed; even now, too late, most of the world believes this is truly her."

Shame coursed through me, hot and bitter. I had failed her not once, but twice, perhaps many times over. We had all failed one another, in so many ways.

"I'm sorry," I said. "Hero? If you can hear me, we're going to save you."

"Don't *talk* to her," the faerie hissed, and the vines tightened about my throat. I gasped, and heard Eddie do the same. Beneath us, the broken shell of the Panthéon swam before my eyes, all but deserted now and entwined with vines. "I told you, she's barely there anymore. I'm not worried about any fight she'll put up if I snap you in two right now."

I didn't believe it: She would have done it already, and she certainly wouldn't be worried about me talking to Hero. Still, I fell silent, for Hero's sake. I'd said what I'd needed to say to her.

"Why are you doing this?" Eddie spoke up. "Perhaps we can bargain."

Her laugh was Hero's laugh, and it twisted my heart. "You? You have nothing that I could possibly want."

"What *do* you want?" I asked. "Does it have something to do with why you killed so many people at Amiens?"

I wished, more than ever, that faerie scholarship had not been forbidden. I knew so little about how the fae behaved, even with Lady Winter's library. But Matthew had been right, and so had Eddie. This was not a usual dryad. I could see it in her face now, feel it in the thorns pressing my skin. She hated us.

"I killed those people at Amiens for the same reason I killed Hero's husband and everyone who tried to stop me in Berlin and now here," the faerie said. "They were in the way."

"In the way of what?" I asked. "Why do you want the locks broken?"

She said nothing.

"The fae aren't usually murderous," I pressed, and felt the vines creep up to my cheek. I swallowed and kept on. "They're tricksters. If they steal human bodies, it's because they want to experience our world—"

"I don't want your world," she spat. "Look what you've done to it. Paved it over, torn it up, poisoned it. I want *my* world. I want the piece of it you carved out hundreds of years ago. I want what was stolen."

This was new, and unexpected. My heart quickened. "What do you mean? What was stolen?"

Hundreds of years ago. We may not learn faerie magic at Camford, but we certainly teach history of modern magic, and even folklore is rich with tales founded on true events. I rifled through my brain, frantic, trying to think of any faerie deal that had gone wrong hundreds of years ago.

"Did someone trick you into giving them an object?" I tried. "A cloak, or a sword, or…?"

"I don't care about foolish trinkets! And I'm not talking about deals or tricks. I'm talking about theft." The vines around us flexed, trembled. "Stay out of my way, you two, or I will break my promise to Hero and take the consequences. This has nothing to do with you."

I should have stopped. As usual, I persisted. "Perhaps we can help. *What* has nothing to do with us? What was taken from you?"

"Clover," Eddie warned me, softly. It was too late. Hero's face had hardened; her lips drew back over her teeth in a low, sharp hiss.

"*Get away from me,*" she snarled, and then the vines cracked like a whip and there was nothing holding us in the air.

I truly don't know if she meant to kill us. My instinct is no. I think her heart was shrieking, her barriers were cracking; I pushed a fraction too far, too keen as usual for information and too sharp, and the faerie wanted to fling us both as far and as fast from her as she could. But that is scant comfort when the ground is coming up to meet you very fast.

My stomach shot into my throat; my limbs were horribly weightless. The Panthéon flashed in photographic stills before my eyes: pale blue sky, dead leaves, columns, tree roots breaking through cobbles. Eddie, beside me, eyes wide with horror. My arms windmilled, frantic, trying to cling to something, anything. There was nothing.

Except, still in my hand, the broomstick that Lady Winter had given me.

It was barely a stick now. The vines had cracked it in two; the twigs at one end were scattered over the ground. Yet it was warm in my hand, and in desperation I found the breath and the presence of mind to yell the word for flight.

The broom heard me. It stopped still in midair, quivering and trembling. My arm caught, my shoulder wrenched, and I clung on with one hand as tight as I could. With the other I reached out, grabbed for Eddie's hand, missed—and, right as my heart cried *no*, snagged his jacket.

I was a fraction past the last possible second, or perhaps I caught it exactly. Eddie came to a sharp stop in midair, limbs jerking like a marionette's, before his coat slipped from my grasp and he fell the remaining few feet to the ground. I heard a sickening crack as his head struck the cobbles, and a faint cry that choked off to nothing.

"No!" I heard my own voice without recognising it. I landed, stumbled, then sank to my knees and crawled over to Eddie. *Please, please let him not be dead. Not him too, not because of me, please...*

He wasn't. When I reached him, he was already stirring, turning over, raising his hand to his forehead with a wince. There was blood above one eyebrow and the beginnings of a bruise already, but not the broken skull I had feared. I had, after all, slowed his fall enough.

"I'm all right," he mumbled, dazed, as I checked him over. "No, I'm fine, really. Are you hurt?"

"You're not fine, you clod." I deliberately ignored the question, because if I thought about it, I suspected I was. Beneath the adrenaline, I could feel agony lurking along my arm and shoulder, waiting to surface, and I was trembling. "But I don't think it's very bad. Can you get up? We need to get out of here."

There was no sign of Hero any longer. The vines that still entangled the Panthéon were as immobile as any other plant. She was gone. Sooner or later, people would trickle cautiously back to the wreckage, looking for survivors. If any of them happened to be Guards, we were in serious trouble—

"I'm fine." Eddie's voice was firmer now, and he pulled himself up with barely a wobble. "Come on. People are looking."

They were: a crowd of stunned spectators, drawing timidly close to the broken monument, looking with wonder at the vines twisting up the columns. One or two, in the front of the line, were already pointing toward us. I didn't know if any of them were Guards, or the French equivalent of Guards. If they weren't here yet, they would be soon. I shook myself firmly.

"Hold tight," I said to Eddie, and offered my poor, faithful, fragmentary broomstick. He clasped it, his hand nudging mine, and I raised it in the air and gave the word. We rose, dangling from a broken stick of wood, up into the Paris sky.

24

It was too late.

The words echoed in my head, even as my body managed to do quite normal things. Alight out of sight, cast a quick charm to cover our tracks so that anybody passing through the area in the next quarter hour would forget they had seen us. Take the metro to the Gare du Nord—there was no point in staying in Paris now, when Hero had what she came for. She would be headed straight to London. We had to do the same.

"Do you have money to get back to England?" I asked Eddie briskly.

"Enough for the crossing." His head was still bleeding, and he was looking very white and dizzy. "Not enough to get out to Calais as well. Clover—"

"Never mind." It was too late. Even if we could get there in time, it was still too late. It had been too late years ago. "We'll improvise. Hold on tight."

We lighted on the roof of a west-bound train, with the very last feeble spark of the broom's magic, and we slipped inside a carriage packed with trunks and luggage and crates. It was leaving Paris, rattling over miles of French countryside, back the way we had come, as though in mockery of our long journey to get here. I didn't care. The words were still ricocheting through my brain, and when I stopped moving, they exploded.

I sank down against a huge leather trunk covered in yellowing labels and closed my eyes against the dim light as the carriage shuddered gently around me, utterly miserable and utterly spent. My head throbbed, my body ached, and I felt shivery and exhausted as though I had the flu. I didn't care about that either. All I could see, whether my eyes were open or shut, was Paris split apart, the Panthéon wreathed in vines, Eddie falling through the air. Hero's body being worn by the creature we had summoned, so many years ago.

As long as we were still on this earth there was nothing that couldn't be fixed. I had believed that, had clung to it through years of war and sickness and beyond. But we couldn't fix this. The sight of faerie magic tearing up Paris had blown away any illusions I had managed to cling to. It was too big for us—that was why the faerie had broken through in the first place, when we were stupid, thoughtless children pretending to be scholars, and it was why we could never hope to put it back now. It was too late to fix anything. The only thing we could have done was never let it break in the first place.

"Clover?" I felt Eddie's hand on my shoulder, then heard a slight catch of breath. "You're hurt."

I opened my eyes and glanced down, with effort. Blood had seeped through the dressing on my arm and through the sleeve of my coat. "Oh. That wasn't from Hero. That's where Lady Winter took the tracking spell from me, a few days ago. It must have opened, I suppose." I hadn't even thought about it since leaving Pendle Hill. Lady Winter had given me firm instructions to change the dressing every few days, but I hadn't had the time or the inclination.

"Let me see."

It hurt to move, much less to ease out of the coat I had been wearing for days, and all I really wanted was to curl up and not think. Eddie was gently insistent, though, and I let him pull down the sleeve of my blouse to expose my upper arm and unwrap the greying dressing.

Whatever he saw made him wince. "No wonder you look rubbish."

I had to laugh, though I suddenly felt closer to tears. "Oh, thanks. You're not looking so clever yourself, you know."

"I just got a bump on the head. It's nothing. I've done worse to myself falling out of trees. That, though, looks like it needs a bit of cleaning, and then a bit of magic. Do you mind?"

I shrugged the shoulder that didn't feel like it was burning up, a little surprised. "Go ahead. Have you done this before?"

"Well," he conceded, "not on humans. But Richard and I nursed a baby fox back to health last winter, so..."

My laugh this time was more real. "Oh, say no more. I'm in good hands."

I was too. His satchel opened; from it came a first aid kit, exactly the sort of thing I was always forgetting, and he patched up the bleeding gash in my arm as deftly as Lady Winter had done a few nights before. Instead of putting on a fresh dressing, though, he pulled out a specimen box with a single flower inside. The bloom was deep scarlet with a faint purple tip. It looked vaguely familiar, though I couldn't place it.

"This is a rose from Camford," he answered my unspoken question. "The same kind that helped your brother. Do you mind if I use it?"

"No, please." I looked at it, interested and wary despite myself. "What does it do?"

"Nothing on its own, it turns out. It senses and enhances magic—faerie magic, especially, which was why it reacted so strongly to your brother's curse. It should help with this as well, if I talk to it right."

"Are you a hedgewitch now?"

I was teasing, cautiously, and I was rewarded with an echo of his old lopsided smile. "Unfortunately not. One came to the house in winter, though, and stayed with us for the coldest weather in exchange for teaching me all she knew. They're miles ahead of Camford when it comes to herbs and potions. Hold still, please."

He pulled off a dark leaf and laid it against my arm, muttering the same healing charm Lady Winter had used. The leaf burned with a sting like a nettle; I hissed on reflex, but when Eddie glanced at me, I nodded to keep going. Beneath the sting, the pain and the dull heat was ebbing, and my thoughts were clearing in their wake. Besides, I trusted him.

"I was worried you'd given up research for good," I said. "When you left Camford."

"Oh no. Never. You don't need a university to learn. Though admittedly it does help. I've bought a lot of books; I would have got a lot further and faster with the Camford Library. There." He pulled the leaf away. "How does that feel?"

"Much better. Thank you." It really did, I discovered as I flexed it. The heavy exhaustion had lifted, and the sting in my upper arm had eased to a faint, muffled throb. I saw before Eddie wrapped it again that the inflammation had faded. I felt less shivery, too, though that hadn't all been the wound. The blaze of those green eyes in Hero's face was still seared into my brain.

Eddie's face was troubled. "I can't believe Alden did that to you," he said. "I knew he would lie to hide what we'd done, but—not this. Not to you. Not to Hero either."

"We don't know how much any of this came from him directly," I reminded him, without much conviction. "It might have got away from him."

"Still. I'm sorry I called him to the house. And I'm sorry I didn't try to do more for Hero all those years ago, when I suspected what had happened." Those eyes were clearly still burning in his head too.

"*I'm* sorry." This time, at least, it sounded sincere. "I let you down."

Eddie shook his head firmly. "I never thought that."

"I knew you were struggling, that last term at Camford. I knew something wasn't right. I should have asked more questions."

"I wouldn't have given you answers then. I *was* angry at you, I suppose, but mostly I was worried for you. You aren't Family, and neither you nor your brother was ever safe. If things were as bad as I feared, I didn't want you anywhere near them."

Guilt squeezed my chest. I had said the same thing to Alden about Eddie, in London, and yet when it came to it, I hadn't hesitated to draw him back in. "You always were a better friend to me than I was to you."

"No. It wasn't like that." He paused, frustrated, trying to find the right words. "It wasn't about *being a good friend*, as though it was a duty I'd taken on, and because I had it was your duty to be one back. Everything I did with you, or for you, I did because I wanted to, because I liked you. I don't like a lot of people, you know. You didn't owe me anything in return."

"I liked you too." It felt inadequate, but the simplicity of it also felt right. "Very much. I knew you were a better person than Alden. I don't know why that doesn't matter when you're eighteen."

"Oh, I liked him too," Eddie said matter-of-factly. "And you had more excuse than me. He admired you, truly, everyone could see it. He never did me. We were friends when we were children because I was dropped off at his house and told to play with him and Hero. He looked after me at Crawley and then at Camford because he felt sorry for me, and perhaps because he could see that in those days I was a little bit in love with him. I'm not sure he ever even liked me."

"He did—he still does." Perhaps I was deluding myself, wanting our summer at Ashfield to be real. I was very capable of delusion where Alden was concerned, apparently. And yet I had seen the look on Alden's face when he had told me we were the only people he had ever loved. It had been an apology, I knew now, for what he was about to do. But he had meant it. "He just isn't going to let it stop him."

Stop him doing what, though, was the question. The easiest answer was simply that Alden was trying to preserve his career, his name, his entire way of life. It was what Lady Winter believed, and it was convincing—I had come close to doing the same, all those years I had put Ashfield behind me, looked the other way, and focused on my academic path. I just couldn't quite believe it of him, even now. He was selfish, ruthless even; he wasn't shallow. Surely if he was going to throw us all away, he needed something better than that. What did he want?

What, for that matter, did the faerie want?

"Clover?"

It was the hesitation in Eddie's voice rather than my name that snagged my attention. I looked at him, inquiring.

"That flower I just used," he said, with a nod at my arm. "The roses that grow in Camford. There's something you should know about them."

"What is it?"

"I saw them on the vines that Hero just used to bind us. They're the same flowers."

My thoughts had been very far from flowers. It took a moment for his words to catch up. "What do you mean, the same?"

"I mean that I haven't seen these roses anywhere except Camford before. Nobody has. I thought they were regular roses, that growing in Camford had changed them. All the plants in Camford are slightly off. But today—the flowers on those vines were the same."

"How can they be?" I asked slowly. "I mean...Are you sure?"

I already knew the answer. When it came to plants, Eddie had always been sure.

The look he gave me confirmed it. "They were holding me suspended in midair, Clover. I got a pretty good look at them. I just don't know what it means."

Something was forming, coalescing. It was my favourite moment of research, the moment when a thousand fragments come together in a blinding flash that illuminates everything. This one I wasn't sure I wanted to see by, but out of sheer stubborn habit, I grasped for the fragments.

This, I reminded myself, was what knowledge was for. Not to bend to our own purpose and our own ambitions, the way we had when we were young. To find the truth, even when that truth is something you wish could be different.

"They respond to magic, you said?"

"Faerie magic, particularly," Eddie said. "The wise woman who stayed at our house thought they might be faerie plants. But that didn't make any sense to me at the time."

And then, all at once, I saw.

The trees that grew around Camford, ash and oak and wild roses. The mists outside the Camford walls, the locked gate, the doors that we stepped through every day when no two places on earth could be connected that way.

I don't want your world, the faerie that was Hero had said. *I want my world. I want what was stolen.*

"It's Camford," I said slowly. "The doors we pass through to reach Camford, at Oxford or Cambridge—they're faerie doors. That's where Camford is. Camford is built on faerie ground."

"But—" Eddie shook his head, bewildered, and winced. "The doors leading to faerie country were all closed and sealed after the Accord. Ashfield only escaped because it had been opened during the war, in secret. If the Oxbridge was a faerie door, we wouldn't be able to enter the university at all."

"Except that every faerie door is twofold." The words were tumbling too fast to stop, trying to keep up with my thoughts. "There's an inner door and an outer door, remember? The Camford door is still open at our side—that's how we get in. The other side—the dangerous side, the faerie side—is closed. It has been for centuries, long before the Accord."

"The door set into the wall surrounding Camford is always locked." Eddie looked very white—though that might have been the blow to the head. "And nothing can be seen beyond it except mist. But the space between doors is supposed to be tiny. A millionth of the width of a hair."

"Usually. This one is the precise size of a university. Once you have a spell, stretching it a little isn't so difficult."

"Why, though? You can build a university anywhere. Why would you go to all that trouble to build one on faerie ground?"

"I don't know, not yet. But that would explain why nobody is ever allowed to know where Camford is. It would explain why you were always deterred from studying the plants that grow there, do you remember? They were the only thing that gave it away. They're faerie plants."

"Hero always thought they knew more about the faerie at Amiens than they were telling," Eddie said slowly. "That's why they were so quick to shut down faerie magic. They knew, or at least suspected, why a dryad might go to such effort to break through to our world, and how dangerous it would be if she succeeded."

"It's nothing in our world she wants at all. She's trying to break down the wall between the worlds and find something at Camford. Not her tree—she'd have died long ago without it, and besides, there are no birch trees at Camford." I could say that with confidence—birch trees were something I noticed, given Matthew's curse. "But there's something we stole along with the land, and she wants it back."

Eddie was silent for a long time. "Oh God," he said at last.

Camford. My home, the haven of knowledge I loved, the place that despite everything I had believed existed especially for me. I had been there my entire adult life, trying to dig up answers about the heart of magic, and I had missed what was buried right under my feet. I had wondered about Camford's location, and then dismissed it, because I'd wanted to fit in. I had grown up in the heat of the dryad's anger and its consequences—my brother's curse, Alden's brother's disappearance, Hero's possession, the trail of destruction she was leaving now in her wake—and I had never tried to find out what might have earned that anger. I was used to feeling stupid—it was the first step to knowledge, I always told my students—but this was different. I had been the worst kind of scholar, the kind who accepts answers without even realising there are questions to ask.

"We need to get there." Eddie's voice pulled me back. His grey-blue eyes were steady, and I tried to let them steady me too. This was the Eddie I remembered, the one who accepted immediately the situation we were in and only looked for what he could do to help. Amidst everything, I felt a flash of shame that the very things that sent me into despair were the things that brought him back. "If Hero's going to Camford, we need to get there first."

I found my voice again. "The Board must know where she's going. They'll evacuate the university. We won't be able to get in."

"The Camford Faculty will help, surely. You're a scholar. They respect you."

"Some of the other scholars do, I hope. Not the Faculty. They've never liked me."

I could say it without sting now. It wasn't as though I hadn't known it from the first. All those long, tiresome fights over grants, the struggle to get even one teaching appointment, the regulations about women scholars that were outdated by the standards of most universities in the world. I had spent so many years shaping myself into what they had wanted me to be, and all it had done was annoy them. They had been delighted when Hero left; they must have been downright thrilled when the two of us were declared criminals.

"Never mind them, then." It was a verbal shrug. Eddie didn't exactly not care what people thought of him—I'm not sure that's possible—but he cared less than anyone I knew. "Is there anyone else who could get us in?"

I racked my brains, trying to channel Eddie's focus. Never mind them. Never mind. "Sam might. He isn't high on the Board, but he knows things. With any luck, Matthew and Lady Winter should have cornered him by now. He might be able to get us in."

"Then that's what we'll do," Eddie said. "We'll go to London as we planned, and we'll go to Sam for help. If we can't stop her in London itself, he can get us into Camford."

"That sounds like a plan." I didn't say that we might still be too late. That even if we did reach Camford, our conversation might not go any better than last time—if anything, it could be worse. My one faint hope had been to save Hero by bargaining for her release. If the faerie made it to Camford, she already had what she wanted.

"We can't just do nothing," I said out loud.

"No," Eddie agreed, as though he had heard everything I had left unspoken. "Not with Hero being held by that dryad. Not now that we've seen it for ourselves. Of course we can't. And it's more than just Hero, isn't it?"

"Yes." I rested my head back against the wall and closed my eyes against the rattle of the train. I was so tired that I felt weightless, thrown about inside the carriage like a loose piece of luggage. "God, Eddie, what did they do, all those centuries ago, that made that faerie hate us so much? Why build a university on faerie ground at that kind of cost?"

"We'll find out." He settled beside me, and in the midst of everything, his shoulder was a comforting warmth against mine. "We're scholars. It's our job."

We came back across the Channel on the early ferry and arrived in Dover to a bright, cold English morning. My limbs had steadied by then, and my nerves with them. My thoughts had found their old wartime groove. We weren't defeated yet. Until the moment we heard the third lock had been broken, we still had time. That could be the very next moment, it was true, but it wasn't here yet. Eddie went to find tickets for the nearest train to London, while I hurried to check the office for a message. I had sent Lady Winter a telegram from Calais; she should have had a chance to reply by now, however cryptically.

My heart was beating a little less rapidly by the time I got back to Eddie.

"Richard's safe," I said, without preamble. "Lady Winter left a message. He reached her and gave her our news."

Days' worth of tension flooded from his body at once, and the first real smile I'd seen in all those days lit his face. I couldn't help but smile in return.

"Good," he said, inadequately. "That's good. How about your brother? Has he reached Sam yet?"

"She said Sam would be ready to talk to us when we arrived. And since she didn't mention London being in ruins, it seems Hero isn't there yet."

"Good," he said again. "Well. I have our tickets. The train will be boarding soon."

Another train journey. It was better than a broomstick, I supposed, but I wasn't sure I could bear the enforced stillness. I had no choice.

Perhaps it was the thought of that train ride that did it—the knowledge that I wouldn't be able to put through a call until we reached London, and then it would be too dangerous and too late. Either way, I glanced at the telephone box on the station platform, and I faltered.

"I need to make a call," I said, before I could change my mind. "Would you mind waiting, just a minute?"

Eddie was startled, but he hid it well. "No, of course not. Is it…?" He trailed off. "Never mind. As long as we don't miss the train."

"We won't. This will just be a second."

I wasn't sure I even remembered the number for Ashfield. I had never called it, after all, only given it to my family a very long time ago. But I'd always had a good memory for number sequences, and I remembered everything about Ashfield. I imagined my call racing across the country, travelling through the wires, through the little hills and rivers of Oxfordshire toward the leaden skies and wild moorland of the north. It was hard to remember, these days, where magic ended and technology began.

A click on the other end, and then a voice, deep and efficient. I wondered if it was Morgan—it had been a long time, and voices sounded different on the telephone. "Hello, this is the butler at Ashfield Manor."

"Hello." I pitched my own voice a little lighter, more formal. My hands were slick with perspiration against the receiver. "Could I speak to Mr. Lennox-Fontaine, please? It's urgent."

It was far more likely that Alden was at his office in London, awaiting developments there. That was his job, as minister for magical enforcement. And yet I wasn't surprised when the butler said, "One moment, please."

Alden must have been waiting for a phone call—probably many of them. His reply was swift, and despite the earliness of the hour it had the brisk efficiency of someone prepared for a colleague on the other end. "Hello?"

"Alden," I said. "It's me."

I don't know what reply I expected. There was none. Silence rang in my ear, the still, frozen silence of a wild thing that knows it has been seen. Only the faintest crackle of static let me know that he was still there and breathing.

"Clover," he said at last.

The telephone at Ashfield was on the first floor corridor, or it had been in my day. I imagined Alden standing there now, amidst the oak panelling and oil paintings and the low slanted beams of sunlight.

"Do you still have nightmares at Ashfield?" I heard myself ask.

"Do you care?"

"I hope you do. You deserve them."

"I do."

I meant this to be a quick conversation. One last chance, and then gone before he could call anyone at the Board or work out where I was phoning from or get under my skin. But he was already under my skin, embedded somewhere deep along with Hero and Eddie and Camford and that summer at Ashfield. It was too late.

"What did you tell the first minister after I left your apartment, Alden?" I asked. "That I was helping Hero? That we were what came of women being educated at the hallowed halls of Camford?"

"No." A faint sigh, as if he'd sat, or leaned back against a wall. "That was what *he* told the rest of the Board, and the papers. *I* told him more or less what I promised to tell him. I spun you a few lies that evening, I'll admit; that wasn't one of them. The first minister already knew that Hero was possessed by a faerie—that much was obvious from the curse. I told him that it had likely happened during our university days, that I had been involved, and so had you. I told him that you had been to my house and intended to tell others. As I foresaw, he wanted to leave my name out of it."

"Nobody wants a scandal this close to elections." My mouth was dry.

"Exactly. I'm too valuable where I am and too dangerous anywhere else, and of course he knows my father. Besides, I was hardly going to tell anybody. You were a different story. The Board wanted you silenced."

"Do you expect me to accept that? That it wasn't your doing, and you didn't know it would happen?"

"No. I'm telling you that I didn't lie to the first minister. Of course I knew what would happen when I told him the truth.

I've lived in this world too long not to know how it works. I needed you out of the way too. For what little it may be worth, I wouldn't have done it if you hadn't come forward, and I did what I could to keep Eddie out of it. If you hadn't gone to him, he still wouldn't be involved. Is he with you now?"

I knew better than to answer that. "That is indeed worth very little." I let my voice drip with irony. "Considering you destroyed his house without knowing if we were inside it."

"Yes." A moment of uncharacteristic silence. "Tell him I'm sorry about that. It wasn't my decision. I'm only the minister for magical enforcement, not the Board. A lot of things are out of my control."

My hand tightened painfully on the receiver. "You know, I truly believed you when you said your political career wasn't what mattered to you."

"You were right to. It isn't."

"Then why?" It was what I'd really phoned to ask, after all. "What do you need us out of the way *for*? Why are you doing this, Alden?"

"The same reason I opened the door eight years ago—the same reason I did any of it. I want to put things right, the way they should have been if I hadn't made one foolish mistake when I was twelve years old. I was never like Hero, you know. I never wanted to change the world. I just wanted it back the way it used to be, before everything fell apart."

That, of all things, I understood. My voice softened only a little, but it softened. "It's too late for that."

"It's too late for some things, I know. Not for everything, not yet." He paused. "I never meant to draw you or Hero or Eddie into this, all those years ago. Please believe that."

"This isn't about what you *meant* to do," I said. "It isn't even about what you did by accident. Everybody makes mistakes. It's about what you did afterwards. And what you did was protect yourself at the cost of everybody else. It's what you've always done, but this time you were old enough to know better."

"I know," he said simply.

I drew a deep breath, forced calm. "If you really want to fix this, then let's fix it together. We're going to put it right, Alden. Eddie and I. And God knows you don't deserve it, but you should be with us. Forget the Board, and your family, or whatever else you have in mind. Please come and help. For Hero's sake, if for nothing else."

"I wish I could." He genuinely seemed to mean that. On his next sentence, though, his voice had shifted. "Clover, are you and Eddie on your way to Camford?"

"Are you going to help us?" I countered, as quickly as I could. I told myself he couldn't possibly read anything from my answer. Even if I'd given myself away, he would wonder if I'd done it on purpose to allay suspicion. Whatever he suspected, he couldn't stop us.

His sigh was a burst of static down the phone. "I can help you this much, at least. Don't go to Camford. I know what the faerie wants there, and you can't give it to them."

"What?" Now my heart was racing for a different reason. "What does she want?"

"I can't say any more," he said, very carefully, "because when I took office I accepted a binding curse before I learned this secret, and if I break it, my heart will quite literally break too. But it's best you leave this alone."

"You know more than what the dryad wants," I said. "Something happened when Camford was created, didn't it? Something terrible, something the Board are trying desperately to hide. You know what it is."

"Yes. Yes, I know now. And I'm sorry about it, but it wasn't my doing. It was centuries before I was even born, for God's sake. Our world was built on the back of it, and we can't undo it without bringing everything crashing down. Believe me, you've a stake in this too. If you go near Camford, you'll only see I'm right."

I found a painful laugh. "*Believe* you? Are you truly expecting me to believe you about anything ever again?"

I heard the soft, sideways smile in his voice. "Perhaps not. It's true nonetheless. Clover—"

I hung up. I had nothing more to say, and there was nothing more Alden could say to me that I wanted to hear.

Eddie was waiting for me outside the telephone box. He must have known who I'd been talking to, but he didn't mention it.

"The train's coming in now," he said instead. "They're saying we'll make good time to London."

"Good," I said, just as Eddie had. My eyes were burning. I ignored them. "Let's go."

25

Even as the train rolled into Victoria Station, it was obvious that something was wrong. The sky was leaden—not the usual cloud cover of an English summer, but the low haze that heralded a nearby bonfire or city pollution. The crowds on the platform were distracted, subdued.

"Perhaps she *has* broken the London lock already," Eddie said to me quietly. We'd both been thinking it, the anxious, too-slow journey back.

The tension in the air didn't quite feel that way, though. I knew the stunned, barely comprehending quiet that followed a disaster, all too well. This was different—the vague dread of something still to come.

"Clover!" I recognised my brother's voice a moment before I turned to see him wave at us from the station entrance. My brief flicker of relief was immediately subsumed in worry. I hadn't wanted Matthew in London at all, much less meeting us.

"Hero broke the Paris lock," I told him in a rush, as soon as we were in earshot of each other.

"I know." It had been a long time since I'd seen Matthew away from Pendle Hill—perhaps not since before the war, when he'd drive us younger ones into Manchester for the day and treat us to lunch and the Sherlock Holmes serials at the pictures. He looked different set against the city: crisper, brighter despite the tension in his face, alive in some way I hadn't realised I'd missed. A still-young man who'd been around the world, and not a weather-beaten extension of the farm. "Lady Winter called me at the hotel. I'd already read about it in the papers. A bombing, they called it, though I was pretty sure your papers would call it something different. Until she called, though, I had no idea if you'd even made it out of England, much less France. Hello, Eddie. Good to see you again."

"It's good to see you too," Eddie said with a smile.

He meant it. He'd got on well with all my siblings, the week or so he'd spent with us. He saw no trouble at all with Matthew being here, in the midst of a magical conflict, and I knew I was being foolishly overprotective to mind it myself. Still, I did mind.

"We're not too late, are we?" I asked.

"Not as far as I know." He glanced about the crowds, understanding the reason for my question without words. "The whole city's on edge, though. They're saying in the papers that the people who bombed Paris might target London, and they're urging people to go into the city as little as possible. I think your lot are expecting Hero at any minute. And before you tell me I shouldn't be here—I'm guessing you need to talk to Sam more than ever?"

"Did you speak to him?" Eddie asked.

"Not as such," Matthew admitted, and my spirits did a quick plunge again. "I tracked him down, but he's still avoiding all my messages and calls. Don't worry, though, Lady Winter got to him. He's finally agreed to meet her at two this afternoon. Not in his house or his office. Somewhere discreet. He insisted on that."

I tried to rally. It wasn't too late, not yet. "I thought Lady Winter was at Pendle Hill."

"Really?" he said, with the exaggerated surprise of someone whose companion is being very dense. "Well, I suppose we'll just have to meet him in her stead, then."

I shoved him. "Where?"

"Somewhere called the Illusion. Do you know it?"

It came back in a painful rush—Hero's hand at my arm, leading me downstairs; the pulse and throb and glitter of the club floor; Alden's hand at my waist, firm and sure; Eddie looking up at me from the cold stairs, the dazzle of stars overhead. I had to swallow hard before I spoke.

"Yes," I said. "I know it. Two, did you say?"

"It doesn't leave long to get there, I know." Matthew glanced up at the station clock. "I have a room in Soho, if you both want to clean yourselves up a bit. Lady Winter paid for it, before you ask, so it's nicer than you're probably imagining."

"No time." I tried not to imagine the possibilities of a room— a chance to wash, to change clothes, to be anchored for an hour or so. Since I had left Alden's, I hadn't stayed in one spot for longer than a single night, and the last few days had been a nightmare of trains, ferries, broomsticks, more trains. Never mind. It wasn't as though I had anything to change into anyway. "Hero will be ahead of us. We need to go now."

The air had the hushed, breathless quality of the heat before a storm.

I hadn't been in the Illusion since my eighteenth birthday. It wasn't the sort of place I'd ever go on my own, and the few classmates I'd been close to over the years would never have gone either. I'd heard it had only grown wilder and more glittering as the twenties had unfolded—tales of extravagances and excesses crept into the *Practitioner*, all with a faintly scandalised air that made it more attractive than ever. I could see traces of those adventures now: the sticky floor, the scratches on the walls, the sparkles still clinging to the ceiling.

Now it was a dull Thursday afternoon, and the place was still waking up. The lighting was grey, the sun not bright enough to filter through the high windows and yet too bright for the glowing lamps at each table to alleviate the gloom. The band was setting up in the corner, still tuning their instruments, and the bartender was levitating chairs into place. We had left Eddie outside, in the same alley where we had sat together all those years ago, watching the street for any sign of Guards. I sat at one of the corner tables, nursing a drink, trying to look inconspicuous when my clothes were stained and slept-in, my hair was a mess, and my photograph had once again appeared in the morning paper. I had found a copy of it lying on the table and checked.

"Could be worse," Matthew said. He was looking at the paper upside down, from across the table. "At least you got pushed to page three this time."

"Such a relief," I said, as dryly as I could. "Hero attacking Paris took up page one."

"There really is a bright side to everything." He shifted in his seat. I saw the familiar flicker across his face, the twitch caught before it could become a wince. I hadn't seen it in a long time, but I remembered.

"Is your shoulder hurting?"

"It's fine," he said, too defensive, on reflex. He caught my eye and relented. "A bit. Just this last day or so. It's a bad sign, isn't it?"

"I think she's already in London." I couldn't imagine she hadn't beaten us there, under the circumstances. "I think she's waiting, and she could strike at any moment of her choosing. Does that seem right?"

He nodded reluctantly. "It hasn't felt like this in a long time. Years. And...I had very strange dreams last night."

"What was strange about them?"

"I don't think they were mine."

He was right: That was a very bad sign. At any moment, as

we stood here, a siren could blare or an explosion could rock the streets, and the London lock could be shattered like its counterparts in Berlin and Paris. The Illusion was built as a bunker in case of air raids, Hero had told me once. Perhaps it was the safest place to be, if what we wanted was to be safe. But if we wanted to stop Hero—to save her—then we were hanging a great deal on a gamble that might not pay off. Perhaps it was best for Eddie and me to seek out the lock for ourselves, try to protect it, or since the Board were already doing that, go straight to Camford and hope to find a way in. And Matthew should be back home, getting our family to safety, being safe himself. I didn't know what I had been thinking.

I was on the brink of running for the door when Matthew nudged me with a sharp elbow. I looked up, and thank God, there he was.

Sam Truelove Wells was making his way downstairs, his three-piece suit and tie uncharacteristically wilted, his fair hair gleaming in the smoky lights. He was alone, and seemed intent on staying so, though he gave the bartender a familiar nod as he stopped at the counter. He took his glass in one hand and sat down at a small table on the other side of the room, far from the band and the other customers.

"Right on time," Matthew said quietly. Now, of all times, he looked ill at ease.

We waited until Sam had settled down and the attention of the bartender was elsewhere. Then I crossed the room and slid into the seat next to him.

"Hello, Sam," I said.

I'd thought Richard had been surprised to see me materialise in a clearing in the Highlands. He'd only stilled. Sam's entire body flinched, like a double take in a Buster Keaton film.

"Clover!" He looked around quickly, as though expecting the room to be crawling with Guards. "How did you even— You can't be here! I can't be talking to you! Did Lady Winter set this up?"

"Well, what was she supposed to do?" Matthew slid into the seat on the other side of Sam. "You weren't answering my letters."

This time he stilled. He never even turned his head. "Matthew."

"Oh, you recognise me, then?" His voice was so light I think only I heard the effort there. Perhaps not, though. Sam had known a version of my brother that I had never known, in places I couldn't imagine. "It's been over ten years."

"I know. I kept meaning to visit, but—" Sam shook himself, his head darting to each of us in turn. "What are you *doing* here? What do you want?"

"Keep your voice down," Matthew warned softly, with a nod toward the rest of the bar. "You were right—if they find you talking to us, we're all in danger."

Sam's mouth closed at once, though he plainly wasn't happy about it. But then, he didn't look very happy at all. Up close, he had the frayed, worn look of somebody who had been awake for long hours doing work they knew wouldn't be enough.

"We need your help, Sam," I said.

"I tried to help!" His voice was now a furious whisper—directed at Matthew rather than me. "As soon as Berlin told the first minister that Lord Beresford had been murdered with a faerie curse, I sent a raven to your farm to warn you to get out. Do you know what would have happened to me if they'd discovered it?"

"I can imagine," Matthew said. "But—"

Sam was still talking. "I wasn't even supposed to know about it. I just happened to be the one to file the report. I expected the information would be made public that evening. Only instead, the murder was blamed on Lady Beresford with no mention of the curse, the Guards were sent to apprehend you as a precaution, and a few hours later, we were all told that Clover was a suspected collaborator and needed to be hunted down at all costs."

"Even the Guards don't know that Hero isn't Hero?" That startled me, despite everything.

"Most of the Board don't even know it. Only the top ministers, apart from me. What happened, Clover? Why did they come after you? Was it because of Matthew?"

I shook my head. "No. No, it's because of me." Even now, I had to draw a deep breath before going on. "Lady Beresford is under the power of the faerie from Amiens, as I'm sure you've guessed. She and I released that faerie by accident eight years ago, at Ashfield, along with Alden Lennox-Fontaine."

"Dear God," Sam said quietly, without real shock. Clearly, it was less of a surprise than the fact we were at his table. "And Edmund Gaskell, I assume. There's a warrant out for him now too, less public—his family, you know. Lennox-Fontaine, though...I can see why they'd want to keep his involvement quiet. They've pinned their election hopes on him. And it would explain why nobody's seen him today, when he ought to be at the forefront of this. What a mess."

"It's worse than that," I said. "Has the university been evacuated?"

His gaze flickered, just briefly. Sam had many wonderful qualities, but he would never make a spy. "Why would Camford be evacuated?"

"I think you know why. I think all the Board do, even the ones who aren't supposed to. Has it?"

"As it happens," he said, with great dignity, "Camford *has* been evacuated. It isn't being publicised, but it isn't a secret either. It's a precaution, that's all. Camford has the greatest concentration of Family members, which makes it an attractive target for a magical attack."

"A faerie attack," Matthew said bluntly. "That's what you mean, isn't it?"

"I mean," he said firmly, "a magical attack. What are you *doing* here, Matthew?" The whisper was straining to be louder.

"It's bad enough that Clover's been mixed up in it all. I sent that raven to you so that you would stay away. This isn't your world."

"You made that clear enough after the war, didn't you?" An edge had crept into Matthew's voice. At eighteen, I would have taken it for anger. Now, I knew that it was hurt. "As soon as the war ended, you wanted nothing to do with me."

"Me?" Sam blinked, his mouth opening and closing without words. "That is…How could you think that?"

"What else was I supposed to think?" I put a warning hand on Matthew's arm; he shrugged me off. "The last time I saw you was at the front, do you know that? They had to tell me you hadn't died. I asked to see you, over and over, all those months they held me. You never came. They told me you'd refused."

"I was fighting for you the entire time! The Board wanted you locked up, if not worse. They were furious with me for not letting you die."

"I know. And I'm grateful for that. I'm grateful for what you did for Clover, too, and for sending that raven. But give me one good reason why that meant you never wanted to set eyes on me again."

"I *did* set eyes on you. Once, at least. It was on a midnight. When the curse took hold. My father took me into the room where you were bound in silver—he said he wanted me to see what it was that I was protecting. You spoke to me. You said what happened was all my fault, and you never wanted to see me again."

Matthew laughed, hard and exasperated and ever so slightly shaken. "That wasn't me! It was never me, those midnights—you were the one who explained that to my family. I'd never have said that."

"You would have thought it."

"How could you possibly have known that?"

"Because it's *true*!" Sam's voice rose sharply; he caught himself, checked to see if anyone was watching, but he couldn't hold back. "This is my world, magic and Families and faerie curses. I was born into it. You weren't. You never should have known about it. That day at Amiens—I ran off to fight that thing, along with every other mage there. You shouldn't have followed me. But you did."

"Of course I did! I wasn't going to let you go off alone, was I? We always looked out for each other."

"I was the one who should have been hit by that curse. It got you because you were looking out for me. And because of that—because one of our kind unleashed death on a battlefield, because you were fighting alongside me, because you saved my *life*—my own family locked you up and tried to leave you to rot. Do you have any idea how that feels? How could I look you in the eye and see that reflected in your face?"

"You saved my life too," Matthew said, far more gently. "We're even on that score."

"We aren't even." Sam had dropped his voice, but it didn't matter. His whisper was hot and furious as a scream. "Do you think I don't know how unfair it all is? The only difference between your kind and mine is that magic comes a little easier to us—and after watching Clover all these years, I'm not even sure how much. And yet the Families keep it secret, then act as though we're the only ones who matter just because we have knowledge we've deliberately kept to ourselves. God, it makes me sick. We could have done so much more to help during the war than we did. We could be doing more now. And we don't. You can't tell me you don't feel the same."

"I do," Matthew said, and I'd never heard his voice so soft and so serious. "Of course I do. But I never blamed you for that."

I had been so blind to so much. I had felt it many times over the last few days; I felt it again now, watching Matthew and Sam, finally seeing the jagged wounds between them. It was as though I'd been walking on rotten ground for years, refusing to look down.

Matthew and Sam were looking at each other with something akin to recognition. I hated to break in. I knew this was a conversation that they needed to have—that they'd needed to have ten long years ago and that had been eating them up ever since, and God knows I had enough painful experience with what happened when unspoken things were left to fester and poison and hurt. But every minute in the Illusion was a risk. And outside, Hero was ready to move.

"The Board know who that faerie is and what she wants," I said. "What is it, Sam?"

It took Sam a moment to drag his eyes from Matthew to me. When he did, he only shook his head. "I don't know."

"The governments of the world agreed to seal off faerie country immediately after Amiens. You were the only Family member who made it out of there unscathed. Whatever brought about the Accord, it must have been something you told them."

"It must have been," he agreed. "But I don't know what—or not entirely." He took off his glasses to rub his eyes wearily. Without them he looked younger, softer—one of the many who had been to war before they had had a chance to live, and survived.

"They questioned me for hours after they pulled me out of Amiens," he said. "Not just the Board. There were people from France as well, from Italy, even from Germany and Japan. They wanted to know every detail, as you'd expect, but…it was the oddest things that seemed to bother them."

I thought of Eddie. "The fact that the faerie was a dryad."

"Exactly. They wanted that kept quiet, even from the other Families. That was why they were so worried about Matthew, you know. His curse didn't just threaten to expose our world to non-mages. It was evidence of what had cast it. A dryad in the human world is unusual enough to provoke questions."

I shivered, despite myself. Across from me, Matthew shifted uncomfortably in his seat.

"They also," Sam added, "didn't want anyone to know that the circles were no longer secure."

That distracted me. "So they *did* know that all along."

"They knew," he said. "The Board hadn't come up with a cover story yet; they were talking about it among themselves in only thinly veiled terms. I assume they had tested it for themselves straight away. Whoever that faerie was, it hated us enough to do what no faerie had ever done before, and now all of faerie country knew how it could be done."

"Then why not say that?" Matthew said. "Why not tell the scholars, so they could find a solution?"

"I can only assume," he said, "because they didn't *want* a solution. They were willing to sacrifice faerie magic entirely to make certain nobody encountered that faerie again—to keep something about it a secret."

"Something," I said, "like the fact that Camford is on stolen faerie ground."

Sam was beyond being surprised now. He only shook his head. "No. That is... Camford *is* on stolen faerie ground. All the magical universities around the world are. I'm not sure how you found that out, it's meant to be a secret known only to the Board and the Faculty, but you wouldn't be the first to have guessed it. It simply isn't a big enough secret to justify all this. Those leaders weren't talking as though there was a threat to Camford, or academia at large. The entire magical world seemed to be at stake. It's something far worse."

"Like what?" Matthew asked.

"I have no idea. If I had to guess, it was something that happened hundreds of years ago, on the day Camford was born. It's a brutal act, you know, to widen the gap between doors. It ate up great swathes of faerie country. They said the fae never quite forgave it. Our dealings with them were different after that."

"And yet we still dealt with them," I said. "This is the only one who's ever wanted to destroy us."

"Exactly," Sam said. "Whatever this faerie wants, it's personal."

There was no time to worry about it now. If all went as I thought, we would have a chance to ask the faerie directly soon enough.

"Whatever it is, Eddie and I need to get into Camford," I said. "If that lock breaks and the doors between worlds open, she's going to go straight there to take what she wants. We need to be there for her."

His surprise rallied somewhat. "Why? Why should you be the ones to step in?"

There were a lot of answers to that. I gave the one that mattered most. "Because Hero is our friend, the way Matthew was yours. It's my fault the faerie took her, just as you feel it was your fault Matthew was hurt. You broke all the rules to save him. Please, let us try to save her."

"If this really is the faerie from Amiens, then you can't. Believe me. It will kill you without a thought."

"She won't." I tried to believe this with every cell in my body, so that Sam would believe it too. "Hero won't let her."

"I admire your faith in your friend, truly, but there's nothing she can do. There may be nothing of her left at all."

"There is," Matthew said unexpectedly.

Sam looked at him, startled, as did I. "How would you know? You don't know anything about faerie lore."

"I don't need to know about the lore." He leaned forward on the table, folding his arms. "I saw what that thing unleashed at Amiens. I had a fragment of it in my head for years, taking over my body inch by inch, whispering to me in the dark. I know how quickly it kills and how little it cares. But it had Clover and Eddie in its grip back in Paris, and they're unharmed."

"At the Panthéon?" He frowned. "You think Lady Beresford stopped it from killing them."

"I think she's the only thing that could have. And I don't know what the Board's planning to combat this thing, but I don't think they stand a better chance than that."

"No," Sam said slowly. "No, perhaps not. But…I still can't help you. Camford has been evacuated. The doors have been locked for the first time in four hundred years."

"You're a member of the Board," I countered. "You must be able to open them."

Sam opened his mouth to reply. He never got the chance.

At that moment, the Illusion shook.

The entire room juddered; the tables and chairs danced, dust fell from the ceiling like rain, and the rotating lamps bumped and collided with one another. Sam grabbed the table; I, ludicrously, grabbed my drink. Matthew swore quietly, and his hand flew on instinct to his shoulder.

"Before you ask," he said to me, too calm, "*that* really hurt."

"She's here," Sam said faintly. He reached into his pocket and pulled out a coin; I recognised the faint glow of a doublet charm. No doubt every Board member in the country—in the world— was feeling that same glow.

Eddie ran in from the back door, heedless now of discovery. He was probably right: Anyone recognising him now would have other things on their minds.

"You can see it from the alley," he said, breathless. "There's a forest rising up on St. Paul's."

We weren't the only ones to run for the back door. The bartender, the musicians, the few other early patrons—we all piled out into the narrow alley that branched onto Fleet Street. The shadowy mound of St. Paul's dominated the view, as usual, its enormous size making it loom closer than it really was. It was covered in trees.

Eddie and I had missed the main attack in Paris. By the time we had reached there, the wreckage had been strewn with branches and leaves, Hero had stood wreathed in thorns, but the forest was still, already growing over a ruin. Now it was alive. Trees erupted from the London pavement, sending cracks spidering through the foundations; ivy already half covered the great white dome, sending tiles crashing to the ground like scales falling from a snake. The church was hundreds of feet high, the tallest building in London, the tallest I had ever seen. The forest was tearing it apart as though it were made of clay.

"I'm going to guess that's the site of the third lock," Matthew said from beside me. He leaned heavily against the wall, hand still pressed to his shoulder, and his face was stark white.

Sam gave a barely perceptible nod. "I'm supposed to be there. I'm supposed to be ready to defend it. I—"

"Don't," Matthew said quietly. He didn't need to say any more. They had both been at Amiens. They knew it would do no good.

"That's the end," I heard myself say. I didn't quite believe my own words. It couldn't be. "It's too late. It took her minutes to break through in Paris. We won't get to Camford in time to stop her."

"We can try," Eddie said. Strangely, or not so strangely, his voice held none of the fear rising in my own. He was worried, but his eyes as he watched the trees thrash and groan were soft with wonder. "She has to get to Camford too. If we start out right now—"

"No," Sam interrupted. His jaw had set, and his eyes were suddenly brighter than I had ever seen them. "We can do better than that. There's another door to Camford. The real door—the first door."

His words took a moment to sink in, and when they did, they made no sense. "The first door?"

Sam turned away from the street purposefully, toward me. "The Oxford and Cambridge doors don't look like faerie doors, do they? Have you not wondered yet which is the original, and where the runes have gone?"

I rallied my thoughts with difficulty. Outside, the screams were beginning to reach us; footsteps thundered down Fleet Street as a city of scared people who had already lived through a war fled from something else beyond their imagining. "I didn't… That is, I assumed it was the Oxford door. Alden told me once that the Cambridge door is the same entrance, just a copy."

"They're both copies. The real one—the first one—is far too dangerous for hundreds of prank-loving students to pass through on a daily basis. It's locked up safe where nobody can touch it except the Board. The last time they moved it was during the war, when the air raids began."

The answer came to me a beat before I could ask. Here. It was here. During the war, the Families had moved their valuables underground, to a bunker that had become a nightclub. While we'd been dancing, all those years ago, the door to Camford had been here with us.

"It's right through those doors, down in the vault," Sam confirmed. "That was one reason I asked Lady Winter to come here. I thought she might not come alone, if she came at all. I thought—I thought whatever happened, we might need it."

"And we do." I tried to keep my voice from trembling. "Please, Sam. Let us try. Whatever we do, we can't possibly make it worse."

Outside, the dome of St. Paul's cracked open like a skull. A renewed cry went up from the street, and the building blazed with a hot white glow.

Sam looked at Matthew, and his face set. He nodded. "Downstairs," he said. "Quickly."

———✦———

The smell of damp and dirt hit me as soon as the vault opened. The room was larger than I had expected, extending well beyond the bounds of the club and under the London streets, and it plainly hadn't been touched for some time. It was packed solid—mostly with crates, though there were several enormous wrapped picture frames and a covered birdcage from which something rustled. On top of everything that was happening outside, the urgency bubbling under my skin, I felt the hairs at the back of my neck rise to attention one by one. The air prickled with strong magic. Everything here was thrilling and dangerous, and everything in my blood knew it.

Most of all, it knew what stood at the back of the room.

Leaning against the far wall was a section of wood panelling that had plainly been cut from a much older building—older than any in Camford, old enough that it would probably have rotted away had it not been protected by strong magic. Inscribed on it in a sweeping arch were the runes I knew all too well. There was no trace of chalk lines here—they had been carved, sure and permanent, and they glittered now with pure moonlight.

This was a true faerie door. Had we been passing through this each time we went to Camford, we would have known it for what it was at once.

"They should have told us," Eddie said beside me, and I knew he was having the same thoughts as I was. When I glanced at him, his face had tightened with that anger he only let out in flashes. "Whatever they did, they had no right to make us part of it."

"No," I said quietly. And yet there was a small, shameful part of me that still wished I didn't know.

I brushed it aside and turned to Matthew and Sam. "You can't come with us," I said. "Especially you, Matty. On the other side of that door is exactly where the curse tried to take you, every time it had you in its power. You can't go."

"I could try," he said, but without his usual conviction. He had stumbled once coming down the stairs, and his eyes had the unfocused, distracted look of somebody working very hard to stay in their own body.

"You'd be lost the moment you stepped across the threshold. You know that's true."

I wasn't surprised when he nodded. "I know." He sighed, frustrated. "Bloody thing. I thought that was all over. I can hear it again, you know?"

"The dryad?" My heart quickened. "You can hear her?"

"Not her. Her tree." There was an odd, remote quality to his voice, beyond the tension that came from pain. "Her tree's somewhere on the other side, in faerie country. It's waiting for her to come home."

"We'll head to St. Paul's," Sam said, with a quick, concerned look at him. "There's going to be people hurt there. Just like last time."

He could have meant Paris. He didn't. The last time for him was another battlefield, the last time they had stood together.

"If Hero's still there," I said, "then don't either of you stick around. You run. Get back home—stop in Manchester and get Iris, if you can—and keep everyone safe. Look after Rose. Please. I don't know what the world is going to be like after today."

"Don't worry," Matthew said, and at least he sounded more like himself. "I'll keep them all safe." He paused, and his voice turned quiet in the way it was very occasionally between us, and never when anybody else was listening. "I know you're a witch, and Eddie's a wizard, and you're more than a match for any faerie. But take care of each other, all right?"

I hugged him tightly. "I will. I know what a risk this is, I promise. It's just that this is what needs to be done."

"Well." He tightened his grip just once, then let me go. "There you are, then. Nothing more to be said."

"One thing," Sam said suddenly. His jaw was set once more. "You'll need this."

With a single shuddering movement, he pulled off his silver ring and held it out. I took it, wondering, a little in awe. Mages never parted with their rings. My own ring was unadorned and woven with the entry spell for Camford only, and yet I couldn't imagine giving it up.

"That will get you through the door there, even with all the Board's safeguards," he said. "It will also get you anywhere you want to go in Camford. Just...don't be too long. If all three locks do break, there are plans in place to reseal them as soon as possible. Whatever the faerie does will have to be quick—an hour, perhaps, no more. That means you have to be quick too. Don't get trapped on the wrong side of those doors when they lock again, or you'll be trapped in faerie country."

The thought of that great ragged wasteland I had glimpsed through the door hit me like a chill. I nodded. "Thank you, Sam. Truly. If we make it through this, I'll do everything I can to make sure this doesn't get back to you."

"I don't care if it does," Sam said stoutly. "This isn't right. Any of it—and I'm not the only one who thinks that. We should have been made aware that we're dealing with a faerie. We should have been told who she was and what she wanted from the start. We should be trying to broker a deal with her, to avoid bloodshed, and we've been forbidden from doing so. We shouldn't be hunting down you and Gaskell without asking questions. Everything's gone wrong, somehow—perhaps it's been wrong for a long time. It needs to be put right."

I could only nod, my throat tight. I gave them both one last quick smile, then turned to Eddie. He had been watching the door the entire time, his eyes thoughtful, his face far away. When I spoke his name, he came back to me with effort.

"Are you ready?" I asked, for all the world as though we were a basket of sandwiches away from embarking on a picnic. It was only that it had struck me, like a blade through the heart, that this might be the last we would see of anyone, ever again. "I mean...would you like to phone someone first? Richard? Your family?"

Eddie shook his head. "My family and I aren't really on speaking terms these days. And Richard's safe with Lady Winter. The only other person I'd call at the end of the world would have been you." He gave me the smallest flicker of a smile, faint and transparent as mist on glass. "Are you ready?"

I couldn't find a smile of my own—the one I had given Matthew and Sam had been my last—but I took his hand in mine and held it tightly. "Let's go."

<hr/>

Together, we stepped forward, and into another world.

Part Four

Faerie Country

26

I had stepped through the door to Camford hundreds of times—thousands. I knew the cooling of the air, the playful gust of wind, the way the university opened in front of me as though I'd come out of a tunnel. This was like nothing I had ever felt before. The ground dropped from beneath my feet. My stomach plunged. Wind tore at my skirts, ice-cold, bringing with it a blast of rain and stone and leaf. I grabbed Eddie's hand in the dark and felt him snatch at mine.

Then, with a stumble as though we'd missed a step in the dark, we were on the other side. Camford lay sprawled before me, its beloved stone towers and crooked streets and winding river as empty as they had been that Christmas break when Alden and I had first broken the rules. Despite everything, it hit me like the glad swell of a wave that I was finally, once again, home. I had feared at times I would never see it again.

There was something different. Something missing. My dazed brain was still fumbling for it when Eddie spoke.

"The gate." His voice sounded strange, numb, barely there. "It's open."

It was. Normally the long, high wall would encircle the university, its gates barred across the mist that lay beyond. Now those gates were ripped apart. They sagged on their hinges, ragged and rough as though they had been clawed by a tiger. The gap in the wall was sickening and startling as a missing tooth. Beyond it lay faerie country.

I had glimpsed it once before, that night we had unleashed the faerie, the moment the door had opened just a little too far. A great, grey-green country, all woodland and thorns and scarlet roses tinged in purple, stretched as far as the eye could see. The wind that always buffeted Camford was stronger now, tearing through the wall and beating at the buildings; the trees and overgrowth tugged and twisted in it, and the rustling of their branches filled the air like a whispered language. And everywhere, even in the light of day, that strange moonlight glow.

"She's already here." I crossed my arms tight against the sudden chill. "Do you see? She doesn't need to come through one of the Camford doors as long as that gate's open. Faerie country is her home. She can make a door to it anywhere, and then make her way across to Camford. She came through that gate as soon as the lock was broken."

He nodded slowly, taking it in without visible fear. But I saw his hands curl into fists at his sides. "Then where is she?"

"I don't know," I said. "We'll find her."

Before I could think too hard about what I was doing, I turned and pressed Sam's ring to the door.

"*Beclysan*," I said clearly, and felt it lock beneath my touch.

It wouldn't keep everybody out—probably other members of the Board could unlock it. With all that had happened in London, though, I imagined it would take the Board a while to get to the door, and they would be less than inclined to open it when they did. In the meantime, Sam couldn't. I didn't put it past Matthew to change his mind about not following us through, and if he did, Sam would be at his side. This way, whatever happened, it was just the three of us.

Eddie's eyes widened slightly, but he said nothing about it. He understood.

"You're right," he said. "We'll find her."

Camford felt different as we picked our way through the deserted streets. When I had passed through it that first Christmas I had come back alone, the plants and stones had seemed half-asleep—waiting, I had thought, for the cold to pass and the students to come back. Now, perhaps, they had what they were truly waiting for. They quivered with life, hungry and eager. The trees lining the pathways thrashed their branches and rustled their leaves in ways that had nothing to do with the wind; the grass and vines underfoot shivered. Once, unexpectedly, a thread of ivy snaked out and snatched at my arm. I flinched back. Eddie at once spoke a spell I didn't know, and the plant withdrew, entwining once more about the lamppost where it grew.

I let out a shaky breath. "Thanks. Where did that spell come from?"

"It was just a calming spell. It's more about—the voice, I suppose. You know how to get a spell to work, you have to hit a particular tone? There's a tone—a timbre of magic—that plants can hear. I've spent a lot of time finding it, that's all. It's not usually so dramatic. Usually I just get the vegetables to grow better."

I couldn't help but smile, albeit nervously. "Do you think they'll listen to you this time when we meet Hero?"

"No. She's a dryad. Their loyalty is to her, as it should be. We're the interlopers."

That was what I felt, with every step, deeper and deeper into the university I loved. Every leaf, every branch, every blade of grass was watching me as though I no longer belonged. Not hostile, at times even curious, but wary, and dangerous. They would kill me if they were asked.

We were drawing near to the centre of the university when Eddie grabbed my arm and pulled me back. My heart flew to my throat; I looked around, expecting to see Hero. But there was nothing—nothing, at least, that I could see. As usual, Eddie noticed more.

"A birch tree," he said quietly.

I followed his nod, and there it was. I could see the leaves and the tops of the branches peeking over the buildings. There was no birch tree in Camford.

"That's the quad," I said. "Come on—slowly."

Hero wasn't in the quad. We saw that as soon as we drew near, coming through the odd little alley behind the Buttery, trying not to make a sound. What was there was far, far worse.

It was Grimoire. He lay on the ground, arms outstretched, head thrown back and glassy eyes staring up at the sky. His face was still and bloodless, strangely peaceful, the lips parted as if about to speak. I had seen death before—this looked different. I might have run to his side to look for signs of life had it not been for the slim trunk of a birch tree erupting through his chest.

I couldn't move. Horror rooted me to the ground; disbelief shuddered in great waves through my nerves, my blood, bone deep and then deeper. The ward of the Camford Library couldn't be dead. Despite what I knew of his name and background, he had never seemed flesh and blood enough to die. He had been a creature of paper and dust, moving around the great labyrinth of shelves as though a part of it, the magic that we had glimpsed the night we had tried to break into the archives always rippling somewhere beneath his skin. It was wrong to see him lying out in the open, under a cloudy sky, the life drained from his body.

His heart pierced by a tree. That shadowed my shock at seeing Grimoire dead: the knowledge that this was the death three hundred had died at Amiens, the death that had been trying to burrow its way through Matthew all those long years after the war. I had never seen it before, the curse I had endangered the whole world to break. Yet again, the conviction came to me that this was far too big and powerful for any of us to stop.

Eddie recovered first. I felt rather than heard him draw a quick breath, brace himself, and go to Grimoire's side. He took up his wrist to feel for a pulse, clearly without much expectation, and then closed the librarian's eyes with a hand that shook only a little.

"She killed him," I said. The words weren't a question, or a statement. They just came of their own volition.

"Yes." Eddie got to his feet slowly, his face stark white. "His ring is gone," he added, almost as an afterthought.

He was right. Grimoire's left hand lay on the ground with the palm facing upwards, as if supplicating. The long white fingers were bare. A flicker came to me: Alden holding that same ring, that night at the archives that had seemed so dangerous and exciting and now just felt ridiculous. The night we had felt the books come alive and heard the inhuman howl.

You became a ward by taking the ring of the old ward, after their death.

I had to swallow hard before I could speak.

"The library," I said. "She's gone to the library."

———————————⟨⟩———————————

It was easy to find the way she had gone.

The blue doors of Camford were locked down, able to open only to Camford graduates. It hadn't stopped her. The enormous door at the entrance to the library had been ripped open; when we ventured in, we saw another door torn from its hinges. We followed the trail of broken doors and scattered books, deeper and deeper, until we came to the great circular dome at the heart of the library.

Without the usual bustle of students and lecturers passing through, browsing the shelves, studying in clusters under the great oak, the hall looked cavernous and empty. Through the glass ceiling, the light came grey through the clouds and cast the room into shadow. The floors and shelves were entwined as usual with thorned vines; the great oak, magnificent as ever, spread its arms over the paved ground.

Beneath it, the faerie that was Hero stood, head tilted back to look up into the branches. For a second, the last time I had seen her in Paris still sharp and vivid in my mind, I didn't recognise her. She was barefoot, her hair had fallen loose about her face, and her fashionable dark suit was torn to rags. Her exposed skin was bruised and caked with dirt, and blood seeped from a cut on her cheek. She had fought the forces of three nations and split open two worlds to get here. Faerie magic and blazing hatred could only stretch so far.

Hero didn't turn; she didn't have to. The vines rushed at us, encircled us, raised us from the floor. I didn't fight this time— only tensed, breathed deep, and braced myself for that horrible dampening of magic the way I might for an insect or clammy frog I needed to pick up. It didn't prepare me enough. These vines were stronger than the ones in Paris, and they were barbed; I felt the thorns dig into my arms, my stomach, the soft point of my throat, sharp enough to cut. The magic in my blood sparked, flickered, then died. A wave of nausea took me; I bit back the cry pushing to get out.

It's for Hero, I told myself. *She stepped into a faerie circle to save you. You can step into this.*

"Hero." I kept my voice as calm as I could. Blood trickled from my wrist, and a single drop hit the ground. "We came to talk to you."

"I told you to leave her alone," the faerie in Hero's body said. Her voice was absent, distracted. All her attention was on the great oak, her palm pressed to the rough bark of its trunk, her eyes tracing the lines of its branches. I could see no glint of silver on her finger. Perhaps, after all, Grimoire had prevented her from taking the ring with his life. "There's almost none of her left anyway."

"I don't believe that," I said, and tried to mean it. The faerie seemed so much less Hero than she had in Paris.

"Why not, Clover Hill? Does the scholarship say otherwise?"

The scholarship was divided, in fact. I didn't say so. "Because you still haven't killed us."

The vines flexed, and the thorns bit my flesh; I winced, but the grip soon relaxed. Hero dropped her hand from the great oak tree, and her face was somewhere between fury and anguish.

"I can't get her out," she said, almost too low to be heard. "I've come all this way, and I can't save her."

Eddie spoke up for the first time. "Who?" He sounded for all the world as though he was only mildly curious. It was the way I'd heard him talk to his pet field mice, to his plants, to Iris and Little John when they were children and he had visited the house. It was the way he asked questions of the world: not challenging, like Alden, or probing, like me, but soft enough to leave no mark. "What did you come here to find?"

Hero laughed, and her laugh was an open wound. "Oh, you want to know that, do you, Edmund Gaskell? You want to see what's at the root of all your precious flowers, and why their magic works?"

"Yes," Eddie said simply. "I do, please."

Hero turned to us at last, slowly, and seemed to grow taller. It took a heartbeat to realise that she had risen in the air, very slightly, so that her bare feet only lightly brushed the ground. It looked strange without wings, grotesque, like a marionette being made to walk. Then she clapped her hands together and spoke a lilting faerie spell.

There was a crack, so loud it seemed the world itself had snapped in two. The paved floor split across the middle, shattered like a mirror, and dropped away in a cloud of dust and grit. Had we been standing on it, we would have fallen with it; as it was, the vines holding us flexed and snapped, and I cried out on reflex.

At the same time, the room kindled into moonlight. It was the light that had glowed at Ashfield, all those years ago, the luminescence I'd seen lurking in hallways and under doors, only this was a thousand times brighter. It seared my eyes and made them sting; I blinked rapidly, and tears spilled down my cheeks and fogged my glasses. The library hall became a chamber of white light and black shadows, the great tree a dark shape blurred against my vision. And then I saw it.

Beneath the floor, covered in stone and rubble, were the archives. They were perhaps ten feet below, a twisted web of shelves that spidered out into the rest of the library, the beginning of perhaps miles of forbidden knowledge. Plunging through the centre was the rest of the great oak, the base that nobody ever saw. It grew up through the earth floor, roots twisted among the shelves.

Inside it was a faerie.

It was visible now as the light blazed: a silhouette, small and inhumanly slender, curled at the heart of the trunk. I had been to the Natural History Museum in London and seen the shelves of insects suspended in amber; this looked much the same, its fibrous wings and frozen limbs buried deep in the transparent glow. Then I narrowed my eyes, and I saw the delicate ribs breathing in and out. It was alive.

Certainly there are secrets buried in the archives that would help us come to some theories about what went wrong. It took me a while to place the memory. The lecture about Amiens, so many years ago; the words that had sent Alden and Hero searching for the archives and cost James Larkin his place at the university. He had known, or suspected. He was trying to tell us what lay buried there. Not books, as we had assumed. This.

A living faerie, trapped within the great oak at the heart of the library.

"Who is it?" Eddie asked.

"My sister." Hero's voice was tight with a rage that I was finally beginning to understand.

I fumbled for my own voice and found it. "How—how long has she been here?"

"How long do you think? Hundreds of years. Since the Families carved this abomination from our country, with her at its core." She sank slowly to the rubble, so that she stood beside the frozen figure, and tilted her chin to look at us. "Did you even know that some of the fae are born from trees?"

The scholarship ran through my head—Dorothy Edgeware had produced the definitive categorisation of the fae in the 1870s, there had been a revised edition around 1913, many of the entries have been disputed in papers elsewhere. Eddie spoke first.

"Yes," he said. "Dryads. You're the dryad of a silver birch, aren't you?"

She inclined her head, a stiff jerk. "My tree is on the other side of the gate. But hundreds of years ago there was no gate. Only a tangle of woodland, ancient and green and wild. The doors opened from your world on the edge, and sometimes the other fae would venture through to play or to bargain or to trick. We never did. Our homes were in our trees. My tree was the silver birch. Hers was the oak. We wanted nothing to do with your kind. And then one day another door opened in the sky, and this one didn't wait at the edge of the trees. It rushed forward in its hunger and it took a great bite from our world. It swallowed elms and oaks and ivy, sky and earth and grass. The whole forest screamed."

It's a brutal act, you know, Sam had said, *to widen the gap between doors. It ate up great swathes of faerie country. They said the fae never quite forgave it. Our dealings with them were different after that.*

I swallowed hard.

"When it was over, I was left on the edge," the dryad that was Hero said. "There was a terrible gate of dead wood before me, and my sister, the dryad of the great oak, was on the other side. For hundreds of years I believed she was dead, and I grieved."

"And then you found out she was still here," he said. "How?"

"Chance," she said bitterly. "Or fate. Another door opened. This time, I went through."

"Why? Your kind aren't interested in our world. You said as much."

"I did," she agreed. "This one interested me for one reason. It was a child on the other side."

My heart caught. Alden. That had been Alden, at the start of the war.

"I'd not seen a human child before," she said. "He was so small, so open, so hungry. He told me a good deal about his brother, and about the war. What he didn't tell me, I read in his heart. It was too young to guard itself from me. But none of that mattered. What mattered was that from the moment I stepped through I knew that my sister was still alive."

"What?" Surprise startled me into speech once more. "How?"

Alden at twelve could no more have known about what lay at the heart of Camford than anyone outside the very highest echelons of magical government. Even had his father known, the binding spell would have kept it from being passed on.

"His blood," the faerie said. "His blood, and yours, and the blood of every Family member in the country. This tree—the great oak—it scatters pollen to the winds all year. You all breathe it in, every one of you human mages. I could taste it spilling through your veins. That tree still stood whole and growing in the centre of this terrible place. Which meant that my sister was still trapped there—stunted, sleeping, bound inside, but alive. After that, I wanted nothing more than to get out to your world and set her free."

"You broke free at Amiens," I said quietly.

"Briefly. I had stepped into a circle once, now—I knew its magic. Faeries had been trying to break those binding runes for years, but they hadn't been built for dryads. We have different knowledge of magic, and unlike most of the fae, we don't easily lose interest. For the next few years I did nothing except work at ways out of that spell, over and over again, until it started to buckle, and at last it broke."

Trees were patient, Eddie had said. It might take centuries, but sooner or later they tore down walls.

"I didn't want to come out on a battlefield," Hero added, as an afterthought. "The safest thing would have been if Alden Lennox-Fontaine had summoned me again. I tried to tell him that. Instead, a soldier summoned me in the midst of his defeat. I stole him and tried to run. But there were too many mages there, on both sides. I burned through hundreds of men, and still in the end they forced me back."

Her eyes shifted, as if looking at a memory. "It was difficult after that. The Board guessed what I was coming for—there are few reasons why a dryad would act as I had acted—and they knew I could break free of the runes. They locked the doors and sealed them. All I had was the half-open door at Ashfield, and Alden Lennox-Fontaine on the other side. It was enough. A door, and someone to open it. I wouldn't leave him alone after that. Every minute he was in the house, I pressed him and pressed him until I thought I would break him. At last the door opened, and I had a body once again. This body."

"It should have been me," I said.

The faerie didn't respond to that. I'm not sure what I expected her to say. It wasn't as though she cared.

"I've used this body for eight years to get here," she said. "I learned where the three locks were. I broke them. I crossed two worlds to find her and bring her home. Now I can't."

"Why not?" Eddie asked reasonably. "She's right there."

Hero's teeth bared in what was almost a hiss. "I *know* she's right there! I'm here with her. But I'm here in this body. And this body cannot become the ward of the Camford Library."

It took me longer than it should have, even suspended by thorns above the library floor. Then I remembered the doors torn apart in the passage, the way the walls had been split open by the roses to clear the way to the centre of the library. Grimoire's body dead in the quad, and the ring stolen from his finger.

"The ward can release the oak dryad from her tree, can't they?" I said slowly. "That's why the ward was banned from access to the archives. They wanted to make sure he never had the opportunity."

"I killed him and took the ring from his finger," Hero said. "That should have been enough to make me ward in his place. Only Camford worked another clause into the spell."

"To protect it from falling into the hands of the fae?"

"No. To protect it from falling into the hands of students. The new ward needs to be a Camford graduate."

It was so bitterly ironic I had to bite my lip to keep from laughing. This, of all things, was what had ruined the plans she had spent years setting in motion. The faerie hadn't let Hero come back to Camford. The magic in Camford would have noticed her presence too easily—besides, she had other plans for her. Hero had wanted more than anything to graduate, and the faerie had kept her from it. And because of that, she had come all this way, in a stolen body, only to find that body had betrayed her.

It meant something else too. Something that, for the first time since seeing the faerie in the tree, gave me a whisper of hope.

"I can do it," I said, and felt rather than heard Eddie draw breath beside me. "I could release your sister. I'm a Camford scholar. I graduated. I could become the new ward."

The words sounded ridiculous, impossible; unexpectedly, in the face of all the terrible circumstances, they brought a heady thrill with them. Me, the scholarship witch, the ward of Camford Library. Even my wildest seventeen-year-old ambitions would never have dared venture there. But I *could* do it. I was the only one present who could. I had always wanted to belong to Camford, more than anything in the world. Now I could be a part of it, powerful and undeniable. Nobody would ever be able to say again I had no place here.

The faerie snorted, in a startlingly Hero-like manner. "Why

would you help me? As you said, you're a Camford scholar. This is your university."

"That doesn't mean I want your sister trapped! Surely no scholar would."

"And yet everyone who reaches the upper echelons of the Board or the Camford Faculty does. Every year, over and over for hundreds of years, they learn what lies at the heart of Camford. None of them ever try to let her go."

That pulled me back down to earth. It was exactly what worried me, it was true. Because why hadn't they, all those centuries of scholars and politicians who had risen to power and learned what was at the heart of the university? If the faerie had only been trapped by accident when Camford was formed, they would have done so. Never mind the cruelty—it was dangerous to have her here, sleeping below the earth while scholars and students milled overhead. Surely there had to be a reason why it was necessary, or somebody would have stopped it long ago.

It was the same question Eddie and I had asked on the train, the question with no answer. Camford could be built anywhere. Why had they built it on faerie ground?

Eddie had thought the same thing. "Be careful," he said, in a voice almost too low to hear. "I'm not saying don't do it. Just be careful."

"If I did agree," I hedged, in answer to the faerie, "what would happen to Camford? Would it survive?"

"I couldn't say," Hero said. "Why? Do you think a university is worth more than my sister's freedom?"

I had read enough folklore to know that *I couldn't say* was one of those ambiguous wordings the fae loved—that there was a very good chance that Camford might in fact not survive the oak dryad's release. I also knew that her question was a fair one.

"No," I said. "No, of course it isn't." I paused. "What would you give us, then, for your sister's freedom? Would you promise to release Hero in exchange?"

The faerie's laugh sounded higher and tighter, less like Hero's than before. "Why would I want this body if I had my sister back? I would take her and leave it behind. We would take a cutting from the oak so her tree could grow anew and flee back to our own country, too deep to ever be found or summoned. You could lock the doors behind us and never speak to us again. This is what I came here for." She paused, and something in her face changed. "Very well."

She threw something toward me, and the vines around my wrists loosened just enough for me to snatch it from the air. It was Grimoire's ring, a tiny smear of his blood marring the Family crest. It burned hotter than it should have, as though it had passed through fire. Even through the plants dampening the magic in my blood, I felt the surge of waiting power.

"Set that on," the faerie said, "and you can be ward of the library. If you truly mean what you say, Clover Hill, then I will make that deal. I will give you Hero in exchange for my sister."

This was it. I had come to make exactly that deal—Hero, in exchange for what the faerie may want—and here it was. Hero's life, a wrong set right, and a power I had never dreamed of attaining, all with one deal. I had said, hadn't I, that I would save Hero whatever the cost?

But I had been thinking of the cost to me, and I had expected a cost I could calculate. I was still missing too much about this. I didn't know what ripping the faerie from the heart of Camford would do. At the very least, it could bring Camford tumbling down around us, and I wasn't certain I was ready for that. It didn't matter how much I told myself that Camford was only a place. It was a place I had loved for my entire adult life.

And it might do still worse. That was the real difficulty, what truly haunted me. I hated making decisions without all the information. I needed months to research this, investigate the possible outcomes, find out exactly what spell had been woven in the founding of Camford and why it needed such a terrible sacrifice. I couldn't just throw everything away to save one person, even a person I loved.

Yet wasn't that what I had done in coming to Camford in the first place?

I had hesitated too long. Hero's face hardened, sharpened, the faerie light flickering once more in her eyes. "I didn't think so," she said, and turned.

I raised my voice, cursing myself inwardly. I was losing her. "No, wait—"

I had no chance to go further. Behind her, the doors burst open.

It was Alden.

27

It was Alden, but at first I didn't recognise him. I had seen him only a week ago, crisp and polished and slicked-down, more façade than person. That façade had cracked now. His clothes were frayed and torn by a thousand branches; his face was scratched and bleeding. His gold hair hung in filthy curls, and his eyes blazed fever bright. Magic throbbed in the air around him, in every taut line of his body.

He had been at Ashfield when I had phoned him this morning, hours before the last lock had broken. It had felt so inevitable, so right, that he should be in the place I always saw him in my mind, that I hadn't thought to wonder why. If I had, I would still not have believed he was planning something so blatantly suicidal. No human expedition had ever made it through faerie country and returned.

Yet that was what he had done. All these years, the Ashfield door had been closed, and the locks held it in place. When Hero had started to break the locks apart, he would have seen the opportunity at once. He had waited at Ashfield, beside the old door, until the London lock had been shattered and the Ashfield door could be opened once more. This time, he hadn't waited for a faerie to come out. He set out across faerie country the same way Hero had come, God knows how far through wind and thorn and wasteland, and found the Camford gate.

It was Alden, and he had at last come for revenge.

The vines rushed to meet him at once, as they had us. He was ready for them. They struck him and burst into flame, recoiling in a shower of fiery roses. (*The books!* my heart screamed, moved by the patterns of a lifetime, but the fire burned out without spreading.) In the same movement, he spoke a word, and a chain of silver shot from his outstretched hand. It whipped through the air, lithe and sleek as an eel, and snapped like a whip around Hero. She crumpled, chain wrapping her from neck to ankles, with a terrible hiss as if she had been burned too.

Alden strode forward through the charred vines and slid down the rubble to the faerie, his movements too controlled, his eyes too dark in his chalk-white face. The cord of silver shrank as he drew nearer, withdrawing into itself or into him. He was perhaps ten feet from her when he clenched his fist. At once, the chain pulled taut, cutting into Hero's flesh. She screamed, an unearthly wail of horror that tapered into a terrible gasp.

"Stop it!" I fought against the vines, furious at my own helplessness, but they only tightened their hold. "What are you doing?"

"Agrippa," Alden said, and his voice was ice. "That was always the problem with his theories, do you remember? To bind a faerie with them, you would have to be standing on faerie ground."

The terrible thing was, there was a small instinctive flicker of me that actually found that interesting.

"Alden," I said, and my own voice was so calm it teetered on the brink of hysteria. "Please. Think about this."

His laugh was little more than a choke. "*Think* about this? I have been thinking about nothing else since I was twelve. Why do you think I left Camford, why I went to so much effort to rise so high and so fast on the Board? Did you think I'd lost interest?"

"No," I said. "I thought you'd given up."

I should have known better. The only thing he had given up on was Camford. There was nothing more to be learned there, as I had proved—not without getting into the archives, and Grimoire had never stopped watching Alden after the first time he had taken his ring. But the restrictions on the study of the fae wouldn't hold back the minister for magical enforcement. In that position, he could have learned everything he needed.

His fist clenched again, and the faerie on the ground let out another cry as she convulsed.

"Stop it." I tried to keep my voice quiet this time. "Alden, please. You're hurting her. Is that really the kind of research you've been doing?"

"It only hurts because it's in a human body," he said. "Human beings hurt. That was its choice. I don't see why it shouldn't suffer for it."

"Hero suffers too." Eddie, who had been talking freely to the faerie in Hero's body, clearly had to fight to get those words out. He really was scared of Alden. I wondered if he had always been—if I hadn't noticed, or if he hadn't. "If you hurt the faerie, you hurt her."

"Hero's gone. That thing devoured her a long time ago." Nevertheless he unclenched his fist, reluctantly, and Hero's body on the ground relaxed. Her face was grey, her eyes half-closed, and her breath came in shallow gasps.

"She isn't gone," I said. "Hero. The faerie just agreed to release her if I made a deal."

"I didn't come to deal." His voice was still tight, but at least it was calmer. "I told you. I came to kill this monster, and I came to take back my brother."

"And what makes you think your brother's alive if Hero isn't?"

"Thomas wasn't possessed. He was taken. I saw him. This thing showed him to me every night I spent in Ashfield growing up: Thomas, in the faerie court, growing paler and thinner every year but no older. You locked him behind the Ashfield door, and however much I learned, I couldn't get him out. I'm here now. I'm not leaving without him."

I knew it was useless to point out that the faerie could have shown him anything in nightmares, that there was no more reason to believe that Hero was dead than that his brother was alive. I had worked with Alden long and intensely enough to know his weaknesses as a scholar, and his greatest had always been in finding evidence to support what he wanted to be true.

"Then perhaps we can bargain for Thomas too." I put every ounce of reason I could into my voice, willing his own to come out of hiding to meet it. "She doesn't want him any more than she wants Hero. She promised to give Hero back if I set free her sister in the heart of the tree. Let me do that. Or you could do it, if you wanted. You graduated from Camford just as I did. You could be ward instead."

"That's impossible." He looked at me for the first time, and I saw a little of him come back to himself. "It tried to kill your brother too, remember. It killed hundreds of people that day. It's just come from killing still more in London. It seduced and murdered Lord Beresford—though God knows he's no loss. Why would you even *want* to deal with it?"

"We stole faerie land and imprisoned a dryad inside her own tree," I countered. "Her own sister. That's why she hates us. That's why she doesn't care who she hurts or kills getting here. You must have known that, for you to come here as soon as the gates opened."

"When I was told about Camford last year, the day I made minister, some of the things it had said to me began to make more sense. It makes no difference."

"No *difference*?" My hands were bound; I nodded toward the door, trying in a sweep to take in the scale of the library, the lecture theatres and halls of residence, the crooked streets outside, all shot through with thorns and forest. I'd always loved that rustling overgrowth, but without thinking about it, I'd always considered it an invasion, weeds trying to colonise buildings that had stood for centuries. We were the invaders. All this time, it had been trying to break free. "We did this! This is what Camford has been, all this time."

"*We* didn't do anything," Alden snapped. "It was done centuries ago. And I'm sorry about it, I truly am, but I didn't do it, and it's too late to do anything to change it now. This has been the foundation of our world for hundreds of years, and perhaps it *is* rotten, but what's been built up around it is sound. We can't just rip it out. Not without destroying Camford and everything that comes with it."

So I had been right—freeing the faerie did mean the destruction of everything around it. I tried not to think about the library cracking apart, the buildings falling. "Even if that's true—does it really matter? Surely Camford can be rebuilt. It's only a school of magic. People can learn magic anywhere."

"It isn't just that."

"What else is it?"

I watched his face tighten, and recognised the tell-tale sign of a binding curse—presumably the one he had mentioned on the telephone only that morning, the one taken by ministers to ensure their silence. His eyes flickered as he sought a way around.

"It's a place where the *Families* come to learn magic," he said at last. "It has been since before there were Families at all." He looked at me seriously, willing me to understand.

And I did. Far too late, but at last I did.

This tree scatters pollen to the winds all year, the faerie had said. *You all breathe it in. I could taste it spilling through your veins.*

"The plants." Around me, as if in answer, the leaves quivered. "The plants sense and enhance magic. Eddie worked that out, a long time ago. When we come to Camford, we breathe them in, through the spores and the pollen, every year. This is why the Families can do magic so much easier than everyone else. It's in their blood in the most literal sense."

"Exactly." Alden gave a small, relieved shiver: the binding

curse letting him go. "We've built our world on the premise that
the Families are born to magic—have a natural, true-born ability to wield it—and that's why we have a right to keep it to ourselves. But it isn't natural. It comes from this, and places like it
all over the world. It always has. That faerie, bound to the tree,
is what keeps these plants alive. We take in their magic, and it
helps us in whatever spell we care to cast—but only as long as
the plants are here and thriving. Without them, our blood ceases
to be anything special at all."

This was it, then. This was why everyone who had climbed
high enough to reach the truth about Camford had been forced
to accept it: because without it, they were nothing. There were no
common people and mages, no magical families with magic running in their veins and ordinary families who didn't matter. There
was no reason for magic to be secret to only a few. There was only a
sprawling university whose doors were guarded, and a faerie at the
heart of it whose imprisonment kept those who were let in special.

"We weren't the only country to do this, you know," Alden
said. "Not even the first—the Romans did it, thousands of years
ago, and the Mongols and the Greeks did something similar. The
French did it, and the Germans, and the Japanese. If we hadn't,
we'd have fallen behind."

I didn't want to hear the justifications. I was still trying to
grasp the implications. "But not every Family member in Britain comes to Camford. Women don't, usually."

"Not everyone has to. Once you've spent time here doing
magic, it winds itself around every cell in your blood and bone and
body, and any child of yours will inherit it too. In that sense it *is*
an inheritance. Just a legacy that comes at the expense of another."

Any child. The image came, with overwhelming poignancy:
a small blond head curved over my hands, watching them as I
brought her wooden farm set to brief, joyous life. A face, blue
eyes narrowed in concentration, as her small hands tried to
work the same charm.

"Rose," I whispered.

Alden frowned. "Who?"

"My daughter." I couldn't remember if I'd ever spoken those words aloud. "Rose Hill. Matthew and Jemima are raising her—I told you she was theirs—but she's mine. She was born in April 1922, nine months after the door was opened. After we spent the night together."

I think it was the only time I'd ever seen him truly shocked. "Dear God," he said softly. All at once, I could recognise him again. The silver cord went slack in his hand. "I had no idea. Why didn't you say something?"

"What would you have done? Married me? I knew you better than that, at least. We weren't even on speaking terms." Another time, those words would have been accusatory; now I didn't even care. "She's very good at magic. It comes naturally to her, the way it does to the Families. I thought...I thought that was from you. I thought it was in your blood. But it's mine as well. I gave it to her."

"I don't know what I would have done," Alden said, as if I'd said no more than the first sentence. "I wish you'd told me, all the same. Whatever you wanted to do, I would have helped."

"My family helped. We didn't need you."

Eddie had said nothing more, all this time. I don't think Alden noticed—he had, after all, always had a bad habit of over-looking Eddie. But I looked sideways at him on instinct, won-dering how he had reacted to hearing about Rose, and had to work not to react myself. His face was locked in concentration, his lips moving very slightly as they formed a spell too quiet to be heard; one hand, bound to his side by the vines, was moving too. I remembered the ivy on the path, the way it had listened to him. Not while the faerie was there, he had said—the plants' loyalty was to her above all. Now she lay on the ground, power-less, unmoving, perhaps even unconscious. Hope fluttered in my chest, unexpected. If he could get us free...

I forced myself to look away. It wouldn't matter what Eddie could do if Alden saw him first. I needed to draw his attention.

"Please," I said, and Alden focused on me as if with great effort. "You have the faerie bound now. Let's work something out, all of us. You said, at your apartment, you didn't want Hero dead."

"Of course I don't." His voice hardened again, but not all the way. Some small part of him was still thinking of Rose—was thinking, perhaps, of the night I had found the faerie gate, when we had been invincible, and our brilliance and our excitement had shone out and bound us together. Sex never meant very much to Alden, Hero had told me, and I believed her. But *I* meant something. We all did. "Not if there's another way. There isn't."

"There is. We can do as she asks."

His eyebrows shot up, as they would have in Camford had I been proposing a theory at once impractical and impressively radical. "Truly? I've just told you what that would mean. Do you really expect me to believe you would let Camford die and see every Family member lose the magic in their blood, on the off-chance a faerie will let Hero go?"

"Not just for Hero," I said. "Because it's the right thing to do."

I hadn't put it into such clear words in my head before—I had been too tangled up with ambitions and consequences and magic. Once I had, I knew it was true.

"The right thing for whom? For the fae? Believe me, they have no such qualms about whatever they can do to us."

"And who's 'us,' Alden?" I returned. "Because I'm not one of the Families. I'm one of the ones they tried to keep from ever knowing magic existed. I only have it in my blood because I forced my way in here, and I was made to feel every step of the way as though it didn't belong to me."

"But it's in your blood now. Have you considered what it

would feel like to lose that, after all these years? The pollen dies if it loses touch with the tree. Those weeds binding you are dampening it now, and I'm sure you hate it. That's how it will feel for the rest of your life, if you destroy Camford. Thousands of people across the country will feel the glow in their veins go dark—our daughter included."

"You forget," I said, as evenly as if everything in my soul didn't curl up and cry at the thought, "that's how I lived my whole life before Camford. I taught myself magic then, with time and study and effort. It was harder—much harder—but it worked. There's no reason we can't all do the same."

"Without Camford? Without this place to teach them? Tell me honestly, Clover, can you live in a world where all this is swept away: the halls, the spires, the lecture theatres, the labyrinth of a library that goes on forever?"

"New universities are built all the time, out there in the real world. People can learn anywhere. There are books of magic in houses across the country, and thousands of people to teach them. I'd rather live in that world if this is the cost of the one we have."

"And what about you?" Alden turned to Eddie. I stiffened, but he seemed to notice nothing amiss. "Do you agree with Clover? Is that the world you'd prefer to live in?"

"I don't think it matters what world we prefer," Eddie said. He was looking at Alden, but I knew the answer was for me. "I agree with Clover that it's the right thing to do."

Alden laughed suddenly, a laugh at once bitter and desperately tired, as though giving up on an after-dinner argument that had stretched well past when both parties should have gone to bed. "Have it your way, then. Do what you want to Camford. Destroy the Families. I don't care, truly. You won't let this monster go." His hand flexed, and the faerie's back arched as the silver tightened. "I've come too far for that. I won't deal with it because there's no deal that will see it dead."

I'd known that, really. He'd hated it too much for too long, through too many long nights of torment from too young an age. It was why, deep down, he'd accepted Hero's death as the only way. The only way to kill the faerie was to kill her too.

I tried again nonetheless. "Alden—"

Alden didn't move. Eddie did.

The vines holding us both up slackened and bowed. The prickle of thorns about my wrists and ankles loosened; for one stomach-dropping second I was falling, then it had caught me again and was lowering me gently to the floor. Eddie was already free. He stepped toward Alden, rose stems and bracken still pulling away from his clothes, and raised his hands. The vines shot from the ground and reared up around Alden.

Alden reacted as before, almost as quickly. Flame shot up in a sheet in front of him; the twigs burned at once, and the thicker branches burst into fire. Yet he was caught off guard—besides, this wasn't a faerie he hated but his childhood friend. The flames were wilder, weaker, less focused. They caught the edges of the great wave of undergrowth surging toward him; it still kept coming. They spread outward across the floor in a great crackling blanket, igniting the roots and trees in their wake. And still, at Eddie's fingertips, the forest kept coming.

"Oh, don't you *dare*, Edmund Gaskell!" Alden hissed, over the spit and fury of the flames. His eyes were blazing blue. "I've come too far to be stopped by you."

"You never did think much of me, did you?" Eddie said. His voice was calm, but I saw in his eyes the same coiled warning that I had glimpsed the morning after we had released the faerie eight years ago. "I knew that, even in school. I put up with it, because you were kind to me, and I thought an awful lot of you. Then you stopped being kind to me, and I put up with that too. I told myself I liked you, because I didn't want to admit I was afraid of you. But I am not letting you threaten the people I love. Not anymore."

The fire had reached the walls now. On the lower shelves, books began to smoke and burn. The air was searingly hot, and I coughed as the acrid smoke caught in my throat. I barely noticed any of it, not even the books. The vines that had been holding me pulled away. One of the thorns nicked my arm as it did so; blood welled and blossomed along the cut, and I didn't feel that either.

The ring was in my hand. Grimoire's ring, the ring of the ward of the Camford Library, and his body lay outside.

It was one of the most important moments of my life, and I didn't think. I didn't even hesitate. I just slipped it on my finger.

Until then, the most powerful magic I had ever felt was the faerie spell that had broken Matthew's curse. That had only ripped through my body. This took it to pieces and left me outside. In one shock of light or thunder I felt every nerve, every muscle, every blood vessel, each one sharp-etched and bright as the after-images that come with a flash of lightning. Then it was gone, faded, and I had gone beyond it into something else.

I was the library. I was the yellow-paged books nestling like sleeping doves on the shelves; the old familiar curves of the stairways, steps worn from hundreds of years of footsteps and railings polished by the brush of thousands of hands. I was the quiet stack rooms steeped in cobwebs, the bright study rooms filled with the memory of students' voices. I was the rooftop that looked over the wall, the circular windows that looked out to the quad, the greenery that threaded through them all. I was the great oak at the heart of the building, bathed in slanted sunlight from the domed roof. Somewhere in the midst of all this were Eddie and Alden and the faerie in Hero's body, but they were so small and fleeting, I barely felt them. I was the ward of Camford Library. I was everything I had ever wanted to be.

Then I was back, doubled over, fighting for breath. Magic crackled under my skin and fizzed in my blood; there was a low buzzing in my ears; I was acutely aware of where I was and everything within it, but I was myself again.

Alden was still locked in his struggle with Eddie. He hadn't seen me. The great oak tree was there, three or four paces away. All I had to do was run to it, lay my hand on the bark, and unlock it as I would any door in Camford. Eddie wanted me to: He had told me so, right before he had broken free. He was putting himself in the line of danger not only to save me, but to give me a chance to do what only I could do.

Yet could I really do it? I had meant every word I had said to Alden. The thought of that terrible door opening and swallowing up faerie country, the image of the faerie kidnapped and bound while her sister grieved outside those gates, the knowledge that we had all been living and working on the bones of her tree and siphoning her magic—it all sickened me. And that was to say nothing of the world that had grown up in its wake. The Families cutting themselves off from the rest of the human race, steeped in tradition and lies, claiming magic as their birthright while keeping it from everybody else at any cost. I thought of the first time I had seen Oxford—the deep twinge of unease I had felt without knowing why, the relief that Camford on the surface was nothing like it. Yet it was. The only difference was that the door had let me in, and so I hadn't questioned who else it was keeping out and why. Matthew and Sam had understood long before I did how unfair it all was, and it had nearly torn them apart forever.

Unfair or not, though, it was the world we lived in. Its roots ran deep, and tearing them up would mean tearing everything else up with it. Did I have the right to inflict that kind of trauma on a world that had already had its foundations shaken to the core? Surely there was still a better way, an easier way, a way to fix everything without breaking it first?

I waited a fraction too long. Alden at last caught a gap between the plants; he took it, and a blast of light hit Eddie head-on. He fell to the ground with a startled cry, and Alden looked up and saw me.

He could have killed me. My blood was coursing with new magic, but it was a confused tangle I had no time to separate. I was off guard, defenceless, and he was ready. Whatever he hit me with, there was no way I would have had time to recognise the spell, think of a counter-spell, and block it. He could have burned me alive or frozen me in ice or turned me to stone.

Nothing came in my direction. I can only think, and believe, that it was for the same reason that he hadn't killed Eddie either— the same reason why, despite all he had said, the faerie in Hero's body still lived. When it came to it, when he looked at us, even through all his anger, he *saw* us. He had been lying about many things, that day in London at his too-new apartment, but one thing had been true. After his brother had been stolen away, the three of us were the only people he had ever loved. I had told Eddie that he wasn't going to let it stop him. But perhaps we don't always get to choose what stops us, what catches us off guard in the middle of a dark road and puts us on another path entirely.

In that hesitation, I ran. The ground beneath me was uneven with roots and slippery with rubble; I fell to my knees once, picked myself up, lunged for the tree. It was still glowing through the falling ash, suffused with moonlight with no moon to be seen. This close, the faerie was etched in precise detail: I could see the brush of her eyelashes against her cheek, the spindly bones and the fine long hair. My hand fell on the bark right above the curve of her elbow.

I looked back over my shoulder, at Eddie and Alden and Hero in the ruins of the Camford Library. Eddie was climbing to his feet, streaked with dust and ash, his pale face watchful and intent. Alden stood very still. His eyes were locked on mine. In the mingled silver and firelight, I saw, irrelevantly, that they had the same flecks of gold as our daughter's.

"Don't," he said simply.

I couldn't. I loved Camford, its lecture halls and its crooked streets and my little rooms in Chancery Hall when the rain lashed the windows. I loved the magic that was coursing through my blood now as strongly as I had ever felt it, the magic I now knew was every bit as strong in me as it was in any of the Families. I loved the library—my library, the library that had just bound itself to me. I had fought so hard to be here, to be exactly what I had become. A witch, a scholar, the ward of Camford Library. This was my home. I loved every stone and every tower and every blade of grass.

I knew what I should do. I knew it was right. Even then, though, with the great oak pulsing under my fingers, I didn't have the strength to do it.

Except that I looked at the faerie bound in silver at Alden's feet, and saw with a start that her eyes were open. They caught mine, as Alden's had only a moment ago. And this time, they weren't the faerie's eyes alone. Hero looked back at me from deep inside her own body, for the first time in eight years. With great effort, she nodded.

The first time I had met Alden Lennox-Fontaine had been in this very library, nearly a decade ago. I had thought then that if I could find a way to make faerie magic safe, *fix* it in some way, I could fix everything. Matthew, my family, the world that had seemed splintered into a thousand pieces. I know Alden had in his own way been trying to do the same thing. It was what had bound the two of us together, for better and for worse. Eddie had wanted to hide from the world. Hero had wanted to make it new. Alden and I, in our own ways, loved the old, safe world— Ashfield and Camford, tradition and beauty, the sunlit days of our childhoods before the Great War.

But the world had never been safe, not for everybody. It had been broken for a very long time, and the war had only shown those cracks for what they were. It couldn't be patched over. It needed to shatter if it was ever to be rebuilt into something glittering and new.

"I'm sorry," I said.

Then I turned back to the trunk of the great oak at the heart of Camford, and I broke it wide open.

28

The university convulsed. All around us, the stones shivered like the surface of a pond rippled by a breeze; the trees rustled and roared as though caught in a storm; the wind tore through the library like a scream. The force of it threw me to the ground, knocking my glasses from my face and the breath from my lungs.

The library writhed and cracked. The books fell from the shelves in a blizzard; I curled up, shielding my head, and so heard rather than saw the domed ceiling shatter, and glass rained down around us.

The great oak didn't move. But through stinging eyes blurred by tears and my hair whipping across my face, I saw something small and slender and insubstantial step from its trunk. She was more shadow than being, a glint of moonlight with the ghost of a branch crown on her head. She looked around, bewildered and dazed, a child woken from a very deep sleep unable to remember where she had been put to bed. Then her gold eyes lit on Hero, bound with silver chains at the centre of the room, and they flashed. She stepped forward, her lips parted, and the silver fell from the faerie's stolen body like rain.

The walls were tumbling down. I couldn't see Eddie. I couldn't see Alden. In all the noise and wind and debris, there was room for only one thought.

Hero.

The faerie was free now, along with her sister, and she had everything she wanted. There had been no bargain made between us, only proposed. There was no reason to keep her word. She could flee the ruins of Camford in Hero's body, and nobody would ever see her again.

I did the only thing I could think to do, in that screaming chaos with the world tearing apart around me. I pulled myself to my knees, fighting the battering wind, and as the two of them passed, I lunged for Hero's wrist and I held as tight as I could.

The faerie hissed as though burned and wrenched back her arm with a strength like the crack of a whip. In response I felt the new magic in my blood flare and catch alight. The movement pulled me forward, knees scoring the rubble, but I held on.

The faerie's voice came in a snarl without words. *Let me go.*

"No," I said. My voice was lost in the roar, but I knew the faerie would hear. "You can't have her. Not this time."

The dryad stretched out her free arm, tilted her head to the sky, and changed.

She was a birch tree shooting up to the sky, a pillar of burning fire, a twisting torrent of water. She was a monster that snapped and snarled with ravening teeth, a creature of rock with a gaping open mouth, a thing of shadow and claw. Pain shot up my arm, burning hot then ice-cold, flesh withering and tearing from my bones, my skin bubbling and cracking like scales.

I held on. I held on as she twisted into form after form, again and again. And then, as the pain and the cold and the fever-heat pierced beyond what anyone could bear, I held on as *I* changed. I held on as my bones melted and my skin turned to shadow. I held on as the howl building in my throat burst from my lungs, as the world rippled and sharpened and ceased to make sense.

I had never seen what Grimoire had become that night we had broken in, but I had heard its cry, and I felt it now in my own heart. Camford Library was falling around us. Until it fell I was its ward, and I was home.

I killed the last ward, the faerie said. *I could kill you.*

It was very likely true. Yet she didn't want to. Whether because I had saved her sister, or because the last part of Hero was still holding on, or because she had at last everything else she had wanted, she only wanted to leave.

Let Hero go, I said. *Let her go, and we'll let you go. We'll let all of you go. We'll see the last of the doors are closed forever. We'll never trouble you again. Just let her go.*

There was no answer. Perhaps the faerie had never heard me at all. I don't know, at that point, if I was human enough for words.

I held on.

The ceiling was falling in. It crashed around us, stone and books and wood in a violent cascade, the sky wheeling overhead and the ground beneath me surging like the sea. I closed my eyes shut, and held on. I put myself on the library roof even as it fell about me: Hero braced like an explorer on a ship, her hair tumbling and her dark eyes amused; Alden lying in the sun, relaxed and playful and at peace; Eddie quiet and shy and pleased, taking in everything; Camford stretched out before us as far as we could see. I held all of them in my mind, and Hero I held closest of all.

She had pushed me from the circle the last time the world was ending. I had let her do it. I had let her keep pushing me until we were no longer a part of each other's lives.

Not this time.

29

C lover."
       The voice was saying my name—gentle, insistent. A
memory caught and sparked: a summer's morning in Ashfield,
lying on the floor, eighteen years old and about to open my eyes
to the new world our mistakes had made.

But it wasn't Alden's voice this time. And when I opened my
eyes, blinking hazily, it was not to the Ashfield drawing room.
I lay on the cracked ruins of the stone floor, rubble and shattered glass strewn about me. Above was the canopy of a forest.
Branches and boughs thick with leaves crossed over my head;
through them filtered grey-gold light, and patches of a cloudy
sky. The wind teased at the branches, and the leaves whispered. I
frowned, wondering, still only half-aware of where I was.

"Clover?" It was Eddie. I recognised his voice with a rush of
relief, and when I turned my head, I saw him crouched beside
me. There was a long crack across one lens of my spectacles that
blurred his face, but he seemed unscathed, and his own sigh of
relief was unmistakable. "Thank God. Are you all right?"

"I think so." Feeling was beginning to come back to my body,
and with it a hundred vague aches and bruises. More importantly,
I was becoming aware of another hand still clasped in my own. I
turned toward it, careful not to let go, and came face-to-face with
Hero. She lay curled on one side, eyes closed, her face pale and still.

"She's alive," Eddie said quickly, before I had time to wonder. "But I don't know who she is. I don't know if the faerie left."

"Neither do I," I said, because the part of me that did know was so tentative, and it felt too dangerous to say for sure. Something had left, though, hadn't it? I had felt it as the buildings fell—a kiss of the wind, a breeze like the air off the sea.

As I watched, Hero's eyelids flickered; her brow furrowed. I sat up quickly, my hand still tight around hers, scarcely daring to breathe. Eddie dropped to his knees beside me; we exchanged quick glances, brimming with hope and fear in equal measures.

"Hero?" I said softly, as though her name were a spell.

Hero gave a single shiver, then her breath caught with a gasp. Her dark eyes flickered open and met mine, and for the first time in eight years they housed no soul but hers.

"Clover," she said, and then my arms were wrapped around her, and hers around me were strong and wiry and frail all at the same time. I clung to her tightly and buried my face in her shoulder. She was trembling; I'm sure I was too.

"Are you all right?" Eddie asked, as we parted. "Is the dryad really gone?"

Hero nodded. "She's gone. She's gone back to her tree."

"I'm so sorry," I said in a rush. I had said it to the faerie many times, hoping Hero could hear. This was the first time I had been able to say it and know she could. "It was my fault, all of it."

"Oh, shut up." It would have been convincing had she not still been shivering as if she would fly apart. Still, her head had its old proud tilt and her eyes their old warmth. "Never mind. It was far from all your fault, and the parts that were I forgave you for when you came for me in Paris."

"I don't know if I can forgive myself."

"I'm the one who spent years trapped in my own body married to a man I hated before going on a murdering spree across three countries. If I can forgive, you certainly should. Oh, hell." She wiped irritably at her eyes, from which tears had spilled, and drew a deep, shuddering breath. Her limbs were stiff and clumsy, the first time in years she had moved them of her own volition. "I swore when I finally got control of my own body I wouldn't let it cry."

"Oh, that old promise," Eddie said, with his crooked smile. "I break that one every day."

Hero laughed, shakily, and drew him into a tight embrace. "God, I've missed you both."

That reminded me, inevitably, of the one we weren't speaking about, the one who was still missing. "Where's Alden?" I made myself ask.

"I don't know," Eddie said. "I couldn't find him. At first I couldn't even find you. The whole building came down. I wasn't sure if the trees had stopped you being buried."

That was where we were, I realised, too late. Still in the midst of Camford, only the library had gone. It had all gone. And the trees...

I looked up at the boughs encircling us. "Did you...?"

"I asked them to shield us." His face was coming into clearer focus now—the blurriness hadn't all been my glasses. He looked white and tired, and there was a cut over one eyebrow. "I don't know if it was me they listened to. What did *you* do? Are you sure you're all right?"

"I'm fine." I meant it now, at least physically. The aches had settled to a dull throb, and that appeared to be where they planned to stay. "But..."

My eyes flickered against their will to the wreckage, the great smashed glass dome overhead and the books strewn and smoking beside us.

"This was the *library*," I said inadequately. It was the library. My library. It had let me in, welcomed me, and I had used that to destroy it. "I don't know if I did the right thing, or..."

"You did," Eddie said, more certain than I'd ever heard him. "It wasn't right. Any of it."

"It wasn't." Hero was calm now, her eyes serious. "I lived in the dryad's head for so long, or rather it lived in mine. Its anger was terrible, day in and day out until I thought I would go mad locked up with it. But it had been wronged. It needed to be put right."

I knew it did. I'd known it as I did it, and I'd done it with all of my heart. Still, looking at the library crumbling around me, the buildings I'd loved for so long torn from the riven ground, my heart was cracked and bleeding in my chest. The magic that had been mine all too briefly was already dead in my veins. And soon, too soon, the rest of our magic would start to die too.

I said none of this. It was selfish and weak, and it wouldn't help. But oh God, I felt it.

Instead, I drew a deep breath and dashed the tears from my eyes. "We need to get out of here."

It was inarguable. The problem was, there was nowhere to go. Camford lay in ruins—the gate was torn open now, and the Oxbridge would have collapsed. We were in faerie country now, with nothing except reclaimed forest and wasteland for miles in either direction.

"Could we make a new door?" Eddie asked, his thoughts clearly running on similar lines. "Is that possible, from this side?"

I shook my head. "No. If it were, the fae would be through all the time. Besides, Sam said there were plans to reinstate the locks almost at once. Faerie country will be closed again by now."

Alden's voice came, quiet and husky. "Ashfield."

We turned, sharp, defensive. Eddie rose to his feet, and the vines around the wreckage twisted and rustled. I think we had all been secretly hoping that Alden had vanished, and we would never have to know what became of him.

I was shocked when I saw him. He was barely standing, supported by a crumpled pillar that had once belonged to the staircase; one arm was at an unnatural angle and he was bleeding from a cut on his temple. All the colour had drained from him—not only from his skin, but from the gold of his hair, the blue of his eyes. Even his clothes were so covered in fine ash that they seemed to have greyed at a stroke.

"Don't worry," he said, with the faintest twitch of his mouth. Had it not been for that almost-smile, I wouldn't have recognised him. "You're in no danger from me. The faerie's gone. It's over."

It was far from over. But the faerie *had* gone, and perhaps it had, at last, gone as far as Alden was willing to go. I didn't quite relax, but I stood.

"What was that about Ashfield?" I asked.

"The door there won't have locked," he said, as though this was a perfectly theoretical conversation we were having in the library years ago. "I left it open when I crossed faerie country to get here. It will stay open, just as it did the first time."

"Could you find your way back?" Eddie asked.

"I found my way here. I don't see why not."

"I know the way too," Hero said slowly. She stood beside me, shakily at first, rapidly regaining her balance. "The dryad knew."

The three of us exchanged uncertain glances. It was strange, after all these years, how easy it was to fall into the old, half-subconscious patterns of communication: I knew, at a glance, that Hero was sceptical but inclined to follow, that Eddie was wary, that both were taking in my own conflict between doubt and hope. Alden clearly knew too, because he gave a short, breathless sigh.

"I'm not asking to be trusted," he said. "I only said I know the way home. You can come with me or not, if you like." He paused, and whatever he claimed he wasn't asking, when he spoke again there was a defensive edge to his voice. "I know you all hate me. I don't care. I know I deserve it, and I don't care about that either. But for what it's worth, Hero, I truly did believe I couldn't save you."

Hero snorted. "Of course you did. It suited you to. You know, I always did think I had no illusions about you, Alden. I thought I knew every one of your faults, and your charm didn't work on me. I had the audacity to warn Clover about you. I underestimated you."

"Perhaps you overestimated me."

"Perhaps." She shook her head. "You were willing to throw us all away for your own ends. The fact you flinched from it at the last moment is neither here nor there. I don't hate you. But that's only because I've been swimming in somebody else's hate for years, and I'm exhausted of it."

"I hate you quite a bit," Eddie offered. "If that helps."

Alden's soft laugh dissolved into a harsh, wrenching cough; he stifled it with a wince and cleared his throat. "I know you do. It's fair. A shame, though, because whatever you think, I've always liked you very much." He didn't look at me at all. "Well? Are you following me?"

"We'll follow," Hero said, after a quick questioning glance in my direction and Eddie's. "Just don't think for a moment this means you're forgiven."

"I'm not asking for forgiveness either," Alden said.

※

And so we set out across faerie country, the four of us, as we had often talked of doing those long summer evenings at Ashfield.

It was a long, hard road, far longer and harder than I could have imagined. Alden had arrived so quickly at Camford that I would have expected us to be at the Ashfield gate within half an hour at the outside. But either we took a wrong turn, the ground had shifted when the gates opened, or time simply didn't have the same meaning in faerie country, because the great grey wastes stretched out forever.

The ground was thick with roots and vines, so that it was

impossible to move without placing your feet carefully or struggling through thorns. Any exposed skin was soon scored by
stinging scratches, and more than once I fell hard on the earth.
And the earth *was* hard, so cold and tight-packed it felt more like
rock. The wind screamed constantly, voices in our languages
and others intertwining, half-understood. It buffeted our hair
and clothes until I felt my reason threaten to tear loose and blow
away with it. Worst of all was the laughter. It swirled in the air,
always just out of earshot, high and lilting and sending shivers
tapping up my spine. I understood now why Alden had arrived
in the state he had.

Eddie was the only one among us who didn't seem to feel it.
At times the trees would raise their roots and the vines would
grip at our ankles; a soft word from him and they settled, rustling their leaves threateningly. I wondered at it, and at his confidence stepping through the foliage, head high and eyes alight
with curiosity.

Hero clearly saw the same thing. "I see you've mastered the
roses." She was breathless, but I could see she was beginning to
settle into her limbs. She was very tired, though. The faerie had
taken her body through fire and battle and the gates between
worlds. "It was very impressive, what you did back there."

"Not mastered," he corrected, with a shy smile. "They'll listen to me, though. Once Alden bound you—the faerie—they
were willing to be persuaded."

He glanced at Alden then, and away again without a word.
None of us had spoken to Alden since we had set out, and he
hadn't spoken to us. He walked a little ahead, not looking back,
an Orpheus with a string of Eurydices whom he had never
meant to bring home.

The great silver sky began to darken and the air to cool. Perspiration turned cold on my skin, and I was soon shivering.
There were rustles and snaps from the surrounding dimness,
and more than once I caught the movement of tiny imps out of

the corner of my eye. If we were still here when night fell, we had every chance of being attacked. I remembered the flashing teeth and screams of the imp at the Bodleian, all those years ago, and felt sick.

"No wonder the fae want to come to our world if this is all they have," I said out loud.

It was a meaningless comment, bravado in the face of exhaustion, but Hero shook her head. "It isn't," she said unexpectedly. "These are the outskirts, where the edges touch the human world and the doors open. That's why we haven't seen any life, except the imps who feed off the deadwood. Toward the centre, the trees grow bigger and wind themselves into great cities, and at the very centre is the fae court, where the queen resides."

For just a flash, I could see it, the great starry court thronged with fae of every shape and description, and I wished with a longing like a physical stab that we could turn aside from our course and see it for ourselves. Hero caught my expression and gave a bitter smile.

"The faerie grew up there," she explained. "She loved the dancing and the great branches glittering like starlight. But she couldn't forget her sister."

"No," I said quietly. I thought of my brother, away all those years in that vast no-man's-land of barbed wire and death; of Alden's brother, growing paler and more distant at the faerie court; of the oak faerie, sleeping in the tree while the students of Camford milled oblivious around her, and of Hero locked inside her own head while we all did the same. We had all done so many foolish and terrible things trying to save the people we loved. The world had been changed because of it, because we had broken it and battered it and held fast until we had reshaped it into what it needed to be. I still didn't know—perhaps would never know—if I had bent it into a better shape. Yet the faerie of the oak was free, and I had Matthew and Rose and Sam and my family safe in the world, and Hero and Eddie were both walking at my side to the edges of the earth. I could live without Camford, without Ashfield, even without magic, for that.

Alden never said a word, but it was more obvious with every passing mile that there was something very wrong. His breathing came shallow and ragged, he flinched spasmodically at each misstep, and more than once he stumbled. When we stopped to rest under the shade of a twisted yew tree, he collapsed, racked by deep, rasping coughs that he tried and failed to stifle in his sleeve. When he pulled his arm away, the shirt cuff was stained with blood.

Hero and Eddie ignored him. They sank down with me some distance away, quiet, recovering our breath. There was some water left in the bottle in my satchel, the one I'd filled at Calais, and I passed it around. They didn't move when, after a moment's hesitation, I pulled myself stiffly to my feet and took the last of it over to Alden—though they didn't protest either.

He looked up, slightly surprised at my approach, and shook his head at the proffered bottle.

"Keep it," he said. "It's not far now."

I put it away. "Are you all right?"

His mouth quirked very slightly. "Do you really care?"

"Yes," I said honestly. "God knows why, but yes."

"Thank you. No, to answer your question, but I'll do." He coughed again, and when he spoke there was a strange quality to his voice—soft, almost shy. "What's she like, our daughter? Rose, I think you said?"

"I don't know her as well as I should." I knelt on the ground beside him and tried to recall my little girl to my mind.

I had taken far too long to realise that she was coming. I'm not sure why—I grew up on a farm, I knew the signs. Perhaps I've always been better than I want to admit at ignoring things I don't want to know. I was back at Camford by the time it dawned on me, and by then even I couldn't ignore that things between the four of us had changed. Hero was gone, Eddie was fast going too, Alden refused to look at me. I was eighteen, fighting for a career in a world that wanted to lock me out, and instead I was on the brink of unwed motherhood. I could have sought a way to get rid of her, with or without magic, but somehow I shied from the thought. She was too tied up in that golden summer, in the glowing days and silver nights before it all went wrong. She would be Family by blood, a magical child born of one precious night when everything seemed possible. I wanted her in the world, whatever it cost.

In the end, it had cost me both too little and too much. Matthew and Jemima were happy to raise her—the more so because Matthew was firmly against having children of his own with a faerie curse still lurking in his blood. I had been very lucky and very stubborn, and I had been able to hide her as she grew inside me for those long months. In the spring holidays, I had told anyone at Camford who cared that my sister-in-law was having a baby and I was going to the farm to help her. I was almost too late—she came early, only my second evening at home, and by dawn there she was, a fair-haired, pink-faced child screaming at the top of her gloriously healthy lungs. After a month I was back at Camford, and nobody noticed that I was exhausted and unwell and sometimes on the verge of tears, until eventually I wasn't.

I loved her, truly. I had seen many babies, my own younger siblings included; I hadn't been prepared for how wondrous she would be, how precisely and exquisitely a piece of my heart would be wrenched from my body and given fragile, perfect form in the world. I hadn't realised how many nights I would cry helplessly alone in the dark as Camford glittered outside, and no work could fill the aching hole that had been carved in me. I didn't realise how scared I would feel for her, all the time. But she was happy with my family—far more so than she would have been with me—and I told myself it was for the best. I had given and taken too much to give up on Camford now. Besides, no matter how I tried, I couldn't shake the feeling that she was Alden's child, not mine. From the beginning, I could see the magic sparking in her blood, and I'd known it had come from him. After that, I began to see him in her cleverness, her charm, the gold of her hair and the delightful lilt of her laugh. I had told myself that Matthew and Jemima were her parents, and what didn't come from them came from the Families. I loved her as an aunt or a godmother, through birthdays and Christmases and letters and presents, and I'd told myself that was right.

And yet her magic hadn't come from Alden after all. It had come from me too. I had breathed it in, and it had blossomed in my veins. I had given it to her, exactly as I'd wished to, and now that I'd taken it away, I could teach her how to find it again with the rest of us. It could all be different, in the new world on the other side of the door.

"She has your hair and eyes," I said slowly, because Alden was still waiting for an answer. "My face, though, which was fortunate because everyone always says how much she looks like Matthew. She loves games, and learning, and magic. She's mischievous and daring, but she's kind too—she'll do what she's told by those she loves, and nobody else. And she never gives up."

It wasn't enough. But it was a start.

His smile was real this time. "God help Camford when she gets there."

"There is no Camford." It was just beginning to sink in, like a wound I would feel every day for the rest of my life. "It's gone."

"Well, there will be something else in its place soon enough," he said, unperturbed. "And then God help it."

⁂

It was obvious when the Ashfield door at last drew near. The ground beneath our feet was the first to change. It smoothed, the roots becoming softer, the slope gentler. Yellow grass began to creep across the thorny stones, and stray wisps of cloud hung in the darkening sky. I thought I heard the burble of water, though that might have been my mind playing tricks. The bottle was long since empty, and my tongue was thick and parched.

And then, there it was: the spare room door, outlined in silver, hanging above the tangled undergrowth. My heart, which had not dared feel beyond the next few steps, skyrocketed in my chest. I started to run, stiffly, stumbling, and Eddie and Hero quickened their pace beside me.

Alden didn't—I don't think he could. He was barely stumbling forward, his face the colour of chalk, blood at the corner of his mouth. But he sighed as he caught up to us.

"There," he whispered. "I said I'd find it."

I looked at him askance, out of sheer habit, and his mouth twitched.

"Well," he amended. "I said I'd try."

Ashfield was on the other side of that door. I hadn't seen it in so long, and amidst everything my chest ached with longing. I would be arrested soon, and Hero and Eddie with me. Alden would probably be given a medal, once they'd cleaned him up enough to take the weight. And yet I had walked through faerie country and come home to Ashfield. They couldn't take that from me.

"Come on," Hero said briskly. "One at a time."

Alden shook his head.

"You three go through," he said. "Go through, close it behind you, and set the whole bloody thing alight. That's the only way to be certain it's closed from our side. It still isn't enough. Last time the dryad was able to keep it open a crack—even when the door became subject to the Accord, and the faerie was loose in the world, the door never quite faded as it should. We can't leave it that way. I need to close it from this side too."

Hero raised her eyebrow, and I recognised it from a long

time ago as a way to cover her surprise until she could work out what to feel. "This is a strange and uncharacteristic time to be a martyr."

"This isn't martyrdom, and it isn't a new decision. I told you, I came to fix what I did all those years ago. I've done some very questionable things to get here, as I'm sure you'll all agree, and I kept doing them over and over, because I told myself that the ends would justify the means, or some such thing…" He paused for breath, a hand to his ribs, and half laughed. "Honestly, I can't remember what I told myself. Never mind, either way the end failed. I can't kill the faerie now; I can't bring Thomas back. I don't even know now if he was alive here to start with. At least I can still do this. I can make sure this door is closed once and for all."

"But…" I swallowed, possibilities turning over in my weary mind. "You'll be trapped here, forever. You'll die here."

"I am aware," he said, very calmly, though I saw his fist clench and unclench. "Thank you, again, for caring. It's very generous of you, under the circumstances."

"Too generous," Hero agreed, "but she's right. Right now, I know this place as well as any on earth, and you *will* die here. If you really want to fix your mistakes, wouldn't it be better to come back and fix them properly for once in your bloody life?"

"Possibly," he conceded, with the faintest ghost of a smile. "But you really do keep overestimating me, Hero. I'm too much of a coward for that. Besides, that won't close the door, and it truly does need to be closed. It's been open too long, all those years with that faerie testing it and trying to break through. It's a weak point in the veil between worlds now. If the faerie doesn't push through it again, something else might, or the Board will find a way to use it from the other side. Either way, I think we've had enough to do with the fae, don't you?"

Against my will, I remembered the feel of Hero's wrist in my hand, and the promise I had made. *We'll see the last of the doors are closed forever. We'll never trouble you again. Just let her go.*

It had been a promise, not a bargain. We weren't held to it. But it was what the faerie had wanted, and she was right. There could be no more deals between us, not safely, not for now. We had broken faith with them too many times.

"Yes," I said. "I do think so. I also think the door should be closed, on both sides if we can. There has to be another way, though."

"I don't *want* another way," he said bluntly. "I mean what I said: I'm a coward. I never once intended to face what I'd done. I'm not even sure I can face the world out there now. I don't think any of you ever realised, but I *liked* things the way they were. The old world suited me. I'm not fitted for a new one."

He meant it, I knew that. It was the same brutal honesty he'd given to me eight years ago on the other side of this very door, as heartfelt and troubling as an unwanted gift. Yet I couldn't help but feel in a great rush how different things might have been if Alden had ever been half as clear-eyed about fixing his deficiencies as he had been in identifying them, how wide the chasm had always been between who he could have been and who he let himself become.

"It's getting dark," he said into the silence. "You don't want to be in faerie country after dark. And, to be frank, if we wait much longer, I might not have the strength left to close the door at all. It's been a very, very long day."

Hero nodded slowly. She, after all, must have known better than any of us how dangerous it could be to leave the door half-open. And he had betrayed her—over and over, in small ways and large, up until the last possible second that should have weighed feather-light against eight years. She had tried to save him once and nearly lost herself. She owed him nothing. But Eddie had been right that friendship is so rarely about what is owed, or even deserved.

"Well, then." Her voice tried for brisk, but it had been a long time since she had used it, and she had lost the knack. "Then I suppose we'd best say good-night, hadn't we?"

She started toward the door. Then, as if on impulse, she turned back and gave him a swift, light kiss.

"Sleep well," she said, very softly, and then she walked out of faerie country.

Eddie had been watching Alden quietly, without saying a word. I thought he was going to leave without a word. Then at the last moment, he too turned.

"I'm sorry you couldn't save Thomas," he said in a rush. "Thank you for standing up for me, back at Crawley. You were the only one who did, and it meant a lot."

"Oh." Alden blinked, slightly startled. "You're welcome. And thank you. I'm sorry too."

He might have meant about Thomas, or he might not have.

Then it was just the two of us, and the night closing in. The screeches of the imps were getting louder, and the air around was cold. It had been cold the last time I had heard that sound, in the Bodleian, when we had unleashed a nightmare and giggled about it helplessly as Oxford had spun into the new year.

For the last time, his eyes met mine. Just for a second, in a searing flash of dust and sunlight and the smell of old paper, we were in the Camford Library with the whole world spread before us. *What are you reading?* he had asked, and he had laughed as if I had meant it when I said, *A book.*

I had loved him from that moment. It was a strange, intense, complicated love, wrapped around Camford and Hero and Eddie and Ashfield and a whole shimmering way of life, embedded in my heart like a climbing rose. I didn't know what to do with that love now, but I was grateful for it nonetheless.

I think something similar must have come to him, because a smile flickered and then faded on his face.

"Don't tell Rose about me, please," he said abruptly. I think it surprised even him. "I'd rather she not think of me the way you'll have to describe me."

In the end, I was the only one who left without a word. I couldn't speak. I nodded tightly.

Then I stepped through the gate, and he was gone. I tried to look back one more time, at the last threshold between worlds, but there was nothing behind me except mist.

The room at Ashfield was bathed in moonlight once more. This time, there was no mystery about where it came from. A cloudy night had fallen outside, but the silvery light of the last faerie door glowed even as I passed through and sank, head spinning, to my knees. The other two were bent similarly, catching their breath in ragged gasps. My body was light, untethered, ears roaring as though I'd stood up too quickly. I found myself gripping the rug, trying not to float away.

My head settled soon; so, less welcome, did every throb and ache of my limbs. I could make sense of the familiar surroundings: the sofa, the fireplace, the door that led to the east wing. I marvelled at how unchanged it was. I shouldn't have, I suppose. Ashfield had stood all but unchanged for centuries.

Hero got to her feet first, rubbing a hand across her eyes, and turned to the wall. I expected her to speak the usual words to close a faerie door. Instead, she lifted her chin, and she raised her voice in the unearthly lilt of the faerie tongue.

The silver lines across the wallpaper evaporated. I turned to her, eyes wide, and she gave me a shadow of her old wicked smile.

"I wondered if that would still work," she said. "I only have a few words left. They're difficult, but I always liked spellcraft linguistics."

"You could write a paper," I said stupidly. My head was still dizzy. "The Faculty—" I broke off, remembering anew the tumbling library and the closed door. Yet why not? There was still a Faculty, after all. The people hadn't gone anywhere. There were many books left, in private libraries across the country. And it only took ink and a page to write a paper.

Eddie was getting to his feet too, stumbling. "Has Alden closed the other side?"

Hero tilted her head to one side, as if listening. For just a moment, I glimpsed the faerie who had been in her head most of her adult life. "It's closed," she said, with a nod. "On both sides."

"It isn't enough," I said. This time, I refused to even think about the ache in my chest. "Alden was right. We need to close it forever this time."

I didn't need to say anything further. We had all been there. It had been vital that both sides be closed—if they weren't, nothing we did to our side of the door would be enough. But even a closed door could be opened.

It needed to be burned. Not just the door, or the room, or even the east wing. The faerie had been able to see over all of Ashfield—the magic had embedded itself throughout the whole house. It all needed to go. Ashfield needed to burn.

"We'd better do it quickly," Hero said, and I nodded.

"I'll go to the servants' quarters," Eddie said quietly. His eyes held mine, sympathetic, then let them go. "I'll make sure everyone gets out."

I turned to the door as he left. I knew the spell to light a fire. I had used it a hundred times, a thousand. I had burned my own motorcar with it only days ago, at what seemed the end of another life. It should have been nothing, after Camford. Yet my fingers felt numb and frozen, and my mind was the same.

The act of freeing a faerie, the act of stepping through a door...those were things that could be done without thought to the consequences. Setting fire to Ashfield felt too deliberate, too much like real destruction. This, of all things, I couldn't do.

Hero laid a hand gently on my arm.

"It's all right," she said. "I'll do it. I told you, I never did like this room."

She drew herself upright, eyes flashing. For the second time, she spoke the faerie tongue.

The wall burst into flame.

Faerie fire blazed a good deal hotter and brighter than even mage fire. By the time we joined the servants on the front lawn, coughing and soot-streaked, the flames had eaten the entire east wing and were licking at the main building. I don't know what Eddie had said to Morgan and the other servants—or, perhaps, he'd had no need to say very much at all. They had lived in that house a long time, and whatever magic their masters had tried to keep from them, they had as many brains and eyes between them as any other group of people. Either way, some of them shifted uneasily; not one moved forward to put the fire out.

I found after a while that Hero was holding my right hand, and Eddie was holding the other—also that I was silently weeping and suspected they were doing the same. A light Yorkshire drizzle fell on the grass, but it didn't touch the blaze. Instead, the firelight caught it, turned it to a million flecks of light that sparked and disappeared in the heat. Through the tears that blurred my eyes, the great manor house seemed surrounded by a halo of gold.

In my head, Ashfield was always golden. Baked in relentless summer sun, yellowing fields around it, sunbeams slanting into the old warm rooms and turning the dust motes into specks of light. It didn't seem right that my last sight of it was on a damp night without even a moon—that I hadn't seen it in daylight since the morning after the door opened, and now I would never see it again.

It takes a long time for a building to burn. Long, heartbreaking hours, as ash falls from the sky like snow and clings to your hair and eyelashes, as ancient staircases and corridors and your funny crooked bedroom are devoured one by one. We stayed those long hours, as the great beams cracked and the roof toppled, as the stones fell, as Alden's last smile flickered in my head over and over.

The sky was turning red overhead when Hero's hand tightened spasmodically around mine and Eddie caught his breath. I might have been dozing, because it wasn't until I blinked that I saw what they had seen.

A figure was walking out of the flames.

He was a young man, perhaps not yet twenty, dressed in a simple dress shirt and trousers with his fair hair cut short and his face clean-shaven. His feet were bare, but he crossed the grass and mud without a thought, as though he were stepping on something else entirely. He might have been a ghost, had his frame not been so solidly built, and had his eyes not so clearly lit on us as he came forward.

"Hello," he said. His brow was furrowed, puzzled, not concerned, like a man who had missed a turning on the road or was trying to remember a dream. "I'm sorry, it's the strangest thing, but can you tell me where I am?"

I wondered only where on earth he could have come from. He was a stranger to me, though I could see he looked familiar in some way: his blond hair, his well-shaped face, his blue eyes. It was only when Hero caught her breath and said his name aloud that I realised I was face-to-face with Thomas Lennox-Fontaine.

Epilogue

I thought about ending my story there. What happened afterwards is history: too big and unwieldy to tell on the one hand, and on the other, told too many times, in too many different forms.

There are full transcripts, should anyone care to read them, of the months-long trials that Hero and Eddie and I underwent, Sam and Lady Winter and a few surprising others fighting for us every step of the way, before the Board were forced to accept that Hero had been under faerie control and the blame was laid conveniently at the feet of the absent minister for magical enforcement. There are newspaper articles of the scandals that emerged during that trial, including the secret at the heart of Camford and the erosion of the Board afterwards. There have been books written, prematurely I think, about the hard year following the breaking of Camford, when magic dulled in our blood and the university scrabbled to reform with nothing but an idea to hold it together.

It *was* a hard year—an impossible year, a year I would have thought none of us could have survived had I not already lived through so much worse. As it was, once the trial was over, the three of us hid up at the Pendle Hill farm and for weeks did nothing very much except talk and sleep and go for long walks and help on the farm and eat and sleep and talk some more. There was something strangely idyllic about this, amidst the grief and the shock and the sick dread of what the world had become. We hadn't been together in such a long time. Richard joined us, of course, and in a strange way he kept the missing place Alden left from feeling too stark.

"I hope you don't mind us all being here," I said to Matthew once. "It's just that we've nowhere else to go. Everything feels broken."

He gave me the look he's reserved since I was a toddler for when I was being spectacularly stupid. "Clove, this is your *home*," he said, and I realised that it was true. Perhaps it had never been Pendle Hill I was running from, but rather some version of myself I feared I'd become if I stayed there; I'd outgrown her now, and so at last I'd grown back into Pendle Hill. "It's where your daughter lives. It's where your family are. Of course you can all stay here as long as you need. Besides," he added, more gently, "you think I don't know what it feels like when everything breaks?"

I might have stayed there forever, all my ambitions smashed. Eddie had never wanted anything more than to hide from the world in the first place. It was Hero who ended it. One morning I came down to breakfast to find her and Eddie and Richard already there. She looked very different now to how she had the day we had met—pale, gaunt, dressed in one of Jemima's old farm jumpers, her hair pulled back into a loose knot. But the determination was back on her face, and with it the glint in her eye that I loved, the one that invited everyone to challenge her and see what they got.

"I've been thinking," she said. "It's time to go."

"Why?" I asked—not because I disagreed, but because I wanted to know what she would say.

"Because they're putting the world back together out there," she said. "And if we're not careful, they'll put it back in the same old shapes. We need to go out there and fight for it."

"I don't think there's a lot we can do on our own," Eddie said cautiously.

She snorted. "Of course not. Still, we can do our part."

We did. That's another thing worth writing about: the way the line between Families and commonplace magic users has blurred over the long years, far too slowly yet inexorably, like a tide coming in. But we've lived that, and it doesn't need telling. If you're reading this book, you must have lived it too, perhaps without even being aware of it. Magic still isn't common knowledge, but it's less and less secret. There are whispers on the street now, books of magic left in libraries and in old bookstores where someone looking for them might find them. The cracks between the old order and the new are widening, and stories seep out. Most people don't want to know, or need to know, but one by one, the ones who do come to seek us out.

Perhaps you, reading this book right now, are one of them. If you are, and you're ready to learn, find us. At the time of writing, a full third of our students of magic come from ordinary families. I hope it will be more and more each year, while those able to identify as Family grow less and less, until one day we'll find ourselves standing in the midst of unfamiliar territory without knowing how we got there. We have such a long way to go.

There are other things I could mention, too, that nobody else has written of, but those are too many. When I try to get them down, I can only catch fragments, like the Imagist poets Hero and I used to read aloud on my floor at Chancery Hall. The books from Lady Winter's library, sending up clouds of dust as she sorts through to find ones to replace those lost in faerie country. Rose's smile the first time I came home, and the rain on the roof of the barn as I sit there with Matthew late at night. Hero battling through months of nightmares on my couch, then emerging on the other side to begin to travel the world. Eddie and Richard in their cottage in the Highlands with flowers growing wild throughout the house. All these things are too small and unruly to push into a narrative, though perhaps it would be worth trying.

And yet, after all, I have a few things left to say.

I write this sitting in a library, as I was all those years ago when Alden Lennox-Fontaine sat beside me. It isn't the Camford Library, of course, although it's *a* Camford library, one of many in the smaller universities that have blossomed and thrived all over the country since Camford itself fell. Some of these universities are made of new brick and some of old stone; some of them are in still more modern buildings of metal and glass. This one is in Manchester, though I teach at several these days, including the one Rose attends in Durham. There are students about me, talking in soft murmurs, and sunlight through the great high windows that transforms the redbrick walls to soft russet. It's the world Alden, so clever and so scared, wasn't certain he could face. I wish with all my heart he had. It's a difficult world, a dangerous world, especially now with a new war looming on the horizon. Still, the world has always been that, beneath the surface. Perhaps we could have helped him through it, and he could have helped us.

This book will be the first time Rose reads about Alden. I kept my promise to him, for her sake rather than for his, waiting for the time she was old enough to understand—which was foolish, because I'm not old enough yet myself, and never will be. But Rose is a scholar now, as am I, and if I've learned one thing, it's that it's the duty of a scholar to find the truth.

I miss Alden desperately, despite everything. I miss Ashfield. I still miss Camford, every day. It comes in intense jagged waves, like grief: One hour I can believe I'll never think of it again, the next I'll catch a glimpse of an oak tree or a stone wall or the smell of old books, and I'll be unable to breathe. Yet it hurts less than it might, because of the dreams.

I never know what nights they'll come. I'll close my eyes, and when I open them, I'll be standing somewhere, anywhere, in Camford. The crooked streets and student buildings and winding river will sparkle under a crisp sky, and the wind will buffet my hair and clothes as though it's welcoming me home. There are no people there, and the plants are even thicker on the ground, and yet it's whole again and perfect, the books back on the shelves and the chalk lying beside the blackboards as though it's just waiting for the end of the holidays. I can wander all night through the empty buildings, skin tingling and heart opening wide. Often I've spent hours in the library, reading the books I've not found it easy to relocate in the real world, and when I wake, the knowledge is always fresh-printed in my head.

At first I thought it was because I was still the ward of Camford Library, that as long as I still live, the library will live too. Lately, though, I've wondered if it isn't something more. Sometimes Hero's work on faerie language comes from places I'm not sure even her experience encompasses, or Eddie's breakthroughs on Camford's plants slip into the uncanny. Even Matthew seems to be learning a little too much and too fast. I've never spoken about those dreams to anyone before, not even to the people I love most in the world, and they've never mentioned them to me. I'm too afraid that if I do, the dreams will go away again, and I have so much more to learn first.

Thomas Lennox-Fontaine is living in York now, about an hour's drive from his parents' new house. I've spoken to him often—he's a kind, brave, honourable young man, with Alden's playfulness, and he's recovered well from his time away, although on certain nights his gaze will shift as though he's hearing something nobody else can hear. He remembers nothing of his years in the faerie court and can shed no light on why he was returned.

But I remember the moment when the worlds were falling apart, and I held on to the faerie in Hero's body. *Let us go*, I said, *and we'll see the last of the doors are closed forever.* There was no bargain struck, not in any magical sense. And yet I made a promise, and together we kept it, Alden most of all. And the faerie of the silver birch kept her promise too, and let us all go, every last one. If I'm right, it's a different exchange of magic to any that's ever happened between humans and the fae, a deal based on trust and goodwill and not on mutual threat. Nothing may ever come of it; if it does, it likely won't be for a very long time. We broke trust with each other hundreds of years ago, after all. It might take hundreds more to earn it back, even thousands. But as far as I know, no faerie has ever lived eight years in a human body and returned to faerie country. If Hero can learn to understand the fae from that, perhaps they've learned to understand us.

It's nothing substantial, I know. Dreams and theories, nothing more, and definitely nothing that a Camford scholar would consider evidence. Officially, nobody has seen or heard from faerie country since the Second Accord. The doors are closed, the locks are unbroken. Faerie magic is being taught again only as theory. Everyone agrees that the fae are best left alone. We have enough problems of our own, in this fragmented and glittering age we've created.

There's just one thing, one solid thing, that might mean nothing or everything. A few years ago, a tree began to grow on the ruins of Ashfield. A tall, slender tree, with a silvery bark and small dark leaves like those on the great oak at Camford. It has yet to flower, and nobody, not even Eddie, can tell us what will happen when it does. For now, it puts down roots, and grows, and waits, a relic of the old world and a promise of something new.

Acknowledgments

As always, a special thank you to my agent, Hannah Bowman, who somehow finds time to answer multiple emails, read my books, reassure me they're not terrible, tell me how to fix them, and generally guide me through the thorny paths of publishing. I so appreciate it. Thank you also to Nivia Evans for taking on this book and for the first round of edits; to Angelica Chong for taking up the reins for the second round and beyond with enthusiasm and insight; and to Emily Byron, for taking such good care of this story across the pond. The book is so much better for all your work.

To the amazing people at Orbit: Thank you to Lauren Panepinto, head of department, and Lisa Marie Pompilio, cover artist—I always know my books are in safe hands with you. Thank you to Bryn A. McDonald, Rachel Goldstein, and Kelley Frodel for your tact and care in copyedits, even when it's very obvious I've left in bits of old drafts and don't know how time works. In publicity and marketing, thank you so much to Alex Lencicki, Ellen Wright, Stephanie Hess, and Natassja Haught for helping this book find its people in the outside world. You are all magic.

Thank you as always to the Bunker for your wisdom, your support, and your friendship.

This book is, among other things, a homage to the writers

of that strange and terrible period immediately before, during, and after World War I, who found themselves in a broken world and were determined to make a new one. So, thanks to them, and thanks in particular to Vera Brittain, Ford Madox Ford, Rebecca West, E. M. Forster, Katherine Mansfield, and T. S. Eliot, whose words all helped bring this book to life in different and unpredictable ways. It's also, of course, a book about academia, and so my endless gratitude goes to every university and university library that ever opened its doors to me.

To the menagerie: Jeremy and Miss Adler, our fashionable cat couple; Fleischman and O'Connell, our overactive and much-loved rabbits; Mr. Norrell and Thistledown, our chaos guinea pigs; and all the members of our mouse mischief, past and present. As usual, you were no help at all. Never stop.

Most importantly, thank you to Mum and Dad for your continual support and love, and especially to Sarah for reading, for brainstorming, for encouraging, for believing in what this story was going to be. The book wouldn't exist without you.

Last of all, if you've read anything I've ever written, including this, thank you. It means everything to me.

meet the author

Fairlie Atkinson

H. G. PARRY divides her time between a tiny flat in Wellington and a house on the Kāpiti Coast of New Zealand, which she shares with her sister and an ever-growing menagerie of small creatures. She holds a PhD in English literature from Victoria University of Wellington and has taught English, film, and media studies.

if you enjoyed

THE SCHOLAR AND THE LAST FAERIE DOOR

look out for

THE MAGICIAN'S DAUGHTER

by

H. G. Parry

*Off the coast of Ireland sits a legendary island hidden
by magic. A place of ruins and ancient trees, sea salt air
and fairy lore, Hy-Brasil is the only home Biddy has ever
known. Washed up on its shore as a baby, Biddy lives a quiet
life with her guardian, the mercurial magician Rowan.
A life she finds increasingly stifling.*

*One night, Rowan fails to return from his mysterious travels,
and to find him, Biddy must venture into the outside world*

for the first time. But Rowan has powerful enemies—forces who have hoarded the world's magic and have set their sights on the magician's many secrets.

Biddy may be the key to stopping them. Yet the closer she gets to answers, the more she questions everything she's ever believed about Rowan, her past, and the nature of magic itself.

Chapter One

Rowan had left the island again last night.

He had done so quietly, as usual. Had Biddy not been lying awake, listening for his light tread on the stairs outside her bedroom, she would have never known he was gone. But he had slipped out of the castle once or twice too often lately while she slept, and this time she was ready. She got out of bed and went to the window, shivering at the touch of the early-autumn chill, in time to see him cross the moonlit fields where the black rabbits nibbled the grass. Her fingers clenched into fists, knowing what was coming, frustrated and annoyed and more worried than she wanted to admit. At the cliff edge he paused, and then his tall, thin form rippled and changed as wings burst from his back, his body shriveled, and a large black bird flew away into the night. Rowan was always a raven when he wasn't himself.

When she was very young, Biddy hadn't minded too much when Rowan flew away at night. As unpredictable as Rowan could be, he was also her guardian, and however far he went she trusted him to always be there if she needed him. In the meantime, she was used to fending for herself. She did so all day sometimes, when Rowan was shut up in his study or off in the forest and had no time for things like meals or conversation or common sense. Besides, Rowan always left Hutchincroft behind to watch over things. Hutch couldn't speak to her when he was a rabbit, it was true, but he would leap onto the bed beside her, lay his head flat, and let her curl around his soft golden fur. It made the castle less empty, and the darkness less hungry. She would lie there, dozing fitfully, until either she heard the flutter of feathers and the scrabble of claws at the window above hers or exhaustion won out and pulled her into deeper sleep.

And in the morning, Rowan would always be there, as if he'd never left.

———————————◆»•═════════•◆◆———————————

That morning was no exception. When she woke to slanting sunlight and came downstairs to the kitchen, Rowan was leaning against the bench with his fingers curled around a mug of tea. His brown hair was rumpled and his eyes were a little heavy, but still dancing.

"Morning," he said to her brightly. "Sleep all right?"

She would have let him get away with that once. Not now. She wasn't a very young girl anymore. She was sixteen, almost seventeen, and she minded very much.

"What time did you get in?" she asked severely, so he'd know she hadn't been fooled. He laughed ruefully.

"An hour or two before dawn?" He glanced at Hutchincroft, who was busily munching cabbage leaves and carrots by the stove. "Half past four, Hutch says. Why? Did I miss anything?"

"I was asleep," she said, which wasn't entirely true. "You'd have to tell me."

She pulled the last of yesterday's bread out of the cupboard, sneaking a look at Rowan as she did so. There was a new cut at the corner of one eyebrow, and when he straightened, it was with a wince that he turned into a smile when he saw her watching.

Biddy didn't think there had ever been a time when she had thought Rowan was her father, even before he had told her the story of how she first came to Hy-Brasil. The two of them looked nothing alike, for one thing. Rowan was slender and long-limbed like a young tree, eternally unkempt and wild and sparkling with mischief. She was smaller, darker, with serious eyes and a tendency to frown. And yet he wasn't an older brother either, or an uncle, or anything else she had read about in the castle's vast library. He was just Rowan, the magician of Hy-Brasil, and as long as she could remember there had been only him and Hutchincroft and herself. She knew them as well as she knew the castle, or the cliffs that bordered the island, or the forests that covered it. And she knew when he was hiding something from her.

He knew her too, at least well enough to know he was being scrutinized. He lasted until she had cut the bread and toasted one side above the kitchen fire, and then he set his mug down, amused and resigned.

"All right. I give up. What have I done now?"

"Where did you go last night?" she asked—bluntly, but without any hope of a real answer.

She wasn't disappointed. "Oh, you know. Here and there. I was in Dublin for a bit, then I got over to Edinburgh. And London," he added, with a nod to Hutchincroft, conceding a point Biddy couldn't hear. In her bleakest moments, she wished they wouldn't do that. It reminded her once again of all the magic from which she was locked out.

"And when did you get hurt?"

"I didn't—well, hardly. A few bruises. I got careless." He looked at her, more serious. "If you're worried, you don't have to be. I'm not doing anything I haven't been doing longer than you've been alive. I haven't died yet."

"Death isn't a habit you develop, you know, like tobacco or whiskey. It only takes once."

"In that case, I promise I'll let you know before I consider taking it up. Is that toast done?"

"Almost." She turned the bread belatedly. "But we need more milk."

"Well, talk to the goats about it." He checked the milk jug, nonetheless, and made a face. "We do, don't we? And more jam. I need to take the boat out to the mainland for that."

This gave her the opening she'd been hoping for. She picked the slightly burnt bread off the fork and buttered it, trying for careful nonchalance. "I could come with you."

"No," he said, equally lightly. "You couldn't."

"Why not? You just pointed out that you've been leaving the island at night since long before I was born, and you're still alive. Why can't I at least come to get the supplies in broad daylight?"

"Because you don't go to the mainland, Biddy. I told you."

"You told me. You also told me it wouldn't be forever. You said I could go when I was older."

He frowned. "Did I? When did I say that?"

"Rowan! You said it when I was little. Seven or eight, I think. I asked if I could come with you when I was grown up, and you said, 'Yeah, of course.'"

She had held on to that across all the years in between, imagining what it would be like. Rowan clearly had no memory of it at all, but Hutchincroft nudged him pointedly and he shrugged. "All right. You're not grown up yet, though, are you?"

She couldn't argue with that. She had tried when she turned sixteen to think of herself as a woman, like Jane Eyre or Elizabeth Bennet or the multitudes of heroines who lived in her books, but in her head she wasn't there. They were all older than her, and had all, even Jane, seen more of life. And yet she was too old to be Sara Crewe or Alice or Wendy Darling either. She was a liminal person, trapped between a world she'd grown out of and another that wouldn't let her in. It was one reason why she wanted to leave the island so badly—the hope that leaving the place she'd grown up would help her leave her childhood behind. Not forever, not yet. But for a visit, to see what it was like.

"I'm not a child," she said instead. Of that, at least, she was sure. "I'm seventeen in December. I might be seventeen already—you don't know. I can't stay on this island my entire life."

"I know," he said. "I'll work something out, I promise. For now, it's not safe for you."

"You leave all the time."

"It's not exactly safe for me either, but that's different."

"Why?" She couldn't keep frustration out of her voice. "It should be safer for me than for you, surely. You're a mage. I'm nothing."

"You're not nothing," he corrected her, and he was truly serious now. "Don't say that."

She knew better than to push that further. Rowan, like her, had no patience for self-pity, and she didn't want to blur the lines of her argument by indulging in it.

"Well," she amended. "I can't channel magic. I'm not like you. I'm no different to any of the other millions of people living out there in the world right now, the ones I read about in books, and they're safe and well. If there's no threat to them, surely there's no threat to me." She hesitated, seized by doubt. "They *are* out there, aren't they? It really is like in the books?"

He laughed. "What, you mean are we the only people left in the world?"

"How should I know?" she pointed out, defensive. "I've never seen anyone else."

"There are millions of people out there. Of all shapes and sizes, colors and creeds, many of them very much like the people in books. Trust me. Where do you think the jam comes from?"

"I don't know where the jam comes from!" This wasn't strictly true—she knew both exactly how jam was made, thanks to the library, and how Rowan obtained it, thanks to Hutchincroft. But qualifying that would weaken her position, so she rushed on. "I've never seen that either. I've never seen anywhere except the island."

"Well, none of the rest of the world have ever seen the island. So you're not too badly off, considering."

"That isn't the point! I know why the rest of the world can't see us. I don't understand why I can't see the rest of the world."

"Biddy," he said, and the familiar note was in his voice, quiet but firm, that had stopped her in her tracks since she was old enough to recognize her name. "That's enough, all right?"

Against her own will, she fell silent, burning with resentment. It was directed at herself as much as anyone. Rowan rarely tried to guide any aspect of her behavior, and yet when he did she never dared to push back. No, *dared* was the wrong word—that sounded as though she was afraid of him, and Rowan had never done anything to make her so. The barrier came from inside her own head, from her own reluctance to lose Rowan's approval when he and Hutch were the only people in her world. She hated it. The heroines in her books would never care what anybody thought. And she hated most of all the reminder that her world was so small.

Rowan must have seen it, because the lines of his face softened. "Look, Bid—"

"Never mind." She laid down her butter knife and pushed her toast aside, trying for a dignified exit. It felt stiff and childish, only signifying that she had lost both the argument and, for some reason, her breakfast. "It was just a question, that's all. I need to see to the goats."

"All right." Rowan didn't sound happy, but he clearly had no intention of prolonging a discussion he himself had stopped. "I'll be in the study if you need me. We'll probably see you this afternoon?"

Biddy glanced at Hutch, who was watching her anxiously from the fireplace, and managed a wan smile for him. Then she went out the kitchen door, into the windswept courtyard where the chickens pecked. She wished, not for the first time lately, the hinges in the castle doors worked well enough to allow a remotely satisfying slam.

There were three rules to living on the Isle of Hy-Brasil, or so Rowan always said.

The first was to never set foot under the trees after dark. That one wasn't much of a rule—Rowan broke it all the time. It was difficult not to in the short daylight hours of winter. The forest covered most of the island, tangled and grey green and wild, and they often needed to forage well into it to collect plants for food and spells. But certainly there was an edge of danger under the branches once the sun went down. The shadows had been known to misbehave; high lilting sounds like laughter or half-heard music drifted through the leaves when the wind was still. There were things in the depths of Hy-Brasil that none of them would ever know, not even Hutchincroft.

The second rule was to watch out for the Púca, and never accept a ride from it. Unlike the rule about the trees, which seemed something she had always known, Biddy could dimly remember being given this one when she was four years old. She had been picking dandelions in the fields beyond the castle, the summer's grass swishing past her knees, when she had seen a black horse beyond the crest of the hill. There were no horses on Hy-Brasil: She had recognized it at once from pictures in her books, and her heart had thrilled. Its golden eyes had held her, beckoned her, and she had been venturing forward open-mouthed to touch its wiry mane when Rowan and Hutch had come from nowhere. She could recollect very little after that, but afterward Rowan had sat her down in the library for a rare serious talk and told her all about the Púca—that it was a shape-shifter, a trickster spirit who loved nothing better than to tempt unwary travelers onto its back, take them for a wild and terrifying ride, and dump them in a patch of thorns miles from home. She had found the thought more funny than scary at the time, but she had steered clear of any golden-eyed creature ever since.

The third was to never harm the black rabbits that speckled the long grass behind the castle, along the cliff paths up to the ruins. This one was the easiest of all. Biddy couldn't imagine why anyone would want to harm a rabbit.

It wasn't until she was a good deal older that Biddy had realized the fourth rule of living on Hy-Brasil, the unspoken one, the only truly inviolable ultimatum and one that applied only to herself. She was never to leave it.

It took her a long time to notice this, and even longer to mind. Hy-Brasil was hidden from the rest of the world by centuries-old magic, only able to be seen once every seven years and only reached by a chosen few. Nobody had ever come to its shores in her lifetime. As a child, she was curious about the world beyond the sea, but in a vague, half-sketched way, as she was curious about a lot of things she read in books. London and Treasure Island and horses and dragons were all equally imagined to her. She thought she would probably see them one day, when she was old. In the meantime, the island was hers to explore, and it took up more time than she could ever imagine having. There were books to read, thousands of them in the castle library, and Rowan brought back more all the time. There were trees to climb, caves along the beach to get lost in, traces of the fair folk who had once lived on the island to find and bring home. There was work to be done: Food needed to be grown and harvested; the livable parts of the castle, the parts that weren't a crumbling ruin, needed to be constantly fortified against the harsh salt winds; the rocks needed to be combed for useful things when the tide went out. She was a half-wild thing of ink and grass and sea breezes, raised by books and rabbits and fairy lore, and that was all she cared to be.

She didn't know now when that had changed—it had done so gradually, one question at a time wearing away at her like the relentless drops of rain on the ruins by the cliffs. She must have asked Rowan at some point how she had come to the island, but she couldn't remember it. It seemed she had always known the story: a violent storm that churned up the ocean and strewn the shoreline with driftwood; Rowan and Hutchincroft walking along the clifftops the morning afterward; the battered lifeboat on the rocks, half-flooded, with the little girl that had been her curled up in the very bottom. Rowan had since shown her the spot many times at her request. She had been no more than a year old when they found her, with a mop of chestnut curls and enormous eyes, wet through and crying but unscathed. There was no trace of her parents, or the shipwreck that had likely killed them. It was as though the island itself had reached out into the deadly seas and snatched her to safety. She liked to think of that—that Hy-Brasil, which rarely let anyone come to its shores, had for its own reasons welcomed her. It had to mean something. Perhaps she was the daughter of somebody important, a queen or a brilliant sorcerer; perhaps, like the orphan girls in her books, she had some great destiny to fulfill. It made up in some small way for not being a mage.

She could, though, distinctly remember reading *A Little Princess* when she was ten or eleven and stopping short at the realization that Sara Crewe, at seven, was being sent from her home to school. She wasn't sure why this struck her particularly—she had read other stories about children being sent to school, after all, without wondering why it didn't seem to apply to her. Perhaps it was that Sara's father, young and full of fun, reminded her a little of Rowan just as Sara reminded her a little of herself. Perhaps it was just that she was ready to question, and books, as they so often did, crystallized her questions into words.

She'd tracked him down to the library that evening. "Rowan?"

"Yes, my love?" he'd said absently. It probably wasn't the right time—he was up on the bookshelves near the ceiling, balanced precariously as he tracked down a volume about poltergeists. Hutch lay on the rug by the fire, flopped on his side in a peaceful C shape.

"Why haven't I gone to school?"

She thought he focused his attention a little more carefully on the books in front of him, but he might have just been trying not to fall to his death. "Do you want to go to school?"

It wasn't what she had been asking, and the possibility had distracted her while she considered. "I think so," she said at last. "Someday."

"Well, then you will, someday," he said. "It might be a while, though. I'll see what I can do."

It was no different to the kind of thing he'd said before, but for the first time, far too late, she realized what he wasn't saying. He was telling her that she couldn't leave yet, and she trusted that he had a good reason. He was telling her that she would leave one day, and she trusted that too. But he wasn't telling her *why*. He never did.

Once she had noticed that, she began to notice other things he wasn't saying, lurking like predators in long grass amid the things he was saying instead.

She knew, for instance, that Rowan had grown up on the distant shoreline she could see from the cliffs on a clear day, the one she used to think of as the beginning of the world. Actually, it was Inishmore, one of the Aran Islands. Beyond it was the coast of western Ireland, and beyond that was Great Britain and then the great mass of Europe, over which Rowan and Hutch had wandered before coming to the island. Rowan would give her all the books and maps she could ever want, and in the right mood he would talk to her for hours about the countries inside their pages. Yet when she pressed him on any stories from his own childhood or travels, he would turn elusive.

"It was a long time ago," he said once, with a shrug.

"So was the Norman Conquest," she reminded him. "And we were just talking about that."

He laughed. "Well, it wasn't *that* long ago!"

"How long was it, then?" she countered. "I know you're a lot older than you look, because Hutch told me that magicians age slowly once they get their familiars. But he didn't know how old that made you, because rabbits aren't very good with time."

"Neither am I. A hundred years or so? I lost count around the Boer War."

She didn't believe that for a minute. Rowan could misplace a lot of things, but surely not entire years. But she had learned to accept it. It was useless to try to make Rowan talk when he didn't want to. And Hutchincroft, who when he could talk would do so happily at any time at all, knew Rowan too well to give Biddy information that she wasn't supposed to have.

Lately, though, things had been different. It wasn't only that she was getting older, more restless, her eyes pulled constantly to the bump of land on the horizon and her thoughts pulled even further. Rowan had been disappearing more and more often; he was bringing back a lot more injuries than he was artifacts, and some of them she suspected hurt more than he was letting on. Hutchincroft was restless when he wasn't there, on edge, possibly in constant silent communication and certainly in silent worry. It was possible, she supposed, that these things had been festering under the surface of her life for a long time, and she was only lately becoming aware of them. Either way, she could feel a bite of danger in the air like the first frost of autumn, and she didn't like it.

⁕ ══════════ ⁕

It should have been a perfect morning. The day had unfurled crisp and bright, the kind to be taken advantage of on Hy-Brasil, where wind was common but sun was rare, and she had gone up the cliffs with a rug, three undersized apples, and a battered copy of *Jane Eyre*. The wind ruffled her hair and the grass behind the castle; the black rabbits grazing there, infected with the chaotic joy of it, flicked their ears and jumped in the air. It made her smile, despite everything. And yet she hadn't been able to focus as she usually did. The argument had tainted the morning like smoke, leaving an acrid taste in her throat and a grey pall over the sky. The world of her book seemed impossibly far away, full of strangers and schools and romances when she had never seen anything of the kind. Her self-righteous fury at Rowan's treatment of her gave way, predictably, to doubts about her own behavior, and then to guilt. It was a relief when shortly after midday a shadow fell across the pages.

"Hello," Rowan said. At his side, Hutchincroft nudged her book experimentally with his nose. "What are you up to, then?"

She shrugged, determined not to give him the satisfaction of a smile quite yet. "Not a lot."

"You're not still sulking, are you?"

"I don't *sulk*. You two sulk. I was reading."

"Any good?"

She glanced down at her book. "'It is in vain to say human beings ought to be satisfied with tranquility: they must have action; and they will make it if they cannot find it. Millions are condemned to a stiller doom than mine, and millions are in silent revolt against their lot. Nobody knows how many rebellions besides political rebellions ferment in the masses of life which people earth.'"

His eyebrows went up. "And that's you not sulking, is it?"

"It's Charlotte Brontë, not me!" In fact, that part had been a few chapters earlier, but she had remembered it to make a point. "I'm just reading what she says."

"Well, tell her to lay off." He must have seen that pretending they hadn't argued wasn't working. She heard a faint sigh, and then he settled down beside her on the grass. "Look, I know it's not fair. I know it's lonely here for you. For what it's worth, I'm sure I did say you could come with me when you were older, and I'm sure I meant it. I thought things would be different by now. They might be soon—I'll do what I can, I promise—but I need more time. All right?"

It wasn't, really. But she knew Rowan was apologizing in his own way, and she wanted to apologize too. She didn't want there to be undercurrents of tension and struggle between the two of them, as there seemed to be more and more often these days. There never had been before. Oh, when she was thirteen and a prickly ball of existential angst, she would shout at him that he didn't *understand* her, and he would retort, a little frustrated and a lot more amused, that she was bloody right about that, and she would storm off fuming. But that had been about her own emotions flaring, easily solved once they settled down again. This was about Rowan, and she had enough common sense to see that if he wasn't going to budge, she could do nothing except keep pushing or back down.

And so she nodded, and tried to mean it.

"Thank you." His voice was so unexpectedly quiet and sincere that it caught her off guard. It was as though a curtain had flickered aside, and beyond it she could glimpse something shadowed and troubled. Then the moment passed, and he was stretching and getting back to his feet in one sure movement. "What time is it, by the way?"

Biddy resigned herself to the subject being closed and checked her coat pocket for her watch. "Ah…almost two."

"That late?" He glanced down at Hutch. "You were right. We do need to get a move on if we want to get back before tonight."

"Are you going somewhere tonight?" She made her voice deliberately innocent, and his look suggested he knew it.

"I might be. For now, I'm going out to the oak. Do you fancy a walk?"

She was half tempted to refuse, just to show she wasn't letting him off as easily as all that. But she *did* fancy a walk, and what was more, she fancied their company after her morning alone. So she got to her feet, brushing grass from her skirt.

"It isn't only about me leaving the island," she couldn't help adding. "I worry about you when I wake up at night and you're not there."

"I know you do. But you don't have to, I promise. I can take care of myself. I'm always back by morning."

"That doesn't mean you always will be."

"It doesn't mean I won't be either," he pointed out, which was technically accurate if infuriating.

They walked through the trees, the two of them on foot and Hutch scampering beside them before Rowan scooped him up to settle him against his shoulder. At this time of year, the path was like a dark green cathedral, dappled with sun, and Biddy told the other two about the words the Japanese had for different kinds of light: Light through leaves was called *komorebi*. Her mood lifted, and the trapped, resentful feeling sank back down in her chest where it belonged.

When they passed the familiar track where the elm trees grew, Rowan stopped.

"Think you can get up there now?" he asked, with a nod to the tallest branches.

She sighed. "Honestly, does it matter? When in my life am I ever going to need to get up a tree?"

"You never know," he said lightly. "Does that mean you can't?"

Reluctantly, she returned his grin. "What do you think?"

Children in the books Biddy read were always told not to climb trees and always getting in trouble for tearing their clothes when they did. Hutchincroft, it was true, did fuss over both her clothes and her safety, but Rowan had been teaching her to climb since she could walk, usually just a little higher and on branches a little more precarious than she would have preferred. Sometimes they made a game of seeing how far through the forest they could get without once setting foot on the ground; sometimes they raced to see who could get to the highest branches first. Rowan always won, but she had grown to her full height over the summer, and she had been practicing.

"Good work," Rowan said approvingly, as she made a grab

for a mossy branch and pulled herself up to him. "You'll be out-climbing me soon."

She rolled her eyes, pleased but disbelieving.

"No, I mean it! You're clever, and you're brave—that's all you need with trees. My reach is longer than yours, but you're lighter, and you're learning how to use that. You're mostly slower now because you're more cautious than me, and that's probably not a bad thing. Probably."

"Well, it means I'm not going to come back in the mornings covered with scratches and bruises," she couldn't resist saying, "so that's a good thing. *Probably.*"

He laughed. "Honestly, you and Hutch. If you had your way, I'd never do anything at all."

There was an edge to the laugh, and she knew there had been an edge to her words too. He couldn't quite hide that he was in an odd mood: restless, distant, too light and playful when he was talking to her and too prone to frowning silence when he wasn't. He took a great deal of magic from the oak as well, when they finally reached it. As though he intended to use it.

She said nothing more. It was his business, she reminded herself, and he had made it clear that he would answer no questions. If she trusted him—and she did, with all her heart—then that would have to be enough. Until she felt like starting another argument, at least.

That night, when she heard his footsteps soft and light on the stairs, she lay quiet. She kept her gaze trained on her window, until a darker speck of black flashed across the clouds and was gone. Then she closed her eyes, and tried to think of nothing at all.

⊷═════⊶

Biddy wasn't sure what woke her, only that she sat up so sharply in her bed that something certainly had. The sky was still dark, but faint traces of grey and gold glimmered on the horizon. Almost dawn.

She swung her legs out of bed and went to the window. The grass under the castle stretched out dark and tangled beneath them. On it, a square of light glowed from Rowan's study window in the turret. When she craned her neck up, she could see the shutters wide open and a candle burning on the ledge. That candle had been left there for a reason: to guide the raven back from its travels. When Rowan returned, he extinguished it. Right now, like the rest of the castle, it was still ready and waiting. A memory stirred uneasily. She frowned, trying through the last cobwebs of sleep to see what it was that troubled her. She had known he was going, after all.

It was then that she heard a sharp, sudden sound; the sound, she knew at once, was what had woken her in the first place. The warning thump of a rabbit's back feet against a hard wood floor. Hutchincroft.

The cobwebs cleared as if in a sudden gust, and her stomach turned cold.

The sky.

An hour or two before dawn, Rowan had said, when she had asked him what time he had gotten back. He had given her the same answer before, on many occasions. It was one sure thing she knew about his nighttime travels, the more valuable for being the only one: Wherever Rowan went, he was always back an hour or two before dawn.

Now dawn was almost here. And Rowan hadn't come home.